It's kind of fun to do the impossible.
—Walt Disney

B

Temptation in a Kilt

VICTORIA ROBERTS

sourcebooks
casablanca

Published by Sourcebooks Casablanca, an imprint of Sourcebooks, Inc.
P.O. Box 4410, Naperville, Illinois 60567-4410
(630) 961-3900
Fax: (630) 961-2168
www.sourcebooks.com

Printed and bound in the United States of America.
VP 10 9 8 7 6 5 4 3 2 1

To my family, for their unwavering support and dedication to this Bad Boy. For my son, who understood at such a young age that Mommy was editing. For my daughter, the only Gaelic-speaking lass in the fifth grade. And for my husband, who makes dinners countless nights. I could not ask for a more encouraging bunch. I love you all, and you have my heartfelt thanks and appreciation. I could have never done this without you.

One

Royal Court, England, 1603

SOMETIMES BEING A HIGHLAND LAIRD WAS A ROYAL pain in the arse.

Laird Ciaran MacGregor of Glenorchy was tired and wanted to be home. It felt as if he had been attending court for more than a fortnight. The courtly games alone were enough to make a man impale himself on his own sword. As soon as he was finally granted the audience he had requested from King James, Ciaran and his men would depart.

Sounds of laughter and snatches of song filled the air. As Ciaran glanced around the great hall filled with several hundred members of nobility, he was thankful to have discovered an unoccupied wall. Frankly, everyone was grating on his nerves. Men socialized and were dressed in their finery. To him, they all looked like exotic birds—peacocks, perhaps. The heat was so unbearable that he did not know how the women managed with so many layers of clothing. He pulled at his restricting silk doublet at the thought.

"Ye have held up exceedingly well, my laird."

"Aye, as well as can be expected in this madness." Ciaran scowled at his brother and knew his vexation was evident, but frankly, he did not care.

"We are all ready to be off," said Aiden, slapping him upon the shoulder. "Have ye given any thought to whether Glenorchy still stands with Declan in your stead?"

Running his hand through his hair, Ciaran sighed. "I think of it often. He had best be out of his cups and have ceased his wenching before we return. I only hope my walls still stand."

Only a king's summons would have forced him to leave his reckless fool of a brother in charge. At least most of Ciaran's actions were defended at court—well, except his skirmishes with the bloody Campbells. Hence the reason for his delayed departure. If upon his return he found Glenorchy destroyed by the bloody Campbells or under siege by Declan's wenches, he would not be shocked. He hoped that leaving additional guards behind would have protected against both.

When Ciaran received the summons, he had no doubt Aiden would prove more beneficial at court. Had he brought his younger brother… he shivered at the mental image. Between constantly worrying about the neighboring clan's machinations and wondering if his home was still in one piece, he needed a drink.

Recognizing his familiar expression, Aiden cast a wry grin. "Ye worry overmuch. He knows the duty that befalls him. I cannae speak to whether he is in his cups, but Aisling would have speech with him if he was wenching within your walls. Of that, I have nay doubt."

"I have noticed your wee wife has found her voice since she is with child."

"Ye've noticed, have ye?"

"Brother, we can hear her bellowing at ye from across the bailey. At least *ye* seem to be the only one provoking her ire as of late." A smile played on the corner of his lips.

"'Tis only because ye run at the sight of her, ye coward." A flash of humor crossed Aiden's features. "She says she cannae find comfort and I must suffer as well because of her condition."

It was difficult not to notice how much his brother had changed since Aisling had become with child. Even though his lady wife would cry, laugh, and call him to the devil in the same breath, Aiden seemed to be both happy and content. Ciaran hoped Aiden's contentedness would rub off on Declan—well, one could always pray to the gods for a miracle.

They exchanged a subtle look of amusement. "And I wish ye luck with that. Praise the saints, I donna yet have a woman to make me suffer. Howbeit I do have enough troubles with Declan," Ciaran grunted, rolling his eyes.

"He may go knee deep into his cups more often than he should and he may also wench a time or two or thrice, but ye know if ye needed him he would be at hand. 'Tis ironic to hear ye speak as such lest ye forget it wasnae long ago when ye fondled a lass with one hand and held a tankard in the other," Aiden smirked. "Granted, ye took your responsibility seriously when Father passed. Listen to reason, Ciaran. All Declan needs is to find a strong woman and wed. Aye, mayhap he will even be lucky enough to find himself a lass with Aisling's ire." A mischievous look twinkled in Aiden's eye.

That was surely something to think upon. Perhaps a wife was what Declan needed. Ciaran could go daft remembering all of the times he had tried to save his brother from himself. His head was starting to throb. No longer interested in having this discussion, he was about to take his leave for some much needed air when a raised voice held his attention. His private wall was no longer his own.

"How many times have I told you to watch that Highland tongue of yours, Rosalia? It makes you sound daft. I will not tolerate your deliberate attempts to thwart your chances with an English gentleman. You are one and twenty. How many chances do you think you have left? No one shows interest in you. Did you notice your midriff is much larger than the other women in attendance? I will not tell you again—do as I say or suffer the consequences."

Ciaran watched the English she-dragon spread her wings and fly across the floor, but not before she pinched the young woman in the arm. Stains of scarlet appeared on the woman's cheeks, but when her heightened color subsided, her features were exhilarating. Loose tendrils of hazel-colored tresses softened her features, and her fully rosy lips beckoned to be kissed. She had more curves than most, but she was a wild beauty.

For a brief moment, her azure eyes met his. He attempted to ease her embarrassment by offering her a gaze as soft as a caress. She returned a shy smile and inclined her head in a small gesture of thanks before she walked off in the wake of the fiery beast.

"Och, I pray for a son," murmured Aiden, a suggestion of annoyance hovering in his eyes. "We need women such as that on the battlefield—aye, brother? Her venom alone would bring a man to his knees."

Ciaran shrugged dismissively, but his eyes still followed the young woman.

"Ye know, Ciaran. Mayhap while we are at court ye should seek a wife." His brother shifted, giving him a better view of the woman.

"How many times must we speak of this? Ye know I cannae seek a wife until my vow to Father is fulfilled."

"Aye, the *vow*," Aiden drawled with distinct mockery. "And ye think Declan will straighten his path because ye made a promise to Father?"

Ciaran's body stiffened in response. "I gave my word." He was tired of having the same speech with his brother. He needed a respite—from everyone.

❧

Lady Rosalia Armstrong of Mangerton was crimson with humiliation. She prayed no one had heard her mother's venomous tongue. When she discreetly glanced around to ensure no one had overheard their words, she saw him standing there, devilishly handsome. She did not know who he was, but his profile spoke of power and ageless strength. Even in a crowd, his presence was compelling.

He was over six feet and stood tall and formidable. He had a generous mouth, a straight nose, and a smile that was a dazzling display of even, white teeth. He had a ruggedness and vital power that definitely attracted her. His full chestnut hair brushed the rich outlines of his broad shoulders which strained against the fabric of his clothing. The muscles under his silk doublet quickened her pulse, and she found it impossible not to return his captivating smile.

Keenly aware of his scrutiny, Rosalia could see that he obviously pitied her. Taking a deep breath, she brightened her smile and straightened her spine. She had to step away from his observant eyes before she was made any more the fool. Seeking her mother and father in the crowd, she finally found them huddled with a man in deep conversation. Upon her approach, the man lifted his head and openly studied her. His dark eyes shifted and seemed to undress her.

A shudder passed through her.

Walking casually to her father's side, Rosalia remained silent, trying to watch that Highland tongue of hers. Her father cleared his throat. "Lord Dunnehl, allow me to present our daughter, Lady Rosalia Armstrong." His eyes were intent on watching Lord Dunnehl's reaction to her.

Lord Dunnehl gave her a low bow and then stood. When she extended her hand, he brushed a brief kiss on top, his expression one of faint amusement. "A magnificent creature indeed. Clearly, she gets her beauty from you, Lady Armstrong."

"You flatter me, my lord." Joy bubbled in her mother's laugh and shone in her eyes.

Rosalia was unimpressed. "A pleasure, my lord," she responded with a nervous smile.

During the discussion that followed, Rosalia did not pay attention. There was no need. Her mother and father entertained Lord Dunnehl with pleasantries and she was happy for the respite. For the first time, Rosalia was grateful for her mother's endless prattle and it gave her an opportunity to inspect the "English gentleman." Rosalia swore if she heard those words one more time, she would surely lose her contents.

Height was definitely not in his favor. Although Rosalia was taller than most women, she was at least a head taller than he. His eyes were of a muddy brown color, and the few hairs he had left on the top of his head were a thin tawny-gold. He was quite large around the middle, and the courtly fashions did nothing to flatter his appearance. A man of his station would be expected to dress in such a manner, but the clothes made him look like a peacock.

With a sigh, Rosalia shifted from foot to foot. Her eyes darted around the room, and when she found the man with the handsome smile, he was looking directly at her. Quickly, she lowered her gaze.

"Rosalia?"

She could not resist another peek at the man. Every time she glanced at him, his gaze returned to her. She tried not to be caught staring and found a joyous satisfaction in studying his profile. Her mother's firm nudge brought her back from her woolgathering.

"Rosalia!" her mother repeated with authority.

"Aye?"

"Lord Dunnehl has taken his leave. You could at least have feigned an interest in the conversation," she said curtly.

Rosalia nodded briefly, turning to her father. "Father, who is that man standing…" When she twisted around to show her father, she spotted *his* broad back walking briskly out of the hall.

Her father glanced around her. "What man?"

"It does not matter what *man*," said her mother, attempting to correct their brogue. "We leave for Mangerton on the morrow. Your father must see to the crop, and we need to prepare for an important guest."

Rosalia raised her brow searchingly. "An important guest?"

Her mother smiled at her knowingly. "Lord Dunnehl."

She paled.

Two

Liddesdale, Scotland

"WHAT DO YE WANT ME TO DO, CAROLINE? THE COIN is almost depleted."

Rosalia wanted to cover her ears to shut out another of her parents' heated arguments outside her bedchamber.

"We shall keep Cook, and Rosalia will need to attend us," spat her mother, her voice ruthless. "I am through with idle chatter, Ronald. You need to offer her hand. It is the only way to fill our purse. Be a man for once in your miserable life. There is no other choice!"

Her father sighed with exasperation. "Caroline, ye cannae fail to notice she is a score and one, and the truth that she has nay dowry isnae too promising for prospective suitors. As ye know, the only prospect from court is Lord Dunnehl and he is most unpleasant."

"He is not unpleasant, and you had best not treat him that way when he arrives on the morrow. Let me ask you, Ronald—have you given thought to how you will provide for me when the coin is depleted? No, of course not. When Lord Dunnehl comes to Mangerton, you shall be opening another means to fill our purse. After all, it is *your* responsibility to see the coffers filled, is it not?" Her voice was laced with sarcasm.

"We do not have to battle on this, Ronald. Offer her hand and you will see all of our worries gone. Furthermore," she huffed, "after everything I do for you, this is the least you could do for me."

Rosalia could not move.

That was the true reason why they had taken her to court. Rosalia was perfectly aware that marriages were arranged for coin, land, or title, but that was not the life she sought. Was it too much to ask for a husband who loved her and wanted her, who would make her feel like the only place she belonged was by his side? She was mindful of the fact that it was past time she wed, but how cruel to have a man as unsavory as Lord Dunnehl selected as her mate. The last thing she desired was to be caught in a loveless marriage—the same fate as her mother and father.

Although her sire had been born and raised in the Highlands, her mother was from England and refused to make the journey to the *barbaric* north. Rosalia had always been told that her father had given up everything upon his marriage to her mother, agreeing to reside at their estate at Liddesdale so her mother could cross the border to her beloved England. And Liddesdale was the northern most part of Scotland her mother was willing to go. Rosalia's *seanmhair*, her father's mother, still had her home in Glengarry, but Rosalia was never permitted to travel there. She had given up on asking the reason why long ago. As a result, her parents were all the family she knew.

Reluctantly, Rosalia proceeded to the great hall where her mother and father were already seated for the midday meal. Wiping her sweaty palms on her day dress, she walked to the table and slid out the heavy wooden bench, attempting to take her seat unnoticed. To her dismay, she failed. Her mother cleared her throat, raised her cheek, and waited. Having no choice, Rosalia grudgingly rose and kissed her mother's uplifted cheek.

Nodding her head in approval, her mother gestured for Rosalia to take her seat for the second time.

"Rosalia, eat, but not too much. Your clothing is getting tighter around your midriff—again. Finish your meal and then we wish to have speech with you."

"Aye, Mother."

She had barely finished her meal when her trencher was yanked away. "That is enough. We have something to discuss with you." Pausing, her mother took a sip of wine. "I want everything prepared and in order for Lord Dunnehl's arrival. I will be inspecting."

Rosalia stole a glance at her father. Clenching her jaw, she struggled to rein in her temper. Unfortunately, that did not assist her in holding her tongue. "Mother, if ye and Da are thinking of offering my hand, donna ye wish to ask my thoughts?"

Her mother rose in one fluid motion and hauled Rosalia from the bench. The fury that shot from her eyes was all too familiar, and Rosalia felt the sting of the slap before her words were finished. She lifted her hands to protect herself, but it was pointless.

Forceful hands continued to strike her.

"You. Ungrateful. Child. Your father and I have provided for you and expected nothing in return! You will wed Lord Dunnehl if we command you to wed him!"

"Mother, I beg ye!" cried Rosalia in a choking voice. Her hands covered her eyes and cheeks, and she wept aloud, rocking back and forth.

"Look at her, Ronald! She is daft. I live for the day when she becomes someone else's burden." Her mother's hard voice held no sympathy. "Rosalia, enough of these tears. You will clear the table now and assist Cook. When you have completed that task, prepare for Lord Dunnehl's arrival. I have had enough of your foolishness."

Hot tears rolled down Rosalia's cheeks and she lowered her head, staring at her hands. She could not bring herself to move. The smell of blood pulled her from her despair. Hastily, she grabbed for a rag on the table, applying it to her bleeding nose.

Her mother's eyes narrowed. "Did you hear me, Rosalia?"

"Aye," she answered, defeated.

After a hushed stillness, her father spoke. "Do as your mother commands and all will be well."

"Aye, Father."

Rosalia pulled herself to her feet and started to clear the table, pausing to wipe her bloodied nose. Glancing up, she saw James, the captain of her father's guard, standing frozen at the entrance of the great hall. His grave expression told her all too clearly what he had witnessed. Rosalia face reddened with humiliation, and she kept her eyes down to the task at hand.

She spent the remainder of the day avoiding him. Several times he tried to capture her attention, but she pretended not to notice him. Rosalia recognized that her behavior was childish, but frankly, she did not have the energy to deal with James. Between worrying about her future and preparing for Lord Dunnehl's visit, she was exhausted.

Rosalia was finally crawling into bed for another restless night when a familiar voice whispered her name through the door. It was senseless to ignore him. She donned a blanket and opened her bedchamber door. Sneaking a quick peek and observing no one in the hall, she walked out quietly and gently closed the door.

All she needed was to have a servant catch her sneaking about. Then she remembered that Ealasaid, the cook, was the only servant in quarters, and she silently chuckled.

Ealasaid was like a grandmother to her, and James, irksome as he was, was her best friend. Never did she have a romantic notion about him, unless she counted the time she made him kiss her to see what it was like. What a terrible kiss. Sharing a romantic kiss with someone who was like a brother was not something Rosalia desired ever to repeat.

Nightfall had arrived some time earlier and the main torches were extinguished. There were only a few lit, but she could have found her way even in the dark, having walked this path so many times. Climbing the steps to the parapet, she called his name.

"God's teeth, woman, hush! I am here. Remind me ne'er to take ye into battle. The enemy would hear ye trampling from a distance before ye even got close enough to draw your sword," said James with a trace of laughter in his voice. "Be thankful I havenae yet taken my sword to ye." He smirked, tapping her playfully on the arm. "Howbeit the fates have tempted me so."

Rosalia pointed a finger at him. "Annoying man—be truthful. The many words that spew from your cheek would put your enemy to sleep. Ye wouldnae even have to draw your sword. Ye would simply *bore* them to death," she said, satisfaction pursing her mouth.

She watched him through the torchlight, his ash-blond locks reflecting the light. Unsheathing his sword, he leaned it against the stone wall. His expression stilled and grew serious. "Are ye hurt, Rosalia?"

She glanced away and out into the darkness. "'Tisnae as bad as the others. My head aches, but I shall be fine."

James approached her and his eyes widened with concern. Raising his hand, he turned her head toward the torchlight. Gently brushing her cheek, he sighed.

Clutching her blanket, Rosalia stared out into the darkness. With a shiver of vivid recollection, she recalled the attractive man with the charming smile. "I saw a man at court. I couldnae breathe, and my heart was beating so fast when he looked at me. I have ne'er felt that way before. He was the most handsome man I ever laid eyes upon."

Her musings were interrupted by his smirk. "Donna speak untruths. Ye know I am the bonniest man ye have ever laid eyes upon."

She swatted at him. "Cease, ye rogue."

"Did ye speak with him?" he asked her searchingly.

Rosalia shook her head. "Nay. When he heard Mother scolding me, the smile he offered was only one of pity." She spoke regretfully, pausing a moment to remember him. "Did ye hear, then? They want to offer my hand to this Lord Dunnehl. Do ye know him?"

James hesitated, measuring her for a moment. When the sound of laughter approached from a distance, he reached out and touched her arm. "The guards come. Quickly, back to your chamber."

◈

After a night of tossing and turning and a tiring day of preparing for Lord Dunnehl's arrival, Rosalia would be paraded like livestock. Perhaps he would think her midriff too big and she would be unacceptable for breeding—one could only hope. Shaking her head, Rosalia willed away her dark thoughts. She pulled at her gown and rechecked her hair. There was nothing further she could do. The time had come, whether she was ready or not.

Taking a deep breath, Rosalia hesitantly approached the great hall. The sound of her mother's laughter made her face turn grim. It was obvious she was trying to impress the man by showing him the fine tapestries. There may be nothing left in the coffers, but they had the finest of wares. Her mother was quite proud of that fact.

Glancing up upon her approach, Lord Dunnehl ambled toward Rosalia in a leisurely manner. "My lady, a pleasure to see you again." He gave her a low bow and she extended her hand. "Your beauty is exquisite. Clearly, she gets it from you, Lady Armstrong."

"So ye have said," Rosalia mumbled under her breath, trying with all of her strength not to roll her eyes.

"You flatter me, my lord," said her mother, her eyes glowing with enjoyment.

"Are you injured, my lady?" he asked Rosalia searchingly.

When she clamped her jaw tight and lifted her brow, her mother quickly explained, "She fell from her mount."

"Most unfortunate. My apologies for your discomfort."

While her mother uttered meaningless chatter, Rosalia quietly reflected.

"Rosalia would love to show you the gardens, my lord." Her mother gave her a pointed look.

"The pleasure would be mine, my lady."

He extended his arm, and Rosalia cleared her throat awkwardly. "Ye and Da are joining us?"

"Surely ye donna require a chaperone. Lord Dunnehl wishes time with ye. A walk in the garden will do ye some good. Besides, the captain of my guard is on watch out there if ye want for anything." Her father narrowed his eyes at Lord Dunnehl.

Having no choice, Rosalia reluctantly took his arm. As they entered the gardens, she glanced up as James walked the parapet. "Have ye… you traveled far, my lord?" She wished her mother would not insist she mask her Highland brogue. It made it much more difficult to carry on a conversation, and she was nervous enough.

"After court, I traveled to my Northumberland home and came from there."

She was instantly wide awake. "I find the courtly

appeal fascinating. I understand King James is attempting to tame the Highland *barbarians*. I personally donna... do not think they are barbarians at all. They fight amongst themselves to keep land that has been rightfully theirs for generations. I admire their courage and their honor," she spoke eagerly.

"And what does a woman know of courtly matters? I can assure you, my dear, those men *are barbarians*. Why don't we speak to the matter at hand, shall we?" Lord Dunnehl stopped and inclined his head, holding out his hand for her to sit on a bench. He glanced up at the parapet before he took his seat next to her.

Taking a deep breath, Rosalia tried to command her emotions to order. "And what matter is that?"

"I am aware you speak freely. Your father has said as much. I do not seek such qualities in a wife. However, I am in need of a wife and you are in need of a husband. More so, I am in need of an heir and I am not getting any younger. We will have an open marriage, and you will be free to do as you will as soon as you provide my heir. I understand the coffers are low, and I am willing to bargain with your father."

Her jaw dropped and she gave him a sidelong glance of utter nonbelief for speaking so bluntly.

He chuckled nastily and forcefully pulled her head toward him. Vehemently, he smacked his lips upon hers. As Rosalia felt bile rise in the back of her throat, he finally broke the kiss. "You may bring that fire into our bed... and I will show you how thoroughly I can put it out. I like my women with some spirit."

Breathless with rage, she sprang from the bench and slapped his hands away. "I believe 'tis enough, my lord. My sire awaits us in the great hall." She flashed him a look of disdain and stormed off.

He quickly caught up with her. "I shall have speech with your father on the morrow. I wish to wed quickly and return to London. I know you will be looking forward to our marriage bed as well, my dear." His gaze rested on her breasts.

He was the foulest of beasts.

Her feet couldn't carry her fast enough. When they entered the great hall, Rosalia thundered past her mother, her temper barely controlled. "I must retire. I bid ye good sleep." Hefting her skirts, she ran up the stairs to her bedchamber and slammed the door.

⤳

Rosalia awoke the next morning with a pounding headache. How could her mother expect her to wed such a man?

Fierce pounding upon her door made her jump. "Rosalia, open this door at once! I will not ask again," ordered her mother in a clipped tone. Pulling herself from the bed, Rosalia unlatched the door and stepped back as her mother pushed through the doorway. "Lord Dunnehl has offered for your hand and we are most pleased."

"Aye, I can see with my own eyes how verra pleased ye are with this match," she bellowed.

Her mother was surprisingly calm.

"Come, Rosalia, your father awaits us in the study." She lifted her hand and gestured for her daughter to follow.

Rosalia trailed after her mother in a trance-like state. The first part of her life had been horrid, but she refused to have the last part of it be the same. This was one fight she could not, would not lose. When she entered the study, her father was seated behind his dark wooden desk. He gestured for them to sit and folded his hands in front of him.

There was a heavy silence.

Sitting forward, he peered at her intently. "Rosalia, as ye know, Lord Dunnehl has offered for your hand and has returned to his home. Once he comes back with the bride price and the banns are posted, ye will be wed in the chapel. He wants to take his leave shortly after to his home in London."

She clenched her jaw, fighting for collectedness.

"Rosalia, you will absolutely *adore* London. There are many advantages to living there. Once you provide Lord Dunnehl with his heir, you will be free to do as you will. That is all he seeks from you," said her mother with a proud smile.

Rosalia glanced back and forth between the two of them in awe. It was apparent they waited for her response, and she was more than happy to oblige.

❦

James knocked once and called her name. When she did not answer, he made another attempt. "Rosalia, how do ye fare?"

She slammed her trunk shut and tried not to flinch. "James, I cannae have speech with ye at the moment."

"Are ye unwell? Let me in."

"Mother and Fath—"

"Are below stairs. Let me in or I will break down this door, Rosalia. *Now*," he ordered with a warning in his voice. She unlatched the door and he swung it open. He strode in and glanced around, studying her chamber. "What was that shuffling I heard?" he asked suspiciously.

She gave him her back and could not find the strength to look at him.

"Rosalia…" He reached out and touched her arm. When she winced, he stepped around her and pushed the hair back from her face. "Och, lass, what has befallen ye? Look at me, Rosalia." His voice caught in his throat.

"'Tis naught. I am fine." She closed her eyes in a futile attempt to hold back her tears. "'Tis my own fault. I spoke in truth to Mother and Father. Father…"

He embraced her lightly while she sobbed.

She pulled back slowly. "James, I must be alone. Ealasaid brought a tray and I only wish to go to bed. We can speak on the morrow. Please, James," she said, gazing at him with despair.

He hesitated, his face full of anguish and concern. "Aye, lass, ye rest. Do ye have a salve for your bruises?"

"Aye, I have some. Please, I must get rest," she insisted.

Finally able to convince James to take his leave, she approached her trunk. Carefully and slowly, she lifted her bundle and placed it on the bed. She sat down and removed her clothing, wincing where it rubbed her ribs. She pulled her dirk from her sack, drawing strength from the feel of it in her hand. She could do this. She had to. It was the only way. There was no turning back now. She leaned over the washbowl and placed the dirk at the base of her neck. One glance at her bruises in the reflection of the water gave her all the confidence she needed. She closed her eyes and cut deeply.

A clump of hair fell into her hand. She tossed it into the fire. She made another deep cut. Her hair was so thick. Why had she thought it would cut easily? She gathered the remaining hair clippings and threw them into the fire. Lifting her arms, which felt as though they were strapped with heavy weights, she bound her breasts and ribs the best she could. The strips she made from her old day dress worked perfectly, but the task took forever. She finally managed to pull on her tunic and don the trews James had given her to practice swordplay. A sharp pain radiated through her side, and she had yet to pull on her boots. She sat down, inhaled deeply, and bent to fasten them.

When Rosalia positioned herself upright, she fought a wave of nausea. Giving herself a moment, she packed the food from the tray Ealasaid had so graciously brought her. Holding her breath, she bent to secure her dirk inside her boot. Once she threw on the hat she had borrowed from the stable boy, her disguise was complete. She hesitated, taking one last glance around her bedchamber. She would not miss it. What was there to miss?

Opening the door, Rosalia glanced down the hall. Thankfully, James had listened to reason and left her alone. She discreetly descended the back stairs to the stables. There was no one about, but she could not be too careful. The stable master, Duncan, would be in the kitchens with Ealasaid. The two of them were inseparable.

Noonie stomped his feet and whinnied upon her

approach. "Shh… we will go for a ride, Noonie, but ye must be quiet." Rosalia managed to saddle her horse and attach her bundle. Grabbing a couple of woolen blankets, she securely fastened them to the saddle. A sharp pain attacked her ribs and she mentally willed it away. There was no time. She needed to move.

She was about to pull Noonie from the stall when she heard a whimper. "Magaidh…" She placed her head to Noonie's, knowing in her heart she could not take her pup. Although Rosalia's heart was breaking, Magaidh would be much safer here with Duncan.

Leading Noonie from his stall, she crept through the back of the garden. The guards would not see her from this angle. She was sure of it. Rosalia made her way to the edge of the forest. The air was warm and the moon was full. She should be able to travel a fair distance this eve.

Standing to the left, she pulled Noonie's mane, the command for him to kneel. Praise the saints for Duncan's training. Rosalia pulled herself upon the horse's back. The pain was excruciating but she managed to secure her seat. Another swift kick and they were off.

When she reached the path toward the loch, she turned north. She would continue to ride into the Highlands, knowing her mother and father would never search for her there. She would seek her *seanmhair* in Glengarry and pray she would take her in.

Seanmhair was never permitted as a topic of discussion. She often wondered what Father's mother had done, but in her heart Rosalia would always love her. *Seanmhair* would send messengers upon occasion who would seek her out and deliver notes or gifts. It seemed Rosalia was never far from her grandmother's thoughts—well, she prayed that still rang true.

At least she managed to get a few hours' head start. When she could no longer hold her seat and every bone in her body ached, she needed to stop. She would pause only a moment to rest and then continue on her way. Rosalia led Noonie into a small clearing. This would have to do. As she tugged on his mane to kneel, she slid from his back and fell hard to the ground with a heavy thud. That was the last she remembered before she welcomed the blackness.

Three

FOR WELL OVER A FORTNIGHT, LAIRD CIARAN MacGregor of Glenorchy had ridden his men hard to flee the madness of the English court. Now back in Scotland, they were all restless and tired, but bound and determined to reach Glenorchy in just a few more days. Ciaran could not wait to return home, sleep in his own bed, and eat at his own table. When his mind filtered back to his leman, Beathag, his memory of her warm thighs and ample bosom made him shift in his seat. He sorely missed Glenorchy. He would continue until he or his men dropped.

After he had had to spend what felt like an eternity at court, his reckless brother had best have everything in order upon their arrival. Fortunately, the bloody Campbells could not have caused too much grief in his absence since they were in attendance at court as well. The greedy lot continued to hold King James's ear, but Ciaran refused to play such games.

However, he was somewhat relieved that his liege held both clans accountable for the skirmishes; at least his head would not be alone on a pike. Expressing his intense displeasure, King James warned them to keep peace in the Highlands or suffer the consequences of their actions. Ciaran had no concerns with his liege's demands as long as the bloody Campbells stayed away from his land and his people.

Aiden slowed his mount and reined in beside him. "My laird, we have been riding for hours this day. Do ye nae think we should stop and rest the horses?"

"What is wrong? The horses are fine. Do *ye* wish to stop and rest?"

"Well…" Aiden murmured, shrugging his shoulders.

Ciaran gave him a pointed look. "What is wrong, brother?"

"Och, my bloody arse cannae take it! I know we are all anxious to return to home, but ye barely stop to let us take a piss," he said through gritted teeth.

Ciaran reined in his mount and yelled for his men to stop. Lowering his voice, he smirked. "God's teeth! Ye are a Highlander and a MacGregor, but if ye wish to rest to save your bloody arse… Donaidh and Seumas, ye scout and we will make camp," he shouted over his shoulder.

❧

Donaidh and Seumas were exhausted, but if scouting meant they could return to Glenorchy sooner rather than later, they would do anything their liege commanded. They searched the surrounding blanket of darkness to ensure there was no possible threat lurking in the shadows and were ready to return to camp when a horse whinnied.

"Didnae we just search that clearing?" asked Donaidh.

"Aye," responded Seumas cautiously.

Both men separated and drew their swords, approaching the clearing from opposite directions. Once they spotted each other, they dismounted. A horse as black as the night pawed at the ground. With the full moon above, the creature cast an eerie glow—as if the beast itself was under some ancient spell.

Donaidh advanced carefully. "Is that someone upon the ground?" he whispered to Seumas.

The beast jostled his reins and pawed at the ground.

"Take caution," Seumas murmured. "It may be a trap." Giving the horse wide berth, he poked at the mass on the ground with his sword. Seeing no apparent movement, he stretched out his leg and kicked it with his foot. "Hold the mount steady and I will turn him over."

Donaidh secured the black beast as Seumas reached down and flipped the darkened figure. "Och, the laddie fell from his mount." Kneeling down beside him, Donaidh placed his ear to the youth's lips. "He lives. Help me get him to his feet."

Sheathing their swords, they each grabbed under an arm and brought the lad to his feet. "He is still out. Lay him back. 'Tis too dark to see how badly he is injured. We will take him back to camp," said Seumas. Reaching out, he clutched the reins of the black beast and spoke in soothing tones. Once the mount calmed, he nodded to Donaidh. "Try again to get the laddie on his mount. Lift his feet."

Donaidh had no sooner hefted his feet than a blood-curdling scream cut through the night. "*Sèimhich*, lad! Ye took a tumble from your mount. We arenae going to harm ye," Donaidh assured him. Kicking and bucking, the boy tried vigorously to release their hold. He let out an agonizing moan before he again lost awareness. Hastily, they secured him to his saddle. "Seumas, have ye seen that horseflesh? Do ye think the lad a thief?" Donaidh gripped the reins and started to lead the black horse back to camp.

Seumas grunted. "I donna think 'tis the laddie's mount. 'Tis prize horseflesh. I wonder where he got him."

"Mayhap he was reiving from the bloody Campbells."

⁂

Ciaran, Aiden, and Calum watered their horses and tethered them to a tree. Aiden started a fire, and Calum pulled out their provisions. They had been in this situation so many times before that Ciaran rarely had to assign tasks. Everyone knew his responsibilities well. Ciaran had been in many a battle with these men, and they always watched each other's backs. They were dependable and he held them in the highest regard.

Aiden and Calum were sitting quietly around the fire, and it did not surprise Ciaran that no one wished to converse. After hearing all of the chattering women at court and their peacocks floating about, the silence was soothing.

Ciaran approached the fire and handed his brother a wine sack. "And how is your arse?" he asked, sprawling out on his own blanket.

"Ye laugh, brother." He took a long swig of wine and handed the sack to Calum.

"Aiden, lass, when are ye going to don your skirts? Mayhap Aisling wears the trews, aye?" Ciaran jested.

Calum spit the wine from his mouth but tried to cover his actions with a cough.

"Ye know, if I wasnae so sore right now, I would take ye both to task." Aiden fell back on his blanket and moaned.

Something gnawed at Ciaran's gut, and he could not quite place his finger upon it. "Donaidh and Seumas should have returned by now."

A scream pierced the night, and all of the men jumped to their feet. A few moments later when a whistle rang out, Ciaran sheathed his sword and let out the breath he held. He strode toward his men as they led their mounts into camp.

"We found a lad in the clearing. We think he fell from his mount—well, *that* mount." Seumas pointed to the horse, shaking his head in nonbelief. "When we tried to pick him up, he screamed as though death were upon him. I think his ribs are broken, but at least he is still out cold."

"Donaidh, Seumas, secure the horses. Aiden, help me move him close to the fire," Ciaran ordered. Pulling the boy from the horse, they carried him to a blanket and gently lowered him to the ground. When Ciaran pushed back the hair from the lad's face, his eyes widened with concern. "Och, his eyes are blackened, his lip is cut and swollen, and he has swelling to the face. And 'tis only what we see. That must have been one hell of a tumble."

Aiden grabbed a blanket and handed it to him. "Here. Lay this under his head."

Lifting the lad's head, Ciaran positioned the cover carefully underneath. "We should check for other injuries." He started by squeezing the injured lad's arms to check for broken bones, but as he applied pressure, the boy started to moan.

"Ciaran, the blackness is probably a blessing for now. If he awakens before first light, we will give him some ale for the pain. I think it may be better to check him on the morrow. Then we can see to what extent he is injured," offered Aiden.

"Aye." Ciaran shook his head regretfully. "There is naught we can do now. His pain will be much on the morrow, though."

The men arranged their bedding in front of the fire while Ciaran took first watch. He knew the path home had been too clear—well, the lad was not at fault. Ciaran would do what he must. If the boy could ride on the morrow, he would take him to the next village and ensure he received proper care. The lad was breathing heavily now and would probably sleep through the night.

Glancing over at the dark horse, Ciaran wondered where he came from. The mount was clearly prize horseflesh. They were at least a day's ride from the English border. Surely, the lad knew better than to steal from an English lord. All Ciaran needed right now was to have a band of men searching for their prized mount. He certainly did not want trouble. All he wanted was to return home to Glenorchy where a warm bed and Beathag welcomed him. He smiled at the thought.

He walked over to the fire and nudged his brother. "Aiden, 'tis time."

Letting out a sound of displeasure, his brother rolled over. "Nay, Aisling, I need a few more moments."

"Aiden, get up, ye daft fool." Ciaran nudged him again with his foot—not so friendly this time.

"Och! God's teeth! I am awake!" Placing his hands over his eyes, Aiden groaned.

"Quiet or ye will wake the men."

Aiden rose for his turn to stand watch and Ciaran took his place, listening to the fire making popping noises well into the night. He loved to sleep under the stars—not exactly for an entire fortnight, but for a night or two. In fact, he was not even aware he had fallen asleep until sunlight beamed in his eyes. When he opened them, Seumas sat next to the boy with a troubled expression.

"He just started to stir. I believe the pain is setting. He seems to be aware."

Pulling himself to his feet, Ciaran walked around the ashes of the fire and knelt beside the lad. He had seen that the youth's injuries were severe by the fire-light the past eve, but in the light of day... He gave the boy a little nudge and he cried out in pain.

"Seumas, we have nay choice. We need to know how badly he is injured or if he can travel. Grab an arm and let us sit him up." Supporting the lad by the upper arms, they placed him into a sitting position. "Can ye speak? Ye fell from your mount. Do ye understand?" Ciaran waited for his answer, but the boy was unresponsive.

"Do ye think he is injured in the head?" asked Seumas with concern.

"Nay. I have seen head injuries before," said Ciaran, studying his bruises. "He isnae injured in the head."

～

The pain was unbearable. Was someone talking to her? Head injury? Rosalia was trying to make sense of it all. She needed a moment to compose herself. Her vision was blurry, and it felt like a dagger was stuck in her temple. She let out a moan as she lifted her hand to her head. Opening her eyes, reality started to creep back in. The last thing she remembered was... falling from Noonie. She searched around the men, the very large men, and spotted several horses tethered to a tree. Noonie was there, but who were these men?

Someone asked her if she understood. Her eyes met his, and she could not answer because something clicked in her mind. It was *him*—the man from court who pitied her. She would recognize him anywhere.

"Can ye stand?" he asked with concern.

Rosalia did the only reasonable thing that came to mind. She nodded. The man grabbed her under the arms and attempted to pull her up. When she yelped and took a sharp intake of breath, he lowered her back to the ground.

"Seumas, help him hold up his arms. I will remove his tunic," the man ordered.

Her eyes widened in panic as an even more terrifying realization washed over her. She became instantly awake, fully aware of her surroundings. What if he discovered she was a woman? This situation could end in nothing short of a disaster.

"Donna worry, lad. Once I remove your tunic, we will check if your ribs are broken or bruised. Mayhap all they need is to be bound." The man he called Seumas hefted her arms, and *he* started to pull up her tunic.

She thought she squeaked. "Nay, I am fine. There is nay need—" she coughed.

"Lad, I willnae hear it. I need to see your…"

God's teeth! Was that her tunic up over her breasts? She'd bound them before she left Mangerton, but she was not sure if the bindings remained intact. Rosalia tried to search his expression as swiftly as he yanked the tunic down.

Turning his head, he coughed. "Seumas," he choked out. He nodded for Seumas and his men to take their leave. His massive body blocked her frame, and she did not think his men had seen her. At least, she hoped not. He stood over her, his hands on his hips, and she was silenced by his dark expression. He whipped around and started to fold blankets and gather supplies. His actions made her nervous and his jaw was clenched tight.

Without warning, his angry gaze swung over her. "When I pulled up your tunic, I was expecting a lad. Ye apparently have some *daft* reason to be traveling alone dressed in a lad's clothing with that prime horseflesh as your means of travel," he curtly stated, pointing at Noonie. "I will have the tale. Now, *lass*," he ordered.

Rosalia studied the man in front of her. She found herself completely at a loss for words and did not have the strength to look into his judging eyes. Tears spilled down her cheeks as she lowered her head, staring at her hands. She did not want to be a watering pot, but she had been through so much and did not need *him* as an added complication.

His expression softened and he cupped her chin

gently, searching her upturned face. "Lass, if I wanted to harm ye, it would have been done. My men and I journey from court, and I must know if someone gives chase to ye," he spoke in a soothing tone, successfully disarming her with his smile, but fortunately not robbing her of her wits.

"I have wasted your time and willnae keep ye further from your journey. Please leave me my mount and I will be on my way." She spoke with as reasonable a voice as she could manage.

He let out a long, audible breath. "I can see ye are going to be difficult." He smiled blandly. "First, I must check ye for injury. Now… I can either do it or have my men return and watch me do it. Ye decide," he said, his lips twisting into a cynical smile.

There was an uncomfortable silence and then Rosalia reluctantly nodded her head in consent.

"A wise choice, lass. I must cut the bindings to check your ribs, but I have supplies to use for binding if there is a need." He pulled out his dirk and started to lift her tunic.

She gasped, reaching out and grabbing his arm. Nervously, she blurted out the first thing that came to mind. "Wait… I donna know your name."

"I am Laird Ciaran MacGregor of Glenorchy." A smile played on the corner of his lips. "Will ye gift me with your name?"

She was not sure where Glenorchy was, but hopefully it was far enough from her home that he would not recognize her name. She glanced down for a brief moment to decide whether or not to speak it. After further consideration, there was not much he could do with a first name. "I am… my name is… Rosalia," she said quietly.

"Rosalia?" He cast a questioning gaze and then his face split into a wide grin. "'Tis a beautiful name." He partially lifted her tunic but left enough material to cover her breasts. Taking out his dirk, he cut her bindings. "Now I must touch ye to check your ribs." He hesitated, waiting for her response.

She nodded her consent.

He applied pressure and she inhaled a sharp breath. Stepping around her, he bent down behind her. "Rosalia, I am going to check your back." He paused for her response.

"Aye," she whispered.

Slowly, he touched her back and then pulled down her tunic. He walked over to his mount and returned with a sack. Sitting down, he dumped the contents in front of her. "I donna believe anything is broke now, but ye do have bruised ribs." He ripped pieces of cloth into sections. "Binding will help the pain."

It was apparent he had done this many times before. She continued to study him and stare at his broad shoulders and the corded muscles on his frame. He was much bigger than she remembered him being. What was the matter with her? She was injured. He just reminded her of James. Sure, that was it. Even though James never seemed to make her breath quicken when he glanced at her. Then again, perhaps it was the pain in her ribs. She wondered if she'd hit her head.

"Where are your men?" she asked, glancing around the small clearing.

"They are around. They will return when I call for

them." He grabbed the strips of cloth and gently lifted her tunic. "Are ye able to hold it up?"

"Aye," she grunted. He wrapped the strips of cloth around her and bound her ribs, tying off the strips. For someone who was so incredibly large, his touch was surprisingly gentle.

"That should help the pain in your ribs, and this should help the pain in your face," he said, holding up a salve. "May I?"

"Aye." She felt the heat rise in her face. Thankfully, the color was masked by the bruising—at least, she hoped it was. He applied the salve to her bruises and seemed naturally kind. She would be sure to thank him before she took her leave.

"There, all finished." The beginning of a smile tipped the corners of his mouth. He gathered up the remainder of the supplies and bundled them back on his horse. Returning with a wine sack, he sat down beside her and offered her a drink. "Do ye think ye can ride, Rosalia?"

She choked. This was not wine. It was… stronger, and it burned her insides.

"Careful. 'Tis my own ale."

Plagued with a coughing fit, she felt like her throat was on fire. She hastily handed him back the wine sack and he repeated his question. "Aye, I can ride. I thank ye for seeing to my injuries, my lair—"

"Ciaran," he simply stated.

"Ciaran. Ye and your men have my thanks." She tried to smile, but her lip cracked open. Instinctively, she raised her hand and placed her finger to her sore lip.

"It will heal with time." He hesitated, measuring

her for a moment. "Rosalia, I must know. Is your husband giving chase?"

"Husband?" Her voice unintentionally went up a notch. "I donna have a husband. I am nae wed." Why would he ask if she had a husband?

A strange look crossed his features before he quickly masked it. "If ye arenae wed, then who did this to ye, lass?"

Lowering her head, she stared at her hands. "Again. I must thank ye for caring for me, but donna let me keep ye from your journey. I am sure ye and your men wish to return home. *Mòran taing.*" *Thank you very much.*

❦

"Mòran taing?"

Did she think he would honestly leave her here to fend for herself? Maybe he should. That would surely teach her a lesson. Did she not realize the dangers of traveling alone? If she were his sister or even his wife, he would throttle her. He briefly wondered where that idea came from. No matter, he would take her to the next village and see to it she received care.

Her sudden, jerky movements pulled him from his thoughts.

"I havenae had an opportunity… What I mean to say is… I need a moment to…" Her flush deepened to crimson and she looked away from him.

"What?" Ciaran realized from her actions what she was trying to convey. He stood and held out his hand. "Let me help ye up. Can ye walk?"

"Slowly, but I can walk." Taking his hand, she

stood and held her ribs. Unsteady on her feet, she took a step back. He caught her by the elbow to assist her and she waved him off. "Nay, please. I can do it myself."

He watched her take unsteady steps into the trees. When he'd lifted her tunic and noticed a woman's breasts, several thoughts had come to mind. Why would a woman cut her tresses and dress in a lad's clothing? And when she spoke her name, something clicked in his mind. Ciaran had a vivid recollection of the woman at court. Her troubled face still haunted his dreams, but when she'd graced him with a smile… Due to the extent of her bruising he was not sure she was the same woman, but he would pull the truth from her eventually. He did know there was only one logical reason for her actions. She was running from someone or something. He most definitely did not need a woman's woes to keep them from returning home.

They needed to move.

He blew out a loud whistle for his men to return and Aiden cast him a questioning gaze. "What the hell was that about?"

Ciaran waved for his men to come near. "Ye willnae believe… The lad is a *lass*. We need to take our leave." When all of his men held similar shocked expressions upon their features, he added, "Aye, she has cut her tresses and wears a lad's clothing. Those arenae bruises from a fallen mount. She was badly beaten. She runs from someone but willnae say who. She says she is unwed but willnae say why she runs. Mount up. I donna want trouble. We will take her to the next village."

The lass emerged from the brush and his men gawked at her. She shifted from foot to foot and stared at her hands.

Silence grew tight with tension.

"We will ride with ye to the next village," said Ciaran, his voice ringing with command.

She immediately tensed. "Nay, ye have done enough. My thanks to ye and your men," she spoke firmly, her eyes proud.

"Lass, we willnae leave a woman, especially an injured woman, alone. We will all escort ye to the next village and seek the healer," he insisted. When she did not move and held her ground, he stared at her, perplexed. No one ever disobeyed his orders and this would not be a first. He grabbed her mount and led him over. Dropping the reins, Ciaran moved to assist her.

She placed her hand on his forearm, and a shiver ran through him from her mere touch. "Please, nay, I can do it."

Was she completely daft? Why was she so insistent on doing everything herself when she could barely stand to take care of her personal needs? Women. She was a frustrating lass. His eyes widened when the black beast actually started to kneel upon the ground.

Wincing in pain, she pulled herself upon his back. She kicked him once and the beast actually rose. "He is mine. I didnae steal him." She spoke with light bitterness.

He shook his head in nonbelief. This woman was an ever-changing mystery. He and his men mounted their horses and moved in single file. He rode behind her for her own protection, but also to ensure she did not flee. For some reason, he would not have been surprised if she tried. They continued to ride in companionable silence for the next couple of miles. It was a slow pace, but at least he was getting closer to home. He longed for the mountains of the Highlands.

The lass was quiet—too quiet. When Rosalia placed her hand at her side for support and stretched her back, he knew she was uncomfortable.

"How do ye fare?" Ciaran asked with concern.

She jumped at the sound of his voice and her horse shied, but she easily controlled her mount. "I am fine. My thanks for asking," she murmured.

He grunted in frustration—loudly. Perhaps he even growled. He was not sure. Was everything "fine" to her? Did she not realize the danger she was in? If someone else had found her, she would surely be… Ciaran shook off the mental image. She was a stubborn lass. It reminded him of why he was not wed. He heard enough of Aisling's ire to be thankful he was not Aiden. He would never understand women, let alone why anyone would want to be shackled to one—obstinate, bellowing creatures.

Aiden stopped his mount ahead on the path and waited for Ciaran to catch up. "Donna ye think we should rest, brother?" he asked, reining in his mount behind Ciaran.

He chuckled. "Why is it ye always ask me to rest, Aiden? Is it your bloody arse again?"

"Nay, ye daft fool. The lass probably needs to stop and rest," his brother chided him.

Ciaran sighed. "I suppose. We will stop at the next

clearing. Howbeit only for a short time. I want to keep moving in case trouble follows."

He halted his men at the next clearing, and Aiden quickly dismounted. Rushing to Rosalia's side, Aiden extended his hand. "Lass, can I assist ye down?"

An easy smile played the corners of her mouth and she remained as still as a stone statue. "Thank ye, sir—"

"Aiden."

"Thank ye, Aiden, but Noonie will go down for me." She pulled on the horse's mane and he went down on bended knee.

His brother shook his head in amusement. "'Tis truly incredible. Noonie?"

"His name." When she dropped Noonie's reins and stepped away, Aiden picked them up.

"Here, lass, I will take him for ye and tether him."

Turning, her movements were stiff and awkward. "There is nay need. He knows to stay when his reins are upon the ground."

"Truly?"

"Aye."

Ciaran pulled out a piece of dried beef from his sack as Aiden approached him. "Do ye know the horse will stay when his reins are upon the ground?" Aiden shook his head in amazement.

"I heard her speak as much to ye."

"Where did she get this mount?"

Ciaran swung his head around as Rosalia struggled to sit upon the ground. "I donna know, but I intend to find out." He patted his brother upon the shoulder and walked toward her with steely determination.

She was going to die. Dropping to the ground, Rosalia attempted to mask her pain. They could not see her suffer. They needed to be gone, and the sooner she could be rid of them, the better. She needed to keep moving. The closer she traveled to Glengarry, the better her chances of escape. The swig of ale she took earlier had only assisted for a short time and was starting to wear off. She winced as she lifted her tunic to adjust her bindings to be more comfortable.

"Do ye need me to assist ye?" When Rosalia yanked down the tunic, Ciaran added, "I didnae mean to startle ye." He handed her some dried beef and the wine sack. "'Tis just wine. Ye may have another drink of ale before we mount. Did it help the pain?" He sat down beside her.

"For a time." She placed a piece of dried beef into her mouth and then cast her eyes downward.

"Aiden tells me of your horse. Where did ye get such a trained mount?" When she took a drink of wine and ignored Ciaran's question, he repeated it. "Lass, ye know I willnae harm ye. I only ask where ye got him." This time his voice held a degree of warmth.

From his demeanor, she did not think men or women often refused to answer his requests or demands. She spoke cautiously. "I've had him since he was young. He was trained that way," she muttered uneasily.

"And where was he trained?" A suggestion of annoyance at her vague reply hovered in his eyes.

Rosalia chose her words carefully. "Er... Scotland, of course."

"And where in all of Scotland might that be, lass?" he drawled with distinct mockery.

Suddenly anxious to escape from his disturbing presence, she spoke hastily. "Pray excuse me. I believe my monthly courses have arrived." Pulling herself to her feet, she bit her lip to keep from crying out in pain. Holding her ribs, she walked stiffly into the trees. She was running out of diversions.

Did she actually tell him her monthly courses had arrived? She was at a loss for what to say and had to think of something quickly, so she spoke the first words that came to mind. That tactic usually worked on James. In fact, it would stop him dead in his tracks and he would always stop questioning her if she broached the subject. Rosalia could never understand why men were so adverse to womanly nature. They had no trouble bedding women, but mention a woman's time or birthing…

❦

Did she intentionally change the subject? Ciaran was usually skilled at getting the answers he sought, but he had to admit he never saw that one coming. He was speechless. She obviously did not want him asking any more questions. When he remembered her response, he had to laugh. She was good. He would give her that.

He gave an impatient shrug as he approached Aiden. "It was all for naught. She would speak of naught. All she said was that the horse was trained in Scotland and she has had him since he was young." Ciaran placed the wine sack in his bundle. "Let us keep moving and see the lass safe to the next village. Besides, I am sure your wee wife wants ye home."

Aiden's mouth twisted wryly. "I am sure she does. Ciaran, ye cannae keep running the lass so hard to get her to the village. She is injured." Ciaran was about to interject when Aiden cut him off. "Let us ride for a few more miles this day, and if we make it to the village, we make it. If we donna, we donna. Ye cannae stress her wounds even more, brother." He spoke in a disapproving tone.

"Aiden, ye know trouble will follow her. We will see her safe to the village, but we didnae ask to be her *champions*. I wish to be home to Glenorchy and—"

"Ciaran—"

He held up his hand to stop his interruption. "Ye know someone will come searching for the lass. If nae her, at least the mount—"

"Ciaran—"

Again, he held up his hand. "And when they do… She is the one who decided to run. 'Tisnae our fight, brother."

Aiden closed his eyes and shook his head downward. Unfortunately, it was at the same moment Ciaran heard someone else gasp from behind him. He spun around as Rosalia turned on her heel.

Aiden slapped him on the shoulder. "Verra tactful."

"God's teeth!" Ciaran moaned, rubbing his hand over his face.

"And I wish ye luck with that, brother."

Rosalia stood next to her horse, patting him on his muscular neck. She would not look at Ciaran, and considering the words that had escaped his mouth, he did not blame her. He placed his hand on Noonie's head and rubbed his ears. "He is magnificent."

She glanced down, her faint smile holding a touch of sadness. "Aye."

"Rosalia…"

"Please donna speak of it, my laird. I am fine. If ye wish to take your leave, please donna feel ye must chaperone me. I am one and twenty, and I assure ye that I donna need a chaperone or a *champion*." Tears welled within her eyes.

Ciaran drew his lips in thoughtfully. "Lass, we have been riding for well over a fortnight and—"

Rosalia set her chin in a stubborn line. "Please, my laird, nay apologies. I am ready to ride. How far to the village?" she asked, her eyebrows rising inquiringly.

"Half a day's ride from here," he sighed. "Rosalia, I didnae mean—"

She pulled on Noonie's mane so he would kneel. "Come, my laird. Ye are wasting precious light." She grunted as she tugged herself onto Noonie's back.

Staring at her, Ciaran stood motionless. Her face was black, she was battered and bruised from head to toe, frightened of something or someone, and he'd told her she was not worth the trouble she brought. Shaking his head, he realized he could be such a dolt.

Aiden brought over his brother's horse and nudged his shoulder. "Take your mount before ye look even more the daft fool."

"Aye, there is that." Before Ciaran mounted, he pulled out the wine sack from his bundle and handed it to Rosalia. "'Tis the ale. Take at least two swigs for the pain."

He could see her weighing her options. After a brief hesitation, she took the ale and drank two healthy gulps, choking both times. She handed the sack back and turned her head away from him.

He was an arse.

Four

"It appears only one room remains. We will sleep in the stable, and ye and your *wife* will be sharing a room," said Aiden, masking a smile. When Ciaran's men pulled Aiden aside as soon as they crossed the threshold of the small inn and then bolted out the door, Rosalia knew something was amiss. This, however, was not what she had expected.

"*What*?" Ciaran and Rosalia spoke at the same time.

Aiden shrugged his shoulders with indifference. "There arenae enough rooms. Donaidh and Seumas thought ye would rather stay with the lass than have any of us stay with her. Besides, Aisling would have my—" he paused, looking down at his manhood, "er… *head* if I stayed with her. They go to seek the healer now, and it was easier to explain if the lass was posing as your wife."

Silence grew tight with tension. Rosalia did not like this—at all. His commitment was to take her to the village. It was not to be sharing a room and pretending to be man and wife. He was asking too much of her. "Nay, I willnae share a room. Ye have done enough, my laird. I will see the healer and then be on my way. 'Tis what we spoke of. Ye and your men have my thanks." She spoke with a faint thread of agitation in her voice.

An unwelcome tension stretched even tighter between them.

Ciaran placed his hand gently on her shoulder. "Rosalia, ye can barely ride and need to rest in a bed. And ye *will* spend the night in a bed. How do ye expect to heal if ye donna take care?"

His hand remained on her shoulder for a moment too long. She felt a shiver run through her body and pulled her eyes away from him. Ciaran placed his fingers under her chin. "Look at me, lass. Ye know there is nay need to fear me. I will sleep upon the floor." She tried to protest, but he left no room for debate. "My men are right. 'Tis less to explain if ye are posing as my wife."

Clearly having no voice in the matter, Rosalia sought her room while Ciaran and his men headed to the tavern. She climbed the stairs, step after miserable step, and could feel a growing pain in her arse that was not from her injuries. Frustration consumed her. She was stuck with these men for another night. And now she had to maintain the pretense that she was his *wife*? The way he barked orders at her—God's teeth! She could not even run away to Glengarry without things running awry. Opening the door to her room, Rosalia felt the scent of fresh-cut flowers tickle her nose. She closed the door and found the space was small with only a bed, a table, and two chairs, but at least it appeared clean. As she sat down on the bed, she noticed the cut flowers bundled on the pillow beside her.

There was a knock at the door and three burly men carried in a tub, followed by a couple of lads with steaming buckets of water. A maid entered, ushering the men out. Rosalia was speechless and needed a moment to gather her wits.

"Your husband ordered a bath for ye, my lady. My apologies ye lost your trunk in the accident. I know 'tisnae much, but I have a worn day dress ye may have. 'Tis at least clean," the maid said, holding up the dress.

Pulling at her tunic, Rosalia muttered the first words that came to mind, "Aye, my gown was badly torn. Ye have my thanks." She accepted the dress from the maid, then panicked because she was unsure how to answer if the maid questioned her cut tresses. Rosalia simply prayed that she would not ask.

"May I assist ye with your clothes, my lady? Your husband says ye are injured from when ye fell from your mount."

Rosalia could not let pride stand in the way of a warm bath. It would definitely soothe her sore and aching bones. How very thoughtful of her *husband* to order it for her! Once she was in the tub, she immediately dismissed the maid. The water felt positively delightful on her bruised skin. She moaned, letting the hot water work its magic. She had not felt this peaceful in days. Closing her eyes, she enjoyed the warmth that surrounded her.

Someone pounded on the door, and for a moment, Rosalia forgot her surroundings. She must have fallen asleep. "My lady, the healer is here for ye," called the maid through the door.

"Just a moment." Grabbing the edge of the tub,

Rosalia pulled herself from the tepid water, not so gracefully exiting her bath. The room was tiny, so the washtub made it more difficult to maneuver. Needing to dress quickly, she dried herself and donned a fresh tunic. "Come."

The maid entered with an elderly man and shut the door.

"My lady," said the gentleman, giving her a quick bow. He placed his bag upon the bed and gently pushed her shoulder to lie down. He examined her bruises and his eyes narrowed. "That must have been some fall. Ye have several cuts and swelling in the face. Are ye light-headed?"

"Only when I stand too quickly," she offered. As he applied pressure to her arms, ribs, and legs to check for broken bones, she closed her eyes to abate the sharp pain.

The healer murmured to himself and then smiled as he covered Rosalia with a blanket. "I donna think ye have broken bones, but I would advise ye to accept a treatment of bleeding."

"Bleeding?" she squeaked. Rosalia was too startled by his suggestion to offer any objection.

"Aye, I donna know if ye have inside injuries, and I find bleeding will prevent fever and infection from setting in."

The door opened and Ciaran simply walked in. It was getting a bit too crowded in the small room. "And how does she fare?" His eyes caught and held hers.

The healer cleared his throat. "I was explaining to your wife that I donna think there are broken bones. I donna know if she has injuries inside so I will bleed her."

"Bleed her?" The lines of attentiveness deepened along Ciaran's brows and under his eyes.

"Aye. I find bleeding will prevent fever and infection from setting."

"Ye willnae bleed my wife," Ciaran said smoothly. His expression was a mask of stone. He reached into his pouch and handed the healer some coin. "For your time."

The healer shrugged indifferently. "As ye will. I will leave a salve for her bruises," he said, searching through his bag.

"Nay, ye have done more than enough. I will care for her." Ciaran ushered the man out the door and then turned toward the maid. "Have the tub removed and inquire on the tray I asked for my wife," he ordered.

"Aye, my laird," she said, bobbing a small curtsy and scampering out the door.

Ciaran stood frozen in the doorway. He would not look at Rosalia, and he surely was not speaking to her—again. He placed his hands on the wall and tapped impatiently. Running his hand through his hair, he stepped aside as the men came back to remove the tub. When they left, he closed the door and his eyes.

❧

When the healer said he would bleed Rosalia, Ciaran had tried to rein his anger. He had needed to remove the man from his sight and quickly. Unfortunately, throwing him through the door was not an option. What was the lass going to do when he and his men departed on the morrow? She had no one to look after her. If he was not here and the man had attempted to bleed her... The thought tore at his insides.

"My laird?" Rosalia said softly, her eyes narrowing.

A muscle quivered at his jaw. "Ciaran," he simply stated.

"Ciaran?" There was a gentle softness in her voice.

"What kind of healer is that?" he bellowed. "Ye have nay reason to be bled." He paced the floor of the tiny room. "I have seen men with injury worse than ye and still they arenae bled. He doesnae know what he speaks."

She sighed. Tossing off the blankets, Rosalia rose from the bed and approached him. Her fingers rested upon his arm. "Ciaran, I am well enough. My cuts and bruises will heal with time. Ye have spoken as much." He stared at her hand upon his arm as there was another knock at the door.

"Come," he said curtly. A maid entered with a trencher of meat, bread, and cheese. "Place it upon the table."

The maid lowered the tray and, as she turned, brushed her breasts against Ciaran chest to pass. The woman hesitated briefly and gave him a pointed look. "Close quarters. If ye need anything, anything at all, please ask for Eilidh," she spoke in a silky voice.

Rosalia brought up her hand to stifle her giggles.

"Thank ye, but 'tis all my *wife* and I need," Ciaran said, ushering the maid out the door. When the door closed, he turned and scowled. "And what do ye find so amusing?"

"She obviously found ye too tempting to pass."

He clenched his mouth tight and pulled out a chair for her to sit at the table. When she sat in the chair, his eyes roamed over her and he discreetly adjusted the front of his trews. "Rosalia, will ye don something other than only a tunic?" Slowly, she stood and grabbed her trews, and he turned around.

"Ciaran, I must thank ye for the food, and the bath was welcome." She grunted as she pulled on her trews. "Ye may turn." She spoke with an air of ease as if she was not almost bare in front of him.

He nodded for her to take her seat. "Please eat." He paused for a moment. "May I ask a small boon?"

"Aye," Rosalia said, stirring uneasily in the chair.

"Ye donna need to thank me for everything constantly. 'Tis something most men would have done had they been in my place." His words seemed to amuse her.

"Hmm… That, my laird, hasnae been my experience." Something flickered in the back of her eyes. "I have a feeling ye arenae like most men." Reaching out, she grabbed a piece of bread and cheese. "Please, ye are going to join me?"

Ciaran nodded and sat down. Breaking off a piece of bread, he placed a morsel into his mouth.

"I donna know if ye brought the ale, but might I have some?" she asked, rubbing her side.

"Of course." He wiped his hands on his trews and rose. Pulling out the ale from his sack by the door, he handed it to her. "Drink a fair amount this eve since we donna travel. It will help ye rest."

"My thanks."

He raised his eyebrow when she insisted on

thanking him again, and she returned his look with a sheepish smile.

❧

Taking another swig of ale, Rosalia noticed how his chestnut hair hung low on his shoulders. She wondered how pushing it back behind his ear would feel. As if he read her mind, he took a strand of hair and placed it behind his ear. She studied his hands. Ciaran had such strong hands. They were rough and worn, but she could not believe how gentle they were when he touched her. She took another sip of ale, and her throat did not appear to burn as it had before. Why was it warm in here? Was he warm?

Ciaran caught her staring and cleared his throat, and Rosalia promptly glanced down at her hands. He obviously did not want to be tied with her, but he did portray a tremendous amount of honor. *Honor.* She wondered if he was from the Highlands. It occurred to her that she had never asked him.

"Ye spoke of Glenorchy," she said as he looked up from the trencher. "Is it located in the Highlands?"

"Aye."

"Is your wife waiting for ye there?" She caught herself too late. Why the hell would she ask him that? She could not believe she had spoken so freely. He must think her daft.

His gaze traveled over her face and seemed to search her eyes before he responded. "I am nae wed. We travel with haste because Aiden's wife is with child. Court took longer than expected and my men are anxious to return home."

"As are ye."

He studied her thoughtfully for a moment. "Rosalia, my apologies for what ye heard. I meant naught. My men are tired and only want to return home—and aye, as do I." His tone was apologetic.

She waved him off. "There is nay need for apologies, my laird. I have sought the healer, and ye have delivered me safely to the village. Ye and your men will be traveling on the morrow. I only hope I havenae delayed your journey too long."

His eyes were gentle, understanding. "Rosalia—"

"Will ye tell me of your home?"

"What?" Ciaran stared at her, confounded.

"Will ye tell me of your home? I wish to hear of it," she said, taking another swig of ale. Her reaction seemed to amuse him.

"What do ye want to know?"

Rosalia handed him the wine sack and he took a healthy drink. "Howbeit we make a compromise?" he asked, handing it back. "I will answer what ye ask, and in return, ye have to answer what I ask."

He waited for her response as she took another sip. "'Tis a deal as long as ye donna attempt to keep me further from *my* journey. Ye appear to be a man of your word. I will have it—your word."

Ciaran nodded his head in consent. "Agreed. Ye have my word."

"Good. Now tell me of Glenorchy."

He chuckled as if he was sincerely amused. Leisurely, he stretched his long legs. "Glenorchy stands at the northeast end of Loch Awe. The northwest side is where the River Orchy enters the loch. The land around Glenorchy forms an island on which sits my home. And where is your home?"

She lounged casually in the chair. "My home is in Scotland but verra near to England's border."

He wiggled his fingers for her to take another drink. "Is that where your horse was trained?"

"Noonie? Aye. Ye forget it was my turn to question," she scolded him.

"Aye." He held up his hands in mock defense and then held out his palm for her to continue.

"If your home is on an island, how do ye get there? Surely ye donna swim," she blurted out as she laughed—actually laughed. She could not remember the last time she had laughed. Why was she so warm?

"Ye can get to my home by boat or by *cabhsair*."

"Can ye view the loch from all sides of your home?" Rosalia put her elbow on the table and rested her chin in her hand.

"Aye, but ye see the mountains on all sides as well."

She sighed. "It sounds beautiful."

"'Tis. And your home? What loch is it near?"

"My home doesnae sit on the loch. 'Tisnae far to travel to it, though. I enjoy watching it and hearing the water."

"Aye. Peaceful," he agreed.

She took another drink and handed him the wine sack. "Is it my turn or yours?"

"Your turn to ask," Ciaran said, handing it back.

"Tell me of your family."

"My family. My mother and father have passed. As ye know, I am eldest. Aiden is my second brother and then I have Declan, the youngest. Tell me of your family."

"I donna have a brother or sister."

"Are your mother and father still living?"

She paused, looking down at her hands. "Aye. How far is Glenorchy from here?"

"Two days. How did ye end up in the clearing where Donaidh and Seumas found ye?"

Rosalia rubbed her hands over her face. "The pain was shooting and I needed to rest. I was only going to stop for a short time. I fell from Noonie and everything went black." She took another swig of ale and handed him the wine sack. "I heard tales of fighting in the Highlands. Men fighting to protect what is theirs and such. Do ye fight or have a need to defend your home from another clan?"

"Aye, the bloody Campbells. Why is your horse named Noonie?"

"'Tis the name to which he has grown accustomed. The bloody Campbells? Tell me. Why do ye fight?"

"Ye didnae answer the question. I asked why such a name for your horse." Ciaran raised his eyebrow and waited for her response.

She was not exactly thrilled to answer him, but she did make a promise. "My mother named him. She often said I ate as much as my horse and I ne'er missed a noon meal. She said we were alike in that regard. Now… I will hear about the bloody Campbells. Tell me. Why do ye fight?"

"'Tis a question that has nay easy answer. Glenorchy was originally owned by the Campbells."

"The *bloody* Campbells," she slurred.

He laughed. "Aye, the *bloody* Campbells. Glenorchy was bestowed upon the MacGregors for allegiance.

The MacGregor Chief at that time helped Alexander II with his conquest of Argyll. The MacGregor Chief was one of the leaders of the Royal army as vassal to the Earl of Ross. When the leaders of the army were rewarded, Glenorchy was bestowed upon us."

"And they still continue to fight for it after all this time?"

"Aye. Who hurt ye, Rosalia?"

She took another swig of ale. "'Tis a question that has nay easy answer," she repeated in the same mocking tone.

"'Tis your turn to answer."

"Aye. 'Tisnae a pleasant tale to tell to recollect," she moaned into her hands.

"Take all the time ye need."

She raised her head and smiled at him. "Ye are too kind, my laird… Ciaran…by far."

There was a moment of silence and Rosalia found it hard to focus. "The family coffers are near to empty so I was to be bargained to an English *lord* in order for Mother and Father to obtain a heavy purse." A heaviness centered in her chest.

They exchanged a subtle look of amusement as Ciaran waited for her to continue.

"Verra well. Mother and Father give me a strong hand—a verra strong hand. I gave the English *peacock* a chance and discovered he was the foulest of beasts. There was also a tale that he killed his own brother for coin. When I told Mother and Father I refused to wed this man… ye can see for yourself." Her voice did not quite reflect the agony she felt. "I travel to Glengarry to seek my *seanmhair,* but the gods were kind enough to put ye in the path of my journey, Ciaran MacGregor. I will have a chance to heal and will be able to continue, thanks to ye."

⁂

Ciaran's mind was racing with questions. Her own mother and father had caused these bruises? Glengarry? The Highland weather this time of year was unpredictable. Was the lass completely daft? He had known something untoward had befallen her and he still was uncertain he had the entire tale. He shifted in his chair and his heart pounded through his chest, a mixture of anger and respect overwhelming him.

"Ciaran, I donna feel so well." Rosalia rubbed her hands over her eyes. "Could we seek our beds now?"

He exchanged a smile with her. "Of course, lass." He rose and grabbed the back of her chair. "Donna stand too quickly, Rosalia." She put her hands on his arms and tried to pull herself up, barely able to balance on her own two feet. He steadied her and she glanced up at him with trusting eyes—eyes that were the color of the sea. A man could easily drown in them.

"Ciaran." Raising her hand, she placed it on his cheek.

He closed his eyes and leaned into her hand. When he opened them, she looked at him so intensely. Her short, cut tresses fell into her face and he brushed them back behind her ear. What was he thinking? Rosalia was injured and, no thanks to him, in her cups. He could not take advantage of her weakened state. Instinctively, Ciaran glanced down at her parted lips, and all sense of reason deserted him. The next he knew, he was bending his head slowly forward as she closed her eyes.

His lips gently brushed hers. She melted into his chest, her fingers squeezing the muscles on his arms. She wrapped her arms around him and he deepened the kiss. When Rosalia let out a mewling sound, he pulled back. The last he wanted was to cause her pain. He kissed her bruised cheek and then kissed her on the top of her head.

She pulled back slightly and raised her fingertip to her lips. "I need to sit before I fall."

"Come," he said. He helped her into bed and covered her with a blanket. Sitting beside her on the edge of the bed, he again brushed her tresses away from her face. When he glanced down, she was watching him.

"Please donna pity me, Ciaran. From ye, I donna think I could bear it."

Ciaran gave her a warm smile and bent down and brushed his lips with hers. "'Tisnae pity ye see upon my face, Rosalia." He rubbed his thumb on her bruised cheek. "Now ye sleep." He bent over and kissed the top of her head. He stood and gave her one last look before he blew out the candles and sought the floor. What the hell was the matter with him?

Not sure why he'd kissed her, he contemplated his actions. No woman had ever gazed at him like that. Although the tale the lass told was not pleasant, Ciaran could not remember the last time he actually sat and spoke with a lass. He and Beathag never really had words, nor would he ever think of being that compassionate to her. Simply, they took their pleasure from one another and then took their leave. That was all he ever desired, nothing more. He had to admit he enjoyed speaking with Rosalia. Was it pity he felt for her? It was definitely not pity. He admired her courage.

As he lay in the darkness listening to her gentle breathing, his mind wandered. How much had actually occurred before Rosalia decided finally to take her leave? She'd cut her tresses and dressed in lad's clothing. He did not know too many lasses who would attempt such a feat. And who was this English lord she was supposed to wed? That was a mystery in itself. Ciaran finally closed his eyes and had fallen into a deep sleep when a piercing scream echoed loudly in the silence of the night.

Startled, he sprang to his feet and grabbed his sword, ready to defend against whatever nightmare had awoken him. He found Rosalia thrashing violently on the bed. Ciaran dropped his sword and quickly approached her. "Rosalia, ye are dreaming," he strongly whispered, grabbing her by the arms.

Surely this commotion would bring the attention of the entire inn upon them. He did not want to think about that outcome. He needed her to stop—now. As he restrained her arms, she shook violently. The lass clenched her fists and tried to hit him. His grip was intense, but she managed to free her legs from the blankets and kick at him, almost hitting him between the legs. As Ciaran repositioned himself, he relaxed his grip on her arms. It was too late. He realized his mistake. She squeezed her hand into a tight fist and took another swing at him. This one landed squarely on his jaw.

He placed his body weight upon her and whispered soothingly into her ear until she started to calm. She was still shaking, and he could feel the dampness of her tears upon his chest. "Rosalia, are ye awake? Ye were dreaming," he whispered.

She was actually trembling now. "Aye." Her tears choked her.

The innkeeper's voice echoed in the hallway as he told everyone to go back and seek their beds. Ciaran closed his eyes at the inevitable.

There was a knock at his door.

"Everything is fine. My wife was only dreaming," he called out with sternness in his voice.

There was a brief pause. "Aye," said the innkeeper as he paused and then walked away from the door.

Ciaran moved to get up, but she wrapped her arms around him and cried into his shoulder. "Please stay with me, Ciaran. Donna leave. I need ye here with me. I donna want to be alone. Please…" Her voice faded to a hushed stillness.

"I willnae leave ye, Rosalia." He moved to her side and wrapped his arm around her waist as she nestled her bottom against his groin. He pushed stray tendrils of hair back from her cheek. "Shh… ye are safe." Her breathing calmed and her tears finally stopped, but he continued to hold her well into the night. Although he was reluctant to admit it, Rosalia felt damn good in his arms. He swiftly pushed back the notion.

He really would like to know what the hell was wrong with him. Maybe he'd had more ale than he realized or perhaps it was simply having a warm woman cradled next to him. He had not bedded Beathag for some time. He could not understand why he was drawn to Rosalia. Ciaran knew for certain he did not pity her, and she was not the type of lass he usually bedded. She had no tresses and dressed in lad's clothing, and he most certainly did not take to men. What was it then? It could be her blue eyes—the color of the sea. When she laughed this eve, it had felt as if the sun bathed his body in warm rays of light.

Rosalia stirred and he held her tighter.

"Ciaran," she murmured sleepily.

"Aye, I am here," he reassured her. God help him. He knew at that moment he needed to enjoy the warmth while it lasted because he had made a decision. Come first light, she would not like it—not like it at all.

His vow of not becoming involved with her was solid, but his honor would not allow him to leave her here unattended. Whether the lass liked it or not, she would travel with him to Glenorchy. Once he delivered her to Glengarry, his conscience would be clear. Rosalia snuggled in closer and let out a sigh. Ciaran closed his eyes, having no intention of permitting himself to get too close to her. No intention whatsoever.

෴

Rosalia was bathed in heat. It was delightful. She breathed in the spicy scent and sighed. Arms tightened around her as she stirred, and she realized that Ciaran slept next to her. Remembering most of their speech last eve, she did not want this to end—well, at least the part of Ciaran sleeping next to her. It felt… right.

"How do ye fare, Rosalia?"

She jumped, having thought he was still fast asleep. "I feel… I donna know," she said, confused.

"'Tis probably the ale. It will pass," he said in a

warm, comforting tone. There was a knock on the door and she stiffened in his arms. "Aye?"

"Ciaran, Calum is readying our mounts," said Aiden through the door.

He sighed. "Give me a few moments."

She was not surprised that he wished to take his leave so early this morn. It was as they had discussed, but Rosalia could not stay the feelings he stirred within her. Glengarry was her destiny, not some Highland laird she met along the way. She needed to quit dreaming and come back to reality. She was never meant to be with someone like *him*.

Raising his hand, Ciaran gently rubbed her cheek. "I will let ye take care of your personal needs and then I need to speak with ye."

She nodded her head in agreement.

He fled the bed fully clothed and sat at the table to put on his boots. He fastened his sword, grabbed the ale and his sack, and gave her a brief nod as he departed. She could be so foolish. Ciaran offered her comfort, nothing more. She was thankful for his kindness toward her because if anyone else had found her, she might not have been so lucky.

Rising from the bed, Rosalia felt slightly better than she had the day before. She was definitely sore, but it was not as unbearable. She took care of her personal needs and approached her sack. Picking up the day dress, she decided to pack it. There could be a need for it. After all, she could not greet her *seanmhair* in trews. She sat down and donned her boots. Grabbing her bundle, she swung open the door and found Ciaran waited for her, leaning up against the wall.

He took her gently by the arm and escorted her back into the room. "Rosalia, I need but a moment."

Turning around, she placed her sack on the bed.

"How do ye fare? Does your head ache from the ale?" he asked, a half smile crossing his features.

"Actually, nay. I feel better than last eve."

"Truly?"

"Aye. What happened to your jaw?" she asked, reaching out to touch it.

"'Tis naught. My mount brought his head up when I was putting on his bridle." He paused for a moment, studying her intently. "When we spoke last eve, ye told me ye travel to Glengarry to seek your *seanmhair*."

Rosalia stiffened. "Aye. And I wasnae that far into my cups to hear ye say ye wouldnae keep me from my journey," she said tersely.

Ciaran tilted his brow, looking at her with uncertainty. "I willnae, but I have something to ask ye."

"And what is that, my laird?" she asked hesitantly.

"Ye will come with me to Glenorchy—"

"Nay! Ye and your men have done enough. Ye need to be home, my laird, and I need to travel to Glengarry. I willnae accept your *pity*."

A swift shadow of anger swept across his face. "*Pity?* Rosalia, ye arenae listening to me," he bellowed. When she jumped and raised her hands in a defensive gesture, he took a deep breath and smiled an apology. "Listen to me. Do ye know where Glengarry is, lass?" he asked, lowering his voice.

"In the Highlands. North," she murmured.

"Rosalia, 'tis verra north in the Highlands. The Highland weather this time of year is completely unpredictable. Ye donna have the supplies needed to make such a journey. Even when my men and I travel that far, we must take every precaution. Ye only have a couple of blankets, Rosalia. There is too much risk to journey there now." She was about to interrupt him when he raised his hand. "Glenorchy is two days north from here. Ye ride with me and stay in my home. When 'tis safe to travel, I will take ye to your *seanmhair*. Ye have my word."

She merely stared, tongue-tied. "And why would ye do that? I cannae impose upon ye. I heard ye speak with my own ears 'tisnae your fight and ye didnae ask to be my *champion*."

"Donna think upon it as I would be your champion." His eyes studied her for a moment as if he knew some great secret. "Think upon it as I am now going to be your *savior*."

She snapped her mouth shut, stunned by his bluntness. She also did not fail to catch the sarcasm in his voice. "My *savior*? Ye *arrogant—*"

"Aye. I am saving ye from yourself."

Rosalia paused and when she mentally replayed his words, she actually laughed. James was the only man who ever saved her from herself—repeatedly. "Why would ye do this for me? Ye said ye donna want trouble. I speak the truth when I tell ye I donna know what follows me."

Reaching out, Ciaran caught her hand in his. "Lass, ye appear to have had a time of it and I want to give ye a chance at the life ye seek. Ye seem to think this will happen if ye travel to Glengarry. When I take ye to your *seanmhair*, ye will have your chance. I donna speak untruths when I say ye willnae make it to Glengarry alone."

There was a heavy silence.

As casually as Rosalia could manage, she asked, "And what of your men? I cannae travel at the speed—"

"Donna worry. I have already spoken with my men. Aiden and Donaidh ride ahead to Glenorchy, and Calum and Seumas will ride with us." His voice was firm and final.

An unwelcome blush crept into her cheeks. "I cannae help but to feel a burden—"

"Cease your tongue, Rosalia. Noonie awaits and we are ready to ride. Do ye join me?" Ciaran folded his arms over his chest and waited for her response.

She nodded her head in consent. "Aye, ye have my thanks."

He rolled his eyes. "Cease your thanking and grab your sack."

❦

They continued to ride north, and Rosalia could not help but wonder if she should feel some guilt for the relief she felt. She would have an escort and be able to travel safely to her *seanmhair*. A new life awaited her at Glengarry, and she could not wait to embrace it. She pushed back her reflection of Ciaran from last eve, but she could still feel the warmth of his embrace and her lips tingled in remembrance of his touch. Taking a deep breath, she closed her eyes at the memory. It was not in her best interest to dwell upon such things. When she opened her eyes, Ciaran smiled as if he read her mind—well, she hoped he did not.

Rosalia had Noonie pick up the pace, feeling guilty she had held these men back for so long. They probably had families anxiously awaiting their return, especially if Aiden and Donaidh rode ahead to Glenorchy and told them the remainder of the men followed—slowly.

Calum trotted up beside her and inclined his blond head. Awkwardly, she cleared her throat. "Do ye and Seumas have family waiting for ye at Glenorchy?"

"Nay," he answered quickly. "Aiden and Donaidh are the only fools, er... men to take that step," he murmured, turning his head away from her.

She could not control the giggle that escaped her. "Ye know, Calum, some women feel the same as ye."

His eyes grew openly amused. "Truly?"

"Truly."

"Then mayhap ye can introduce me to one that doesnae want to shackle me." His expression grew serious. "I am glad ye decided to journey with us, Rosalia. I am sure it wasnae easy for ye to agree to such, but I know our laird can be verra persuasive. Ye will like Glenorchy... and our laird." Kicking his mount into a gallop, he rode ahead of her.

She had to will her mouth to close. That was rather embarrassing.

Without warning, Ciaran stopped his mount and whipped his head around. "We will stop here this eve. The next part of the journey is into the mountains and 'tis too dangerous to start now. Our horses will need to be sure-footed and it will be dark soon enough. There is a stream over there to water the horses." He nodded in the opposite direction.

After the horses were watered, Rosalia pulled

blankets from her sack. Calum started a fire and Seumas pulled out provisions. These men were efficient, and she noticed that Ciaran did not have to tell anyone what to do. Awkwardly, she lowered herself to the ground and sat on her blanket. She felt out of place with the men working around her. She should be doing something other than sitting on her arse. It was the least she could do for their escort.

Ciaran handed her the wine sack and she raised her eyebrow questioningly.

"'Tis just the wine," he smirked.

As she tried to stand, he extended his hand to help her up. Leaning closer, she whispered, "Ciaran, I need to do something."

He had a puzzled look upon his features. "Like what?" he murmured back.

She pointed to the men. "Calum is starting a fire. Seumas is preparing our meal, and I am sitting on my..." She gestured with her hands and blushed, feeling unhappy with herself.

"Rosalia, my men know what to do. Do ye actually want me to tell them to let a lass help them with their duties?" Ciaran's response held a note of impatience.

She shook her head. "Nay. I just feel—"

He placed his arm around her shoulder. "I have a task for ye. Ye are to sit here and rest. Ye need to heal, and 'tis a *verra* important task." He helped her to the ground and smiled.

She rolled her eyes. "Aye, but I donna like it."

"I didnae ask ye to like it." He walked away and returned a moment later, handing her some dried beef and an oatcake.

Rosalia nodded her head. "My thanks."

His voice was heavy with sarcasm. "How many times will we be discussing your thanking me?"

She bit her tongue.

Everyone finished their meal and sat silently around the fire. Due to the lack of conversation, Rosalia's eyelids became heavy and she had difficulty keeping them open. "Rosalia, seek your bed around the fire. Calum will take first watch," said Ciaran.

Rising slowly, she gathered her blankets and settled near the fire. She bunched up a blanket to use as a substitute pillow and turned on her side. Ciaran watched her through the flames. His gaze held hers and she could not look away. He was a handsome and honorable man. When Rosalia could no longer fight sleep, her eyelids slipped down over her eyes and she smiled. She would surely dream of him.

❧

Even through her bruises, the lass was beautiful. Ciaran fought his own battle of personal restraint. It was difficult to remain rational when Rosalia was so close to him, but thinking of his vow to his father managed to give him new resolve. He was only her escort, nothing more. Her problems were her own, and he clearly had enough of his own. Ciaran ensured that Calum maintained his post and then sought his own bed—as far away from the lass as possible. Once he returned to Glenorchy, he would seek Beathag and all of this foolishness will be gone. He had been far too long without a woman's touch. No sooner did he fall asleep when shrill screams awakened him.

He approached Rosalia's temporary bed. "Rosalia, ye are dreaming." He dropped down beside her and gave her a little nudge.

"*Cha tugadh an donas an car asad!*" she screamed. *The devil couldnae get the best of ye!*

His men sat up and he waved them off. Drawing on his experience the night before, Ciaran wrapped his arms around her waist, whispering soothing words into her ear.

"James! James, please help me! James!" Rosalia yielded to compulsive sobs that shook her.

"Shh... 'tis me, Ciaran," he said soothingly. Her eyes flew open, tears streaming down her cheeks. Her body trembled with fear. "Lass, who is James?" Ciaran asked, just before he felt a cold, hard blade at his neck.

"Me..."

Five

"Give me reason to slit your throat, ye bloody cur," James bit out, pressing the blade against Ciaran's throat. Rosalia slowly pulled away from Ciaran and not so gracefully stood. As she paused to catch her breath, she needed a moment to process the scene before her. James held his sword to Ciaran's throat with a look of murderous intent upon his face. Calum lay still upon the ground at his post, and a man held a blade at the throat of Seumas as well. She turned her attention back to James as he glowered at Ciaran.

"James…" Fortunately, no one noticed the tremor in her voice.

He may have momentarily ceased glowering at Ciaran, but now James glared at her, looking upon her as though she were filthy vermin. "I see ye are well, Lady Rosalia. Where have ye been? Your betrothed anxiously awaits your return." His curt voice lashed at her.

She glanced around nervously and recognized some of her father's men, but not all of them. From her count, there were roughly eight. James had a reputation of prowess on the battlefield, but she prayed she did not have to witness it firsthand. She had to make an attempt to calm him. Ciaran's life depended on it.

"James—"

"Donna speak, wench! Ye have disgraced yourself and your family. 'Tis a wonder Lord Dunnehl still wishes to wed ye." A chill hung on the edge of his words and he seethed with anger. Ciaran shifted beneath the blade that held him and James whipped his head down. "Donna even attempt escape lest the wench sees your blood spilled upon the ground," he growled, repositioning the blade at Ciaran's throat.

Icy fear twisted around Rosalia's heart. Why would he not calm down? He was not even giving her a chance to speak. She had to try to soothe his ire. "James—"

He gave her a hostile glare. "I told ye to cease your tongue, *wench*!"

She jumped and panic welled in her throat. She had never seen James so hostile toward her. When she glanced at Ciaran, she saw a lethal calmness in his eyes. Rosalia recognized that steely determination. Blood could not be shed. She had to stop this—now.

"Howbeit your mother anxiously awaits your return and I am here to see ye safely delivered. Ye will come back with me to wed Lord Dunnehl, but first I must ask ye…" James paused, cocking his head at Ciaran. "Would ye rather me cut off his head for looking at ye or his hands for touching ye?" Lifting his eyes, James gave her a conspiratorial wink.

The men around her laughed as something clicked in her mind. James would never *force* her to wed, let alone return her to her mother. She glanced around to see most of the men watching their exchange. It finally dawned on her that James had a plan. Rosalia would follow his lead and play along, but from the coolness in Ciaran's eyes, the plan had better be a darned good one.

She grunted and bent to pick up Ciaran's sword. It was heavier than it looked. How could men lift such things? She raised her head and straightened herself with as much dignity as she could muster.

"Nay, Rosalia. Donna…" Ciaran murmured, the pressure of the blade cutting off his speech.

James laughed. "Ye can barely lift the sword. What damage do ye think ye can bestow upon me, wench? A lass with a sword dressed in a man's clothing. Ye know to strike me with the pointy end right?" When he gazed down at the sword pointed at his manhood, she could swear he paled.

"Aye. What damage could I possibly bestow on ye? One move of my wrist and I cut off your most prized possession, ye *arrogant* beast."

Amusement flickered in the eyes that met hers. James blew out a loud whistle as several of the men that encircled them dropped to the ground at the same time. She dropped the sword, and James released his hold on Ciaran.

"Verra well done, Rosalia. Ye actually looked a wee bit pale. For a moment, I didnae think ye understood the need for distraction," said James. Glancing down at Ciaran, he extended his hand to pull him up, but Ciaran would not take it.

Ciaran grabbed his sword and climbed to his feet, rubbing his neck.

"See the men are secured," James shouted to his men, who left them alone as they moved to the task at hand. Turning, he gave a brief nod to Ciaran. "I couldnae take the chance and needed Rosalia to confirm ye werenae a threat."

She placed her hand on Ciaran's forearm. "Are ye well?" she asked with concern.

"Aye." He stepped around her and moved to stand within a hairsbreadth of James. His eyes were hard and filled with dislike. "The next time ye draw your sword on me, ye best be prepared to use it," Ciaran warned, his voice ruthless. He slammed into James's shoulder as he stormed past.

James shrugged his shoulders with indifference and Rosalia flew into his arms. "I have worried so. Please tell me ye are well," he spoke quietly, rubbing his hands over her cut tresses.

"I am well." Tears blinded her eyes and choked her voice. "I miss ye terribly already. My apologies if I caused ye worry, but there was naught I could have done differently."

"I know. I struggle over the feeling I failed ye, lass." His voice dropped in volume.

Pulling away from him, Rosalia held him at arms' length. "Failed me? Ye showed me love as a brother, James. Ye *are* my brother. I love ye and ye havenae failed me. I donna know what I would have done without ye. Ye are my family." She did not understand why he would blame himself. If not for him, she would never have made it as long as she had.

Smiling, he fingered her clothing. "Rosalia, correct me if I err, but isnae that *my* tunic I just had made?" He quirked his eyebrow questioningly and she returned a sheepish grin.

"Aye, but your clothes always fit so much better than my own—much more comfort, ye know."

He rolled his eyes. After a moment, he nodded to Ciaran. "Lass, who is that man? I should have his name lest he kills me with the looks he passes my way." His lips puckered with annoyance.

She turned, gazing at Ciaran. "James, he saved me. I owe him and his men my life." She continued to survey Ciaran kindly and James stepped in front of her, blocking her view.

"When I saw him touch ye, I had to be sure he meant ye nay harm." He hesitated, measuring her for a moment.

"Ciaran is a good man." Realizing her slip of the tongue by the expression on his features, she gave an anxious little cough.

James raised his brow. "Ciaran? Ye call him by his Christian name?"

"Aye, Laird Ciaran MacGregor of Glenorchy. Ye will ne'er believe what I am about to speak. He is the man I spoke to ye about from court. Ye know, the one who overheard my mother. They return to Glenorchy and his men found me. He tended my injuries so please donna cause him further grief. I owe him much."

He searched around his men. "Howbeit we speak of it later? There are things to which I must attend."

James's men ensured the brutes were bound and still motionless and unaware while James continued to study Ciaran who still cast looks of death upon him. In an attempt to keep the peace, she walked over to Ciaran as he attended to Calum. "How does he fare?" she asked with concern.

He pulled the bloodied cloth from Calum's head. "He has a knock to the head, but he will live. His head will ache and he will probably wish for death on the morrow because of your…"

"Brother," she simply stated.

"Brother?" Ciaran choked out. He looked at her doubtfully and stood to his full impressive height.

"Aye. Nae a brother by blood, but we have been together since we were bairns. He is also the captain of my father's guard. Ciaran, he is a good and honorable man," she said convincingly. Hopefully, he believed her. For some reason, it was important to her that he did.

"We shall see," he said, his voice hardening.

Rosalia gave Calum a sympathetic smile. "Calum, my apologies. Are ye well?"

"As well as can be expected from receiving a blow from the hilt of a sword, my lady," he murmured, rubbing his hand over his bloodied head.

"My *lady*?" she gasped. "And ye, Seumas. Are ye well?"

"No injuries, my lady," he simply stated.

"My *lady*? Why the sudden formalities? Ye were both calling me by my given name, Rosalia." She scowled at them both.

"Ah, your *brother* approaches." Ciaran's tone was velvet, yet edged with steel.

"Dunnehl's men are secure," announced James. He nodded at Calum. "How do ye fare?"

"I live," he replied.

Ciaran touched her shoulder. He raised his hand as if to touch her cheek and then placed it down at his side. "Rosalia, ye need to rest. Go and sit before the fire," he murmured.

"I donna know how long Dunnehl's men will be out, and I need to speak with both of ye," interrupted James, gesturing for Ciaran and Rosalia to follow him away from the men. Ciaran grabbed a blanket and spread it out on the ground. Assisting her down, he sat and took his place beside her, motioning for James to sit.

James extended his arm to Ciaran—again. "I am James Montgomery."

Ciaran glanced down at James's extended arm and did not take it. "Laird Ciaran MacGregor," he simply stated.

Lowering his arm, James turned his attention to Rosalia. "How much does he know, lass?"

"Enough," Ciaran answered for her.

James ignored his response. "Ye were discovered missing by the midday meal and when Noonie wasnae in his stall, your mother and father had me search the loch. I delayed them as long as I could, but they know ye fled."

She shivered and Ciaran grabbed her hand while James scowled at him—continuously. Removing her fingers from Ciaran's grasp to pull James from his murderous thoughts, Rosalia folded her hands in front of her. "I bet they were furious," she spoke quietly.

"Your mother was as expected. Your father was… silent. They sent me to scout for ye, and of course I told them I couldnae find ye. Then Dunnehl arrived."

"Dunnehl?"

James huffed at Ciaran's interruption. "Aye, Charles Reymore."

Ciaran cast a questioning glance. "Dunnehl was the match ye spoke of? Your mother and father were going to match ye to Dunnehl?" he asked in nonbelief.

"Do ye know him?" asked James.

Ciaran gave a brief nod. "He frequents court and I understand King James barely tolerates him. In fact, I donna think many tolerate him. Why would her mother and father attempt such a match with that man?" he asked disgustedly.

James shook his head. "'Tis clearly a tale for another time. As I spoke before, Dunnehl arrived with the proper papers, and when Rosalia wasnae there, he refused to pay the bride price. Your mother attempted to delay him, but he was aware something was amiss. When he discovered ye'd fled, he was simply going to take his leave. But your mother had us scout for ye again and insisted some of Dunnehl's men accompany us. She didnae trust I would bring ye back and she isnae giving up. If we donna return within two days, Dunnehl takes his leave and willnae pay the bride price."

Ciaran shrugged. "So he takes his leave and there is nay bride price. The matter is finished then."

"'Tisnae that simple, MacGregor. Dunnehl's men now know Rosalia is found. I will have to lead them astray and tell them a tale. Otherwise, they will attempt such a feat again. If they do something on their own, I donna know what dangers they bring even to ye or yours." He paused for a moment. "Where do ye take Rosalia?"

Ciaran raised his brow, and she nodded her head in consent. "My men and I travel to Glenorchy. When 'tis safe for travel, I will take her to Glengarry."

"I thought as much." James rose, gesturing for her to remain. "MacGregor, I need a word."

∼✄∼

Ciaran was following Montgomery out of Rosalia's hearing when Montgomery turned around abruptly. "I need to know your intentions toward Rosalia," he bit out.

Ciaran smirked, taking one step closer to him. "Ye are in nay position to give me demands, Montgomery." Who the hell did the whelp think he was speaking to? The only reason Ciaran did not run a sword through the man was because Rosalia had been through enough. She obviously cared for Montgomery on some level, but frankly, he had no idea why. Ciaran could barely tolerate him. No man ever lived that pointed a blade at him. He was still not sure why he made an exception—well, it was never too late to change his mind.

Montgomery sighed and ran his hands through his hair. "See here, MacGregor," he said, taking one step back. "I cannae simply take my leave unless I know Rosalia is safe. She is a sister to me, and ye have nay idea what she has been through. Glengarry is where she needs to be. I will do everything in my power to protect her. I have nay claim on her, but as I am sure she said, she is my family and I will see her safe."

Ciaran studied him for a moment. Montgomery did appear to have a certain bond with Rosalia, and she apparently trusted him. "I find the lass has been through enough and I have nay intention of adding to her pain. I will see her safe to Glengarry." He answered in a tense, clipped voice that forbade any questions.

Montgomery gave him a curt nod. "If ye or yours mistreat her, I will have your head or *something else*," he replied with a steely edge in his voice.

Ciaran simply raised his brow, folding his arms over his chest. He was casually amused by Montgomery's attempt to threaten him. He had no idea who this man was, but his actions did seem to be more those of a concerned brother than anything else. He was about to dismiss him when Montgomery grabbed him by the arm. "I need something from ye, MacGregor."

He spoke his request and Ciaran could not stay the smile that played his lips. "That *isnae* a problem." He pulled back his arm and punched Montgomery square in the jaw. Grabbing him by the tunic, Ciaran swung again, knocking James to the ground with a thud.

"Ciaran, nay!" Rosalia screamed. She sprang to her feet and ran to Montgomery, holding her ribs. She knelt on the ground beside him, tears falling down her cheeks. "'Tis all my fault. I am sorry," she said, attempting to wipe his bloodied lip.

Montgomery pushed her hand away. "Rosalia! Donna wipe blood on my new tunic!"

"What?" She hesitated, blinking with confusion.

When Ciaran extended his arm to Montgomery and pulled him up, Montgomery rubbed his jaw and smirked. "Ye had way too much pleasure in that task, MacGregor."

He shrugged dismissively. "Aye. One for me and one for Calum."

"Fair enough."

"I donna understand," said Rosalia, looking back and forth between the men.

Montgomery gave her a brotherly kiss on the cheek. "MacGregor will explain. I will return."

"He has a plan. We will tie him and his men with the rest of Dunnehl's men and take our leave. When they awaken, he will spin a tale and send them on the wrong course. They will think he didnae have a part in this."

"'Tis why ye hit him?" she asked searchingly.

A deep chuckle answered her. "I cannae say I didnae have pleasure in the task, but aye. Come," Ciaran said, gesturing her toward the horses. "We must prepare to take our leave. Once we reach Glenorchy, ye will be safe."

❧

Gathering her blankets, Rosalia fastened them to Noonie. She'd never meant for any of this to occur. By running from Liddesdale, she had now involved James in this madness. She had to leave, but she'd thought she would be taking chances on her own. It was not her intention to involve James or Ciaran. These were two honorable men in her life and she had placed them directly in harm's way. Placing her arm on Noonie, Rosalia felt his warmth and used it for subtle encouragement.

Ciaran placed his hand at her back. "'Tis time, Rosalia." He led her over to where Seumas was getting prepared to tie James. She searched her friend's battered features and could not stay the guilt that plagued her. This was entirely her fault. Seeing his injured jaw made something gnaw at her gut. Perhaps she should have stayed at Mangerton and accepted her fate instead of trying to create a new one. She looked down at her hands. "I appreciate what everyone has done, but I cannae do this. I cannae have ye placing yourself in danger for me."

Turning to Ciaran, she reached out and held both of his hands. It did not help when he gave her a warm smile. She briefly closed her eyes to gain courage. "Ciaran, I cannae travel with ye to Glenorchy. I donna know what trouble follows, and I willnae put anyone else in further danger because of me. *Mòran taing* for everything ye have done."

"Rosal—"

She whipped around to James and stood tall. "I will return with ye and your men and accept my fate. I was wrong to run." She clenched her jaw to kill the sob in her throat.

Ciaran stepped to her side and James shook his head slightly. "Look at me. 'Tis nay request, Rosalia. How many times did we stand upon the parapet and converse upon your future? Ye willnae return with me to Liddesdale. Ye are worth so much more, lass. Ye insult my honor and the MacGregor's. I *demand* ye take your leave with him now. I have his word he will see ye safe to Glengarry. Start a new life for yourself and be well. 'Tis all I ever wanted for ye. Nay sister of mine will tell me she isnae worth the trouble." He nodded to Ciaran. "MacGregor…"

His hand came down on her shoulder. "Ye either say farewell or we take our leave now. 'Tis nay more time. We must make haste." His voice rang with command.

She lifted her hands to James's face. "*Tha mi duilich! Tha gaol agam ort!*" she cried. *I am sorry! I love you!*

He did not embrace her but gave a curt nod to Ciaran and turned his back on all of them. Seumas tied him, ensuring his bindings were secure. As soon as Seumas finished binding James's ankles, Ciaran nodded his head for them to take their leave.

"Ye have my word, Montgomery. No harm will come to her, and I will take her to Glengarry," said Ciaran. His tone was almost apologetic.

"I will lead them astray. Make haste. It looks as though rain will be upon us and will help to cover your tracks."

"Aye." Ciaran turned abruptly, leading her over to Noonie. "Mount up, Rosalia. We ride."

She mounted Noonie and refused to look back. She would not remember James this way. They would travel quickly and all arrive at Glenorchy safely. Anything less was unacceptable.

The sun was just starting to rise over the horizon and the land in front of her was changing. It was becoming rockier and much more mountainous as they continued their journey north. "Are we in the Highlands?" she yelled to the men ahead of her.

Ciaran slowed his mount and let Calum and Seumas pass, waiting for Rosalia. "Aye. We need to slow the horses through this pass. They will need to be sure-footed along the trails. Let Noonie find his own way. Donna guide him."

"Aye. Noonie will take care," she said, patting him on the neck.

"How do ye fare?" he asked with concern, letting Noonie pass in front of his mount.

"I am well." They had bigger issues to think of than

the pain in her ribs and face. Her injuries were nothing in comparison.

There was a heavy silence.

"Rosalia, donna concern yourself overmuch with Montgomery. He has a good plan and knows how to take care. All will be well," Ciaran said reassuringly.

"Aye," she replied lightly, waving him off.

"I know he wouldnae want ye worried over him. He spoke as much to ye."

James may have spoken the words, but it was not that simple. If it were ever discovered that he had aided her escape... she closed her eyes at the thought. Ciaran was right about his plan, but knowing that did not make her feel any better. These men had placed themselves in danger because of her.

When Rosalia did not respond, Ciaran added, "He will lead Dunnehl's men on a chase, and they willnae suspect him. Montgomery appears to be wise in battle. He willnae let anything untoward happen and appears to be a man of his word."

"And when did ye decide that, my laird? Before or after ye hit him?" she asked.

"I..."

Ciaran was obviously struggling for something to say when she turned and smiled at him over her shoulder.

"I suppose it was after I hit him. He does seem to care for ye as a brother," he said sheepishly.

"Donna ye mean to say what I already stated to ye, my laird?"

He shook his head. "Why do I get the feeling 'tis only the beginning of many of these kinds of conversations I am going to have with ye?"

"A wise man would already admit defeat." She chuckled as she felt the first drop of rain brush her face.

Ciaran must have felt it too because he spoke straight away. "Rosalia, we will have to ride in the rain. 'Tis too soon to stop and we must make haste. The rain will also help cover our tracks. We donna have a choice. If we make Glenorchy on this day, we will have a warm bath and a warm meal."

"It sounds delightful. Lead on, my laird." As they headed up the rocky pass, she made the mistake of glancing down. If Noonie faltered, it would surely be their death. Looking ahead at Calum and Seumas, Rosalia noticed that the steep drop did not appear to bother them. She wanted to speak to Calum to see how he fared, but she was afraid to speak in case the horses would startle.

As if Ciaran read her mind, he spoke soothingly. "Ye are doing fine."

"'Tis verra steep. Has anyone ever taken a tumble?" she asked, gesturing below.

"We are almost through the pass. Ye are doing fine."

The skies blackened and pellets of rain stung Rosalia's face. She attempted to look ahead of them, but the heavy rains lashed her bruises. She rode with her head down against the wind and rain. When a rumble of thunder echoed through the pass, she had to trust that Noonie could see in front of him. They continued to ride at a slow pace that seemed like an eternity. Rosalia was cold and drenched, and her clothes felt heavy as they weighed on her body. A warm bath and a warm meal sounded delightful. That idea gave her the encouragement she needed to keep moving. These men were risking their lives for her—complaining was not an option.

Lightning struck and Noonie shied, losing his footing. "*Sèimhich*, Noonie." She spoke in a soothing tone, patting his neck.

Ciaran let out a whistle for his men to stop. "We cannae ride in this. Make haste to the crofter's hut in the glen and we will make camp," he yelled through the relentless rain.

"Aye," answered Seumas and Calum as a bolt of lightning lit the sky, followed by a loud crack.

As they carefully treaded down the mountain, Rosalia clung to Noonie's mane as if it were a lifeline. Maybe it was. At the angle they were riding, she felt as though she could fall over his neck. If she actually had her choice, she would rather meet her maker by a bolt of lightning than chance plummeting to her death and breaking her neck.

"Rosalia," Ciaran shouted. "Lean back in the saddle and place your feet more forward. It will help Noonie for balance, and ye willnae feel as though ye will fall."

She did as he instructed. These types of issues never arose in Liddesdale. There were no steep mountain passes in which she chanced falling to her death. There was only the occasional hill to travel to the village. What was she thinking? She always said she wanted to travel and see the Highlands—well, she'd certainly gotten her wish. Next time, she would be careful what she wished for.

When they finally reached the crofter's hut, Seumas dismounted and took Noonie's reins. This was one time she did not argue. She ran through the door, panting, as water dripped from her. The hut was small and would barely accommodate all of them, but it was dry and would suffice. There was a dirt floor and a small place to light a fire. A worn tankard sat in the corner beside a small pile of wood, which from the looks of it had not been used in some time. Not the comforts of home, but at least they were out of the storm.

The men strode through the door, shaking off the rain. Seumas handed Rosalia her bundle from Noonie.

"My thanks."

Seumas nodded. "Aye. Hopefully something is dry."

She pulled out a couple of blankets from her sack, one damp and the other thankfully dry. Seumas gathered a couple of dry branches that had been left in the corner and started a fire, throwing curses when it did not light as swiftly as he would have liked.

Ciaran pulled out some dry clothes and gave her a smile. "Ye may want to turn your back. We will change clothes."

She was sure her face turned many shades of red and she promptly turned her back. While the men changed their clothes, Rosalia pulled the worn day dress from her sack. She did not have a chemise, but at least the dress would be dry.

A warm voice spoke from behind her. "We will turn our backs. Go ahead and change your wet clothes," murmured Ciaran.

She twisted around to make sure they did not peek. She removed her tunic and trews, the fire warming her bare skin. Rosalia attempted to pull on the day dress, finding it difficult since her hair and body were still damp. What the hell was wrong with it? It clung to her and did not want to budge. Besides, she could not pull it fully over her head due to the soreness in her arms. The dress was the one piece of clothing that was dry. She would make this work. She had no choice in a hut full of men.

As she grunted and maneuvered to don the dress, Ciaran spoke. "Do ye need assistance?"

God's teeth! It was stuck on her shoulders. "Donna turn around!" she spoke hastily.

"I didnae, but ye sound as if ye need help. Are ye sore?"

Rosalia tried to reposition the dress. "Aye. Howbeit I will manage. Please donna turn around," she pleaded.

As a last resort, she gave the dress a firm tug, hearing the fabric tear at the same time. The dress covered her, but it was way too tight for her frame. What was she going to do? Her mother said Rosalia ate as much as her father's men. She should have listened. Not only did the dress not fit, but now she could not lift her arms to remove it because it was far too tight. Never had she been so humiliated. She was not even sure how she'd managed to pull it on as far as she had.

Her blood pounded and her face grew hot with humiliation. Searching her bag for something else to wear, she found that everything was soaked. She closed her eyes and sighed. This was truly a nightmare. Rosalia again attempted to lift her arms but the dress continued to cling to her frame as a second skin, not moving an inch for her to maneuver it. Whether she wanted to admit it or not, she needed assistance.

Her embarrassment quickly turned to annoyance.

"Umm… Ciaran?" she whispered. The thought of speaking to him about this almost made her cry.

"Can I turn around?"

"Nay!" She reached out and pulled Ciaran two steps back away from his men. She stole a glance at them as they tried to look occupied with their backs still turned. She yanked on his tunic and he lowered his head toward her. She whispered her dilemma.

"What?" he asked, not even attempting to lower his voice.

She swatted at him. "Shh…" Thankfully, Seumas started talking to Calum. "I put on the day dress from the maid at the village and it doesnae fit. I cannae remove it and I need your assistance," she repeated, mortified.

Ciaran paused for a moment. "Do ye have something dry to put on?" he murmured.

"Well… nay. I will just wear what I had on," she spoke quietly.

"And ye will catch the ague," he said with cool authority. Grabbing his sack, he rifled through it and pulled out a tunic. Seumas looked at him, and she could swear he smiled. Why did men have to be such beasts? Stepping backward, Ciaran reached behind his back and handed the tunic to her. "'Tis at least dry," he whispered.

There was an uncomfortable silence.

"Do ye still need me to assist ye to remove your clothing?" He spoke in an odd, yet gentle tone.

"Aye," she sighed. Her humiliation could not be alleviated.

"I will have to turn around," he whispered.

"I know. I will give ye my back." Mercifully, he could not see the crimson in her face.

⁓

Shaking his head, Ciaran could not believe he was having this conversation. Rosalia actually needed his help to remove her clothing. This was definitely a first. He turned around and saw that the tight dress clung to her body like a wet cloth. No wonder she could not remove it.

Closing his eyes, he took a deep breath. "Lift your arms," he instructed. She lifted her arms as high as she could, and he reached down and grabbed the bottom of her dress. As he hefted the dress up and over her buttocks, his trews became uncomfortably tight. Rosalia's white, creamy flesh was bared before his eyes. He wanted nothing more than to explore her soft curves and mold them to his hard body.

Clenching his jaw, he tried to ignore her. The cloth was so tight at her waist that he had to yank hard to pull it over her head. She raised her arms to don his tunic, but not before the light had rippled on her creamy, ivory breasts. *God's teeth!* How much could one man be expected to bear? He had been too long without Beathag's expert touch.

He was going to burst.

He spun around quickly and grabbed a dry blanket for her to wrap around her waist and legs. A lass had never worn his clothing—ever. It was—well, he was not sure what it was. Approaching his sack, Ciaran grabbed the ale and took a long, hard swig. Seumas looked at his obvious discomfort and chuckled.

Ciaran made a mental note that the first matter he would attend to when he returned to Glenorchy was to seek Beathag. His body reacted as though he were an untried lad. He was sorely in need of a woman, and she would surely cure him of these urges. Perhaps he would stay in his chamber and ravish her for days until they could not walk. That would surely sate his hunger.

Rosalia sat down on the blanket. Calum and Seumas moved closer to the fire. Praise the saints for his men—let them entertain her.

"Lass, let me place your clothes closer to the fire to dry," said Seumas.

"My thanks, Seumas. Calum, how do ye fare?"

Calum smirked. "My head aches. Mayhap if our laird would share the ale, I could numb the pain."

Ciaran handed the ale to Calum as Seumas laughed. Grabbing his own blanket, Ciaran sat down—as far away from Rosalia as he possibly could in the little crofter's hut. The more distance he placed between them, the better. She snuggled into her blanket and twisted away from him. At last his ardor had managed to cool. Reaching for a piece of dried beef, he tapped her on the shoulder.

"Thank ye. I am nae hungry," she said, turning back into her blanket.

Ciaran faltered in the silence that engulfed them. "Ye must eat. I have an oatcake if ye want it," he offered.

She shook her head and would not turn around. "Nay. Thank ye, my laird. I just wish to sleep."

Surely she was not still pining after Montgomery. Ciaran placed his hand on her shoulder in a comforting gesture. "Lass, I told ye Montgomery will be fine. Ye must eat and keep your strength. Ye donna want to catch the ague," he whispered. He had given his word to Montgomery that he would see to her. If she did not eat or continued with this melancholy, he was sure she would catch something, and that would only be one more obstacle to delay his return to Glenorchy.

Leaning back, Rosalia cast him an expression of incredulity. "Ye think... Ciaran, I am nae worried over James—well, I am, but nae as ye think. My apologies for being such a burden," she whispered.

"What?" What was she apologizing for? He glanced over at his men. At least they *appeared* to make attempts at conversation. The lass made no sense, but he should not be surprised. Why could women never speak their thoughts in terms he could understand? After having Aisling under his roof for so long, he had ceased trying to figure out women. He would leave that task to Aiden.

Her eyes darted around the room in frustration.

"I saw ye and Seumas with my own eyes laughing at my... mishap," she blurted out. "My midriff is always an issue with everyone," she said, her spirits sinking even lower.

"Your midriff? I donna understand what ye speak. I know naught of this. Seumas wasnae laughing at ye. He was laughing at my... discomfort," Ciaran whispered. The reason she was troubled was about her midriff and the dress? Why would she think such things? He could not for the life of him figure out why women held such trivial things in the highest regard.

"*Stop*, Rosalia. Just cease this now." Seeing she was

not going to relent, he bent closer, placing his lips so close to her ear that he was sure she could feel his breath. "The only reason I had discomfort was because I saw your bare, creamy bottom in front of my eyes. Ye are beautiful and ye almost unmanned me, lass." Ciaran kissed her lightly on her cheek before returning to his blanket.

❧

Rosalia could not think and remained frozen. Ciaran said she was beautiful. James was the only man who had ever told her she was beautiful and she had never believed him. He would say that as a brother. She was sure he said such things offset her mother's venom, but Ciaran… Her face was badly bruised and she'd humiliated herself beyond belief. Yet, he said she was beautiful. In truth, it warmed her heart.

She tossed and turned well into the night. Calum and Seumas, or perhaps both, snored loudly. She twisted to her side to try to find a comfortable spot, making a futile attempt to block out the noise. Opening her eyes, she saw Ciaran gazing at her through the firelight.

He smiled. "My men are dependable and trustworthy, but I didnae say they werenae annoying."

"Aye," she laughed.

"We will arrive at Glenorchy on the morrow, and ye will have your own chamber. The heavens know I cannae wait until I see my own chamber and seek my comfortable bed," he growled.

"Ye deserve to be home. I am sure ye missed it. Do ye think Aiden's wife had her babe?" she whispered.

"I donna know. I hope so. Aisling's bellowing was irritating when we took our leave. I cannae imagine what it would be now," he laughed.

"Ye men always think of the inconvenience to ye. She is probably tired and worried about the babe," she chided him.

"Ye havenae heard her bellowing, lass," he said, his brows drawing together in an agonizing expression.

"At ye or Aiden?"

Ciaran grunted. "At everyone she sees. I should take her to battle. She has frightened even the fiercest of my men."

They exchanged a look of subtle amusement.

"I am anxious to make her acquaintance. I am nervous about your family. I mean to say, what will they think of all this—of me?" The thought gnawed away at her confidence.

"Ye worry overmuch. Ye forget that I *am* laird." His voice was a velvet murmur.

She rolled her eyes. "Aye. Keep reminding me of your greatness."

Ciaran smirked, grabbing his chest. "Ye wound me, lass. Try to sleep. We will ride soon enough."

Rosalia must have fallen asleep because the next she knew, the men were stirring. She sat up slowly, and Seumas pointed to her trews and tunic. "Your clothes are dry. As soon as we pack up, we will take our leave and ye can dress."

"Aye. Calum. How is your head?" she asked with concern.

He shrugged. "Stiff, but I will be home this day, which makes it feel that much better."

"I am sure," she agreed. Seumas and Calum took their leave, and she packed up her blankets. Rummaging through her sack, Rosalia spotted the day dress. She pulled it out and sighed—how truly embarrassing. Without giving it additional thought, she tossed it into the ashes of the fire. "I hope ye burn and rot," she said through gritted teeth.

A deep chuckle answered her. She turned around to see Ciaran leaning in the doorway, his arms folded over his chest. "Ye arenae bringing the dress with ye to Glenorchy then?" he asked in his casual, jesting way.

She blushed and knew he teased her affectionately, not maliciously. His playful bantering amused her. "That would be a fair assumption, my laird. I am ready to wipe my hands of yestereve. This day will be much better. Ye are going home."

"Aye. There is that. Are ye going to don some trews, or will ye ride to Glenorchy with a bare bottom, lass?" Ciaran's eyes roamed over her figure.

At least her bare bottom was covered by his tunic. She shooed him out the door. "Will ye please take your leave so that I may dress?"

"Aye. Make haste. We are only half a day's ride from Glenorchy," he exclaimed with excitement.

She nodded and shut the door. Once they reached Glenorchy, she would breathe a sigh of relief. Thinking of James for a moment, she said a silent prayer that he was well. He had to be. Rosalia opened the door and saw the men already gathered around the horses and ready to depart. She approached Noonie and fastened her sack as quickly as she could. She would try to make haste so she did not hold them back any longer than necessary.

"Ye didnae eat last eve. I assume ye are hungry. Can ye eat and ride?" As she turned, Ciaran held out an oatcake.

"Aye. My thanks."

He raised his brow and gave her a challenging look.

Waving him off, she rolled her eyes. "Get used to it, MacGregor."

Turning away from her, Ciaran grabbed the reins of his mount. "Saucy wench." He spoke under his breath, but loud enough for her to hear.

They continued to ride north to Glenorchy. At least they were through the death-dropping passes. The leaves on the trees were bathed in colors of golden hues, and a warm breeze brushed her cut tresses. It felt delightful after riding in the pouring rain. She turned Noonie and loved the sound of his shuffling feet through the freshly fallen leaves. It was so quiet and peaceful. For once in her life, she felt everything would be all right.

They approached a clearing and Rosalia stopped. Never had she seen anything so beautiful. A flowing river with rushing water cascaded through jagged rocks. The smell of pine overwhelmed her senses. She took a deep, penetrating breath and closed her eyes. To her left, pine trees clustered along the river. There was a clear path along the water that led into trees the color of honey and bronze. To her right, the clearing was much more open. Pines gathered in sections, but she did not see a path. The water soothed her mood.

Ciaran rode up beside her. "Rosalia?"

"'Tis just a beautiful sight. Truly, it takes my breath." She sighed, glancing from side to side.

He chuckled. "If ye like the view here, wait until ye see my home."

The sound of thundering hoofbeats caught her attention and she gasped. At least five men were riding toward them at breakneck speed with swords drawn.

"*Cruachan!*" they bellowed.

Rosalia whipped her head to Ciaran for direction, and nothing but hatred played upon his features. In fact, it was the same look Calum and Seumas held. Something cautioned her not to ask.

"My laird?" Seumas said through gritted teeth.

A muscle quivered at Ciaran's jaw. "We have nay choice. We ride to Glenorchy and outrun them. Calum is injured, and I willnae chance Rosalia getting hurt." Curses fell from his mouth—creative curses she had only heard once before from James.

"Ciaran?" Her stomach was clenched tight.

"Bloody Campbells."

Six

"RIDE NOW, ROSALIA!" CIARAN YELLED, HIS EYES BLAZING.

Noonie felt her unease and bolted onto the path into the trees, almost causing her to lose her seat. Her heart was racing and felt as though it would spring through her chest. Seumas slowed his mount and gestured for her to pass him.

"Ride, my lady! I will watch your back," he shouted.

Rosalia rounded a bend and saw Calum stopped in front of her. She yanked on Noonie's reins to halt, gasping and panting in terror. At least ten mounted men surrounded him, swords unsheathed. Thundering hooves rode directly toward her hard and fast.

She was surely going to die.

As she closed her eyes, the sound of racing hooves passed her by. She sat upon Noonie, frozen still and breathing a short sigh of relief, although she was aware of the danger. Positioning Noonie a safe distance from the path, she gawked at the scene before her.

Ciaran rounded the bend, his face a mask of rage. He shouted commands to the men, and they all turned their mounts… directly into the path of the bloody

Campbells. He gave a curt shout to Calum who approached her, issuing a firm warning not to move. Move? She did not think she could budge if she tried.

Galloping hooves approached rapidly but stopped abruptly when a wall of armed men greeted them. Curses flew and the clanking sounds of battle echoed through the air. Ciaran's arm muscles rippled as he hefted his sword, effortlessly deflecting a blow from a Campbell. Turning, he pummeled his enemy square in the face with the hilt of his sword. The man fell to the ground with a thud. The Campbell men retreated, leaving their fallen comrade behind. A few of Ciaran's men gave chase while two others pulled the fallen Campbell to his feet.

Ciaran dismounted and placed his sword to the throat of the Campbell. "I could kill ye now," he bit out. "I will let ye live to deliver fair warning to your laird. I will follow King James's command, but make nay mistake… I *will* protect my people. If I find any *bloody* Campbell setting foot on my land, it will be the last step he takes," he warned, turning to his men. "Put him on his mount and get that *arse* off my land."

The remainder of Ciaran's men trotted past her, not glancing her way. Did every MacGregor need to be so impressive in size?

"Donna fash yourself. Ye are safe." Little beads of sweat shimmered on Ciaran's skin. A lock of thick chestnut hair fell onto his cheek and he pushed it back. She realized he still spoke to her. Why was her mouth suddenly so dry? "Come. We are home," he said, leading her back onto the path.

They cleared the trees and a huge, gray stone

castle stood before her on an island surrounded by green, grassy moss. Mangerton could have fit inside it three times over. It was an elegant castle with a stone barbican with round turrets and square towers. With the changing of the leaves, the mountains surrounding the castle were inundated with color.

She was speechless. Pivoting on Noonie, she tried to scan everything around her. The clean breeze of the loch teased her senses. The water mirrored a deeper color of the sky as small, white waves crashed into Ciaran's island home. She closed her eyes, trying to imprint the picture into her mind.

Riding single file, they headed to a *cabhsair* that extended over the water to the island. Traveling under a huge portcullis, they continued through to the courtyard, which bustled with men, women, and children who came out to greet their laird on his return.

Ciaran dismounted and warmly greeted his clan. He did not immediately turn toward her, giving her time to gather her wits. Pulling on Noonie's mane to dismount, she noticed an older man with a warm smile approaching.

"*Fàilte. Ciamar a' tha sibh?*" he asked with a smile. *Welcome. How are you?*

"*Tha gu math, tapadh leibh.*" *I am fine, thanks.*

"*Is mise Niall.*" *My name is Niall.*

"*Is mise Rosalia.*"

Niall nodded his head in approval. "Verra good, lass. Here, I will take him for ye," he said, holding out his hand for Noonie's reins.

He reminded her so much of their stable master, Duncan. "My thanks, Niall."

A strong, warm voice murmured from behind. "Niall, his name is Noonie. Make sure he gets a good brushing and give him some extra oats."

"Aye, my laird." Niall nodded to Rosalia. "My lady."

She turned and saw that Ciaran had an irresistible grin upon his face, clearly glad to be home.

"'Tis about time ye returned. As ye see, your walls still stand."

Rosalia had to will her mouth to close at the sight of a man dressed in a red-and-green-patterned kilt with a flowing gray tunic and shimmering with sweat and masculinity. His golden-brown hair hung well below his shoulders in two braids. He had a strong chiseled jaw and blue eyes—piercing blue eyes. He was… beautiful.

Realizing that she was gaping, the man laughed. "I see ye brought me a gift, my laird. Pray introduce us," he said silkily.

She heard a grunt and thought it came from Ciaran.

"Lady Rosalia, my youngest brother, Declan." She detected a hint of censure in his tone.

"And the bonniest of the brothers." Declan grabbed her hand and bent to kiss it, gazing into her eyes the entire time.

He was good; she would give him that. She had no doubt that many a woman had fallen under Declan's spell, and she was not foolish enough to be added to the list. The arrogance of beautiful men never ceased to amaze her.

"How can ye bring such a beautiful lass within my sights, brother?" he asked, with an arrogant tone in his voice.

Ciaran was about to speak, but Rosalia held up her hand to stay him. "Empty flattery will get ye naught," she chided Declan. "I dress in a man's clothing, my tresses are butchered, and my face is battered and bruised. Donna insult me with your honeyed words."

Ciaran chuckled.

Declan raised his brow, clearly caught off guard by her response. "I meant nay insult, my lady. I tend to see what is in the heart of a lass and nae what beauty is upon her face," he simply stated, giving her a slight bow.

She rolled her eyes.

"Pray excuse me," said Declan, dipping his head slightly and turning on his heel.

Ciaran chuckled. "Ye wounded his pride."

"My apologies. James is the same. They think because they are beautiful, they can behave as rogues."

"Nay need for apologies. My brother is a rogue." Touching the small of her back, he guided her toward a set of stairs. "Come. Let me show ye my home," he said proudly.

They walked into the enormous interior of the great hall. Corridors shot out in all directions. She would surely lose her way. A staircase swept down and lovely tapestries hung on the wall. A beautiful painted-glass window was displayed at the top of the staircase, and colored prisms danced against the wall. There were two fireplaces in the hall, each adorned with wooden carvings of animals and pine. Long wooden tables and benches graced the floor, and a raised dais boasted several intricately carved chairs.

He watched her intently.

"Your home is truly magnificent."

He smiled. "My thanks. 'Tis good to be home. Welcome to Glenorchy, Rosalia."

"I see ye are safe, my brother." Aiden stood at the top of the staircase, holding a bundle.

Ciaran ran, taking the steps two at a time. "Aisling had the babe," he spoke joyfully.

Aiden glanced down at his bairn and smiled. "Aye, my son. Two days past. His name is Teàrlach after Aisling's father," he said proudly.

"And Aisling?" Ciaran asked searchingly.

"Is fine and recovering. She is still abed."

Rosalia climbed the stairs. The baby was beautiful with his porcelain-white skin and curly red hair. "He is a beautiful bairn," she said, rubbing her hand across his soft curls.

Aiden broke into an open, friendly smile. "My thanks. Welcome to Glenorchy, lass."

An unwelcome blush crept into her cheeks.

Holding out his arms, Ciaran nodded to Aiden. "Time to give him up, Brother. I want to see how strapping the new MacGregor is. Mayhap he takes after his laird," he boasted.

Aiden released his son to Ciaran and Rosalia's heart melted. Ciaran looked natural as a father and was so kind of heart. Surely he would not match his only daughter to an unsavory English lord for coin. She willed away her dark memories. Ciaran placed his hand over Teàrlach's little head, and she noticed how much strength he possessed. And not just physically; he was so confident in every move he made.

The beginning of a smile tipped the corners of his

mouth. "I have had his attention long enough." He held out Teàrlach and placed him in her arms.

A wave of apprehension swept through her and she shook her head. "Nay, Ciaran. I cannae. I havenae held a bairn before. I donna want to hurt him."

His eyes were gentle, understanding. "Here. I will assist ye." He walked behind her, placing his arms around her. "At this time, ye need to support his head and ye place this arm under his bottom."

Rosalia leaned lightly into Ciaran, tilting her face toward his. He was so close to her lips that she could feel his breath.

"There. Ye are doing it," he choked out.

She could swear she heard him swallow. For a long time, she gazed back at him. Holding the bairn and having Ciaran so close made her wish she held their son for the first time. They both remained frozen and she thought briefly that he felt some- thing, too, but then Teàrlach cried and the moment was lost. Ciaran stepped away and gently handed Teàrlach back to Aiden.

"Rosalia, when ye get settled, I know Aisling would love to make your acquaintance," said Aiden.

"Of course. I am anxious to meet her as well."

As Aiden turned and hummed to his son, she smiled. "He is so proud. He will be a wonderful father."

"Aye. Come. Let me show ye to your chamber. I will order a bath for ye, and then we will have a warm meal."

"That sounds wonderful."

When they reached the end of the hall, Ciaran opened the last door on the right. They were imme- diately bathed in sunlight. He gestured for her to enter a room adorned with bright-colored tapestries. A decoratively carved writing desk and stool stood in the corner and a large stone fireplace took up the center wall. As she turned, it was difficult to miss a huge bed with tall carved corner posts and counterpanes of gold cloth. The chamber was twice the size of her bedchamber at Mangerton.

"Ye havenae yet seen one of my favorite views." He led her to the window that overlooked the loch in all its splendor. As she gazed out, the colored trees reflected off the loch. She was breathless. She could not imagine waking up to this view every blessed day.

"Whose bedchamber is this?" she asked, still glancing out at the loch. Placing his hand on her shoulder, he smiled and she shook her head adamantly. "Ciaran, nay. I cannae stay here." Why would he grace her with such a room? She was merely a guest.

"It doesnae meet your approval?" He raised his brow and waited for a response, folding his arms over his chest.

"Of course it does. 'Tis beautiful," she muttered hastily.

Ciaran nodded in approval. "Good. Then 'tis settled."

"Nay. Surely there is a much... smaller chamber."

"There isnae. Ye will stay here," he ordered, turning his back on her and walking toward the door. "Your bath will be here soon. I will then meet ye in the hall for a warm meal." He turned around and gave her a warm smile and closed the door. Apparently, he was not open to her suggested change of venue.

Rosalia sat down on the window bench that overlooked the loch. And she had believed her mother always had the finest of everything. But it did not even begin to compare to this. The loch glistened in the sunlight. Closing her eyes, Rosalia let the warm rays bathe her face. It was delightful.

There was a knock on the door and a maid entered, carrying a bundle of... dresses? "M'lady," she said, bobbing a small curtsy. "I am Anna. M'lady Aisling wants ye to have these." She placed the clothing on the bed. "She said there are many sizes to choose from, and she will greet ye after the midday meal."

Rosalia could not believe the kindness she had received from strangers. They treated her better than her own family. "My thanks, Anna. Ye may tell your lady that I look forward to meeting her as well." Anna nodded her head and bobbed a curtsy as she departed.

Approaching the bed, Rosalia sorted through the dresses, finding at least eight to choose from, as well as two chemises. She closed her eyes and said a silent prayer that one of them would fit. Another knock at the door broke her ponderings as four burly men brought in the tub. A couple of lads dumped the steaming buckets of water just as Anna came back with another bundle.

"M'lady thought ye might be needin' these, too." She held out a couple pairs of silk slippers and a scented bag. "Do ye need me to assist ye with your bath, m'lady?"

"Nay, Anna. Ye have done enough. I thank ye for... everything," Rosalia said, gesturing to the bed.

The girl looked at her in surprise. "'Tis m'lady's doin'. She is kind of heart."

"I will be sure to thank her."

Anna departed and Rosalia opened the scented bag

filled with lavender. She spread some of the contents in her bath and disrobed. Climbing clumsily over the side, she sank into the tub. It felt so warm and soothing. Rosalia stuck her head under the water and let it wash away her worries. When she came up, she heard Ciaran speaking. Wiping the water from her face, she grabbed the drying cloth and covered her breasts. Even though it would not conceal her completely, it was better than having nothing at all. As she searched around the room, she saw it was empty. Was she going mad? Maybe she'd imagined his voice.

"My thanks. That will be all."

A door closed and she glanced to where the sound was coming from. Another door was in her chamber. She wondered why she had not noticed it before. Her eyes widened in surprise. Surely Ciaran was not in the room next to hers. Rosalia remained perfectly still and heard the sound of splashing water and a grunt. *God's teeth!* Ciaran was in his bath as well—now. He was in the room next to hers with no clothing. All she had to do was open the adjoining door and she would see him in the tub.

She closed her eyes and moaned.

This would be torture. Not only would he be bathing in the room next to hers, but he would also be sleeping in the room next to hers. She wondered if his bed was big. It had to be big. He was big. She could not do this. As soon as she finished her bath, she would tell him so. Why would Ciaran give her a chamber so close to his own? Another thought came to mind and a lump caught in the back of her throat. He placed her in the lady of the castle's chamber. For what purpose?

If he believed for one moment that she was going to be his mistress…

Finishing her bath, she blocked out all mental images of Laird MacGregor—with or without clothing. She tried on the dresses and praised the saints when a couple of them fit. Donning her chemise, she picked up a dress of deep blue. Perhaps it was not the best choice since it would match the bruising on her cheeks, but she would not be able to hide her injuries, no matter what she wore. It would have to do.

Rosalia slipped on the silk slippers, and even though she found much more comfort in her boots, she would dress as a lady. She had to admit that she grew tired of wearing trews and tunics. Besides, her dagger was rubbing and beginning to make marks upon her leg. She stood and noticed a mirror on the stand next to the bed. Should she dare? She had second thoughts about picking it up, but curiosity got the best of her.

The face looking back at her was shocking. Her tresses were butchered and her visage was several different shades of purples and yellows. She had not realized how bad she looked. Running her hand over her tresses, she shook her head. There was nothing she could do now. She wished she could hide in this chamber, but that wouldn't work. Someone would eventually search for her.

Gathering her courage, Rosalia opened the door and poked her head out. Observing no one in the hall, she walked out quietly and shut the door behind her. She reached the top of the stone staircase and admired the painted-glass window. A golden bejeweled crown with matching adorned claymores surrounded a rose-hued cross as though securing it in a protective embrace. She loved how the bright colors reflected off the wall.

"Beautiful. Is it nae?"

Rosalia jumped as Declan walked toward her. "Aye," she said, placing her hand over her chest.

Stepping in front of her, he gave her a slight bow. "Pray allow me to start anew. I am Declan MacGregor, Laird MacGregor's youngest brother. I am pleased to make your acquaintance."

She smiled at his effort to make amends. Giving him a slight curtsy, she extended her hand. "And I am Lady Rosalia Armstrong. I am honored to make your acquaintance, sir."

Declan brushed a kiss on the top of her hand and promptly released it. Extending his arm, he waited. "May I escort ye to the hall, my lady?"

Placing her hand on his arm, she smiled. "Only if ye call me Rosalia." She paused, waiting for him to respond.

"Rosalia? 'Tis a name of great beauty for such a bonny—"

She rolled her eyes. "Only if ye donna start being foolish."

He patted her hand. "Aye. I will call ye Rosalia if ye call me Declan." He hesitated and cast a wolfish grin like she was the main course for the noon meal.

"By all the saints," she huffed. "I see we are to have these conversations constantly," she said as they descended the stairs. "I donna mind sparring with ye, but 'tis *all* it will ever be… sparring," she said curtly. Rosalia knew that he only sought to get a response from her, but she was annoyed.

Declan gave her a look that would make most

women weak in the knees and leaned in close—very close. "We shall see," he whispered. Then he left her… standing in the middle of the great hall, probably to seek out some other willing lass. Her eyes darted around the room nervously, not seeing any familiar faces. To make matters worse, people were starting to stare. Trying to look occupied, Rosalia showed an interest in the servants as they placed food on the tables. After all, she did not want to appear to have been abandoned in the middle of the great hall. She finally spotted Calum and Seumas. Upon her approach, both men stood and smiled.

"My lady," they said at the same time.

"Rosalia," she chided both of them—again. "May I sit with ye? I donna find any faces that are familiar."

Both men looked uncomfortable. "I believe our laird would request ye sit with him at the high table," whispered Calum.

She waved them off. "Donna be ridiculous. I am nae family. Now does someone sit here or nae?" She raised her brow and waited.

Calum relented and waved his hand for her to sit. She sat on the bench next to him and could not help but feel out of place. Rosalia was thankful when Seumas handed her a tankard of mulled wine. Glancing around the hall, she saw that everyone was conversing. They all seemed… close. Maybe that was how a family was supposed to be. The Armstrongs were never so jovial and everything with them seemed forced.

A sudden shout rang through the hall and she jumped.

"Three cheers for our laird's return!" yelled a man. Standing at the entrance to the great hall were the three MacGregor brothers in full Highland regalia. She had never seen so many beautiful men. They stood well over six feet and were very muscular with broad shoulders. But, there was only one she felt drawn to.

Ciaran's chestnut hair was still wet from his bath and touched his shoulders. He was dressed in the same tartan of red and green, which she now gathered were the MacGregor clan colors. He wore a white, flowing tunic and a MacGregor plaid over his left shoulder. A small bag which looked to be made from the skin of a rabbit grazed his hips and rested on top of his... Rosalia heard herself swallow. The flashes on his stockings were the same color as his kilt, and he wore white hose that clung to his muscular legs. His doeskin boots were low enough that she could tell how very muscular those legs were. Her heart turned over at the vision that appeared before her. The sights of Glenorchy were indeed exhilarating.

❧

Ciaran spotted Rosalia as soon as he entered the great hall, noticing she wore one of Aisling's dresses. He hoped she was pleased with her bedchamber. He wanted to make her as comfortable as possible. The lass had been through much.

What was she doing sitting with Calum and Seumas?

He was taken aback by her sudden aloofness. She was not looking at him—at all. In fact, her eyes were to the floor. He did not understand what was amiss and was unnerved by her sudden change in demeanor. "Are ye unwell?"

"I am fine. My thanks," Rosalia said with an air of

indifference. She looked away swiftly at the sight of his scowl.

Ciaran hesitated, blinking with confusion. Bending over behind her, he whispered in her ear. "What are ye doing?"

"Taking my place for the midday meal," she answered, whispering in a rush of words.

He was momentarily speechless in his surprise. Was she daft? Why would she think to sit with his men? Standing to his full height, he held out his hand. "Your place is with me. Come." When the lass did not move, he cocked his head to the side and raised his brow. Why did she have to be so stubborn?

"Oh, verra well," she relented, placing her hand in his and standing.

He escorted Rosalia to the high table, and his smile was without humor. "What were ye thinking?"

"I was thinking I took my place for the noon meal. Isnae this table for family?" she asked, barely lifting her voice above a whisper.

"Family and guests. Ye are my guest, are ye nae?" he asked, his tone patient. They reached the table, and he pulled out her chair for her. It just so happened to be the chair next to his. If she thought to sit with his men and their families, she was mistaken. He did not understand her reasoning. Why did she have to be so difficult? Perhaps he should speak with Aiden to see if he had any ideas. After all, his brother was an expert. He had Aisling.

Aiden and Declan took their seats and the entire hall went quiet as Ciaran stood, demanding their attention. "As ye know, King James continues to be pleased with our support in the Highlands. I thank ye all for your efforts while we were at court. Upon my return, I discovered there is a new MacGregor among us. Everyone raise your tankards to my brother, Aiden, and give thanks to the gods for delivering him a healthy son. To Teàrlach!" he said proudly, raising his tankard.

"To Teàrlach!" the men shouted in return.

"Ye may also notice a new face among us," he said, holding out his hand for Rosalia to stand. "This is Lady Rosalia, and she will be our guest. I want ye to make her feel as she is one of us."

"To Lady Rosalia!" one of the men yelled.

Ciaran gave her a mock salute with his tankard, his eyes never leaving hers.

❧

They took their seats and Ciaran filled her trencher. There were several different types of meat, breads, and cheeses. Everything looked and smelled delightful. Rosalia could not wait to taste the fresh biscuits. Maybe they would even be as good as her cook's.

Ciaran peered at her intently, making her nervous, so she turned to Aiden for a much needed distraction. "And how is Teàrlach?" she asked, taking a bite of biscuit.

"He sleeps. He wakes up to feed or because he is wet, and then he sleeps and sleeps again. 'Tis good now since it gives Aisling a reprieve," he said, pausing to drink from his tankard.

"Aye," she chuckled. "I must thank your lady wife for the dresses. Do ye think she will be well enough to speak with me after the meal?"

"Aye. She asked me to escort ye after we finish."

Nodding her head in agreement, Rosalia focused on her trencher because when she thought of Ciaran sitting next to her, her heart turned over in response. His nearness was overwhelming. She could smell his spicy scent, and it did not help when his leg brushed against her thigh. Her mind burned with the memory of his lips upon hers. This could not bode well for her. How was she supposed to keep her wits about her when he was dressed in a kilt and distracted her in ways that she did not understand?

"How do ye fare, Rosalia?" asked Ciaran, leaning back and taking a drink from his tankard.

"The food is delightful," she said, turning her attention back to her trencher.

"If ye want for anything, ye need only ask."

She studied her tankard, playing with the rim. "My thanks, but ye have been much too accommodating already, my laird."

Ciaran leaned close. "I cannae help but ask. Is something amiss?"

"My laird, I am grateful for all ye have done, but I must insist ye change my bedchamber," she spoke firmly.

Pulling back, he gave her a curious look. "Change your bedchamber? Why would I do that? What is wrong with your chamber?"

"What is wrong with Rosalia's chamber?" asked Declan, leaning across Ciaran.

Shaking her head, she closed her eyes. Now the rogue was involved in the conversation as well. Could she at least have one conversation where she was not embarrassed? She was thankful when Ciaran took him by the reins. "Since when do ye call her by her given name?" he huffed.

"Since the lady asked me to, *my laird*," said Declan with a smug look upon his face.

Inclining his head toward Rosalia, Ciaran looked for confirmation. She gave a forced smile and a tense nod of consent. "Aye, 'tis true. I had but a momentary weakness."

"What is wrong with your chamber, lass? We have several to—"

"There is naught wrong with her chamber, Declan," Ciaran bit out.

Rosalia reached out and clutched Ciaran's arm, immediately realizing her mistake. He felt like a rock underneath his tunic. She became aware of his strength and the warmth of his flesh. She lowered her gaze, but when she looked down, his kilt was parted and showed part of his muscular thigh. It was torture and the room was getting so warm.

Carried away by her own response, she failed to notice that he was still looking at her, waiting. She tingled as he spoke her name. Tenderly, his eyes melted into hers. She could not find her voice. She could barely breathe, and she hungered from the memory of his mouth upon hers. Praise the saints. What was the matter with her?

He leaned in close and whispered in her ear. "Lass, your eyes show me what ye are clearly thinking. I suggest ye remove your hand from my arm and your eyes from my kilt."

Mortified that he'd spoken to her so directly,

Rosalia hastily withdrew her hand—but not before her eyes betrayed her by darting to his kilt one last time to see it was clearly tented. She cleared her throat, pretending not to be affected.

"What chamber did ye give her?" asked Declan. Ciaran answered, but she was unable to hear his response. "Truly?" he asked surprised. "Mother's? Ye know what statement ye make by placing her in that chamber then?"

"Enough, Declan," responded Ciaran, clenching his jaw.

"They will assume she is to be your—"

"Enough!" he said sternly.

Declan's eyes narrowed. "Aye, *my liege*," he said with heavy sarcasm. "Ah, look… here comes your… Beathag, how are ye?"

The woman approaching Ciaran had long, brown curly hair and wore a very form-fitting dress. Her bosom seemed sure to burst out of the gown with any sudden movement. Rosalia could never imagine herself wearing such clothing, but it worked well on this woman. She was slender and beautiful—clearly, everything Rosalia was not.

Moving behind Ciaran, the woman placed her hands on his shoulders. She bent down and kissed him on the cheek. "My laird, how I have missed ye so," she purred, placing her hands underneath his tunic. The woman was clearly running her hands all over his chest.

He stilled her hands. "Beathag, 'tis good to see ye," he choked out, patting her hands. She gave him a wanton smile and actually had the nerve to run her hands down the front of Ciaran's kilt and touch him—there.

"Ye did miss me, Ciaran," she said with female satisfaction.

Mixed feelings surged through Rosalia—shock and anger and a touch of sadness. She knew Ciaran would never truly desire her. Why would he when he had Beathag? She was such a fool, she thought, and mentally kicked herself. He was her escort to Glengarry and nothing more. She tucked away the thought by squeezing her tankard until her knuckles turned white.

⤜

Removing Beathag's hands, Ciaran placed them back on her person. He was not about to tell her that she was not the cause of his attention. "I will speak with ye later," he bit out.

"Later?" Beathag pouted, raising her brow at Rosalia. "Of course, my laird. I didnae see ye had a guest." She studied Rosalia openly from head to toe, and when she took a step closer, he held out his arm to stay her.

"Did ye nae hear me? I said later." His contemptuous tone sparked her anger.

Beathag stopped, glancing at his restraining hand upon her. Turning, she gave Rosalia a chilling smile. "Aye, *Ciaran*. I will meet ye in your chamber, and we will finish where we left off."

"Rosalia, are ye finished? I think Aisling waits," said Aiden with a warm smile. This time Ciaran was thankful for his brother's intervention.

"Aye, Aiden." Rosalia pulled back her chair as Aiden assisted her to stand. "Pray excuse me, my laird. I see ye have your hands... verra full," she said in a cynical tone, casting a glance at Beathag, who continued to throw daggers her way.

Ciaran watched the play of emotions upon Rosalia's face, waiting for some sign of objection, but she merely looked hurt. For some reason, he was confused by why that bothered him. She looked beautiful in a dress, but he had to admit he was partial to her trews. They molded to her luscious bottom and legs when she moved.

Obviously, nothing was wrong with her chamber. She either thought it was too close to his or realized it was the lady of the castle's bedchamber. Frankly, he did not care, nor was he concerned with what anyone else would think. After all, he was laird and could do as he damn well pleased.

Casting a glance at Beathag, Ciaran stood. "I need a word with ye." Taking her by the elbow, he escorted her out of the great hall.

"Aye, my laird," she purred.

Once they reached the courtyard, he turned toward the stables. Noticing the direction they were headed, Beathag gave him a smug look. "I cannae wait as well, my love."

"Since when do ye call me 'my love'?" he asked, surprised.

Pushing up on her dress, she gave him a clear view of her bountiful breasts. "Donna be that way. Ye clearly missed me as much as I missed ye," she chided him.

When they reached the stables, Ciaran gestured to a bench. "Sit, please. There is nay way to speak this but only to be clear. Our time together is at an end. I thank ye, but we cannae be together again."

Although he would stay true to his task and not allow himself to get too close to Rosalia, he had not failed to notice the painful expression on her features when Beathag made her presence so clearly known. He could not have his leman flaunting herself so openly before his guest. The gods knew he had needs, but he would rather take it upon himself to satisfy his own desires than to bear the sadness he'd seen in Rosalia's gaze.

"What?" Beathag cried, her eyes welling with tears. "Ye know naught what ye speak, Ciaran. We are good together. Ye have said as much. *I love ye!*"

He grabbed both of her arms gently. "*Love* me? Donna place something there that wasnae. We were good together, but ye know that was all it was."

She wiped her tears. "How can ye speak such words to me?"

Ciaran sighed. "Beathag, ye know this wasnae going to last. We have spoken as much. I didnae seek more than what was offered and I always spoke as much to ye. This shouldnae come as a surprise."

She gazed at him searchingly. "Tell me. Is there another? Do ye already bed that *lady*? I am bonnier than she, and her face is—"

"Nay!" he spoke with more conviction than he wanted to portray. "'Tis time that we part. Ye did naught wrong, and I donna want ye thinking ye did. 'Tis just time."

Wiping away her tears, she stood. "Of course, *my laird*. Whatever ye wish." She gave him a small curtsy and scurried off.

He actually stunned himself by ending his liaison with Beathag, but his decision was made. To honor his vow, he never stayed with one lass too long. He'd kept Beathag longer than most, but only because she satisfied his needs. He had meant to speak with her this eve, but he had not expected her to make her presence known in the middle of the noon meal.

Even though he'd had to address her sooner than he'd wished, he was momentarily relieved it was over between them. The last he needed was two women pining after something they could never truly have— although if Rosalia's eyes continued to undress him, he would not be responsible for his actions. He was astutely aware that the lass was not as unaffected as she pretended to be. Apparently, she greatly approved of his Highland attire. He smiled at the memory.

Walking back leisurely to the great hall with a smile upon his face, Ciaran was completely unaware that Beathag stood in the shadows, watching his every move.

"Have a care, MacGregor whoreson. Enjoy that smile upon your face. It will be your last…"

Seven

AISLING'S BEDCHAMBER WAS LOCATED IN THE SAME corridor as Rosalia's but situated on the opposite end. At least she would not be lost. When Aiden offered to escort her, she jumped at the chance to escape. She did not need to see Ciaran's leman paraded before her eyes. Besides, there were much more important matters that required her attention and she did not need to be distracted by romantic notions. Determined, Rosalia would set about building a new life for herself—one that did not involve a particular Highland laird.

Aiden reached out, grabbing the latch on the door as wailing cries echoed from within. He opened the door to reveal a beautiful woman with flowing red hair sitting in a chair and trying to console Teàrlach. Tears glistened on her pale, heart-shaped face, and her eyes were red and swollen.

Walking toward her swiftly, Aiden knelt down beside her. "What is wrong, *a ghràidh?*" he asked, placing his hand gently on her head.

Aisling leaned into his broad shoulder. "I donna know why he cries. I cannae get him to cease. He is fed. He is dry. I donna know what to do." She gulped hard, tears slipping down her cheeks.

"Where is Bessie?" he asked, rubbing his hand over her beautiful tresses.

"I told her I would sit with him while she had the midday meal. He willnae cease and I donna know what ails him. Teàrlach doesnae want his mother," she cried, wiping her tears.

Aiden gave her a warm smile. "Of course he wants his mother, Aisling. He will cry if he is hungry, wet, hot, cold, or for any reason. 'Tis how he speaks, sweeting." He rubbed his hand affectionately over her shoulder. "Ye are a good mother, Aisling."

She looked at him and smiled as if she did not believe him. "Thank ye, but ye have to speak as such. I am your wife."

"Nay, I donna. Ye are a wonderful mother and wife. I say so freely. Do ye want me to walk with him? It seems to calm him." He stood, holding out his hands for his son.

"Aye." She handed Teàrlach to Aiden. "Thank ye, Husband."

Rosalia saw the heartrending tenderness of his gaze, and it was as if something unspoken passed between them. She smiled at the sentiment. This was clearly a love match. "My lady, do ye wish for me to come back another time?" she asked, feeling as though she were intruding on a private moment.

Aisling looked at her as if she'd just realized Rosalia had been standing there. "*My lady*? We arenae so formal here. I am Aisling." She wiped her tears and gestured for Rosalia to sit in the opposite chair.

"Aiden, could ye please seek Bessie?" she asked him with tear-stained eyes.

His mouth curved with tenderness. "Sure, sweeting. I will check on ye later." He winked at his wife and closed the door.

"Are ye sure ye donna wish to speak another time?"

"Please, Rosalia. I need to have a woman's company. I am sorry for my distress. They say 'tis normal to have these spells, but I donna have to like it." She laughed.

"Nay, ye donna. I must thank ye for the dresses, my lad—" Aisling raised her brow and Rosalia giggled. "I must thank ye for the dresses, Aisling."

"I hope they fit ye. I wasnae sure so I pulled out what I could."

"Five of them fit. I will return the rest to Anna." Rosalia smiled her thanks, and Aisling waved her off.

"'Tis fine." She studied Rosalia closely, hesitating before she spoke. "Ye know, Rosalia, I have nay women companions to speak with—well, other than Anna. I understand ye are to be with us for a time. I would be honored if ye would be a friend to me." Leaning forward, she tapped Rosalia's leg. "Besides, 'tis about time we had another woman to even things out. 'Tis hard enough to keep Aiden on a straight path, let alone Declan and Ciaran. I am afraid we are sorely outnumbered."

"I would be honored to have a friend and a face that is familiar. There are so many faces here and everyone seems close." Rosalia hoped they would be as friendly and close at Glengarry.

"Aye, we are. Ye have met many new faces then?"

"Besides Ciaran, Aiden, Donaidh, Calum, and

Seumas, I also met Declan, Niall, and Beathag." Masking her features, she smiled politely.

"Niall is a kind man. He has been with us for some time." She shifted in her seat and there was a brief silence. "And what did ye think of Beathag?"

Glancing down at her hands, Rosalia spoke softly. "I really didnae get the chance to speak with her. She was," she cleared her throat, "*occupied* with Laird MacGregor."

Aisling shook her head in disapproval. "How can I put this delicately? Ye know Ciaran is an unmarried man and men have certain… *needs* that only a woman can provide." Nodding uncomfortably, Aisling blurted out, "Beathag offers Ciaran her favors."

Rosalia's eyes widened and she heard herself swallow. She did not find joy in having the obvious confirmed. There was an awkward silence, and she gave a silent prayer of thanks when Aisling changed the subject.

"Ye also met Declan?" She gazed at Rosalia and smiled as if they shared some great secret.

"Aye."

"Declan is the youngest. I am sure ye already have an opinion, and it would probably be correct. Most of us are fairly harmless, though."

Rosalia smiled. "He is much like my brother, James."

"Ye have a brother?"

"Well, he isnae my blood brother. We grew up together and he is my family."

Aisling gave her a knowing look. "I have three brothers. All of them rogues. Ye should have seen the time they gave Aiden when he courted me."

"*Three brothers?* I can only imagine if they are as

protective as James. If ye donna mind me speaking as such, ye and Aiden seem verra happy and verra much in love." Rosalia could not stay the slight ring of jealousy in her voice.

Aisling's smile broadened. "'Tis the truth. Why would I mind? Aiden is wonderful." She paused. "Tell me. Do ye have someone, Rosalia?"

"Nay," she spoke softly, shaking her head.

"How is it that ye came upon our laird?"

"Ah, 'tis a verra long tale," Rosalia hedged. A tale she did not really feel the need to share with Ciaran's sister by marriage at the moment.

"Ye know, Rosalia, I think we will be friends. Ye can speak to me freely." Aisling gave her a warm smile and a little encouragement.

Rosalia weighed her options. Aisling was Ciaran's sister-by-marriage and he apparently trusted her. She supposed she did not have to speak the whole tale. Besides, she could use a woman friend. She'd never had one and it would be advantageous to have one now. With a new sense of resolve, she intentionally lowered her guard. "I was upon my horse and blacked out. Donaidh and Seumas discovered me and took me back to camp."

Aisling regarded her with a somber curiosity. "Surely there is more to the tale."

"Your laird tended to my injuries. He will take me to Glengarry when 'tis safe to travel," she muttered uneasily.

A soft gasp escaped Aisling. "Glengarry? What is in Glengarry? 'Tis verra far north in the Highlands."

"My family." Shifting in her seat, Rosalia became

slightly uncomfortable. She was not sure how much to disclose.

"Why are ye so far from your family?"

"My *seanmhair* lives in Glengarry and was a MacDonell before she wed." Rosalia paused, glancing down at her hands. "I am an Armstrong and from Liddesdale," she finally relented.

Aisling had a look of attentiveness upon her face. "Liddesdale? I donna know that."

"'Tis verra close to England's border." Rosalia stirred uneasily in the chair.

"And ye were riding *alone* from Liddesdale to travel to Glengarry? I envy your courage, Rosalia. I know the dangers of traveling. I cannae even imagine journeying with nay one to accompany me. Ye must have been verra frightened. *I* would have been verra frightened."

"Aye." Rosalia smiled sadly.

"It must be some tale to make ye go to such lengths. Does it have anything to do with your bruises?" Aisling held a sympathetic look upon her features, and when Rosalia did not immediately respond, Aisling slapped her hands on her thighs. "Ye know? I think I must rest again. Do ye mind assisting me to the bed?"

Rosalia rose. "I donna mind." She walked Aisling to the bed and propped up a pillow at her back.

"My thanks. 'Tis much better," she said, adjusting herself into a more comfortable position.

"Do ye want me to seek Aiden for ye?"

Aisling's eyes lit up in surprise. "Ye arenae yet taking your leave, are ye?"

Rosalia glanced nervously around the room. "I thought ye needed to rest."

"Aye, I need to lie down. I am nae dying." She patted on the bed beside her. "Come. Join me and we will speak." After a brief hesitation, Rosalia sat as straight as an arrow on the edge of the bed. "Donna be so formal. Sit and relax. Ye will be here for a while, and we need to get acquainted." Positioning a pillow, Aisling gestured for her to sit down next to her.

Rosalia moved herself further onto the bed and leaned against a pillow, placing her feet quickly to the floor. "My slippers. I will take them off."

"Donna worry upon it. Aiden crawls upon this bed with his boots on constantly. The bed will survive your slippers." Aisling ran her hands through her tresses. "I cannae wait to remove myself from this chamber," she groaned.

Placing her feet back upon the bed, Rosalia laughed. "How much longer?"

"I escape on the morrow."

Glancing around Aisling's bedchamber, Rosalia saw it was smaller than her *temporary* bedchamber. Female touches were throughout the room, such as books and flowers, but she also noticed traces of Aiden. His boots and a sword leaned in the corner, making his presence seem so permanent. They both had a place they shared and called their own. Aiden and Aisling were fortunate to be wed and have a love match.

"So what do ye enjoy doing?" Aisling asked, grabbing her tankard from the bedside table.

"I enjoy riding. My horse, Noonie, enjoys it as well. He loves to splash in the loch."

"Well, he came to the perfect place. Look around ye. Water is everywhere. Luck is on your side. My horse, Aiden, doesnae like the water." As if she caught her slip, Aisling chewed her lower lip.

"Aiden?" Rosalia chuckled.

"Aye. I will give ye the tale, but Aiden gets annoyed with me when I speak it. 'Tis just between us?"

Rosalia nodded her head in agreement. How could she not?

"I couldnae think of a name for my horse, which was a gift from my father. One day the beast halted and ceased to go further because there was a stream of water. For some reason, he doesnae like the water and refused to cross it. He wouldnae *budge*. I told him he was just as stubborn as Aiden and—well, there ye have it."

Rosalia brought her hand up to stifle her giggles, tears glistening in her eyes. "Och, what did Aiden speak to that?"

Aisling shrugged her shoulders indifferently. "What could he speak? 'Tis the truth and he knows it."

Now Rosalia laughed with sheer joy. This actually felt quite nice. For once, she did not have to worry about what to say and could be herself. Thinking upon it, she never had another woman to speak openly with. Visibly relaxing, she sat back and started to enjoy the warmth of the company. "And what do ye enjoy, Aisling?"

"Well, I know this may sound daft, but I so enjoy spending time with Aiden. We have so much fun and laughter together and enjoy sparring back and forth."

"It seems that way. I am joyful for ye." Rosalia spoke with sincerity.

"So tell me. How do ye like Glenorchy thus far?"

"'Tis truly beautiful. I have ne'er traveled to the Highlands before, and there are many beautiful sights."

"And beautiful men." Aisling chuckled.

"Pardon?" Rosalia was caught off guard by her newfound friend's comment.

"Rosalia, I am wed, but I am nae dead. How do ye find our handsome Highland men or mayhap one particular Highland laird?" asked Aisling, raising her brow questioningly.

Glancing down at her hands, Rosalia was sure she blushed. "Everyone is verra kind to me," she hedged.

"Mostly everyone is kind. Have ye seen the view upon the parapet yet?"

Rosalia shook her head. "Nay."

"'Tis wonderful when the sun goes down. Mayhap our laird will take ye. Aiden willnae let me go there alone for fear of me falling to my death. I tell him he should have fear of me pushing him off."

They were laughing hard when Aiden walked into the room.

He hesitated, measuring them for a moment. "I donna know if I should run or hide. 'Tis ne'er a good sign when Aisling... are ye plotting against me, Wife?" He spoke with a trace of laughter in his voice. Standing to his full height, he simply folded his arms over his chest and waited.

"Ye are far too suspicious, Husband," Aisling scolded him.

"And I learned to be that way from my experience with ye," he countered.

Rising quickly, Rosalia felt out of place. "Donna let him frighten ye off," said Aisling.

"Nay, I should let ye rest." Rosalia ambled toward the door and stepped around the huge mass that was Aiden.

"Visit with me later? I will have your word," Aisling ordered.

"Ye have my word." Nodding at Aiden, she walked out and shut the door.

❧

Ciaran sat behind his desk in the solar and reviewed the accounts with his steward to ensure everything was in order. The desk was one of his most prized possessions. Remembering the countless hours his father had sat behind this same piece of furniture studying the accounts, he wondered idly if his father would be pleased with his decisions.

He stood, stretching out his legs as he closed the books. Praising his steward, he was pleased with his competency. Everything had been kept in meticulous order while he was at court, and he was thankful to have dependable men. His coffers were full; his walls still stood; and everyone was safe. Now if he could only have his reckless brother—well, not be so reckless. Perhaps then he could finally focus on his own life.

Ciaran was hesitant to admit that Rosalia consumed his thoughts. He was not even sure why. The lass had been through much and he had yet to hear a single complaint—well, other than about the chamber he had assigned to her. Her courage and determination were like a rock inside her. Without a doubt, she had a purpose and would travel to Glengarry with or without him. Her strong stubborn streak drove him mad.

She reminded him a lot of... himself. Regardless, he had no time for foolish fancies. His vow to his father was unbreakable. He would see to Declan before settling himself with a wife—a duty he would complete, even if it killed him. There was no promise, however, that blood would not be shed in the process. Leaving his solar, Ciaran walked through the great hall and stopped suddenly in his tracks.

Sitting in the laird's chair, his chair, on the dais was Declan. His head was rolled back, his eyes were closed, and his lips were slightly parted. One hand was on his tankard and he was already in his cups. If he was already passed out at this time of day, Ciaran was going to kill him. There would be bloodshed in the middle of the great hall, no less.

"Declan!" he bellowed. A few choice curses might have escaped his mouth.

Raising his head, Declan broke into a leisurely smile.

"Come," Ciaran bit out, gesturing for him to follow. There was no time like the present to speak with his brother about his reckless behavior.

"I just did, my liege." Pushing back Ciaran's chair, Declan extended his hand to a serving wench who stood up from under the table. Glancing up at her, he flashed a smile of thanks and patted her bottom as she hurried off. "And how is his lairdship?" Declan slurred, raising his tankard in mock salute.

Ciaran approached the table in disgust. "I havenae even returned a day's time. Ye are already a drunken sot and wenching within my walls."

"Now, Brother... I ensured that your walls stood strong while ye were at court doing," he flicked his fingers with an air of indifference, "whatever 'tis ye do. Ye could at least be *grateful*."

He was going to kill him. "Grateful?" Ciaran's voice hardened ruthlessly. "Declan, ye are destroying yourself. Ye wench and drink until ye pass out. Mayhap one day ye will even get yourself killed," he spat.

Declan waved him off. "Nay, my lairdship. How can I be killed when I have your greatness to protect me?" A flash of humor crossed his features.

"Keep as ye are doing and I will surely be the one to kill ye, Brother." Ciaran spoke through clenched teeth.

He waved him off. "Now donna go and get your kilt all twisted, Brother."

They stared at each other through a heavy silence. Declan needed to wake up. One day he would hurt himself. Maybe not intentionally, but Ciaran could not chance having his dim-witted brother cause harm to someone else as well. He was a threat to himself and others, and the most dangerous part was that he did not even know it. While Ciaran was deep in thought, Declan made the mistake of speaking.

"Ye know? I have been thinking, your greatness," he said, tapping his finger to his chin.

"Well, there is a first time for everything," Ciaran retorted in cold sarcasm.

Declan ignored his brother's words, a small smile tipping the corner of his mouth. "I should find me a sweet lass who will tame my wild heart," he slurred.

"Declan, I donna think any lass would be up to that challenge." Ciaran's response held a note of impatience.

"Nay? What of Rosalia?" His eyes grew openly amused.

Ciaran laughed to cover his annoyance. "What *of* Rosalia?"

"Think ye she would tame my wild heart?"

"Nay, I donna. I think she might place a dagger through it. Ye leave *off* Rosalia," he ordered, speaking in a tone that made the fiercest of his men jump quickly to do his bidding. "I suggest ye find your path, Declan, with much haste." Turning his back on his brother, Ciaran growled. With mounting frustration, he sought Aiden.

When Ciaran knocked on his brother's bedchamber door, Aiden bid him enter. Ciaran swung open the door to see his brother was sitting on the bed with Aisling—with his boots on. Ciaran was surprised she was not bellowing at her husband for that, considering she hounded him about everything else.

"Aisling, ye look well," said Ciaran, grabbing a chair and placing it beside the bed.

"As I've told Aiden *repeatedly*, I feel well enough to escape my chamber."

"And ye will go out on the morrow as we discussed," Aiden chided her.

She rolled her eyes and Ciaran redirected his attention to assist his brother. "The new MacGregor is a strapping laddie. I see he has your red tresses. With much luck, he has your ire as well."

Aiden coughed and Aisling folded her arms over her chest. "And what does that mean, my laird?"

He held up his hands in mock surrender. "I only mean to say he will be a fierce MacGregor warrior."

She visibly relaxed. "Aye, as is his father."

Ciaran coughed. "There is that." He tried desperately

to suppress his laugh. Now was probably not a good time to mention that he could take Aiden to task with one hand tied behind his back. "Did ye meet Rosalia?" he redirected.

"Aye. She came and we spoke," said Aisling.

He nodded. "My thanks. I am sure it was comforting for her to have a woman to speak with."

"Rosalia may speak with me anytime. I like her a lot." She studied him intently. "She has been through much."

"She told ye?" he asked, surprised.

She shrugged her shoulders. "I am sure I donna have the entire tale, but it must have been terrible enough to have her attempt to travel to Glengarry alone, especially as a woman. Do ye plan to take her to Glengarry then?"

"Aye, when 'tis safe for travel."

There was a heavy silence during which Aisling had a look of determination upon her face. Ciaran suspected this did not bode well for him. Why did he get the feeling this was the calm before the storm? "Rosalia said she met Beathag." And there it was. Folding her arms over her chest, she waited for him to respond.

Why did Aisling always make him feel as though he was being scolded by his mother? He had to admit that her actions took him by surprise. She'd become quickly defensive of Rosalia, and he detected a hint of censure in her tone. "And what did she speak of?"

Aisling leaned back, studying him. "Ye should have shielded her more from your leman," she suggested, simply raising her brow.

When Ciaran glanced at Aiden for help, his brother only shrugged his shoulders helplessly. It was a sad day when a MacGregor was more afraid of his wife than his laird. "I told Beathag we are done," Ciaran said, not comfortable explaining his actions to Aiden's wife. After all, he was laird. He didn't need to give an explanation to his sister-by-marriage, but he was not in the mood to be lectured—or tortured. Reluctantly, he chose the easier path.

"Then ye are free to take Rosalia as your leman," Aisling simply stated.

"What?" he gasped. "Rosalia willnae be my leman. She is... What I mean to say is... She is—"

"And what exactly is she, my laird? Since ye placed her in the lady's chamber, I take it she is to be your wife," said Aisling as she retorted tartly.

"My *wife*?" he choked out.

"Aye," she said with a smug look upon her face. "Ye care for her."

"Aye," he answered hesitantly. "She has been through much."

"But yet ye place her in your mother's chamber, and I cannae help but wonder why that is." She gave him a pointed look.

Ignoring the mocking voice inside that made him wonder why he'd placed Rosalia in that particular chamber, he repeated to himself that she was injured and he wanted her to be comfortable—nothing more. "Aisling, she will be with us until we travel to Glengarry. I placed her in the most comfortable chamber since she will be with us for some time. Donna read more into this. There willnae be a wedding, so put away your scheming ways. As ye both know, I made a vow to Father to see to Declan." He swung his gaze to Aiden. "Cannae ye keep your wife controlled?"

"Controlled, my laird? Ye have obviously ne'er been in love. I have as much control of Aisling as she has upon me," he said.

"And that isnae much," she said, elbowing Aiden in the side.

"Ye both have been wed for some time and act as though ye are still courting. 'Tis disgusting." Ciaran scrunched up his face in annoyance.

"Only an unwed man would say that, Brother," Aiden countered.

He rose, placing the chair back across the room. "I need to take my leave of ye… both."

"Aye. Tell Rosalia donna forget to pay me a visit later. Remind her that she gave her word," said Aisling with a curt nod.

Raising his brow, Ciaran nodded as he closed the door. As if he needed Aisling planting ideas into Rosalia's mind—two women conspiring against him. He shivered at the mental image. Proceeding down the corridor, he wanted to see how Rosalia fared or if she wanted for anything. He knocked on her door, and she bid him enter. She was seated at the window bench overlooking the loch, appearing to be more at ease since the last time he had seen her. For some reason, he felt relief that she would be.

He sat down beside her. "Before I lose my thought, I was to tell ye, donna forget to visit with Aisling. She said to remind ye that ye gave your word."

She laughed. "Aye. 'Tis so beautiful here," she said, looking back at the loch. "Aisling said the view from the parapet is wonderful at this time. Do ye have a moment to take me?" she asked hopefully.

Standing, he held out his hand. "Aye. How do ye fare?"

Rosalia shrugged her shoulders. "I am sore, but the pain is lessening."

"It takes time to heal. Donna push yourself." She stood and he placed his hand at the small of her back, guiding her to the door. "I meant what I spoke before. If ye want for anything, ye need only ask."

"My thanks. And donna scold me for saying so."

They walked down the corridor in silence. Opening the door to the stairs, Ciaran let her in front of him, a decision he should have thought twice about. How could he help but notice her swaying hips before him? He pulled his eyes away from her and focused on his feet. When they reached the top of the steps, they found that the door to the parapet was bolted.

"Just slide the latch and it will open," he instructed.

Reaching out, Rosalia made several attempts to open it, but it would not budge. "I cannae move it."

Placing his hand on her arm, he smiled. "Here, let me have at it." Ciaran stepped up as she stepped down, feeling her breasts rub against his chest. As soon as his eyes met hers, she looked away. He pulled the bolt and the door opened easily.

"I am pleased I was able to loosen it for ye," she said with a trace of laughter.

He chuckled. "Aye. Ye loosened it so much it came right open. Ye have my thanks, lass." As soon as she walked out onto the parapet, she shivered. "Are ye cold?" he asked, draping his arm over her shoulders.

"Nay, just a brief chill."

Blue, red, orange, and gold hues glistened on the horizon over the loch. Because they were standing so far from the ground, they seemed to be looking directly into the heavens. She was obviously enchanted by the view. Having seen this sight many times before, Ciaran was starting to take it for granted. It was refreshing to appreciate it again through her eyes.

"I have ne'er seen anything so beautiful in all of my life," she whispered.

"I agree with ye," he murmured. Rosalia did not realize he was gazing at her when he spoke. Standing there with her bruised face and cut tresses, she glanced upon the view with a serene look upon her features. Neither one of them spoke as the setting sun kissed a final farewell.

Rosalia hugged her arms around her.

"Come," he spoke softly, nudging her away. "Ye are chilled."

"Please wait, Ciaran. 'Tis so peaceful here." She pulled back slightly and sighed at the loch.

"Ye arenae frightened?" he asked, quirking his eyebrow questioningly.

Her lips parted in surprise. "Of what?"

"The height." He extended his hand to the ground far below.

Amusement flickered in the eyes that met his. "Nay. As long as ye donna push me off, I am nae afraid."

Placing his hands on her shoulders, he gazed down at her and smiled. "That willnae happen."

They stood in silence.

"Rosalia…" He had no idea what he wanted to say to her, but he felt he should say something. Now that he had her close, he did not want to let her go. Her breath was becoming fast and uneven. When her eyes glazed over, he knew he had to kiss her.

Ciaran leaned in close and she closed her eyes. At first, when his lips finally covered hers, he was gentle. He was not too urgent, but his kiss was that of a hungry lover. Licking her lip, he forced her to open her mouth to him. The moment his tongue found entry, she did not resist. He wanted to devour her softness.

"Och, Rosalia," he moaned, his hands nestling her bottom closer. He clutched at her as if he could not get enough.

Her hand slid hesitantly over his back, his skin afire where she touched him.

It still was not enough. His lips left her mouth, trailing down her neck to her collarbone. She moaned at each touch, her mewling sounds firing his passion even more. Reaching for the top of her bodice, he pulled back, giving her the opportunity to deny him. She only looked at him with glazed passion in her eyes.

He ran the back of his fingers over the swell of her breasts and she shuddered. Closing her eyes, she took a sharp intake of breath. Instead of pulling away as he thought she might, she merely arched her back and let out a soft moan.

He molded her to him, his arms wrapping around her like a vise. Her breasts flattened against his chest and he shuddered with desire. Wedging his thigh between her legs, he could feel her heat pouring through her skin.

She gently pulled away from him, breathless. "Nay, Ciaran." She placed her hands on his forearms.

Instead of releasing her as he should, he pulled her close. "We will cease, Rosalia, but donna pull away from me. Let me simply hold ye."

Rubbing his hands over her back, he felt her hands on his chest. What the hell was he thinking? His vow of not becoming involved was shattering. He'd almost lost control. God's teeth! If she would have permitted him, he would have taken her standing there. That wasn't necessarily true. He still had some self-control. He would have at least taken her to a bed.

Reluctantly, he pulled away from her. "Come. I will escort ye back to your chamber. Do ye want me to have a tray sent up for ye?"

She could not look him in the eye. "Aye. My thanks."

Neither one of them spoke as he escorted her back to her chamber. He did not know what to say. Opening her door, he waited, both of them remaining perfectly still and afraid to speak to their thoughts.

"Ciaran..." She spoke softly, her eyes focused on the floor. "I donna understand all of what is between us, but I donna want ye to just take me for a tumble—"

His eyebrows shot up in surprise. "A tumble? Rosalia, look at me," he said, raising her chin. "I donna understand all of this either, but I assure ye, my intentions arenae just to take ye for a tumble." At least he spoke the truth. He was not sure what his intentions were.

She entered her bedchamber and turned around and smiled. "Good sleep, my laird," she said, slowly closing the door in his face.

Why the hell did she stir such thoughts? The question hammered at him until something clicked in his mind. If he fulfilled his vow to his father, he could move on with his own life—his own desires. Damn. Declan needed to find his path... quickly.

❧

Declan's head felt as if it had been run over by a stampede of horses. Staggering through the bailey, he could not see straight. Someone really should remind him not to get so fully into his cups. He took another drink of ale from his tankard and headed toward the stables. Perhaps Aiden would keep him company. If anyone saw him drinking with Aisling's horse, they would surely think him daft. What the hell did he care anyway? He could damn well do as he pleased.

"*Halò*," said a soft voice.

He looked up from his tankard and smirked. "And what could *ye* possibly want? His lairdship is sure to be somewhere... lairding," he slurred.

"I donna seek Ciaran. I was seeking ye," Beathag spoke silkily. Slithering toward him, she took his arm, leading him into the stables.

"Now what could ye possibly want me for?" he asked, trying to keep his head from moving and finding it difficult. Everything was spinning.

"Ye know? I have always found ye the most handsome of the brothers," she said in an alluring voice.

Declan raised his tankard in mock salute. "Ye know it." He took another swig of ale.

"Your brother underestimates ye at every turn. I see how ye took charge when he departed. Ye are a strong and handsome man, Declan MacGregor," she purred, rubbing her hands over his chest. "The men respect ye, Declan. Ye are a true leader."

"Well, nae everyone around here thinks as ye." He caught himself as he almost toppled over.

Beathag steadied him.

"What do ye want, Beathag?" he asked, annoyed. Could a man not have a simple drink and talk with his faithful companion alone?

"Ye," she said, pulling him close. Kissing him, she ran her tongue over his lips.

He pushed her away, still holding one hand on his tankard. "I may be in my cups, but nae enough to know ye are still my brother's—"

"Nay. I am not." Grabbing his cock, she began to stroke him.

He stilled her hand. "What are ye about?"

"Just take what I give ye," she murmured as she resumed her purpose.

"And ye donna think my brother will have a say?" He tried to keep focused on the conversation and not to be distracted by her ministrations.

"He doesnae want me. He told me so. We are done," she bit out.

So that was the truth of the matter. "And ye are here with me because…?"

"I always favored ye best," she purred. "Ye want me. I can tell," she said, still stroking him.

"And what makes ye think I want ye?" he asked through clenched teeth.

Glancing down at his apparent arousal, she had a smug look upon her face. "Besides the obvious? I know ye and your brother well, Declan. Ciaran thinks too much, but ye are as me. We donna care about anyone." She knelt on the ground before him and lifted his kilt, attempting to take him into her mouth.

He pushed her shoulder away from him with his free hand. "Ye know, Beathag? There is something ye donna know about me and my brother."

Fighting his restraining hand, she leaned in close, licking the tip of his manhood. "And what is that?"

Declan poured the rest of his tankard over her head. "We donna share whores." What a waste of good ale, he thought, pulling down his kilt.

Eight

Rosalia barely slept. Memories of Ciaran's hands and skillful mouth touching her body replayed in her mind. He was so warm, so big, and so very strong. How could she grant him such liberties? What was wrong with her? Thinking of his kisses, she actually did not understand his intentions. Perhaps he sought some enjoyment before he took her to Glengarry and believed such liberties were his payment for escorting her. Nonetheless, she could not let herself get attached to him. What would happen when she took her leave for Glengarry? Her heart would be shattered. How she wished James was here so she could seek his counsel.

Her pain had lessened from the day before. After seeing to her morning needs, she dressed, cringing when she remembered her promise to Aisling. Aiden's wife would be cross with her, but there was nothing she could have done differently. Ciaran tangled her mind and muddled her thoughts. Opening the door to her chamber, Rosalia took a deep breath. This was a new day. She would not allow him to affect her.

As soon as she walked by Aisling's door, Aiden swung

open the door and smiled. "Are ye going to break your fast?" he asked, closing the door behind him.

"Aye. Where is Aisling?"

He rolled his eyes. "Escaped. Early this morn." He chuckled.

"I hope she wasnae too cross with me for nae coming back yestereve. It was late and I thought she would be resting," she explained, hoping she was not in hot water.

He shook his head as they descended the stairs. "Nay. She thought Ciaran took ye upon the parapet."

Heat rose in her cheeks and she glanced away from him.

They approached the dais where Aisling was already seated. Placing his hand on the back of her chair, Aiden bent to kiss his wife on the cheek. "Good morn, sweeting. I see ye escaped before I even awoke this morn." He pulled out his chair and sat down.

"Of course, Husband. My confinement is over," she said as if the answer were obvious. Turning her attention to Rosalia, she raised her brow.

"And how is our Laird MacGregor?" Aisling asked.

"I am just fine," said a warm voice from behind Rosalia.

Ciaran sat down at the table. "I see ye are up and about early this morn, Aisling."

"Aye. I am finally freed from the walls of my prison," she said, pausing to take a drink from her tankard.

"And how are ye this morn, Rosalia?" asked Ciaran, huskiness lingering in his tone.

Why did he have to look at her so knowingly? Memories of their embrace on the parapet replayed in her mind and she answered quickly, choking on her words. "I am fine, my laird." Clearing her throat, she studied her trencher. Maybe a change of subject would be a good idea for them both. "So what do ye do on your first day of freedom?" Rosalia asked.

"Now donna push yourself too soon, Wife," said Aiden, a hint of censure in his tone.

"Husband, ye worry overmuch. Howbeit ye worry about ye, and why donna ye let me worry about me?" she chided him.

"And what do ye do, Rosalia?" Ciaran redirected.

Besides thinking about your lips kissing me and your hands…

"I donna know. I wanted to visit with Noonie and also see how he fares to ensure Niall doesnae spoil him."

Ciaran chuckled. "Well, there is that. I train with my men this morn in the bailey, but I can take ye to see more of my lands if ye want. Mayhap after the noon meal."

"Aye. I would love to see your home, my laird."

Seumas walked forward, stopping in front of them. He nodded to Ciaran. "The men are ready when ye are. We shall meet ye in the bailey."

"I will be there shortly."

"Aye, my laird." Seumas gave Rosalia a slight bow. "My lady."

She groaned as he walked away. "Why do Seumas and Calum insist on 'my ladying' me when I tell them time and time again that they had been calling me by my given name? After all we have been sharing as of late, ye would think they would accept that," she said with irritation.

"Probably the same reason why ye keep 'my lairding' me, lass," Ciaran noted. "They only show respect."

"Well, 'tis annoying."

"As I told ye before, my men are dependable, but I didnae say they werenae annoying." Tossing the last of the biscuit in his mouth, he rose. "I will meet with ye later."

"Aye—well, give Seumas another swing upon your sword and be sure to let him know it was from me."

"It would be my pleasure, lass." He nodded to Aiden. "Do ye come now, Brother?"

"Aye." Aiden rose, but not before he kissed Aisling on the cheek. Rosalia wondered if the gods would ever grace her with such a marriage.

Aisling tapped her on the arm. "Now that they take their leave, I will go and see to Teàrlach. Do ye want to come along?"

"Aye." Rosalia pushed back her chair and stood. "He is such a beautiful bairn, Aisling."

Aisling portrayed the image of a proud mother. "My thanks."

They entered the nursery where an older woman who Rosalia assumed to be Bessie was holding him. "He sleeps," the woman whispered.

Aisling stretched out her arms and cradled her son. She sat down in a chair, rubbing her finger over his tiny cheek. Glancing up at Rosalia, she smiled. "'Tis my favorite time with him. He sleeps and has such a look of peace upon his face."

Rosalia bent down beside her. "He is so small. Aiden is right. Ye are so good with him. Have ye been around many bairns before Teàrlach?"

"I just remember my youngest brother, Ailig, when he was a bairn. 'Tis verra different when ye have your own."

Rosalia could not remember sharing this type of closeness with her mother. She hoped one day she would be able to have the same experience with her child. Closing her eyes, she tried to shut out her mother's voice chipping away at her sanity and telling her she was already more than likely barren. Granted, she was one and twenty. Although, studying Aisling, she noticed that the new mother did not appear to be much younger than herself.

Aisling stood with Teàrlach. "Sit in the chair, Rosalia." When a panicked expression crossed Rosalia's features, she added, "Donna battle with me. Come now. Sit in the chair." Rosalia reluctantly sat down in the chair, and Aisling placed Teàrlach gently in her arms. "All ye need to do is support his head. He cannae hold it up by himself yet. Ye are doing it. Ye see? 'Tisnae hard."

Rosalia rubbed her hand over the baby's tiny curls as a warm glow flooded her with emotion. Gazing into his tiny face, she caressed his cheek lightly with her finger. He was so soft. It amazed her that such a little life could be brought into the world. His innocence brought her sheer joy. She sighed and as soon as she started to relax, Teàrlach screamed loudly—well, now he was not so peaceful. Bessie came over and took him from Rosalia's arms.

"Ye know? I need to walk. I think some fresh air will do me good. Bessie, I will be back for Teàrlach before the noon meal," said Aisling, kissing Teàrlach on the head.

"I was going to visit with Noonie. Do ye want to walk to the stables with me?"

"Aye."

They had just stepped out into the bailey when the sound of banging swords and grunts caught their attention. "Ah, the men still train," said Aisling, pointing to the other side of the bailey. "Do ye want to watch for a time?"

"They donna mind if we watch?" Rosalia asked, her voice rising in surprise.

"And give them a chance to show off their prowess?" Aisling paused, tapping her finger to her chin. "I think… nae."

As they walked to the other side of the bailey, the clanking sound of swords was much more prevalent. Some of the bailey was shaded, but the men practiced their swordplay in full sun.

"Nay! I told ye to wield your sword in a high arc! As such…" Ciaran shouted as he approached the center of the circle of men. He raised his hand and wiped the sweat from his brow. His bare chest glistened and his kilt rode low on his lean hips. He was as chiseled as a statue, his sculpted muscles rippling with every move he made. No wonder he was as hard as a rock when she touched him. She continued to survey him kindly. He was so wet and her mouth was suddenly so dry.

"Now!" he yelled. The other man attacked him with a low swing. Ciaran raised his sword in a high arc and descended on his opponent's sword, knocking it out of the man's hands. Ciaran gave the man a curt nod and handed him back his sword. Turning, he addressed his men. "Now do ye see what I speak?"

"Aye!" the men yelled.

He gestured for the men to continue.

Aisling leaned lightly into Rosalia and whispered close to her ear. "So what do ye think?"

Her words hurled Rosalia back to earth, and she tried to think with clarity. "Of what?" she choked out.

Giving her a knowing look, Aisling nodded to Ciaran. She stammered in bewilderment. "Ciaran is... kind."

"Kind? Ye have feelings for him, do ye not?" Aisling's voice was edged with curiosity.

She glanced around to ensure no one overheard their words. "Aisling, it doesnae matter what feelings I have or donna have for Ciaran. Even though I will be here until I travel to Glengarry, I will still travel to Glengarry. Besides, Ciaran has Beathag," she whispered, turning her head back dismissively and studying the men.

"Nay, he doesnae. He told her they are done," Aisling whispered back.

Rosalia managed to shrug and say offhandedly, "Aisling, one day he will wed a wife who will bear him many sons."

They sat silently for some time.

"Aye, he will. What is the matter?" Aisling stared at her, a slight hesitation in her eyes. Reaching out, she touched Rosalia's arm.

She stirred uneasily on the bench. "Please donna do this," she pleaded. When Aisling narrowed her gaze, Rosalia knew her friend was not going to relent. Fine. If Aisling wanted the truth, she would spill the shocking truth. Perhaps then Aisling would cease her matchmaking.

"I am a score and one and I will soon be a score and two. I havenae yet wed. I am sure to be *barren* and your laird will want many sons. Besides, Laird MacGregor is a powerful Highland laird and is granted audiences with King James. A match with me would ne'er happen. My father is but a lowland Scottish laird and my mother is English. There isnae coin in the coffers and I have nay dowry. I have naught to bring to a marriage," she said curtly. That should surely cease Aisling's matchmaking.

Declan staggered toward them with a wolfish grin upon his face.

"And how are the two most beautiful lasses in all of Glenorchy?" asked Declan silkily.

Aisling rolled her eyes. "We are fine. And how is the biggest rogue in all of Glenorchy?" she repeated in the same mocking tone.

Rosalia laughed.

"Donna speak untruths." Approaching the middle of the bench, he attempted to sit between them.

"Declan, what are ye doing?" asked Aisling, a critical tone in her voice.

"Sitting between two beautiful women," he simply stated.

Rosalia and Aisling huffed, moving to the side of the bench as Declan sat down between them. "Why donna ye train with the men, Declan?" Rosalia asked, regarding him searchingly.

Aisling's voice was laced with sarcasm. "Howbeit he was up late last eve wenching and into his cups."

"Now, Aisling… Ye are sounding more and more like my brothers all the time." Signs of annoyance hovered in Declan's eyes.

"And one day ye will know we speak the truth, Brother," Aisling chided him.

Declan stiffened briefly as though Aisling had struck

him, but then he relaxed and cast her a roguish grin. "If it wasnae for me, ye would have naught to speak of. Ye must admit, I kept ye entirely entertained while my brothers were at court doing—well, whatever 'tis they do at court." Placing his arms around them both, he leaned back casually against the stone wall and crossed his feet at the ankles. "Besides, if I straightened my path, I wouldnae have the enjoyment of ye taking care of me."

Aisling elbowed him in the stomach and he took a sharp intake of breath.

"Och, what did ye do that for?"

She shoved his arm off her shoulder. "Cease. Now."

"Declan!" Ciaran bellowed. His face was a glowering mask of rage. The scene unfolded before them in a matter of seconds, the men looking at Declan with stern glances of consternation. Ciaran stood in the middle of the circle, powerful and alarming. His chest was heaving and he had his sword pointed at Declan. "Come. Take your place," he ordered.

"Well, ye see, *Your Majesty*, I cannae. I donna have my sword. At least nae the kind of which ye speak," Declan smirked.

Aisling moaned into her hands.

Storming through his sea of men, Ciaran thundered toward the bench. His purposeful swagger made Rosalia involuntarily sit back. She imagined that when he was at his fiercest, he was not a man to be reasoned with. "Remove your *arse* from the bench," he said through clenched teeth. Forcefully, he pulled Declan up by the tunic and dragged him away. One-handed, Ciaran slammed his brother into the stone wall, holding him there.

Declan grunted.

"What ye call me when we are alone, I have tolerated. Ye *will* show me respect in front of my men. I will *give* ye a sword and I expect ye to practice your swordplay. Naught has changed, Brother," Ciaran spit out. "Do we have an understanding?"

"Aye," said Declan through gritted teeth.

"Aye, *what*?" Ciaran did not budge.

"Aye, *my laird*."

Releasing him, Ciaran thundered back to his men. Declan followed him in the wake of the storm, rubbing his neck.

"Aisling, can we go to the stable now?" Rosalia whispered.

Aisling was already on her feet. After the uncomfortable turn of events with Declan and Ciaran, both women were eager to escape to the confines of the stables. They walked in companionable silence until they saw Niall brushing one of the horses.

"Good morn, Niall," said Aisling.

He glanced up, surprised. "My lady, how wonderful to see ye up and about. I am thankful ye and your son are well. Your husband has brought him around to show us all. He is a strapping young laddie."

"My thanks. Niall. Ye have met Lady Rosalia?" she asked.

"Aye, I have had the pleasure." Giving her a slight bow, he smiled. "My lady."

"*Madainn mhath*, Niall." *Good morn, Niall.* "'Tis good to see ye again. And how is Noonie? Ye arenae spoiling him overmuch?"

"Nay, only as our laird instructed, my lady. I did

give him a good brushing, and he may have received some extra oats a time or two. I also had to separate him once from Aiden. He clenched his teeth into Aiden's hind quarters, he did."

Rosalia gasped. "He did? He normally doesnae bite. Is Aiden all right?" she asked, concerned.

Aisling laughed. "He probably deserved it, Rosalia."

"No worries, my lady. They are just getting acquainted with one another," Niall reassured her.

Why did Noonie have to cause trouble? Rosalia cringed. At least he did not bite the laird's mount in the arse. She guessed it could have been worse. "Do ye want to meet Noonie, Aisling?"

A flash of humor crossed Aisling's face. "I am willing to meet anyone who can put Aiden in his place. Ye know I am speaking of my *horse* Aiden?"

"Of course," Rosalia said, a glint of humor finally returning.

When they approached Noonie's stall, he pawed at the ground. Placing her head to his, Rosalia rubbed him behind the ears. "Och, Noonie. *Ciamar a tha sibh?*" *How are you?*

"He is magnificent. His coat is so verra black and sleek."

"Aye. He is a good horse—well, when he isnae biting other horses in the arse," she chuckled, quickly covering her mouth with her hands. "My apologies, Aisling. My mouth sometimes speaks before I am able to stop it."

Aisling waved her hand in a dismissive gesture. "I told ye. I have three brothers and I live with the MacGregors. I have heard worse and even spoken worse. Thankfully I met ye after I birthed Teàrlach. If ye would have arrived before then, we wouldnae be friends. Ye should have heard the words spewing from my mouth. I threatened everyone around me, even poor Anna." Leaning in closer, she lowered her voice. "Aiden insisted on being with me when Teàrlach was born and I actually threatened to cut off the part of him that makes him a man."

Rosalia glanced at her in nonbelief. "Ye didnae."

Aisling shrugged offhandedly. "I did."

Noonie nudged her arm. "Niall did a great job with him. We were caught in the pouring rain and he was covered in mud."

"I am nae surprised. Niall really loves all four-legged creatures. Come. I will show ye Aiden."

The stalls were filled with many beautiful and impressive horses. Ciaran apparently knew his horse-flesh. Why did this come as no surprise to her? In the last stall, a chestnut-colored horse with white markings whinnied. Although he was a couple of hands smaller than Noonie, he was a striking horse.

"And this is Aiden," said Aisling, rubbing his nose.

Rosalia pointed to the horse's coloring. "He has perfect white markings on all four of his legs. I have ne'er seen a horse with perfect white markings. He is beautiful."

Aisling's smile widened in approval. "My thanks. When I am nae so sore we can ride together."

"I would enjoy that. How do ye fare? This is your first day out. Do ye feel the need to rest?"

Aisling moaned and rolled her eyes. "Please, I beg ye. Donna sound like Aiden. I am still fine, but I will rest after the midday meal."

"I am sure your husband would be thankful." In that moment, Rosalia realized she had much in common with Aisling—including that neither of them wanted to be lectured.

"Did ye see the garden? My apologies, Rosalia, I didnae know how much Ciaran had showed ye. It might be easier if ye tell me what all he has shown ye."

Passion…

Awkwardly, Rosalia cleared her throat. "I have seen the view upon the parapet but havenae been anywhere else."

Linking her arm with Rosalia's, Aisling led her out of the stables. "Then come. I have much to show ye."

⁓

Ciaran finished training with his men and was burning. Not just from the swordplay, but from Declan's self-destructive behavior. Declan always made it a point to address his oldest brother sarcastically, but when he called Ciaran "your majesty" in front of his men, that sort of behavior clearly had to cease.

Grabbing a drying cloth, Ciaran decided he needed a dunk in the loch to calm him. He walked over the *cabhsair* with long, purposeful strides and placed the cloth on the ground. Removing his kilt and sword, he stood in all his Highland glory. It was getting too late in the season to be swimming in the loch, but he desperately needed it. There was only one way to do it.

He dove in headfirst.

Freezing water rushed over him from head to toe. As he surfaced, he let out a roar that surely frightened away any four-legged creatures that were about.

Hearing laughter upon the barmkin wall, he gave his men a hand signal only they would understand. When they roared with over-exaggerated merriment, he shook his head because on the morrow, his men would all be practicing their swordplay... extensively.

A sudden splash caught his attention. Ciaran whipped around, but there was no one there. As he looked around cautiously, his battle-hardened senses came into full awareness as something grabbed him below the waist. Reaching down into the water, he felt... an arm?

He hefted the mass out of the water.

"I have missed ye, my love," purred Beathag, wiping the water from her face and pressing herself against him.

"What are ye about?" he asked, pushing her away from him. She did not wear any clothing, and when his gaze lowered, so did his voice. "What is the meaning of this, Beathag?"

He did not understand her purposeful disobedience. Prying her vise-like grip from around his neck, he twisted around and spotted Aisling and Rosalia standing on the *cabhsair*.

Rosalia paled. Beathag glared at Rosalia with a smug look upon her face. "Now I see the truth. 'Tis why ye nay longer want me. How sweet," she spoke with bitterness. "Tell me, Ciaran. Does she take ye into her mouth as I do?"

He stood to his full height. "I donna know what games ye play. Unless ye want yourself removed from Glenorchy, I suggest ye cease your scheming. We are done. I told ye," he said. Beathag meant nothing to him. She was a means to satisfy his lust—no more. He refused to have his life ruined due to an error in judgment. After all, he was laird and he would be obeyed.

Turning his back on her, he stormed out of the loch. Grabbing his drying cloth, kilt, and sword, he twisted around to see her still standing in the water. "I told ye we are done. If anything like this happens again, I will personally remove ye from Glenorchy with naught but the clothes on your back. Do ye understand me, Beathag?"

"Aye. Perfectly, *my laird,*" she said, icy contempt flashing in her eyes.

&c&

The garden still displayed autumn's blooms. A warm breeze blew the scent of blossoms and tickled Rosalia's nose. Aisling had already taken her leave to see to Teàrlach, so Rosalia was thankfully left to her own devices. She needed time to compose herself. When Aisling suggested a walk across the *cabhsair* to the loch, Rosalia had imagined it would be refreshing. She did not expect a display of Ciaran and Beathag in a lovers' tryst. At times, she could be so daft. She was a fool to think she meant anything to him. What she needed was to focus on her goal. Her mission was to start a new life in Glengarry—not Glenorchy.

Sitting on a garden bench, she enjoyed the solitude and tranquility. In a few months, she would have a new beginning at Glengarry. She prayed that all of her efforts would come to fruition and that her *seanmhair* would welcome her with open arms. All too quickly, she was running out of diversions. No matter how she tried to occupy herself, her mind would not let her rest. The mental image of Ciaran with Beathag plagued her. At least, Rosalia told herself, she was not foolish enough to believe her embrace with Ciaran on the parapet had meant something. Frankly, she was tired of dreaming about such romantic notions. It would be the last time she would make such an error in judgment.

"I am such a fool," she murmured, slapping her hands to her head.

"Now, lass… Ye couldnae be a bigger fool than me," Declan chuckled.

She jumped.

"My apologies if I startled ye." He gave her a warm smile. "May I?" He gestured to the bench.

She shrugged with indifference. "Aye, but I am in nay mood for your charms."

"Donna worry. I am in nay mood to be charming," he countered.

They sat on the bench in silence. Her thoughts continued to torture her, and Declan was being… Declan. "My apologies that my brother took me to task in front of ye and Aisling. Ye didnae need to see such."

She raised her brow in surprise. "Declan MacGregor, is that a sincere apology?"

He gave her a sheepish grin. "I suppose 'tis sincere."

"Ye know, Declan? My brother is much as ye are. We spoke constantly about everything. If ye ever want to speak to me…" She thought it better to keep her invitation open ended.

Closing his eyes, he took a deep breath.

"It must have been hard for ye being the third son of the MacGregor," she said sympathetically.

He threw up his hand in the air. "Hell, it wasnae easy, if that is what ye're saying."

"Declan, ye are a score and…?"

"Three," he simply stated.

She shook her head. "One day ye will wed and have a family of your own."

"Ye sound like my brothers and Aisling," he said bitterly.

"Nay, Declan, I envy ye." When he raised his brow, Rosalia gave him a gentle smile. "Aye, envy. Ye donna have Ciaran's responsibilities. He must care for everyone and ensure the coffers are full, King James is pleased, the men are trained to defend your home, and I could continue." She reached for his hand. "Ye donna have to worry overmuch on that. Ye are free to choose your wife as ye will and make your own life. What ye make of that life is your choice. Ye donna understand," she spoke passionately. "Ye have a choice, Declan. And aye, for that I envy ye. Donna be too quick to choose the wrong path and throw away your life and your chance at happiness only because ye are angry."

She paused. For a moment, she believed she actually reached him.

"And what of your choice, Lady Rosalia? If ye had to choose, would ye choose me or the MacGregor?"

By all the saints…

"In truth? Neither." She rose in one fluid motion.

Nine

ROSALIA LONGED FOR THE DAYS AT MANGERTON WHEN she could sit easily in the kitchen and eat the noon meal. Memories flooded her as everyone ate in silence. Aisling was sulking; Aiden was quiet; Ciaran was brooding; and Declan was giving her wooing looks from down the table. What was he about? The stillness was suffocating, and she could no longer stand the tension. She'd had enough of it at Mangerton and adamantly refused to be the cause of it at Glenorchy.

She reached out and touched Ciaran's arm and then promptly removed her hand. "So my laird, do ye still wish to show me your lands or do ye have other—"

"Nay, I can take ye if ye still want to go," he said in a dull, troubled voice, looking at her with something akin to regret.

"Of course. The sun is shining and 'tis a beautiful day," she said cheerily. Maybe a little too brightly, but she wanted him to know that she was unaffected by his actions. His behavior was not her concern.

"I could easily take ye, Rosalia," said Declan with an underlying sensuality in his words.

Why did she feel the words he spoke always contained a hidden meaning? Aisling scowled at Aiden, and he shoved his elbow into Declan's side.

Declan rubbed his ribs. "Och, what did ye do that for? Ye and your wee wife keep…"

Aiden cut off his speech with only a glare.

Rosalia ignored them both. "Ye know, my laird? I am finished with my meal and will meet ye at the stable." She pushed back her chair with as much confidence as she could muster.

Looking as though someone had died, Ciaran nodded his head and went back to studying his meal.

Let him brood. She smiled brightly at Aisling and took her leave, feeling Ciaran's sharp eyes boring into her as she walked away.

❧

Once Rosalia left the great hall, Aisling stood, giving Ciaran a sidelong glance of utter nonbelief.

Her husband abruptly grabbed her arm. "Donna, sweeting. Leave it be," he pleaded, shaking his head in disapproval.

Under different circumstances, she would have obeyed her husband. But someone ought to keep the MacGregor brothers on a straight path, and since she was the only married woman in attendance, she felt it was her duty. She was their sense of reason when they lost all sanity. Besides, someone needed to remind the rogues that their actions held consequences.

Shaking off Aiden's hand, she pulled out Rosalia's chair and sat down next to Ciaran. "God's teeth! What were ye *thinking*?"

Looking like a scolded child at his trencher, Ciaran shook his head. "'Tisnae as ye think."

Her jaw dropped. "Nae as I think? And what do ye think Rosalia thinks? We saw ye in the middle of a tryst with Beathag, Ciaran. What else is there to think? Ye say ye care for Rosalia—well, ye have quite a way of showing it," she spat out.

He sighed. "I told Beathag we are done, and she doesnae listen. I didnae even know she was there. She did it on purpose while Rosalia watched." He pushed his food around on the trencher.

"That *whore*," she bit out. "What were ye thinking of, getting yourself tangled with her? Now look at the mess she has created. Ye men, always thinking with your—"

"Leave off, Aisling," he ordered. "Beathag will nay longer be a concern."

"Of course she willnae. Now that she has Rosalia thinking ye are still bedding her, her purpose is complete," Aisling said sarcastically. Leaning forward, she said in a controlled voice, "Ye need to make amends with Rosalia."

He leaned back, his eyes cold. "And ye donna think I know that?" he bellowed.

The great hall went quiet.

Aiden rose from his chair and pulled back Aisling's. With his powerful hands, he yanked her to her feet. "Come, Wife." He gave her an intense but secret expression that did not leave room for debate. "Now, Wife."

❧

Recovering from Aisling's reprimand and after giving himself a reasonable amount of time to sulk, Ciaran went in search of Rosalia. Hesitantly, he approached the stable where she was brushing Noonie. She had a troubled look on her face as she brushed her horse with long, forceful strokes. Ciaran did not enjoy seeing her that way. He needed to make this right. Stopping a few feet in front of her, he realized she had yet to hear his approach. His mind went blank. *I am sorry ye saw… My leman means naught… I donna care…*

"Are ye ready?" Perhaps that was a good place to begin.

"Aye."

"I will get my mount." Ciaran waved off Niall and saddled his mount. He tried to stall to gather his thoughts, but he knew he could not hide in the stable forever. Besides, he was no coward. He was laird—a warrior. He should certainly know how to speak to a lass.

Leading his horse out of the stable, he approached her. "Are ye well enough to ride?"

"Aye, my laird," she said brightly.

He paused. "Rosalia…" His gaze came to rest on her questioning eyes.

"Aye?"

As he shook his head, his words failed him. "'Tis naught." Mounting his horse, he continued to sit patiently while she adjusted and then readjusted her skirts, and he chuckled when she let out a frustrated grunt. "Would ye rather change into your trews?"

She raised her brow. "Ye wouldnae mind? 'Tis just much more comfortable for me. I donna enjoy battling with skirts."

He dismounted. "Of course I donna mind. I will wait here for ye."

"My thanks."

⁓

Rosalia walked hurriedly to her chamber, knowing she would ride with much more ease in her trews. Although it was the custom for women to ride in skirts, she did not enjoy it. It was much too restricting. Besides, she was not trying to make an impression on *Laird MacGregor*. What he thought of her mattered not. By the look upon his features, she could tell he was still out of sorts, and she wished he was not so brooding. He should be joyful that he no longer needed to hide Beathag in her presence. She quickly changed, laughing as she donned James's tunic. She could only imagine him shaking his head in disapproval. She sorely missed him.

As Rosalia went to close the trunk, she spotted Ciaran's tunic and pulled it out. She had yet to return it from their time together in the crofter's hut. Holding it up to her face, she closed her eyes and took a deep breath, smiling as she realized it still held his scent. Knowing that she must cease these ridiculous notions, she whipped it back into the trunk and slammed the lid shut. Any feelings she had for *Laird MacGregor* needed to be suppressed.

Ciaran was speaking with Niall when she returned to the stable, and she tried to mask the guilty look upon her face. If he discovered what she'd been doing with his tunic, Rosalia did not think her pride would ever recover. Turning around upon her approach, Ciaran gave her a heated glance from head to toe. What was wrong with him? He had Beathag and should not be throwing heated glances her way. Pulling on Noonie's mane to kneel, she pulled herself upon his back.

"I thought to show ye the village." He shifted in the saddle.

"Lead on, my laird," she said, gesturing with her arm.

They rode to the village in uncomfortable silence. She centered her attention on Noonie's clip-clopping feet and quickly became entranced by the soothing rhythm. When they arrived, Ciaran pointed out sights, continuing to show her about. Every time she asked a question, he gave her a clipped reply, and she politely nodded at all of his dry remarks.

This was not how she wanted to spend the remainder of her time at Glenorchy. He was obviously uncomfortable around her. She'd thought her actions would make him realize that she cared not about him. Apparently, Ciaran did not understand that. When they took their leave from the village, conversation was still not flowing from either direction.

Abruptly changing course, he headed up a mountain pass. After continuing to ride at a steep angle, they eventually reached a clearing. He dismounted and tethered his mount. When he turned around, she had already dismounted and Noonie's reins were upon the ground.

Ciaran looked at her with a raised brow.

"He knows to stay when his reins are upon the ground."

"'Tis truly incredible," he said, shaking his head in awe. "Aye."

He gestured for her to come closer to the edge, and she prayed his intention was not to push her off.

They stood on top of a mountain that overlooked Glenorchy and the loch. No matter where her path took her, she would always be thankful to have traveled the Highlands. These beauteous views would be forever imprinted in her mind. She stood complacently, gazing upon Glenorchy in its splendor.

The leaves were a rainbow of colors that reflected off the loch. Ciaran did have a truly magnificent home. Rosalia sighed as a warm breeze blew some short tendrils of hair into her eyes and she brushed them away. It would be so simple to imagine Glenorchy as her home and the man standing beside her as her husband. She would not do this—she could not do this. She had to cease these images. Her heart was being trampled.

Ciaran broke the silence and spoke quietly. "She means naught to me."

A tear fell down her cheek and she wiped it away. "It doesnae matter—truly," she whispered.

He reached out and gently brushed Rosalia's arms. When she closed her eyes to avoid his probing gaze, he raised her chin with his finger. He did not speak until she opened her eyes. "It matters to me," he said solemnly. Ciaran wiped her tears with his thumb. "I told her we were done when I returned to Glenorchy. She wasnae pleased. I didnae know she was there, Rosalia. She saw ye and Aisling and threw her body upon me."

She could not help but smirk. "Her verra bare body, my laird."

Ciaran paused for a moment, a spark of some indefinable emotion in his eyes. "I didnae notice, Rosalia. All I saw was ye," he whispered, slowly bending his head toward her.

She did not know if she was responding to the words he spoke or if she was only caught up in the moment, but she needed this. She needed him.

His warm lips touched hers and she shuddered. She pulled him close, running her fingers through his shoulder-length hair.

Placing his hands behind her head, Ciaran deepened the kiss. Their tongues intertwined instinctively and she let out a soft moan. Rubbing his hands down her back, he pulled her bottom close, letting out a guttural moan as they made contact.

Rosalia was not sure what was occurring, but she knew she needed more. She rubbed her hands over his chest, feeling the strong, chiseled muscles that she knew lay beneath.

She wanted… more.

Ciaran smothered her lips with demanding mastery. His hands slowly maneuvered under her tunic until he felt the bare skin of her back, the gentle touch of his fingers sending currents of desire through her.

She slowly pulled out his tunic from his kilt, running her hands over his bare skin. "Ciaran," she moaned.

Trailing kisses down her neck, he slowly raised his hands to cover her breast. She melted into him and arched her back into his grasp.

She had never felt this… hot. She was burning for him.

"I have to see ye, lass." He pulled back with passion-glazed eyes and waited for her consent.

She nodded and closed her eyes.

Ciaran lifted her tunic and bared her breasts. "Och, Rosalia. Ye are beautiful," he whispered.

He bent and suckled one of her breasts while

kneading the other with his hand. He licked her taut nipple and she thought surely she would die.

Running her fingers through his hair, she pulled him closer. "Ciaran," she moaned. If his arms were not supporting her, she would have fallen to her knees.

❦

Ciaran paused, knowing if he did not cease now, there would be no turning back. He'd made a promise to his father, and duty always came first. Besides, he could not take her this way. Rosalia was to be gently wooed, and her first time should be in a bed with her *husband*—something he could never be—at least, not now. He could not offer her anything, but maybe in time. For right now, she needed to know that he cared for her and would not intentionally hurt her. That was important to him.

He stopped his ministrations and dropped to his knees, nestling his head into her chest. Wrapping his arms around her waist, he continued to hold her in a tight embrace. "Forgive me," he whispered.

Rosalia placed her hand under his chin. "There is naught to forgive, my laird," she whispered back.

He rose and pulled her into his arms. "My apologies that I caused ye pain. If I could have changed what ye saw—"

"There is nay need to explain. I only…" she paused.

"Ye only what?" he asked. He pulled back slightly and nodded for her to continue.

"I donna want my heart to suffer. I will travel to Glen—"

He gently placed his fingers over her lips. "Shh…

Howbeit we donna speak of it and we just enjoy our time together?" he suggested, rubbing the back of his hand over her cheek.

She kissed his palm. "Aye."

Neither one of them spoke as they reached a silent understanding. Why glance to the future when they should live in the now?

～

Returning to Glenorchy with lighter hearts, they led their mounts to the stable. Rosalia began to wonder just what she wanted of Ciaran. After all, she would still travel to Glengarry and he would still be the laird of Glenorchy. What he said was logical. Why dwell upon what was to be? Every day away from Mangerton was a day to be cherished.

Reaching out, Ciaran took Noonie's reins. "I donna see Niall."

"'Tis fine. I can care for Noonie," she said, taking back the reins. Ciaran placed his hand on the back of her neck. Slowly bending forward, he kissed her. The touch of his lips sent a shock wave through her entire body.

"'Tis about time ye returned, my liege."

Rosalia jerked away from him, an unwelcome blush creeping into her cheeks even though she did not think Declan had noticed their embrace.

"What do ye want, Brother?" Ciaran scowled.

Declan shrugged with indifference. "*I* donna want anything. There are men here from the village and they want to speak with ye—something about missing goats or the like. Ye better run along. Duty calls, your greatness." With an arrogant swagger, he approached Ciaran and took the reins of his mount. "I will see to your mount."

Ciaran shook his head regretfully. "I must take my leave, but I will see ye later," he said to Rosalia, his eyes sending her a private message.

"Of course." Somewhat disappointed, she understood Ciaran's duty and all that it entailed. Simply, his clan and his people would always come before his own wants or needs. After all, he was laird.

"Donna worry. I will see to your mount *and* Rosalia," said Declan, his mouth twitching in amusement.

"Declan," Ciaran warned.

Declan waved him off. "Get your kilt untwisted, your greatness. I only want to take Rosalia upon the parapet."

Something clicked in her mind. "The parapet?" she squeaked. "Why?" Her memory of Ciaran was pure and clear. She would never forget a single detail of his face or his touch. The idea of sharing the same place with Ciaran's brother gave her sourness in the pit of her stomach. "Umm… I donna really want to go to the parapet, but I could use a walk if ye wouldnae mind escorting me," she offered.

Declan was disheartened by her hesitation, but thankfully agreed while Ciaran took his leave to see to the villagers. She led Noonie into his stall and Declan saw to Ciaran's mount. She would never pretend to understand the relationship between brothers. Declan was an ever-changing mystery to her.

The stable was quiet except for an occasional whinny and pawing hooves. She was enjoying the peace of no one arguing when Declan's voice spoke in a soothing tone.

"Why are ye the only one that loves me, Aiden?" he asked in a childlike voice.

Rosalia poked her head out of the stall to see that Declan had his head placed to Aiden's and was scratching the horse behind the ears. Looking up, Declan gave her a roguish grin. "I know what ye are thinking. Donna laugh. Aiden is the only one who doesnae cause me grief and understands me. Aye, Aiden?" he asked in the same childlike voice.

She walked down to Aiden's stall and rubbed his muscular neck. "He is a beautiful beast. I told Aisling that I have ne'er seen such perfect white markings as are upon his feet."

Declan nodded his head in agreement. "Now speak the truth and tell me why ye donna want me to take ye upon the parapet, lass." He abruptly changed the subject.

He'd caught her off guard and Rosalia swallowed hard, trying to manage a feeble answer.

Aware of her discomfort, Declan chuckled. Standing a bit too close, he gave her a wolfish grin. "Donna ye trust yourself alone with me? I donna bite." His silky voice held a challenge and his eyes clung to hers, analyzing her reaction.

It was much like having a conversation with James. If she did not put him in his place now, he would continually torment her until she traveled to Glengarry. Of this, she had no doubt. She reached down, holding his eyes the entire time. "Did ye ever think *why* Aiden is the only one that understands ye?

Mayhap 'tis because ye can both relate to being a horse's arse," she said, her voice unwavering.

Startled, Declan glanced down to find a very sharp dirk pointed at his heart. He stood there blank, amazed, and stunned.

"Aye, I ne'er leave without it. If ye cease thinking with your…" she gestured to his manhood, "ye would have seen me reach for my dirk and wouldnae have been taken by a mere lass."

He stepped away from her. "Now 'tis clearly where ye are mistaken, Lady Rosalia. Ye see… I donna mind being taken by a mere lass."

Sheathing her dirk, she let out a frustrated grunt. "I yield, but I give ye fair warning. I will be here until your brother takes me to Glengarry. I donna want to do battle, but I willnae let ye speak to me as if I toss my skirts. Will ye be a gentleman and escort me on my walk or nae?" she asked, placing both of her hands upon her hips.

"Och, ye are so much as Aisling." Placing his arm around her shoulders, he led her out of the stables. "Ye have my word as a gentleman. A walk would be fine."

⁓

Finally exhausted, Rosalia sought the comfort of her bedchamber. Fatigue settled in pockets under her eyes. Perhaps she would sleep this eve. Weariness enveloped her as she crawled into bed. Her mind kept turning to Ciaran and his comforting embrace.

"Rosalia, what have you done?" her mother bellowed.

She turned around and stiffened. How she had come to despise that tone! Of course she knew she had done something wrong. She always did something wrong. Considering what she could have missed, she felt her thoughts escape her.

"Look at the dirt! I thought you scrubbed this table!" screamed her mother, pointing to the table.

Rosalia gasped, realizing a shiver of panic. "I did scrub the table. I am still cleaning." She grabbed the cloth and started to wipe the table. It was coming. She knew it was coming. Sheer black fright swept through her.

"Look underneath the table, Rosalia. You did not scrub under the table!" With one quick movement, her mother reached her. She pulled her daughter by the hair and slammed her head down on the table. "Look, Rosalia! You did not scrub under the table!" Yanking her up by the hair, her mother again slammed her head into the table with a loud crack.

"Donna touch me!" Rosalia screamed. *"Mo mhallachd ort!"*

"Rosalia, 'tis Ciaran. Ye are safe. No one will hurt ye," he whispered. "Ye are safe."

A hot tear trickled down her cheek. "Ciaran?" she asked, disoriented and raising her hand to his cheek. She closed her eyes, reliving the pain of that final scene. The memory was like an old wound that ached on a rainy day. The picture froze in her mind until she heard Ciaran again call her name.

He watched her open her tear-stained eyes, his eyes darkening with emotion. She drank in the comfort of his nearness. He was a vision that pulled her out of the darkness. He was her light. He was her... savior. His body was partially covering hers and he was whispering soothingly into her ear as she tried to recover from another round of painful memories.

He kissed her hand. "Ye had a nightmare is all." Ciaran rubbed his hand over her tresses, and his eyes brimmed with tenderness and passion. Suddenly, he clenched his jaw and his eyes slightly narrowed. He moved to rise, but she stilled him.

"Please stay with me," she begged. "I donna want to be alone." Rosalia pulled him into a tight embrace. The harder she tried to ignore the truth, the more it persisted. Whether she wanted to admit it or not, there was something special about him.

"Rosalia…" said Ciaran huskily, pulling her arms off him and springing to his feet.

"Ciaran! Ye have nay clothing!" she squeaked. Sitting up quickly, she pulled the blanket tighter around herself. Her heart jolted and her pulse pounded. She could not help but stare at him intently—all of him. His vitality captivated her. She gave him an involuntary examination and found his closeness so male.

She could not tear her gaze away from him. The glimpses of his strong body made her heart beat more rapidly, and a delicious shudder heated through her. For a long moment, she felt as though she were floating. She glanced up at him and her heart lurched madly. At that moment, she began to recognize her own needs.

Realizing she was still gaping, she lowered her gaze. She had only seen James once before when he was in his cups and she helped him undress.

Turning his back to her, Ciaran mumbled an apology and she stuttered through her nervousness.

He stole a glance at her over his shoulder. "I heard

ye scream, and I didnae think to grab my clothing. Besides, from the way your eyes were looking at me, I didnae think ye minded," he chuckled. "I will—"

She whipped her pillow at his back. "Go put on your—"

"Kilt?" he asked with a raised brow, seeming to enjoy the gentle sparring.

Seeing the amusement in his eyes, she laughed. "Nay!"

He cocked his head at her outburst and turned up his smile a notch. "Nay?"

"Mayhap trews," she suggested.

Ciaran walked back to his chamber. "And I suggest ye do the same," he called over his shoulder.

≈∾

Donning his kilt with no tunic, Ciaran returned to Rosalia's chamber with ale. Thankfully, she had also donned her trews and a tunic and sat peacefully before the fire. The glowing embers cast her in a serene light. He simply enjoyed watching her.

Taking a seat in the opposite chair, he poured her some ale. "'Tis the ale." He held out a tankard. "It will help ye to sleep."

"My thanks." She reached out and took the tankard.

"My apologies I didnae get to speak with ye again. The men from the village took longer than expected." When she was getting ready to question him further, he quickly added, "'Tis naught ye should be concerned about." He did a double take and chuckled, noticing something very familiar. "Is that *my* tunic, lass?"

Rosalia's eyes widened and she started to mumble something he could not understand.

"Ye actually wear my tunic… to bed?" He found that fact very satisfying.

"Leave off, MacGregor," she threatened.

"Have ye always had nightmares?" he asked softly. She took another swig of ale and gazed at her hands. "Do ye remember them when ye awaken?" He paused. "Rosalia, do ye trust me?" Lifting his tankard, he took a swig and glanced at her over the rim.

She looked up at him with curiosity. "Of course I do. Why would ye ask that of me?"

He could not help but notice how bonny she looked in the glow of the firelight. He would have to be a blind fool not to notice. He remembered how beautiful she was at court but would never tell her so. She would be embarrassed. He could not believe he was here with her now. "Every time ye become nervous or donna want to answer something ye stare down at your hands."

Instinctively, she glanced down. "'Tis habit. When I become uncomfortable, I know I do that. Mother used to tell me frequently. My apologies."

"Rosalia, there is naught to apologize for. I merely…" He made another attempt. "Do ye remember your nightmares?"

Looking him dead in the eye, she held up her tankard in mock salute. "Aye, every last one of them," she said, taking another swig of ale.

"How long have ye had them?"

"For as long as I can remember."

Ciaran was surprised by her response. She had been through so much as of late that he'd assumed her nightmares were a result of all the events that had recently occurred. Reaching over, he squeezed her hand. "Was it that unpleasant for ye, lass?"

"Aye," she simply stated.

He waited for her to continue. As far as he was concerned, he had all eve.

She huffed. "Ciaran, ye donna want to hear my woes…"

"'Tis where ye are wrong, sweeting. I want to know all about ye," he said softly. He could tell his use of the endearment took her aback, but it was how he felt. Why not speak it? She sighed and he knew she was eventually going to relent.

"Mother and Father ne'er paid me much attention unless it suited them. I was always lonely, but I kept a few of those close to my heart such as James; Duncan, our stable hand; and Ealasaid, our cook." Gazing into the flames of the fire, she began to speak as if she were in some faraway place in the corner of her mind.

"What I didnae tell ye before was that Father is a Highland laird. After he married my English mother, they lived in Liddesdale. I donna know much about their past or their families, but it wasnae for lack of trying. When I would ask, the subject would always be changed.

"My *seanmhair*, Father's mother in Glengarry, would send a messenger on occasion. He would always seek me alone outside of Mangerton's walls and deliver messages or packages. It seemed my *seanmhair* did want to see me or I was ne'er far from her thoughts, but I was ne'er permitted to travel to the Highlands. I heard Mother once say that she didnae have a choice but to wed Father, but 'tis all I know. Do ye wish to know more, my laird?" Her eyes never left the flames.

He squeezed her hand. "Ye may speak to me about anything, sweeting." She smiled into the flickering light and he continued to hold her hand for reassurance.

"Mother has a verra bad ire. Ye cannae imagine. Everything must be done her way. If it wasnae, everyone around her paid a price—mainly me. Those close to us knew of her ire. To others, she would portray the doting wife and mother. Father has experienced her wrath as well. He does everything in his power to ensure peace, even sacrificing my future to keep her joyful.

"He gave her everything without question. Mangerton was decorated with the finest of wares, tapestries, anything worth a lot of coin. He provided her with the finest gowns and the finest of everything. The coffers are now empty and all servants, except a handful, have been dismissed. In order to replenish the coin, I was to be forced to wed the English beast— Lord Dunnehl. I refused. I paid the price."

She sighed and took another swig of ale. "My entire existence has been spent wondering how Mother felt from one day to the next. I ne'er mattered. In fact, in her eyes I did not exist. Would I be beaten because I gave her a look? Would I be slapped because I didnae act proper? Would my tresses be pulled out because I didnae kiss her in greeting?

"Every move I made was under constant scrutiny. I couldnae think for myself. I couldnae speak for myself. Every moment of time was planned for me, and I was always told what to do and when to do it. At times I couldnae even breathe. I didnae even know who I was. When I was ordered to do something, it was because I was ungrateful or unappreciative. I have been told this my entire score and one. I donna know any different."

She paused, rubbing the rim of her tankard. "When James found us, I was tempted to return to Mangerton. He shouldnae have to suffer because of me. I know marriages are arranged for coin, land, or title, but I ne'er cared about such things. I was foolish enough to think I could find a love match. I only wanted to find happiness. I didnae want to think only of myself, but I knew in my heart I could ne'er return. I would rather die by my own hand than live another moment there. Now ye know, my laird. I am weak and I am a coward." She spoke with bitterness.

Ciaran was breathless with rage, but he swallowed hard, trying not to reveal his anger. The lass was distraught enough. He did not want to add to it. Leaning forward, he intertwined their fingers. "Nay one should ever touch ye that way, Rosalia. What she did wasnae right. I know of men who beat their women into submission, and I think your mother is nay different. She wanted ye submissive. What I donna understand is how your father turned his eye. Ye are his only daughter.

"I donna understand how ye can say ye are weak and a coward. Lass, ye have more courage than most men. Ye cut your tresses and dressed as a lad. Ye were battered and bruised, riding Noonie for many miles before ye passed out from the pain. Ye are a courageous woman, Rosalia. I only wish I knew how to take away your pain," he said softly.

"I am hoping in time my dreams turn to faded memories. I donna enjoy reliving the moments time and again. It feels as if I am still there."

Ciaran rubbed his thumb over the back of her hand. "Ye are safe. No one will touch ye while ye are within my walls."

She smiled her thanks. "I am frightened this will always be a burden for me to bear. I just want to find peace. I want to find… me."

"And I hope I am able to help ye with that. Take all the time ye need, lass," he said, smiling at her with compassion.

"Ye have heard enough of me. Please tell me of ye, my laird." Abruptly, she changed the subject.

"Me?" Sitting back in the chair, Ciaran was surprised by her request. No one had ever asked him to speak of himself. "And what would ye want to know of me?"

"Tell me more of your family."

He rubbed his brow. "My father and mother loved each other verra much. They raised us to be honorable men. I cannae say Aiden and I didnae cause our fair share of mischief, but Father raised us to be able to eventually take his place as laird while Declan was kept under Mother's wing. At nay fault of my father. He did what he thought best. Declan was the third son, even though we ne'er made him feel that way. Father made Declan train with us and tried to mold him, but when he took nay interest, Father didnae pressure him to do so."

Rosalia smiled in understanding. "That gives some reason why Declan acts—"

"As an arse?"

"Well, that wasnae exactly what I was going to say." She chuckled.

"Declan wasnae always as he is now. Nae until Mother died. He and Mother became verra close. Father was busy training Aiden and me, and Declan would be with Mother. She loved us all, but we know she favored Declan. Mayhap she tried to intervene because Father spent so much time with Aiden and me. It is difficult to say. After she died, Declan kept to himself. He didnae want to speak with any of us, nay matter how hard we tried. He started whor—er… wenching and getting into his cups."

Ciaran ran his hands through his hair. "It was as if he was trying to destroy himself along with Mother. We all told him that Mother had died and he hadnae, but he wouldnae listen to reason. Father tried to help him but couldnae."

"That had to be difficult for all of ye. Nae only did ye lose your mother, but ye had to watch Declan lose himself," she said quietly.

"Aye. We hoped when Aiden and Aisling wed that Declan would try to find a lass and wed himself, but he wants naught to do with seeking a wife."

There was a heavy silence.

"And what of ye, my laird? Ye ne'er thought to seek a wife?"

Leaning forward, he grabbed her hand. "'Tisnae as if I havenae thought of it, especially as of late…"

"Ciaran, my apologies. I loosened my tongue too much. I had nay right to—"

"Shh… Ye should know the truth." He paused. "I

made a promise to Father before he died that I would set Declan on a clear path. Father felt he'd failed my brother and made me give my word I would help him. I didnae realize that promise would be a battle of wills. I cannae break my vow. To be truthful, it has ne'er caused me too much concern until now. Rosalia, I cannae wed until—"

She stood and placed her hand to his lips. "Shh, my laird. We agreed nae to speak of such things and to enjoy our time together."

He nodded his head in consent.

"'Tis late. I thank ye for the comfort, Ciaran."

He pulled himself to his feet and raised his hand, placing an unruly lock of hair behind her ear. "I am here for ye, lass, if ye need me for anything." Ciaran brushed a gentle kiss across her forehead. Pulling away slowly, he smiled. "Get sleep. I shall see ye in a few hours." He gave her one last glance before he closed the adjoining door.

Knowing sleep would not come now; Ciaran approached his desk and lit a candle. He penned a missive, confident in his strokes. He did not need to compose much, knowing what he had to write. Completing his task, he stretched out his back. Placing the MacGregor seal into the melted wax, he breathed a sigh of relief.

It was done.

His chamber brightened with the golden hues of the peeking sun, making him realize he had not slept at all. No matter, he would send the missive by special messenger this morn to Glengarry—well, as soon as the messenger was awake.

Ten

ROSALIA DESCENDED THE STAIRS TO BREAK HER FAST, still smiling at the gift that had been placed upon her chair early this morn. She thoroughly enjoyed being able to bare her soul last eve to Ciaran. As she remembered their conversation, she prayed he did not think her daft. The last thing she wanted was for him to think she was some foolish chit. After all, she was not a delicate flower. She just needed someone to offer her comfort and he was a wonderful listener. She was comforted by the fact that James was not the only man she could speak with openly.

As she approached the dais, Ciaran was already breaking his fast with Aiden. Odd, Declan and Aisling were not in attendance. Aisling was probably with Teàrlach, and Rosalia hoped Declan was not cowering somewhere recovering from a night of debauchery.

Both men stood upon her approach.

"And how are ye this morn, sweeting?" asked Ciaran.

She was startled not only because the endearment was spoken, but because it was expressed so freely in front of Aiden. She cast Aiden a nervous glance, but he just smiled and went back to his meal as though nothing were out of the ordinary. "I am well. And ye, my laird?"

He kissed her on the cheek and heat rose in her features. Pulling out her chair, he whispered closely, "I would think after last eve ye would call me Ciaran."

Turning another shade of crimson, Rosalia sat down on the chair.

"I left something for ye this morn. Did ye get it?" he asked softly.

"Aye," she whispered back, trying desperately to remove the color from her face.

"I thought ye might want another one for mayhap when we ride again or if ye wish to wear it to bed." He cast a roguish grin. "After all, ye donna want to wear out my other tunic. The one I left ye was recently made."

Her eyes started to stray to her hands, and she forced herself to look him in the eye. "Ye have my thanks." Rosalia paused, touching him gently on the arm. "Ciaran, about last eve…"

"What about last eve?" slurred Declan, staggering to the table.

When Ciaran grunted, she thought it best to redirect. "Aiden, where is Aisling this morn?"

"She is with Teàrlach," he mumbled, throwing looks of displeasure at Declan.

"Hmm… And what do ye do this day, my laird?" Rosalia asked Ciaran as Declan tumbled into his chair, knocking over a tankard.

"Before or after I battle with Declan?" Ciaran spoke through gritted teeth. Leaning forward, he narrowed his eyes at Declan. "Break your fast. Then we practice swordplay with the men in the bailey."

Ignoring him, Declan took a leisurely drink from his tankard. When Declan turned his head, Ciaran was annoyed to see how glassy his younger brother's eyes were. "But my great liege, I already practiced my swordplay yestereve." Declan nodded to two serving wenches who were giving him smoldering glances from across the hall. "*Twice*, I do believe. Howbeit ye will be pleased to know they said I mastered it verra well," he said arrogantly.

Ciaran and Aiden sprang to their feet, flanking Declan. They moved so quickly that Rosalia jumped. Hauling Declan forcefully from his chair as if he only weighed as much as a mere bairn, they shoved him in the direction of Ciaran's solar. The hall went quiet as everyone gawked at Declan being abducted while breaking his fast. Rosalia only prayed there would not be bloodshed.

After finishing her meal alone, Rosalia went in search of Aisling. She did not need to look far. The sounds of Teàrlach's screams were piercing as Aisling descended the stairs. "Good morn," Aisling said loudly, closing her eyes in an apparent attempt to bear the sound of Teàrlach's shrill screams. "I take him outdoors for a walk. I cannae promise it will be soothing, but ye can come along if ye want."

"Of course," said Rosalia, rubbing her hand over his tiny curls.

Aisling bounced him gently in her arms, and when they reached the bailey, Teàrlach stopped crying almost immediately. "Ye see? He has Aiden's stubbornness already." She cocked her head and raised her brow. "Well? Come now. Tell me all of what occurred with Declan this morn." When Rosalia gave her a questioning gaze, Aisling smiled. "Anna. She tells me all."

They leisurely made their way toward the stable. "It wasnae good. Declan could barely stand when he came to break his fast. Ciaran told him after his meal that he would need to practice his swordplay with the men, and I do believe Declan said he had already practiced his swordplay with two serving wenches— *twice*." She cringed and Aisling sighed. "Aiden and Ciaran dragged him away. To Ciaran's solar, I believe. I donna know what occurred after that. I didnae really want to stay and find out."

Aisling kissed Teàrlach on the head. "Och, Declan has done it now. He doesnae listen to anyone. I wonder if Aiden and Ciaran finally beat some sense into him. 'Tis up to them now. There is naught we can do." Aisling studied her for a moment and smiled. "Ye seem lighter of heart this morn. Could it have something to do with a certain laird?"

"It may be possible," Rosalia said. Even her walk had a sunny cheerfulness.

Aisling grinned. "I am joyful to hear it. Do ye want to go and fetch your cloak?"

"Nay, I am fine," she said, shaking her head.

Aisling stopped. "Rosalia, do ye *have* a cloak?"

She was silent for a moment. "Ye will think me daft, but nay, I donna. When I took my leave, I took only clothes to travel and blankets. I didnae—"

"It doesnae matter. Ye are in the Highlands and ye will need a cloak. I will see to it."

Aisling had given her so much already—they all had. "I already have your gowns. I cannae accept—"

"Ye can and ye will. Come," Aisling said in an authoritative tone, leading her back indoors.

⚜

Ciaran thrust Declan into his solar and slammed the door while Aiden pushed Declan further into the room and shoved him unwillingly into a chair. Aiden took a seat in the opposite chair as Ciaran sat behind his father's desk. Briefly closing his eyes, Ciaran took a deep breath before his ire got the best of him.

"So why the silence, your worship? Now I have to wait the same as a wee lad until ye are ready to give me a scolding?" Declan smirked.

Ciaran's eyes flew open and he was just about to kill his brother when Aiden sprang from the chair, pulling up Declan by the tunic. "Ye go too far, Brother. If Father were still alive—"

"Aye, but he isnae," said Declan sarcastically.

Aiden punched him square in the jaw.

Ciaran flew from his chair, rounded the desk, and pulled them apart. Shoving them forcefully into their own chairs, he then sat on the desk between them. Aiden rubbed his hand as Declan rubbed his jaw. What would his father have thought at such a sight?

"Declan, for once ye are correct. Father isnae here, which means I am laird and I *will* be obeyed. Ye are still my brother and my responsibility. I willnae continue to watch ye drowning yourself in yer cups and destroying everything and everyone around ye." Ciaran spoke in a voice that demanded attention.

"Nor will I," Aiden concurred.

"So what do ye say, Ciaran? Just speak the words ye are holding back," Declan bit out, leaning casually in the chair.

Ciaran glanced at Aiden, and he nodded his head in silent confirmation. "As your brother, I cannae stand by and watch ye continue to destroy yourself. The gods have taken Father and Mother, but they havenae taken ye—at least, nae yet. If ye donna straighten your path, ye willnae be far behind them. How can I continue to watch your back when ye donna watch your own?"

He paused as Declan studied him intently. "As of now, ye will cease drowning in your cups. Ye will cease wenching within my walls. Ye will practice your swordplay daily with the men, and ye *will* straighten your path."

His brother yawned, stretched his legs out in front of him, and crossed his feet at the ankles. "And if I donna?"

"Ye are on your own—removed from my walls with only the clothes upon your back. Before ye speak, think upon this. Ye are my brother, my blood. I cannae watch ye continue on this path ye have chosen. Ye care for nay one. Ye made this mess and only ye can clean it up. 'Tis all your choice, Brother. I only hope ye choose wisely. Make nay error in judgment, Declan. I am your brother, but foremost, I have a duty as laird. I will be obeyed and willnae be made the fool in front of my men." His voice rang with command.

"Declan, Aisling and I have tried to help ye. We *want* to help ye, but we cannae if ye donna even try to help yourself. Ciaran is right in this matter and he has my agreement. If ye donna cease, ye are on your own, Brother," Aiden said tersely.

There was a heavy silence.

Declan rose. "Well, ye two have obviously decided my fate."

"Nay, Declan. Ye make your own fate," Ciaran countered. "I will see ye in the bailey with the men."

"So I am simply being dismissed, your greatness?" Declan walked leisurely to the door and turned around. He gave a forced smile and a tense nod of consent. "I will meet ye in the bailey."

When the door closed, Ciaran and Aiden visibly relaxed. "Do ye think he heard ye?" asked Aiden with concern.

"I donna know. I hope for his sake that he did." Ciaran ran his hand through his hair. "I donna know how Father handled such things."

Aiden laughed. "Ye donna think he felt the same as ye when he was laird?"

He shrugged. "I donna know."

"Ciaran, he had three sons. Ye donna remember the trouble we caused Father? How could ye forget my wenching ways before Aisling? Ye yourself had quite the appetite for the lasses. And let us nae forget one of the many times when ye were in your cups and placed your kilt around your horse," he chuckled. "I also recall the first time *ye* were a drunken sot and were caught by the blacksmith taking liberties with his daughter. Father had a lot of explaining to do. I am sure he felt the same as you do. Ye will know more of the same when ye have a son. Speaking of—"

Ciaran scowled. "Donna start with me, Brother.

Declan will be on a clear path soon enough, even if I have to strap him down and hold him on it."

"And Rosalia will wait until that time?" asked Aiden, raising his brow searchingly.

"Rosalia knows I made the vow to Father."

"How verra understanding of the lass." Aiden chuckled. "Ciaran, will ye take advice from a man that has been wed?"

Ciaran held up his hand to silence Aiden, but his brother simply waved him off. He would have to remind him again soon who was laird.

"I donna care what ye speak. I give it freely. Love doesnae happen often in a marriage, and when it does, ye grab hold with both hands and donna let go. I see ye care for the lass. Why donna ye wed and be done with it? Surely ye donna plan to take her to Glengarry. Ye promised Father to see to Declan, but ye didnae say ye would wait to wed."

Ciaran slumped down into the chair next to Aiden and sighed. "We have been through this, Brother. It was understood."

"By ye or by Father? He would ne'er ask ye to wait to wed."

They sat silently for a long time. The lines of awareness deepened along Aiden's brow and under his eyes. Ciaran knew he was deep in thought. This could not bode well for him. He was about to stand to escape Aiden's lecture, but his brother spoke before Ciaran had the chance to flee.

"Think upon this. Your duty as laird is to beget a legitimate heir. The only way to accomplish that task is to wed. And I think ye are sorely lacking in your responsibilities as of late." Aiden folded his arms over his chest. "I bet ye ne'er thought of it that way, aye?"

Ciaran sat back, shook his head, and moaned. "Why do the gods grace me with such brothers? One pains me in the arse and the other pains me in the head."

"Promise me ye will think upon it or my wee wife will be keeping me up all eve speaking of ye. Surely ye can understand that I donna want to be speaking of *ye* in my marriage bed, Brother. I donna want to be *speaking* at all."

Rising, Ciaran held up his hands in surrender. "Cease, Aiden. I donna want or need to know what ye and Aisling say or donna say in your marriage bed. Besides, I thought she cursed ye out of her bed."

Aiden shrugged, giving him a sheepish grin. "It wasnae exactly *me* she cursed out of her bed. It was my—"

"And that is another reason why I donna rush to wed," Ciaran said, laughing.

❧

Aisling gave Rosalia a cloak that was too small, but at least it matched her shortened gowns and would keep her warm. Why did she have to have her father's height? When she reached Glengarry, she would need to seek proper attire. She did not want to embarrass her *seanmhair*. As Rosalia walked through the bailey, she saw that Declan had joined Ciaran and Aiden with swordplay. Apparently, everyone had survived the confrontation in one piece. When she reached the stables, she scanned the area but did not see Niall. She enjoyed his company. He had a warm and caring personality that reminded her of Duncan.

Noonie stomped his feet and whinnied upon her approach. She reached out and rubbed her hands on his sleek black coat. "And how are ye this morn, Noonie?"

"What an interesting name for a mount."

Whipping her head around, Rosalia saw Beathag walking toward her with a sly grin. "He is a fine beast."

Rosalia shifted her weight, trying to center her attention on Noonie. "Aye."

There was an uncomfortable silence.

Beathag continued to study her intently, but Rosalia refused to display her nervousness. Attempting to keep her focus on her horse, she would not give Ciaran's former leman the satisfaction of knowing how entirely uncomfortable she felt.

"What are ye doing here?" Beathag asked, her tone coolly disapproving.

"I see to my horse," she remarked, pleased at how indifferent she sounded.

Beathag's eyes narrowed. "Nae that. Why are ye here at Glenorchy?"

To Rosalia's dismay, her voice broke slightly and she stammered in bewilderment. "I only stay until 'tis safe to travel to Glen—" she paused. It was probably not the best idea to advise Beathag of her plans.

When Beathag recognized her hesitation, she chuckled. "Ye mean to say when 'tis safe to travel to Glengarry—Lady Rosalia Armstrong of Liddesdale. Do ye nae?"

Rosalia paled.

"I cannae help but wonder why a *lady* would be traveling alone—well, nae unless she runs from something or someone. Donna worry overmuch,

Lady Rosalia. I keep my mouth closed to anyone that would mayhap find an interest in these facts… as long as ye stay away from Ciaran," Beathag warned. "Ye wouldnae want anything untoward to befall ye or our laird now, would ye?"

Rosalia was speechless and shook her head until the words came to surface. "Nay, of course," she spoke quietly.

"Naught will ever happen as long as ye keep your distance from Ciaran." Taking another step closer, Beathag closed the distance between them. Raising her hand, she fingered Rosalia's cut tresses. "I donna know what ye *think* is between ye, but Ciaran will always care for me. We are close—*verra* close. Tell me, *Rosalia*. When he is between your legs, does he tell ye how beautiful ye are? Does he tell ye how he loves your body?" She shook her head with disgust. "Nay, of course he doesnae. How could he? Look at ye." Beathag ran her hands over the front of her body. "And look at me."

Rosalia was sure she turned brilliant shades of red. She was completely aware of the fact that she was no great beauty, but to have it thrown at her in such a way irritated her beyond belief. She had never met someone so completely venomous. "Pray excuse me."

"Of course. Run away, wee mouse. Pray excuse me," she snickered. "Did I say *wee*?"

Rosalia bit her lip to keep matters from becoming worse. If Beathag knew who she was, it would only be a matter of time before men would be pounding on Ciaran's front gate. Maybe Dunnehl's men. Beathag would try to cause her grief—of this she had no doubt. Not wanting to provoke Beathag further, Rosalia chose to remain silent when what she wanted to do was pull out her dirk and ram it down Beathag's whore-ish throat.

Rosalia stormed out of the stable, needing to breathe. Her forceful strides brought her quickly to the parapet door. She would break it down if it did not open. The bolt slid easily and she sought solace in the place she had shared with Ciaran. Beathag's words replayed in her mind. Rosalia needed a release and quickly. Gaelic curses flew from her mouth as fast as she could think them. She whipped them out like stones. Even the cool breeze could not stop her racing heart or cool her raging ire.

After grunting every curse she knew at least twice over, she sought the comfort of her bedchamber until she could figure out what to do.

❧

Ciaran had not felt this lighthearted for some time. Declan trained with the men, actually putting forth an effort. Perhaps his brother was back on a course. Ciaran was pleased and he prayed his threats would work. They had to. He slapped Declan upon the shoulder, giving him a sign of approval.

"Donna touch me. Donna even breathe on me," said Declan, gasping for breath. Sweat poured down his face, and his jaw had turned several shades of purple and yellow.

Ciaran laughed. "Ye havenae practiced your sword-play for a while, Brother. It will come back to ye."

"Before or after I die a slow death?" Declan moaned.

"Ye did well this day, Declan." Ciaran nodded his head in praise.

Declan leaned up against the stone wall and closed his eyes, grimacing as he lifted his arm to wipe the sweat from his face.

"Is he dead?" Aiden chuckled.

"I wish," Declan grunted.

"Ye did better than a lass for nae practicing for so long," said Aiden, giving him a playful punch to the shoulder.

"*That* is supposed to make me feel better, Brother? If I wasnae so sore, I would take ye to task."

"Ye willnae touch one hair on Aiden's head, Declan MacGregor."

All of the men turned at the same time. Aisling stood with her hands placed on her hips, scowling at Declan.

"Ye better listen to my wee wife," said Aiden, placing his arm around her shoulders. "She may take *ye* to task." Aiden kissed the top of her head and she smiled.

"As of now, she probably could drop me on my arse." Declan pushed himself from the wall. "I seek the comfort of a warm bath to soothe my aching… everything."

"It appears ye have come into contact with a fist," said Aisling in a motherly tone. "Make sure ye see to your face as well."

He rubbed his jaw. "I have your husband to thank for that."

A devilish look came into her eyes. "I am sure it was naught that wasnae deserved, ye rogue."

Declan winked. "Ye know it, lass." He limped away, rubbing his aching muscles.

Aisling handed Aiden a drying cloth. "Do ye think ye hit him hard enough to beat sense into him?"

Wiping his sweaty face, Aiden shrugged his shoulders. "I donna know. Time will tell if he ceases his ways."

Ciaran grabbed a drying cloth, wiping his wet face. "He'd best cease his ways if he knows what is good for him."

"Ciaran, I wanted to speak with ye. Ye may want to see to it that Rosalia has proper clothes. Ye know she has some of my gowns, but she didnae have a cloak. The one I gave her has seen better days."

"I ne'er thought of a cloak. Aye, she will need... Do ye know enough of her to have some gowns and a cloak made by Cylan?" he asked, thrilled he would come up with such an idea for her.

Aisling smiled. "What a *great* thought, my laird. Of course." Behind Ciaran's back, she winked at Aiden as he tried to suppress a smile.

"Speak with Cylan and buy Rosalia whatever she needs. She isnae fond of fanciful gowns, but have one made for her as well."

Raising his brow, Aiden gave him a sly grin. "My laird, how *delightful* that ye actually know Rosalia isnae fond of fanciful gowns," he said, mimicking a lass.

Aisling elbowed him in the stomach. "Cease, Husband." She glanced at Ciaran. "I am sure Rosalia will love your gift."

"She cannae remain in the Highlands without proper clothes. She will catch the ague. And donna play me, Aisling. Ye know she willnae take these willingly. We will have to ensure that she does."

She waved him off. "If she is as light of heart as she is this day, we willnae have a problem."

Ciaran attempted to look occupied. The last thing he wanted was his sister-by-marriage to see the blush upon his face. He hoped he was the reason Rosalia felt so light of heart, but obviously he was not going to share such matters with Aisling.

After finishing his practice in the bailey, he went in search of Rosalia. Odd, no one had seemed to have seen her as of late. He approached her bedchamber door and knocked.

"Aye?" Rosalia called from within.

"'Tis Ciaran."

There was a pause. "Can I speak with ye later?" she asked, her voice sounding unnatural.

"Ye arenae well?" If she caught the ague because he did not provide proper clothes for her, he would never forgive himself.

"I need to rest." A tremor laced her voice.

Jiggling the latch, he tried to open the door. "Rosalia, unbolt the door." What was she about? There was another bout of silence between them.

"*Please*, my laird. I need to rest," Rosalia pleaded.

A moment later, Ciaran walked through the adjoining door.

                            ∾

Rosalia sat on the window bench, gazing out at the loch. When she heard Ciaran's footsteps walk away from the door, she prayed he would leave her alone until she was able to gather her wits. She decided to distance herself from him and would not take the chance that Beathag would live up to her threats. Her brief solace was interrupted as he walked casually through the adjoining door she had forgotten to lock.

Damn.

Ciaran strode toward her with a worried look upon his features. Raising his hand, he felt her forehead. "Are ye unwell?" Switching hands, he checked her again for fever.

"I am well." She glanced at her hands.

He dropped down beside her, facing her. "Then why wouldnae ye open the door?"

Closing her eyes, Rosalia shrugged. "I needed a moment to rest."

By the look upon his face, he clearly did not believe her. If she was to keep him at bay, she needed to be much more convincing. She mentally chided herself. What would she speak to James? "My monthly courses have arrived and I—"

"Have fallen into that trap once. I donna fall twice," Ciaran said, shaking his head. "Ye can still have your monthly courses and speak with me." Rubbing his palm over her cheek, she shied away. "What has changed since this morn? Aisling said ye were… er, fine." He shifted his weight, clearly becoming agitated. He was not going to relent.

Maybe a little honesty but not the entire truth would satisfy him. "Did ye ever have something occur ye knew would have several different outcomes depending upon how ye addressed it?" Rosalia asked.

He thought for a moment and glanced back at her. "Aye. Life."

She smirked. "'Tisnae that simple, Ciaran."

He intertwined their fingers and smiled. "In my experience, most things are ne'er as bad as they appear as long as ye have someone to share them with." He raised her chin with his finger, his eyes gentle and caring. "And ye have me. What could be so verra bad ye couldnae share with me?"

Smiling, Rosalia placed her hand into his. Looking into his eyes, her breath quickened, her tongue darting out to wet her suddenly very dry lips. The prolonged anticipation was almost unbearable.

Ciaran leaned in close, brushing her lips. His kiss was slow and gentle. Her heart beat faster, and she could not hear through the blood pounding in her ears. She pulled him closer, her body aching for his touch. She deepened the kiss, running her fingers through his hair. She was powerless to resist him.

When his fingers gently brushed her, he fueled a gently growing fire.

"Ah, sweeting, ye taste sweet as honey," he murmured, the huskiness lingering in his tone. His hand roamed intimately over her breast and she leaned into him. The mere touch of his hand sent a warming shiver through her. She had no desire to back out of his embrace. Her trembling limbs clung to him and she could no longer deny herself his touch.

Ciaran pulled back and his gaze fell to the creamy expanse of her neck. "Ye are so beautiful."

She stiffened and every muscle in her body tensed as if he had slapped her. Those were the words he had said to Beathag. Why would he speak the same to her? Her throat closed up.

Feeling her change in demeanor, he gazed upon

her searchingly. "What is wrong?" Ciaran repeated the question, and still she could not answer.

Rosalia jerked to her feet and tried to put as much distance between them as possible. He rose in one fluid motion, quickly closing the gap between them. With his powerful hands, he turned her to him. He had a habit of muddling her thoughts when he was so close.

He reached out, holding her at arms' length. He studied her intently and refused to waiver. "Something troubles ye and I will have the reason now. 'Tisnae a request." When his eyes suddenly filled with a fierce sparkling, she stared wordlessly. Her heart pounded and her voice would not come. "Rosalia," Ciaran warned, his vexation was evident.

Her eyes quickly darted around the room. "I-I-I… I cannae."

"Cannae or willnae?" His tone demanded an answer. She remained silent in a futile attempt to find the words she wanted to speak when his anger became a scalding fury. "Damn it to hell, Rosalia! How can I help ye if ye donna trust me to tell me what troubles ye? I thought we were beyond this."

When she lifted her trembling hands in a defensive gesture and cowered before him, it infuriated him even more. "I have *ne'er* raised my hand to a lass, let alone ye. The fact ye even *think* I would strike ye… I give ye nay reason to fear me, but your lack of trust in me is disconcerting." He worked off his anger by pacing.

A wave of apprehension swept through her, and she attempted to clutch his hand. "Ciaran, please." Pulling his hand free of hers, he continued to storm back and forth, throwing heated looks her way. Nervously, she ran her hands through her tresses. "Ciaran, this isnae—please, come and sit," she offered, gesturing to the chair.

A sudden icy contempt flashed in his eyes and he smirked but, to her relief, eventually took a seat.

He glared at her, frowning.

Rosalia hesitated, torn by conflicting emotions. She wondered if she should confess her doubts to him. Now it was her turn to pace. "I meant nay offense to ye. When ye raised your voice, my body only reacted as I am accustomed," she explained. Taking a deep breath, she tried to relax, but his expression was thunderous. His angry gaze swung over her and he continued to clench his jaw.

A tense silence enveloped the room.

She stopped in front of him, easing into a smile when he simply raised his brow and folded his arms over his chest. Why did men have to be so frustrating? He was as stubborn as James. In an attempt to calm him, she knelt before him and reached out for his hands.

"Ciaran, I know ye wouldnae strike me. I honestly donna have control over how my body reacts. I have had a thrashing so many times that I come to expect it. My apologies if I offended ye and I meant nay disrespect. I *do* trust ye. I trust ye with all of my heart." She caressed his hands with her fingers.

"But nae enough to tell me the reason of what troubles ye," he said, coolly disapproving. "Ye say that ye trust me and yet ye donna."

Rosalia bit the inside of her cheek, attempting to have more time to weigh her options as Beathag's warning replayed in her mind. She did not understand all of what was between them, but of this, she had no doubt. She truly cared for Ciaran and did not want him hurt, or perhaps worse. If she told him the truth, would he believe her? If something happened to him, could she forgive herself because she did not tell him? Placing her head down on his thigh, she moaned in total frustration, feeling his muscular leg immediately tense. After a moment, she lifted her head.

His head was leaned back and his eyes were closed. Slowly and hazily, he opened his eyes and smiled. "I think it best if ye sit in the chair, Rosalia."

Out of all the responses she thought to get, that was not one of them.

She sat in the chair, and began, "Ciaran, I do trust ye. I have caused ye enough concern and if I speak to ye on this matter, I may bring naught but trouble to your door."

Pausing, he gazed at her speculatively. "And why donna ye let me decide? I am listening, sweeting," he said gently.

She cast her eyes downward, playing with the fabric of her skirts. "I will speak with ye as long as ye promise me we will *speak* on this and ye willnae bellow at me. I will have your word, Ciaran MacGregor."

"Ye have my word."

⁂

When Ciaran watched Rosalia cower before him, he had to willfully rein his temper. After all he had been though with her, it infuriated him that she would think he would strike her. When she explained she did not shy away from him intentionally, he felt some relief. At least they were speaking now. He knew he would have the tale of what was troubling her eventually.

It took nearly an hour's time for him to pull the entire tale from her. He was aware that Beathag had played her tricks, but he had had no idea she would threaten Rosalia. This changed matters completely. As promised, he did not bellow. He merely sat and listened while Rosalia spoke of Beathag's tangled web. In fact, his only thought was that Beathag would be removed and banished from Glenorchy. Where she traveled, he cared not. He looked forward to having such a conversation. After all, he did give her fair warning and he was a man of his word.

"Ciaran, ye have barely spoken. Will ye tell me what ye are thinking?"

He frowned. "What I am thinking? My thoughts are quite clear, I assure ye. Beathag will be removed from Glenorchy." He would see to it that Rosalia no longer had to worry about her.

She stirred uneasily in the chair. "But Dunnehl's men—"

"Arenae your concern. I told ye nay harm will come to ye while ye are within my walls."

Rosalia's eyes widened with concern. "Aye, but ye cannae stop them from coming to your gates. I am concerned for *ye*, Ciaran." Glancing down, she studied her hands. "Mayhap we should travel to Glengarry soon and I can seek protection from my family. I cannae put ye and your family in danger."

He rose and knelt down before her. Clutching her hand, he raised it tenderly to his lips. "Nay one threatens me or mine. Ye are under my protection, and I will see to it that nay harm comes to ye."

Pushing him away, she jerked to her feet with a purpose. "I release ye from any duty ye feel toward me."

He laughed as if sincerely amused. "Release me? What is this ye speak?" He stood up and folded his arms over his chest.

She took an abrupt step toward him. "Ye found me and cared for me. Ye offered to escort me to Glengarry. Ye donna have a duty to protect me, Ciaran MacGregor."

He mimicked her stance. "I donna have a *duty* to protect ye, Rosalia Armstrong. I do so willingly." He had to admit that he did not understand where any of this was coming from. Why would she even think he would not offer her protection?

She swiveled quickly, turning her back on him. Approaching the window, she stared blankly out at the loch. "Why?"

He came close and turned her toward him. His fingers trailed down her temple. "Ye donna know?" he asked searchingly.

Rosalia cleared her throat, pretending not to be affected. "Nay, I donna."

Slowly and seductively, his gaze slid downward. "I… care for ye."

A look of disappointment passed over her features. "As ye cared for Beathag?" she asked thickly.

Ciaran straightened to his full height as if he'd received a strong blow across the face. "I didnae care for Beathag."

"Pray excuse me if I donna understand, my laird. Ye say ye didnae care for Beathag, but ye speak the same words to me as ye spoke to her," she said in a clipped tone.

"Pray excuse me if I donna understand, my lady. I tell ye I didnae care for Beathag, but ye donna trust the words I speak," he repeated in the same clipped tone.

Rosalia's eyes were clouded with tears. "Ciaran, she said ye told her she was beautiful, and ye tell me the same," she cried, wiping her falling tears. "I donna understand why ye would tell me. She *is* beautiful and I know I donna look… as her."

This was her concern? Rosalia was nothing like Beathag. Why would she ever compare herself with her? How in the hell could he make her understand the difference? He placed his head to hers. "What men speak in the throes of passion are simply empty words to satisfy their lust. What a man speaks to someone he loves are meaningful words to bring her into his heart." Pulling back, Ciaran smiled, wiping her falling tears. "Donna ye know ye are in my heart, sweeting? I lov… er, care for ye deeply and ye *are* beautiful."

Eleven

CIARAN SWUNG OPEN THE BEDCHAMBER DOOR. IF Seumas was surprised to see him in Rosalia's chamber, his expression did not show it. "My laird, two riders are at the front gates and insist to speak with only ye. They also have a woman traveling with them."

"Aye." Ciaran turned his head around. "Ye stay here until I speak to ye otherwise." His voice was low and commanding.

The man simply muddled Rosalia's mind. Now that he took his leave, she was on safer ground and could pull her drifting thoughts together. She could not keep doing this. She had left Mangerton to create a new life, and she could not do it successfully if she kept dwelling upon the future or the past. She needed to stay focused on the present to put things into perspective. Although Ciaran spoke the words, they were only that—words. She needed to cease analyzing everything.

Seumas appeared at the door to her bedchamber with a grim look upon his face. "My lady, our laird requests your presence in his solar at once."

"Of course, Seumas. Is everything all right?" She was unable to mask the nervousness in her voice.

He escorted her down the hall. "I donna know, my lady."

Seumas knocked on the solar door and Ciaran bade him enter. Opening the door, Seumas gave her a reassuring smile.

"Lass, there is someone here to see ye." Ciaran's smile was almost apologetic.

He stepped aside as Duncan and Ealasaid rose from their chairs. "Och, lass. *Ciamar a tha sibh?*" *How are you?* Ealasaid cried. Her face split into a wide grin, and then Rosalia ran into her arms and wept aloud with relief. Ealasaid was everything that was good and pure in this world, and her mere presence brought Rosalia the support she so desperately needed. She did not even realize how much she had needed her until now.

Ealasaid rubbed her hand over Rosalia's short tresses. "There, there, lassie. Ealasaid is here," she spoke in a soft and clear, soothing voice.

A strong hand rubbed Rosalia's back as she reluctantly pulled away, wiping her tears. Those same hands turned her and pulled her into a crushing embrace. "Duncan," Rosalia cried.

He held her the circle of his arms. "Och, lass. 'Tis so good to see ye. We have missed ye overmuch."

Giving them both a warm smile, Rosalia embraced them again at the same time. She did not want to let them go. "I am so joyful to see ye, but I donna understand how ye are here."

Ciaran placed his hand on her shoulder. "'Tis a long tale. Why donna we all sit, and Duncan will explain."

Ciaran gestured to the chairs, and everyone composed themselves and took their seats. Pulling her cut tresses away from her face, Rosalia tucked unruly strands behind her ear. She must look quite the sight.

Clearing his throat, Duncan spoke hesitantly. "Lass, 'tis nay easy way to speak what I must, but I will try." There was a pensive shimmer in the shadow of his eyes. Giving him a reassuring smile, she nodded for him to continue. Wiping his brow, he cast a nervous glance. "When James returned with Lord Dunnehl's men…" He paused, looking away from her.

As his expression darkened with an unreadable emotion, Rosalia stirred uneasily in the chair. "Duncan, what has happened? Is James well?" Her voice faded into a hushed whisper.

"James is fine, lass." He hesitated another moment and his face was closed. "Lord Dunnehl became enraged when they couldnae find ye and accused your father of trying to cheat him out of coin. He… your father is dead, lass," Duncan said solemnly.

The color drained from her face. "What?" she exclaimed, rubbing her hand over her forehead. Her father was dead—dead because Dunnehl killed him and dead because of her. She stammered in bewilderment. "*Tha mi duilich.*" *I am sorry.*

Strong arms pulled her up and embraced her. "Rosalia," Ciaran murmured. "'Tisnae your fault, sweeting." He rubbed her back. "'Tis but what happens when you try to make a deal with the *Diabhal.*" *Devil.*

Her mind was spinning. "*Chan eil mi a' tuigsinn.*" *I do not understand.* "Why would Dunnehl kill Father? *I* am the one who ran and *I* am the one…"

Ealasaid rose, placing her hand at Rosalia's back. "Och, lassie. Ye arenae at fault. Ye know there was nay coin in the coffers, and your father and mother would have done anything to fill them. If it wasnae your father, it would have been ye—of that, I have nay doubt, my sweet lass."

Ciaran gently rubbed Rosalia arms. "Look at me," he said in a calming voice. "*Tha mi duilich*, Rosalia, but I know what ye are thinking and I want ye to cease. Ye arenae at fault. Ye knew ye couldnae stay there as much as ye couldnae have wed Dunnehl." His gaze was steady.

She nodded her head, in a daze. "I know, but I cannot fathom that my father was killed by the English beast. I didnae think he would hold Father responsible for—"

"Duncan, there is ale on the stand," Ciaran interrupted, nodding toward the stand.

Placing her head to Ciaran's chest, Rosalia closed her eyes and his comforting arms encircled her. Her collectedness was cracking. When Ciaran pulled back, Duncan handed her the ale. Slumping down on the chair, she gulped a healthy, burning mouthful. Perhaps the fiery liquid would take away the numbness she felt.

"Easy, lass," murmured Duncan.

Rosalia laughed. "'Tis Ciaran's own ale. I am quite used to it, I assure ye." Ciaran rubbed her shoulder, and spoke in hushed tones to Duncan.

"If there is more, my laird, I will hear it. Ye donna have to shelter me," she chided him.

He watched her with a critical squint. "Are ye sure? Ye have been through—"

"I am sure." Turning to Duncan and Ealasaid, Rosalia gestured for them to sit. "Please, ye have traveled far to see me. I will be fine."

Duncan and Ealasaid reluctantly sat down. Duncan hesitated before he spoke. "When James returned with Lord Dunnehl's men, he discovered your father's body. Lord Dunnehl had already taken his leave and left word for his men to return to Northumberland. He doesnae search for ye."

Clearing his throat, Duncan wiped his brow. "Your father repaid his debt with his lifeblood, lass. The remainder of your father's men disbanded, and there was only Ealasaid and me. James sent us straight away to ye and had one of his trusted men escort us. He has already taken his leave. James told me that ye were here with Laird MacGregor at Glenorchy. He didnae want to take a chance he was being watched so he sent us to deliver this message.

"He will ensure Lord Dunnehl nay longer searches and will meet ye at Glengarry in the spring when 'tis safe for him to travel to ye." Duncan turned toward Ciaran. "And if Laird MacGregor will have us, we will travel to Ealasaid's sister in the spring."

Ciaran nodded. "Ye are welcome to stay at Glenorchy for as long as ye wish."

Perhaps it was her own uneasiness, but something was missing in Duncan's words. "And what of Mother?" Everyone turned to stare at her with blank expressions. Something cautioned Rosalia not to ask, but she must know the truth—all of it. She turned to Ealasaid, repeating the question.

Ealasaid played with the fabric of her skirts, then

gave her a sympathetic smile. "She is with Lord Dunnehl, lass." She spoke sympathetically and cast her eyes downward.

She gasped. "The *beast* took my mother? He killed my father and *took* my mother?" Rosalia jerked to her feet and started to pace.

Ealasaid gave her a sheepish grin. "Nay, lassie. Your mother went willingly."

She stopped dead in her tracks. "She *what*?" she bellowed. "She went with him *willingly*? That English cur killed my father, and my mother went *willingly* with the man who had killed my father. Is that what ye are telling me?"

"I think Rosalia has had enough," Ciaran interjected.

She whipped around and glared at him. "Och, nay. I will have the entire tale, Ciaran." She turned back to Ealasaid, who was studying her skirts and would not lift her eyes to hers. She certainly did not want to frighten Ealasaid, but she needed the truth and she would have it.

Raising her head, Ealasaid glanced at Rosalia with compassion. "Aye, lassie. She claimed there was naught more she could do at Mangerton and wanted to go back to England."

Rosalia could not think through the blood pounding in her ears. Ciaran opened the door to his solar, ordering someone to show Ealasaid and Duncan to their rooms.

Duncan approached her, placing his hand to her shoulder in a fatherly gesture. "Ye are safe now, lass. 'Tis all that matters."

"Aye, lassie. Ye rest and come see us later," said Ealasaid, giving her a look of comfort.

Rosalia embraced them both. "My apologies. I am glad ye are both here and safe. I will speak with ye later." She embraced them both again. "I am truly joyful ye are both here."

❧

Ciaran ordered Seumas to have one of the maids fetch Rosalia's cloak. The lass stood in front of him looking so lost and alone. He was not sure how to comfort her. Although she had been mistreated by her father, he was still her father nonetheless. She should mourn his passing, but Ciaran would not allow her to blame herself. Her sire chose his own fate. He never respected a man who raised his hand to a woman or sat by while someone else did harm.

He smiled his thanks when the maid returned with Rosalia's cloak. His memory strayed as he remembered the pain he had felt at the loss of his own father.

He gently wrapped the cloak around her shoulders. "Come, sweeting," he said tenderly. He pulled her close to his side, and they walked together. He led Rosalia to the parapet, hoping fresh air would bring her some relief. She stared blankly out at the loch, and he was caught off guard by the sudden vigorousness in her voice.

"I always wanted to travel to the Highlands, but I ne'er expected such an adventure," she said solemnly.

He wrapped his arm around her shoulders and she leaned into him. He kissed the top of her head.

"I cannae believe my father is dead, let alone that my mother went with my father's murderer."

He squeezed her shoulder. "Your father and mother made their choices, lass. Ye needed to make yours and ye did what ye had to, Rosalia." Turning her to face him, Ciaran smiled gently. "I know ye are distraught and ye have reason to mourn your father, but ye donna have reason to blame yourself. I willnae allow it," he ordered, brushing his fingers lightly on her cheek.

She smiled. "Ye know ye can be verra persuasive, my laird."

"So ye have said," he whispered, lowering his head and brushing a soft kiss on her lips.

Wrapping her arms around him, Rosalia nestled her head into his chest. "Ciaran, I feel so many ways. I donna know what to do. I cannae think clearly."

He placed his chin on the top of her head. "Let me help ye. Let me be here for ye. Let me share your burden, but donna close yourself from me."

She sighed. "I struggle with the words ye speak. Ye *are* laird and are already burdened. Ye donna need me as well. Isnae Declan burden enough?"

Ciaran chuckled. "There is that, but I want ye to think upon this." He paused, placing his lips close to her ear. "I am stuck with Declan, but I *choose* ye."

Pulling away, she glanced at him searchingly. "And I choose ye, Ciaran MacGregor. If I am thankful for anything that has happened of late, 'tis that I met ye. Ye are a great and honorable man."

He knew his face colored and he turned his head away from her. After all, he was a Highland laird, a warrior. "Come now before ye swell my head."

Rosalia ate her meal in her bedchamber. She should have been more attentive to Ealasaid and Duncan after they had traveled so far, but she could not bring herself to entertain them with pleasantries. She needed time to recover.

There was a knock at the door and Aisling entered. Giving Rosalia a sisterly embrace, she expressed sympathy for her father's passing. "Come," said Aisling, guiding her to the bed. "I know just what ye need." Propping up pillows, they lounged casually upon the bed. "Now tell me, how do ye fare?" she asked with concern.

Rosalia leaned back and briefly closed her eyes. "I have seen better days. I assure ye." She adjusted the pillows at her back. "I cannae yet believe my father was murdered and my mother—well, I donna even have the strength to put into words how I feel."

"'Tis all right to be angry and hurt, Rosalia. Donna keep these feelings all to yourself lest ye go mad," said Aisling, patting her on the leg.

"I know ye are right. I blame my father for many things, but he was still my father."

Aisling grabbed her hand in a comforting gesture. "I understand. I think ye need to focus on the present. Ye are starting a new life. Look how far ye have come, Rosalia," said Aisling in an encouraging tone.

"I actually had the same thoughts this morn. Ye are a wise woman. Thank ye for your counsel, Aisling." She enjoyed having a woman she could speak with freely.

Aisling waved her off. "Please, we are as sisters. 'Tis but what we do. I almost forgot." Leaning over the side of the bed, she pulled up a covered basket that Rosalia had not even noticed through her doldrums. Aisling uncovered the bundle and reached in. "I was instructed to give ye these." She handed her a biscuit.

Rosalia grinned. "Ealasaid?" She took a bite, immediately knowing the source that created such splendid bliss. "Och, Ealasaid," she moaned.

Grabbing another biscuit from the basket, Aisling pointed to Rosalia. "Donna keep them all to yourself," she said, tossing a piece into her mouth. She moaned. "'Tis truly incredible," she said, closing her eyes in enjoyment.

"What is truly incredible?" asked Ciaran, walking into the room through the adjoining door.

"Ye men," Aisling smirked. "Always at hand when food is present, but if we need ye for something, ye arenae to be found."

Reaching out, he took a biscuit and sat down on the bed next to Rosalia. Placing a piece into his mouth, he grunted. "These *are* truly incredible. Where did ye get them?" he asked, wiping the crumbs from his chin.

Rosalia giggled. "Ealasaid. They are my favorite," she said, wiping the crumbs from her chin as well.

"I can see why."

"What can ye see?" asked Aiden, also ambling into the room through the adjoining door.

Aisling laughed. "Ye see? Always at hand when food is present but conveniently disappearing if we call upon them."

"Are those biscuits?" asked Aiden, reaching into the basket.

Aisling slapped his hand. "Aye. There is only one remaining and they were made for Rosalia," she chided him.

He had such a look of disappointment on his face that Rosalia handed him the last one. "My thanks." Aiden gave her a sympathetic smile and took a bite. He closed his eyes and grunted.

She laughed. "Ealasaid. Her biscuits are much comfort."

"And how long will she be with us?" he asked hopefully.

"Long enough for ye to get your fill of biscuits, Husband," Aisling chuckled.

Aiden wiped the crumbs from his chin. He turned his gaze back to Rosalia.

"As I am sure my brother has said, if ye need anything, ye need only ask," said Aiden with sincerity.

"Ye all have my thanks—truly."

Aisling stood up abruptly. "Well, 'tis getting late, Husband. Shall we take our leave?" Her voice sounded odd, her eyes widened, and she gave a slight nod for Aiden to follow.

Aiden stared at her, confounded. "'Tisnae late, Aisling." When her eyes bore into him with silent expectation, it was if something clicked in his mind and he turned on his heel. "Aye, Wife. 'Tis late."

Ciaran laughed as they departed. "Ye would think they were newly wed," he chuckled, studying Rosalia for a brief moment. "Ye seem lighter of heart. How do ye fare?"

She shrugged her shoulders. "Now that I am away from Mangerton, I see the truth of how my life really was. 'Tis quite maddening actually. I couldnae think while I was there. Now that I have been away, I am able to think more clearly."

His mouth curved with tenderness. "I know of what ye speak. I find if I am troubled, I am able to think much clearer if I am away from what troubles me."

Lifting one hand, she caressed his cheek. "Then I hope I donna trouble ye, Ciaran."

He kissed the palm of her hand. "I love the sound of my name upon your lips," he murmured.

When her mind relived the velvet warmth of his kiss, she yanked him closer until his lips were almost touching hers. "Ciaran," she whispered, bringing his mouth to hers. She boldly kissed him with a hunger that belied her outward calm. She was shocked at her own eager response, giving herself freely to the passion of the kiss.

She leaned back on the bed and pulled him close. Reclaiming his lips, she crushed him on top of her. Any reflections Rosalia had, she willed away. She was tired of thinking.

Ciaran pulled back slightly and traced his fingertip across her lip. His smoldering look burned her deep within her soul. God help her. At that moment, she realized the truth. She loved him.

She slid her hands under his tunic as she felt the evidence of his desire rise between them. Her heart pounded furiously against his. He was so hot. She melted into him.

Pressing kisses along his jaw, she savored the hint of salt and the scratch of his jaw against her lips. She sensed he was holding back, but she would not have it.

She rubbed her body against him and closed her eyes, enjoying the sudden rush of heat between them. She felt passion rise in her like the hottest fire, clouding her brain, her senses. She wanted—him.

❧

Ciaran was on fire. He had never been more aroused in his life. Rosalia's innocent touches were driving him mad. All of his honorable intentions were forgotten. All he could think of was tearing off her gown and thrusting up high inside her until the burning stopped.

His kisses became demanding. He wanted her to know what she did to him. Never had he experienced this kind of urgency. His tongue delved into her mouth with eager abandon. She was so hot and willing. He could not get enough.

His tongue circled hers, probing in an anxious rhythm that mirrored his pulsing erection. Her soft mewling sounds only heated his desire for her. He slid his hands down to her waist and over her hips, molding every sweet curve closer to his body.

He loosened her bodice enough to pull it past her shoulders and molded her breasts into his hands. The soft pink flesh was more than enough to fill his hands, more lush than he remembered. He lifted her breast to his lips and encircled her nipple with his tongue. "Rosalia, ye taste so sweet," he murmured.

He cupped her mounds with his rough hands, and she groaned as he caressed their softness. She was like velvety fruit that was ripe for the picking. He wanted to savor her sweetness.

He eased his hand up the edge of her skirts, sliding

up the center of her silky thigh, and she moaned against his ear. *Hell.* She was so damn responsive. His finger swept her sex... so wet. She was more than ready for him. He wanted nothing more than to strip off every piece of clothing and bury himself deep into her warm, welcoming heat.

He teased her with his hand, and her hips started to arch against him. He would make her come. Her tiny whimpers increased in urgency as she grabbed his arms, sculpting his muscles. *God's teeth!* She was going to come apart in his hand.

When he felt her break apart, he pressed his finger against the sensitive part of her. His tongue delved into her mouth with the same rhythm as his finger pressing against her womanly heat.

She arched her back and cried out his name. He could not take his eyes off her face. She was so damn tempting with her lips parted and her passion-glazed eyes. Her desire and responsiveness drove him wild. She was so damn beautiful.

He needed to be inside her.

He unfastened his trews and her eyes widened, forcing him to address the sudden wave of reality that came upon him. Closing his eyes, he took a deep breath, pausing for a moment to pull himself together. "Rosalia, I know ye are distraught so I must think for both of us. If we do this—"

"Donna think, Ciaran," she pleaded.

"Rosalia..."

"Donna think. Take me, Ciaran," she said, pulling him to her.

He choked. *God's teeth!* She was going to unman

him like some untried lad. His insecure, sweet lass was a siren! He was a battle-hardened warrior—at least, that was what he kept telling himself. Control. He must regain control.

Ciaran closed his eyes for collectedness. "Ye arenae yet mine to take," he bit out, trying to calm his racing heart.

"What? Ye cannae offer me such a gift and then say I am nae yours to take," she said, gasping for breath. "I donna understand."

He rolled onto his side and gently caressed her bare shoulder. "'Tis the only gift I am able to give ye now—at least, nae until…"

"*Nae until…?*" she asked.

He had already spoken too freely. He needed to regain control, and to his dismay, there was no other way. Reluctantly, Ciaran rose from the bed. "Your pleasure was what I sought, lass. Pray excuse me," he said abruptly and walked through the adjoining door. He would seek his own release and then his mind would be clear.

❧

Rosalia did not have the strength to dwell upon Ciaran's words, but she had to admit she was concerned about his actions. He sprang from the bed and took his leave without as much as a backward glance. Granted, she was not skilled in the ways of what a man and a woman shared. Ciaran offered her pleasure and held back from seeking his own. That's why she was caught off guard when he took his leave so abruptly after their—well, she was not sure exactly what that had been.

Slowly rising from the bed, Rosalia straightened her clothing. Her legs could barely support her, and she had a gentle, calming sensation as well. What was that about? Wicked memories of Ciaran plagued her. She sat in the chair before the firelight, still smiling at what had occurred between them. It was a welcome distraction—a very welcome distraction. In fact, she would enjoy being distracted much more often.

He entered her bedchamber and his expression was not as tight as before. Smiling, he approached her and brushed a soft kiss to her lips. His mood seemed suddenly buoyant.

"I didnae think ye would return," she said searchingly.

"Of course I would return," Ciaran said, sitting in the opposite chair. "I enjoyed being with ye, lass." He gave her a roguish grin.

Rosalia was almost embarrassed at how happy that made her, and she flushed miserably. "I enjoyed being with ye as well, my laird."

Leaning forward, he grabbed her hand. "We need to speak about Beathag."

She moaned and rolled her eyes. "Do we need to do that now?"

His expression stilled and grew serious. "Aye. I will speak with her on the morrow and she will take her leave before ye break your fast."

"Aye," she sighed. She wondered where Beathag would go or if she had family that would take her in.

He smiled at her knowingly. "Rosalia, ye cannae save everyone. After all she said to ye, she doesnae deserve your pity. Besides," he said, patting her hand, "save your compassion for me when I unintentionally fire your ire."

"Ciaran, ye are a man and predestined to fire my ire," she chuckled.

Sitting back in the chair, he bobbed his head. "Aye, so Aisling tells Aiden, Declan, and me—repeatedly."

She shrugged her shoulders. "What can I say to that? Aisling is a wise woman." She yawned and raised her fingers to her lips.

He stood and held out his hand. "Come. Ye will feel better after a good sleep."

Placing her hand into his, she stood. "Ye know? This is one time I think I agree with ye."

He brought her fingers to his lips and kissed the top of her hand, looking into her eyes with warmth she had come to savor. "Good sleep, my lady."

"My thanks, Ciaran… for everything."

He nodded his head and turned toward the adjoining door, pausing after he stepped through it. Turning, he winked at her and then proceeded to gently close the door.

Rosalia sighed in contentment. She fell back on the bed and did not even worry about changing into her nightclothes. She would only rest her eyes for a moment.

∼⌘∼

Ciaran had not tossed and turned in total frustration for a long time. Even his own release did not satisfy the burning hunger he felt for Rosalia. She would have actually permitted him to bury himself deep within her luscious body. Sometimes his honor and chivalry were a pain in the arse. A few years ago he wouldn't have second-guessed himself. She would be his in mind, body, and soul. His mind raced as he thought of what he must do to proceed with his own life. First, he must see to Beathag. Second, he would need to ensure Declan was on a straight path. How he regretted his promise to his father.

Having no tolerance for sleep, Ciaran threw the blankets from the bed and dressed. The sooner he could be done with the first task, the sooner he could see to the second. He descended the stairs in search of Beathag. He found her in her bedchamber and nudged her awake. "Get dressed," he said tersely. "I will wait outside the door."

Appearing moments later, she did not seem surprised to see him. He escorted her into his solar and closed the door. He had many words he wanted to speak to her, but he would not make this more difficult than it needed to be. He must maintain his purpose, and that was solely to remove Beathag from the walls of Glenorchy.

"I gave ye fair warning and ye disobeyed me. Ye are to take your leave of Glenorchy and ne'er return. Ye arenae welcome here," he said with steely determination. Beathag smiled at him with a cold, soulless glare. Her lack of emotion caught him unaware. He was prepared for battle, but she did not even raise her verbal sword. In fact, she did not speak a single word.

Grabbing her firmly by the elbow, he escorted her to the front gates as the rising sun cast its first rays of light. Beathag took her leave with not even a fare-thee-well or a backward glance. He would not dwell on her further; she was not worth it. At least she could no longer cause Rosalia grief within his walls.

As Ciaran walked through the bailey and into the

great hall, he spotted Declan breaking his fast—the second task to which he must attend. He prayed this was not a hopeless task. He was anxious to move forward with his own life and have a wife of his own. He knew the perfect woman.

Beathag grudgingly stepped away from the front gates. She refused to look back and give the MacGregor *whoreson* the satisfaction. She had to remain calm, focused on her plan. She would get the coin promised to her and leave this wretched land forever without looking back.

Men and their games—what they did not realize was that she could be just as dangerous and deadly as any man.

Twelve

"NAY. I WILLNAE ACCEPT THESE." ROSALIA FOLDED her arms over her chest, shaking her head in disapproval.

Ciaran rose to his full height. "Ye can be such a stubborn lass," he said, exasperated. "Ye are in the Highlands. The first snowfall is upon us, and ye need suitable clothing lest ye catch the ague."

She huffed. "I have Aisling's—"

"And they donna fit," he countered.

"Ye arenae going to leave me in peace, are ye?"

He shook his head and smiled in return. "Nay."

Pausing, she glanced at her trunk. "If ye insist I accept the clothing, ye can at least grant me a boon," she said as she bent over to open the trunk. When he stood behind her and placed his arms around her waist, she jumped.

"And what boon might that be, my lady?" he whispered silkily into her ear. She pulled out of his embrace and shoved a pouch into his hands. He held it up and cast a questioning glance at her. "What is this?" He shook the bag as clanging noises came from within.

"Coin. 'Tisnae much, but 'tis all I brought with me

from Mangerton. 'Tis but the least I can do to repay your kindness, my laird. Ye have offered me shelter, clothing, bed me…" She immediately caught her slip of the tongue and blushed. When he smiled with male satisfaction and simply raised his brow, she swatted at him. "Fed me. I meant to say ye *fed* me, clothed me, and I could go on as such."

Giving her an amused grin, he tossed the coins back into the trunk and slammed the lid shut. "Please save us both the time. I willnae take your coin and ye *will* take the clothes." Approaching her, he gently grabbed the bottom of her chin. "Ye are so stubborn, but I know ye can be sensible as well. 'Tis how I know I will see ye wear the newly made clothing." He kissed the tip of her nose. Turning, he walked to the door. "I must go to the village. I will return for the midday meal."

"Ciaran?"

He spun around. "Aye?"

"Will ye please take Noonie? I am sure he needs a run." Nodding his head, he opened the door. "And Ciaran? Ye have my thanks for the clothing."

"Ye may thank me later," he said with a roguish grin, slowly closing the door.

Rosalia's heart hammered against her ribs. She wondered if he would ever stop affecting her that way. She shook her head as she glanced at the bed. Holding up a newly made cloak, she wrapped it around her and smiled when she realized that it covered her perfectly. It was finely made and perfect for her height. Placing it back upon the bed, she lifted a day dress and held it up in front of her. Stacking it back on the pile, she counted five dresses. There was no way she could ever repay his kindness. As Rosalia tried to lift the gowns from the bed, something caught her attention. Shifting the dresses to the side, she gasped in astonishment.

A beautiful gown was *conveniently* hidden beneath the other clothing. The fabric was of fine quality and beautifully made. It was a lovely blue, the color of the sky, accented with gold ribbon and a low bodice. Why would Ciaran have bestowed such a gift upon her? This was clearly a gown to be worn in London amongst King James's royal court. Such niceties were not something to be worn at Glenorchy, or Glengarry, for that matter. Where would she ever wear such a gown? She held it to her frame. Pulling out the skirts to the side, she spun around and smiled. She could almost imagine herself among royalty. Better yet, she could almost picture herself on Ciaran's arm as his wife, dancing away into the wee hours of the night. She smiled when she realized she must look like quite the fool.

Lowering the gown back onto the bed, she hefted the day dresses and was hunching over to place them in her trunk when she spotted a pair of doeskin boots sticking out from under the bed. Setting the dresses on her trunk, she bent over and scooped up the boots. Not only did Ciaran have clothing made for her, but she had warm boots for the winter solstice. As she examined the boots, she was astonished to discover matching blue slippers stuffed inside them—slippers that matched her radiant gown. Ciaran was clever. She would give him that. He knew she would never accept all of this willingly.

She fled her bedchamber in search of Aisling since she was sure her friend had a hand in Ciaran's plotting. She finally discovered the culprit in the nursery with

Teàrlach. When Rosalia entered, Aisling was down on all fours in an apparent attempt to make Teàrlach smile. "Is it working?"

"Stubborn as Aiden, I tell ye. I get on the floor with him and try to make him laugh, but he stares at me like I am daft. I have yet to make him smile. Declan even makes him smile, but his own mother doesnae. 'Tis quite annoying actually," she mumbled under her breath.

"Come now, Aisling. Teàrlach is obviously a lad with much sense. He already laughs at the men," Rosalia countered, sitting down on the floor.

"There is that."

Teàrlach gnawed on his tiny fist and Rosalia rubbed his red curls. "Did ye know that Ciaran went to the village?"

"Aye. Aiden as well." Aisling rose and picked up Teàrlach from the floor. "Could ye please hand me his blanket?"

Pulling herself to her feet, Rosalia handed her the blanket. "I had quite a surprise in my chamber this morn."

"Ye did? And what might that be?" Aisling asked innocently, wrapping the blanket around Teàrlach.

"Now why do I get the feeling ye are playing me, Aisling? I think ye know Ciaran had clothes made for me, and I cannae help but wonder if ye had a hand in that as well." She folded her arms over her chest and waited for her friend to respond.

Aisling studied her. "Och, ye have been in Ciaran's presence too much. Ye two are sounding and looking much the same."

"Mayhap, but I will know the truth if ye had anything to do with the clothing."

"And if I did?" Aisling shrugged with indifference and did not wait for Rosalia to respond. "Ye said yourself that ye havenae been to the Highlands. Our Highland weather is much more severe than what ye are accustomed to. Ye need proper clothes for the winter solstice and now ye have them. Ye should be thanking me instead of attempting to scold me."

"I truly thank ye. They are beautiful." Rosalia relented.

"And ye would have done the same for me. Ye cannae tell me ye wouldnae." Aisling gave her a knowing look. "And how did ye like the gown?" she asked, rubbing Teàrlach's back.

"'Tis truly verra beautiful, but I donna know where I would wear it. 'Tis as if I should be attending King James's court."

"Donna think too much upon it. Mayhap Ciaran just wanted ye to have something fanciful to wear, should something of importance present itself." Aisling smiled and nudged her arm.

Rosalia rolled her eyes. "Cease your plotting."

"Now what is she plotting?" asked Declan, strutting into the nursery. He smiled at both of them in amusement. "If she is plotting, I would run, Rosalia—far, far away."

"Cease. Both of ye. I donna plot. I merely strongly recommend, and if it happens, it happens," Aisling countered with a trace of laughter in her voice.

"And how does my wee nephew fare?" asked Declan, rubbing Teàrlach's curls. As if on cue, Teàrlach's face lit up and he grinned from ear to ear. Aisling moaned and rolled her eyes. "What?" Declan asked with a questioning glance to Aisling.

"Ye see? I try everything to make him smile and he doesnae. Ye walk in and simply ask how he fares, and he smiles for ye."

A lively twinkle came into his eyes. "'Tis because he knows his Uncle Declan. He more than likely doesnae want to be around ye *women* all day."

"*Women*?" Aisling's voice went up a notch and Rosalia cleared her throat.

"Why donna we go and see if Ealasaid prepared biscuits for the midday meal?" she redirected.

"I am right behind ye," murmured Declan, promptly following Rosalia out the door.

"Coward," Aisling smirked.

"Ye know it," called Declan from down the hall.

⚜

Ciaran rode to the village with Aiden to collect the rents and ensure everything was in order. He would also be sure to thank Cylan for Rosalia's clothing. A smile played on his lips as he realized Rosalia was softening toward others providing for her. She had not put up too much of a battle when she was presented with her dresses—although, he chose the coward's way out and took his leave before she found the fanciful gown or the boots, for that matter.

"Did Rosalia spar with ye about the clothing?" asked Aiden.

"At first, but I took my leave before she had the chance to scold me further."

"Coward," his brother chided him.

"I learned from ye. Your wee wife *still* frightens ye."

"There is that."

In an apparent attempt for freedom, Noonie tried to pull his head. He was spirited this morning, and if his prancing feet and agitated movements were any indication, he obviously wanted to run. "Why donna we let our mounts run to the village?" Ciaran patted Noonie on his muscular neck. "He wants to run."

Aiden kicked his mount, making a mad dash off. Ciaran gave Noonie his head, and it was not long before he thundered by Aiden. With the sound of pounding hoofbeats in his ears, the cool breeze whipping him in the face, and the rush of blood pumping through his veins, he could not help but let out a blood-pumping battle cry. Aiden reined in beside him and followed suit. The two of them looked as if they were riding into battle instead of enjoying a brief moment of horseplay.

As they approached the village, they slowed their mounts, seeing that dense, black smoke billowed through the air. Riding to the center of the village, they were greeted with expressions of terror upon the faces of women and children. Shrill screams pierced the air. It was a state of sheer panic and chaos.

"My laird!" screamed a lad, stepping out in front of Noonie. "The stable is burning!"

"Is everyone out?" yelled Ciaran, approaching the stable.

"I donna know," screamed the lad in return.

Reaching the stable, Ciaran saw that smoke was rising fast and furious, and they jumped from their mounts. He was met by a woman with soot on her face and her young daughter, who was in tattered, soot-covered clothing. He recognized the woman as Mary, the stable hand's wife.

"My laird!" she coughed. "My husband is still in there trying to get the animals out," she rasped. "Please help him!" she begged, bending over and gasping for breath.

Releasing Mary into Aiden's care, Ciaran ran into the stable. At first, he could not see anything in front of him. The heat was so overwhelming that he could barely breathe. He shouted for the stable hand and received no reply. The stable started to collapse. A heavy wooden beam crashed beside him to the ground in a fiery blaze, its smoldering ash billowing into the air. He called one last time before he had no choice but to turn back.

As soon as he came out of the stable, Aiden handed him a wet cloth. Ciaran took a couple of deep breaths to clear his lungs and coughed uncontrollably. A crowd gathered as some of the men made futile attempts to douse the flames. He glanced over to see a few of them covering themselves with wet blankets and held up his hand to stay them. The stable was falling apart. He could not chance anyone else getting in harm's way.

Mary approached him with a questioning look. "My laird?"

Aiden intercepted and draped his arm gently around her shoulders, pulling her away. He glanced at Ian's daughter as tears streamed down her smeared, sooty face. Something twisted inside him like a punch to the gut. Taking another look at the blazing flames, he covered his mouth with the wet cloth. He heard Aiden's warning shouts in the distance as he raced back into the stable.

He kept the wet cloth firmly pressed against his mouth and nose, but it did not assist his watering eyes. He proceeded quickly and cautiously, working his way further into the stable while avoiding the falling debris. When he thought he saw something on the ground a few yards in front of him, he pushed himself even further. Ian lay motionless on the ground before him.

He dropped the wet cloth and managed to swing Ian's arm around his neck to pull him up, but his lungs felt as if they were afire. Just as Ciaran was about to collapse, someone grabbed him and pulled him to his feet.

Aiden grabbed Ian's other arm, supporting his weight, and led them back through the maze of falling debris.

When at last they stepped out of the stable, Mary ran to their side. "Ian! Ian! Please be well," she sobbed.

They carried Ian a safe distance away from the blazing flames and laid him down on the ground. Aiden saw to Ian while Ciaran stepped away, bending over and gasping for breath. All he could hear between his gasps for air and the intensity of his coughing were the piercing sobs of Mary and her daughter.

"Papa! Papa! Please donna leave me! I love ye! I love ye, Papa!"

Ciaran was weighted with a heavy heart knowing those words would be forever imprinted in his mind. As he turned, Aiden somberly shook his head.

Ian was dead.

Aiden pulled Mary away from Ian's lifeless body

and she embraced him. "He was my life," she sobbed. "Why would anyone want to kill him?"

"*Kill* him?" Aiden asked, throwing a questioning glance at Ciaran.

Ciaran approached them, and Mary gazed back and forth between them. "Aye. Eallie and I were in the pasture when three riders approached." She pointed in the direction the men came from. "They threw something on the walls and then lit it afire," she cried, wiping her tears.

"The fire spread right quick. We ran into the stable, and Ian was trying to get all the animals out. We tried to help him, but he ordered Eallie and me to take our leave. He wouldnae leave the animals until every last one was out. My Ian was a gentle soul and ne'er hurt anyone. I donna understand why they killed him!"

Cylan approached and embraced Mary and Eallie. "My laird, I will take them to my cottage if ye donna mind. They have been through much this day," she said sympathetically. He nodded his head in consent, and as Cylan led them away, Mary and Eallie looked back at Ian's lifeless body. Cries of grief made Ciaran shiver to his very core.

He walked to the men who were still trying to douse the fire. He glanced at Ian. "Someone cover him with a blanket," he coughed out. One of the men draped a blanket over the stable hand's body, and Ciaran nodded for Aiden to gather the men close. He tried to speak, but his voice was failing him. He nodded for Aiden to take the lead.

"I speak on behalf of our laird. Three riders encroached on Glenorchy lands and murdered one of

our own. Rest assured they will be repaid in blood,"
Aiden bit out as the crowd screamed for vengeance.
"If any of ye saw these riders or know from where
they hail, I ask ye to step forward." He and Ciaran
glanced over the crowd, and most of villagers shook
their heads in disgust.

"I saw 'em, my laird!" A lad stepped forward.

"Come forward," said Aiden.

Ciaran walked to the boy and placed his hand on
his shoulder. "Ye saw the men who did this?" he
choked out.

"John!"

Cylan's husband pushed through the crowd and
stood behind the boy. "John is my nephew. He stays
with Cylan and me as of late." He turned the boy to
face him. "I want ye to think and I want ye to tell
our laird everything ye can remember—everything,
John. Donna think something is unimportant. Speak
everything ye know."

John nodded his head in understanding and faced
Ciaran. "I did see 'em, my laird. I saw 'em approach
from that way," he said, gesturing with his finger.
"They rode in fast and there was three of 'em, there
was. They didnae get off their horses. They threw
something at the stable and then set it afire with a
torch, they did!"

"Did ye see anything else?" Ciaran rasped out,
trying to catch a breath.

"Did they ride out in the same direction?" Aiden
countered.

"Aye. They rode out as fast as they came in—*bloody*
Campbell cowards," the lad snarled.

Ciaran and Aiden exchanged a carefully guarded look, neither one of them wanting to confirm or deny John's claim. The bloody Campbells were a pain in the arse with their petty reiving, but there was never bloodshed. He would need to be damn sure the Campbells were behind this feat or he would start a bloody war.

"John, 'tis verra important. I want ye to tell me…" He coughed again uncontrollably and Aiden intervened.

"John, how do ye know it was the Campbells?" asked Aiden.

"I can spot them Campbells from far away I can. My Da told me to watch out for 'em. He hated the *bastards*!" he spat.

"John," said Cylan's husband in a reprimanding tone.

"But he did, Uncle!" John shook his head in confirmation.

Ciaran cleared his burning throat. "John, how do ye know it was the Campbells?"

He huffed, shifting from foot to foot. "My laird, they wore the Campbell colors of blue, green, and black, and I heard 'em yell '*Cruachan*' with my own ears, I did. I know that is the cry of 'em bastard Campbells! I told ye my Da hated the bastards, he did!" He smiled sheepishly at his uncle. "My apologies, Uncle."

John's uncle squeezed his shoulder. "Would ye be needing anything else, my laird?"

"Nay, I have heard enough," Ciaran bit out.

Reaching out, Aiden patted the boy on the shoulder. "Ye did good, lad." John's uncle escorted him away and Ciaran pulled Aiden close.

"We donna discuss this matter here," he whispered. Aiden nodded his head in agreement and glanced to Ian. "We need to seek the priest and have a proper burial." As if a second thought crossed his mind, he added, "Should we send out scouts?"

"Nay. They are gone and have crawled back under the rock from which they came."

∾

The noon meal came and went, and when the men did not return from the village, Declan ordered a few of the guards, including Seumas, to ride to the village and locate their laird. Rosalia and Aisling continued to keep themselves occupied with Teàrlach, neither one of them wanting to admit to the other that they were worried about Ciaran and Aiden.

"Why donna we go to the kitchen and mayhap Ealasaid will show us how to make her biscuits?" Rosalia asked.

"'Tis a wonderful distraction," countered Aisling.

When they entered the kitchen, Ealasaid was sitting at the table making bread. Rosalia inhaled deeply and patted her on the shoulder. "It smells wonderful."

"Thank ye, lass," she said, glancing up from the table. Ealasaid looked over Rosalia's shoulder, spotting Aisling and Teàrlach. "I didnae know Lady Aisling was here as well with her wee bairn. To what do I owe this pleasure?"

"We thought that mayhap ye would show us how to make your biscuits."

Ealasaid laughed. "Ye want me to show ye and Lady Aisling how to make my biscuits? Lass, ye ne'er showed interest in making them, only eating them," she giggled. "Why would ye want to learn now?"

"Well," she paused, glancing down at her hands. "Truth be told, the men took their leave early this morn and said they would return for the midday meal. They havenae yet returned and 'tis well past the noon meal. We are attempting to occupy our thoughts."

"Lass," Ealasaid addressed them both, her voice reassuring. "I am sure your men are well and they know how to take care. Ye donna need to know how to make biscuits." She patted Rosalia's hand. "I will be able to occupy your thoughts." Ealasaid rose, wiping her hands on a cloth. She pulled out the bench for them to sit. "Ye both sit." They plopped down on the bench, grateful for the distraction. Ealasaid cut a couple of slices of warm bread and placed them on a trencher before the two women. "Food is always much comfort."

Ealasaid went to check on the other loaves, and Duncan entered through the other side of the kitchen. Having a mouthful of bread, Rosalia was unable to greet him. If his actions were any indication, he did not see them sitting at the table.

He approached Ealasaid with a roguish grin upon his face. When he squeezed her bottom, she squealed in surprise, turning around and swatting at him with a cloth. "Och, I love it when ye hit me," he murmured, leaning in for a kiss.

"Duncan!" she squeaked. "Lady Rosalia and Lady Aisling are here!" She nodded toward the table.

He turned several shades of red, but he approached the table and smiled. "Lady Rosalia. Lady Aisling." This was certainly a welcome distraction. Rosalia had always believed that Ealasaid and Duncan shared feelings for each other. Now she knew for certain. Their bantering made her smile. It was obvious they loved each other. She was joyful for them both. Duncan rubbed his hand over Teàrlach's curls. "And how are ye, laddie?"

Teàrlach smiled openly, and Aisling rolled her eyes and moaned. "I give up," she said, nudging Rosalia in the ribs.

"Probably a wise choice."

Everyone froze when there was a sudden ruckus in the great hall. Aisling and Rosalia sprang to their feet and walked briskly into the hall. Ciaran's guards spoke in raised tones, and angered voices rang out among the men. Impatiently, she scanned the crowd for Ciaran, and when she spotted him, her jaw dropped.

He was completely blackened from head to toe. He looked as tired and worn as if he had been through a fierce battle. The shock briefly held her immobile, and there was a heavy feeling in the pit of her stomach. She ran to his side, and he gave her a tired smile. He smelled strongly of smoke and ash. "Och, Ciaran. What has happened? Are ye injured?"

Turning his head away from her, he coughed uncontrollably. She yelled for a maid to bring him some water. If she could not get answers from Ciaran, she would get them from Aiden.

"Aiden, what has happened? What has befallen ye?" She tried to mask the panic in her voice.

"There is much to say, but now isnae the time nor the place." He frowned, his eyes level under drawn brows.

Nodding, she spun back to Ciaran. He had finished drinking some water, and his expression was pained. "My laird?" she asked him searchingly.

Placing his arm over her shoulders, he pulled her close, lowering his lips to her ear. "My voice has failed me. Let me bathe and we will speak. Rest assured I am nae injured. Only my voice suffers, and it should come back in a day or two," he rasped. Hesitating, he turned his head and coughed again.

Rosalia nodded her head in consent and assisted Ciaran toward his chamber. He opened his bedchamber door and she followed him in. He turned to smile at her, but his smile did not seem to reach his eyes. He looked so drained. When he attempted to speak, his voice was so raspy that he started to cough again.

Pulling her close, he whispered into her ear. "Donna worry overmuch. My voice only suffers. I will bathe and then join ye."

She studied him thoughtfully for a moment to ensure he was well. "Aye." She entered her bedchamber through the adjoining door and slumped down on her bed. She was so thankful that Ciaran and Aiden were not injured, but she could not help wondering what had befallen them. Rosalia closed her eyes and prayed it had not been Dunnehl's men.

❦

Ciaran scrubbed himself raw. He could not forget the haunting images of Mary and her daughter as they mourned the loss of a husband and father. Cylan was kindhearted enough to take them in. He would be sure to provide them whatever they needed. He was proud of his clan. They all pulled together. Since the winter solstice was upon them, he needed to ensure that the animals lived and his people would be fed.

He had to admit that Declan had surprised him. At least he'd had the sense to send out the guard when he and Aiden did not return. He would be sure to tell him he was pleased. Declan had heeded his warning since Ciaran had not seen his brother in his cups for well over a fortnight. That was probably the longest time his brother had kept to a straight path. He was proud of him—well, pleased with both of his brothers. They were dependable and their father had raised them well. After all, family was the most important aspect in life.

Ciaran finished his bath and dressed. He grabbed some much-needed ale and met Rosalia in her chamber. He had grown accustomed to talking with her in front of the fire. It took all of his strength to take his leave every eve, but he did it—barely.

"Och, Ciaran. I was worried so. Please tell me ye are well," Rosalia said, rising to embrace him.

His arms encircled her, and he placed his chin on the top of her head. "Just let me hold ye," he whispered. "Ye feel so good to me." They stood silently until he pulled away and noticed the tray of food.

"I thought ye might be hungry since ye did not return for the noon meal." She handed him a chunk of bread.

"My thanks," he whispered. He placed the bread back on the table and poured himself a tankard of ale.

"Do ye think that wise? If your throat is troublesome, mayhap water would be better."

"Lass, when ye hear what I have been through this day, ye will understand why I drink ale." He told her of the fire and Ian's death. What he did not address was how the fire started and how the bloody Campbells might be responsible.

They sat in silence and he finished his meal, welcoming the numbness the ale brought. Too bad the bath and the ale did not help him to wash away the day's events.

"I feel terrible about Ian," said Rosalia as she sighed. "How did the fire start?" When he hesitated too long with his response, she repeated the question. "Ciaran?" Leaning forward, she touched his arm. "What is wrong?"

The lass had become extremely talented at reading his mind, and it was getting much more difficult to keep things from her. But he did not want her having something else to worry about.

"Please donna tell me it was Dunnehl's men," she gasped.

He immediately grabbed her hands to reassure her. "It wasnae Dunnehl's men," he simply stated.

She had a confused expression upon her face. "It wasnae? If it wasnae Dunnehl's men, then what happened and what arenae ye telling me?"

Sitting back in the chair, he rubbed his hand over his brow. He'd had no intention of speaking with her about this and was bewildered when it all came out in one blurted breath. And he did not stop there. In between coughs, he continued to tell her of his past encounters with the bloody Campbells—from their thirst for land, power, and greed to their gaining of King James's ear.

"They are full of greed. I will ne'er pretend to understand the ways of men and their need for such power and so much land. Glenorchy is your home, and ye have a right to protect what is yours, Ciaran. The Campbells—my apologies, the *bloody* Campbells—have so many other lands. Why do they keep attempting to claim Glenorchy?" she asked solemnly.

"I think I am the only one who takes a stand against the Campbell. I have come to think he enjoys the challenge. As I said, my clan earned Glenorchy and we maintain it by right of sword. I willnae give up my home, but I also donna want to start a war over the mere words of a lad. I need to be certain they were responsible. Of this I am sure, if they were the cause of Ian's death, there will be bloodshed," he said sternly. "I willnae put my men in harm's way until I am certain."

"What will ye do?" she asked with a look of concern.

"I have already spoken to Seumas, and the guard is increased around the borders, should another attempt occur. I donna see another attempt so soon. The *bloody* Campbell will expect me to increase my guard on the borders." He sighed. "I have thought on this and will send him a missive on the morrow. If he claims responsibility, blood will be shed, I assure ye," he said tersely.

She smiled.

"What?" he asked her searchingly.

"Ye are a wise man, Ciaran MacGregor. I think most men would have raised their swords, charged his gates, and nae waited to hear if he was responsible," she simply stated.

"And at what cost? Many men would lose their lives foolishly. Many lives have been lost by men rushing into battle with only their hatred or anger to guide them. My father always told me ne'er to act on feeling alone. A planned move is best."

"He sounds like a wise man."

"He was… the wisest. I am tired of speaking." He studied her dress and smiled. "'Tis one of your new dresses."

"Aye. Ye paid to have these made for me. The least I can do is grant ye the boon to see me in them."

"Come," he said, holding out his hand. She rose, placed her hand into his, and let out a squeal when he quickly pulled her onto his lap. "Ye look beautiful, lass." He lifted her tresses behind her ear. "The dress suits ye." She blushed and placed her lips to his. When she pulled back, he growled. "Declan best stay to the path. I donna know how much longer I can bear this torture, Rosalia."

"Neither do I, my laird," she whispered.

❧

Archibald Campbell, seventh Earl of Argyll, sat in the great hall and reread the missive that had been delivered a short time earlier. He shook his head in complete aggravation. Out of all the lairds he defeated and all the lands he seized, the MacGregor of Glenorchy was always out of his reach. If he could only claim bordering Glenorchy from that blasted MacGregor, his lands would be massive. Hell, he would own most of Scotland himself and, with King James's favor, rule most of it.

He would be unstoppable.

There was no reason this scheme should not have worked. After all, he'd killed one of *them*. His men swore they were seen by some in the village. The MacGregor should have demanded Campbell blood and stormed his gates. He was anxious to see the look upon the MacGregor's face when he realized he was sorely outnumbered. He wanted him slaughtered to pieces. Perhaps even have his head displayed on a pike. Campbell smiled at the thought but banished it quickly because now the arse had to send him this missive.

Damn. He needed to provoke the MacGregor into storming his gates so he could kill him and claim his lands. He couldn't very well do that if the whoreson sent him missives that could be intercepted by King James's men. King James was tired of the Highland lairds and their squabbles. His Majesty demanded order and the fact that the Campbell personally vowed to enforce peace in the Highlands did not bode well for him if he was to be discovered.

He sighed as he realized his plan no longer served its purpose. He weighed his options because although he held King James's ear, he was not sure he could persuade his liege to act in his favor—especially if he replied to the missive admitting such a feat. Hell, either way this scheme was out. The MacGregor was clever. Campbell would give him that.

Approaching footsteps pulled him from his plotting. "Now will ye listen to reason? I told ye it wouldnae work. He is much too cunning."

Another look at the missive and it did not take long for the Earl of Argyll to decide. "I am listening."

Thirteen

MOTHER NATURE WAS RIGHT ON CUE: THE SPRING equinox arrived and warmed the bitter chill of winter. The winter solstice had brought frigid temperatures along with harsh-blowing winds that cascaded over the loch. Glenorchy had been a desolate blanket of glistening white for far too long. Rosalia could not believe she had actually survived the entire winter at Glenorchy. She was eager to escape outdoors.

She walked unhurriedly to the stable—as unhurriedly as she could while trying to avoid the mud. She hefted her skirts and lifted her face, enjoying the feel of the sun against her skin. A slight breeze blew against her rosy cheeks and she sighed. She truly welcomed the warmth and vigorousness of spring. She heard laughter and soon realized she was not the only one taking advantage of a warm day.

Niall was conversing intently with Duncan—again. Ever since Duncan had arrived, the two of them had been inseparable. Niall had told her repeatedly that Duncan's keen horse sense was far superior to anything he had ever seen. He sought his counsel often, and Duncan always welcomed Niall's eagerness to learn. With a pang of regret, she was aware that it would not be long before Duncan and Ealasaid took their leave and traveled to Ealasaid's sister. She enjoyed their company and would sorely miss them.

As she opened the door to the stable, she saw Declan with his head placed to Aiden's and speaking in hushed tones. Under normal circumstances, she would have been quite surprised to see a man engaged in conversation with a horse; however, she had become quite accustomed to Declan and his many speeches with Aiden. He jumped when she reached out and patted Aiden on the neck.

"And how is Aiden this morn?"

One corner of Declan's mouth twisted upward. "Didnae anyone ever tell ye nae to sneak up on a man?"

Rosalia's eyes widened. "I wasnae sneaking."

He looked as though he did not believe her. "Escaping the walls, my lady?"

"Most definitely. I cannae stay indoors any longer lest I go daft. I think Ciaran is ready to throttle me." She laughed.

He chuckled. "I think Aiden is ready to throttle Aisling as well. Did ye ever think it just might be something to do with ye *women*?" He winked at her.

Seeing the amusement in his eyes, she swatted him in the arm. "Ye better cease. Ye know how Aisling gets her ire up when ye speak of us that way."

"And why do ye think I do it?" he said, smirking.

Glancing over Declan's shoulder, Rosalia noticed his horse saddled in the other stall. "Are the men practicing their swordplay in the bailey?" she asked in an innocent tone, scratching Aiden behind the ears.

He rolled his eyes. "I know. I know," he said, holding up his hands in defense. "I donna feel like practicing my swordplay this day."

"Why? 'Tis much warmer."

He shrugged his shoulders. "I donna really want to speak upon it," he hedged and a melancholy frown flitted across his features.

"Well, mayhap ye will speak on it with Ciaran when he searches for ye to find out why ye donna practice with the men." She raised her brow, folding her arms over her chest.

"Och, Rosalia. Aisling and I donna agree on much, but ye and Ciaran are sounding and acting much the same." He shook his head in amusement.

"I only look out for ye. Ye know Ciaran will come searching for ye. Why donna ye practice your swordplay and be done with it? Why do ye want to battle him?" she asked, wanting to put all of the pieces together.

He paused briefly. "I go to the village," he said with quiet emphasis.

"The village? For what purpose?"

"Rosalia," he warned, half seriously.

"Donna *Rosalia* me. Why do ye go to the village?" She cocked her head to the side and waited for him to respond.

Running his hand through his hair, he moaned. "Ye and Aisling ne'er cease. And they wonder why I donna wed," he mumbled under his breath but loud enough for her to hear. "Ye donna understand. This day is difficult for me." He looked away from her.

"How so?" Declan had been practicing his sword-play with the men and ceased overindulging in ale, but as of late, he was always seen with his tankard full. If there was a chance she could pull the reason from him, she would try.

He fingered the latch on the stall. "My mother died on this day," he finally spoke solemnly with sadness upon his face.

From her prior conversations with Ciaran, Rosalia knew that Declan and his mother had been very close. She was sorry for the loss he still carried with him.

"Ciaran doesnae want me to wench or get into my cups within his walls and I havenae—well, I havenae wenched. I donna want him to know I take my leave to the village. He will think I am back to my ways and I am nae. I need this one day. I will have your word ye willnae tell him," he ordered, pointing his finger at her.

She shook her head in frustration. "And what of when Ciaran searches for ye and cannae find ye? He isnae daft, Declan." He attempted to speak, but she raised her hand, cutting him off. "Ye know, I think ye misjudge Ciaran. I donna think he would battle with ye on this. Ye have done what he asked of ye for several months' time. Why donna ye just tell him? Surely he would understand."

A corner of Declan's mouth quirked with annoy-ance and he rubbed his brow. "'Tisnae that simple, Rosalia. I donna need another lecture from him. I have had enough of them to last my life. He will think I am back to my ways. Besides, he knows Mother died on this day and he shouldnae seek me out. I will have your word ye willnae tell him. If he asks ye, tell him ye know naught. I will return on the morrow." He entered the stall and she blocked his way out.

"Declan, donna put me in this place. I cannae tell untruths to Ciaran."

He shrugged, amused at her attempts to obstruct the stall door. "Then tell him what ye will."

She did not need to start a battle between the brothers. They had been getting along so well. "I willnae tell him, but if he *asks* me…"

He waved her off. "Tell him whatever ye wish. Just give me my day, Rosalia," he said, pushing past her and leading his horse out of the stall.

"Ye will have a care. I will have your word, Declan MacGregor," she yelled after him.

"Ye have my word. I shall see ye on the morrow," he said, giving her his back and waving his hand in the air.

Men.

She glanced at Noonie and yearned to take him for a ride. Niall and Duncan would both have her head if he would return a muddy mess. She would need to find something else to occupy her. She carefully lifted her skirts and was making her way back across the bailey when someone grabbed her abruptly from behind.

"Didnae I tell ye it wouldnae be long before ye were outdoors?" asked Ciaran, whispering into her ear.

Pulling out of his hold, she turned around and swatted at him. "Aye, ye did. Howbeit I wish to stay out all day. I can nay longer bear the inside walls," she moaned.

"Then donna. Let us ride to the village. I am sure Noonie wants to run," he said, leading her back to the stable.

She stopped and avoided his eyes. "Umm… I didnae really want to go to the village this day. Do ye think we can ride around the loch instead?" she asked hopefully. "Mayhap there wouldnae be too much mud."

"I suppose. There shouldnae be too much mud if we stay to the rocky path." He gave her a warm smile. "Go and change into your trews and I will see to our mounts." Taking a quick glance and observing only a few men in the bailey, she stood on the tips of her toes and brushed her lips to his. When she pulled away, he gave her a smoldering look that thawed the winter chill. "Go and change," he choked out.

She made haste and donned her trews, her mind plaguing her about Declan. It tore at her insides not to speak the truth to Ciaran, but she would be bound to tell him if he asked her. She would have to pray he did not.

❧

Rosalia arrived back at the stable, and Ciaran thought it was a shame she still needed to wear her cloak. He so enjoyed the view when she wore only her trews. Dresses should be outlawed. Men did not realize what they were missing. He handed her the reins and smiled. "Your mount, my lady."

Noonie's prancing feet almost stepped on Rosalia's, and she jumped away from him. "My thanks, my laird. I think our mounts are both anxious to take their leave."

"Aye. Keep a tight rein on him and donna yet give him his head lest he runs with the wind. Are ye sure ye donna want to ride to the village?" he asked, mounting his horse.

"Quite sure," she said quickly. "I think the loch will be fine. I just need to escape these walls."

He laughed. "Then come. Let us ride and escape the madness." He would have to be a daft fool not to recognize the harsh winter chill was taking its toll on her. He also experienced the closeness of the walls and needed to escape to the outdoors. This was one of the most severe Highland winters Ciaran could ever remember. His only saving grace was that the Highland weather made it difficult for the bloody Campbells to further scheme and plot their next course.

When he received the missive from the Earl of Argyll, the *bloody* Campbell, he was not fooled for a moment by Campbell's denial into believing his people were safe. King James demanded peace in the Highlands, but Ciaran would do what he must to make sure no further harm befell his clan.

Rosalia grunted as she held a tight rein on Noonie, but Noonie continued to prance. "Ciaran, I think we must return. He pulls too much on my hands." She held up her hand, showing the imprint of the rein imbedded into her red palm.

He dismounted and approached her. He was not ready to take her back—they needed the outdoor respite. "I donna think we need to return. Ye will ride with me and we will lead Noonie."

"Are ye sure? I donna want to trouble ye," she said as she dismounted from Noonie.

He smiled. "I am sure. I am nae ready to return. Ye will ride with me. Come," he said, holding out his hand to her. When she paused and still did not move, he raised his brow and folded his arms over his chest. "Rosalia, I will have the reason for what troubles ye."

She gave a nervous laugh. "Donna be absurd, my laird. 'Tis naught troubling me."

"Then why do ye nae want to ride with me?" he asked, his eyes sharp and assessing. There was a heavy silence, but that was fine with him. He could be just as stubborn. He would simply stand here until she spoke the tale.

She huffed and stared at her hands. Noonie's reins held much interest to her. When he did not budge, she blurted out, "How will ye get me on your mount?" She colored fiercely.

"What do ye mean?" He stared at her, perplexed.

Rosalia glanced away from him and started to twirl Noonie's reins between her fingers. "Your mount doesnae kneel, and ye cannae simply lift me on him," she said quietly.

"What? I donna understand what ye speak."

She swallowed hard, lifted her chin, and boldly met his gaze. "Ciaran, your mount doesnae kneel, and I willnae be able to get upon his back," she said with a flush upon her face.

He was momentarily speechless in his surprise. So that was the truth of the matter. He could not understand why she believed the size of her frame bothered him. This issue was becoming old, and he would settle this once and for all. He strode toward her and bent down slightly. Before she was able to figure out what he was about, he tossed her over his shoulder. He chuckled as she yelped.

"Ciaran! Put me down! Ye will hurt yourself," She wiggled within his grasp.

"Will ye cease? Your fidgeting is going to make me drop ye." Bending his knees, he playfully pretended he was going to let her fall.

She squeaked.

He laughed and pivoted her from his shoulder into his arms. "Ye underestimate my strength and your self-worth, my lady," he murmured, brushing his lips to hers.

"Ciaran, please put me down," she begged.

"If ye insist." He gently dropped her to her feet and placed his hand to her cheek. Hearing her breath quicken, he knew he had to kiss her. He bent his head slowly forward, but she pulled away from him before he had the chance, giving him a slight smile of defiance.

"Come, my laird. We are wasting precious light," she said, approaching his mount.

He grabbed her waist and easily lifted her onto his mount. "Ye see? Ye worry for naught." Swinging up behind her, he placed his arms around her and grabbed the reins. With Noonie in tow, they rode up the mountain pass as he started to think this was not one of his best ideas.

She was too close.

He could smell her lavender scent and feel her body nestled between his legs. The gentle rocking motion of his mount tightened his groin. His arms pulled her closer. She felt so damn good. He shifted his weight, his groin heavy and painful with lust. Her cut tresses allowed easy access to the creamy expanse of her neck, and he wanted nothing more than to bury his face in her softness. The lass was so disturbing to him in every way imaginable. Every day, he found his feelings intensifying, and every eve, he fought to stay them. Damn, how he wanted her.

Curse his reckless brother.

That idea barely crossed his mind before another followed. He would wait until the last possible moment to tell her. He had no choice. By the end of the sennight, they would take their leave to Glengarry.

✺

When they returned to the stable, they released their muddy mounts into Duncan and Niall's care. Ciaran took his leave to review the accounts while Rosalia sought Ealasaid's company in the kitchens. She had been taking every opportunity to spend time with her as of late. Who knew how many chances she would have left?

Rosalia walked into the kitchen and inhaled deeply. "Do ye have any biscuits, Ealasaid? I smell something wonderful."

Ealasaid chuckled. "Ye always know when and where to find them. I just made a fresh batch there," she said, pointing to the table. "I would grab them right quick before the laird's brother gets to them."

Nodding her thanks, Rosalia pulled out the bench at the table. "Aye, Aiden would have them finished before we even reached for one. What would I ever do without ye, Ealasaid?" she asked, sitting down on the bench and grabbing for a biscuit.

Ealasaid patted her on the shoulder and sat down

beside her. "Ye may have to find out soon, my sweet lass." She smiled warmly, but her eyes held a glimmer of something attune to regret.

Rosalia put down the biscuit, trying to swallow the lump that lingered in her throat. "What do ye mean?"

"Lass, we have overstayed our welcome. We are grateful for Laird MacGregor's hospitality, but we must journey to my sister's." She smiled with compassion.

"Why? Ye donna have to take your leave. Ciaran would understand if ye wished to stay," Rosalia pleaded in a panicked tone.

Ealasaid's eyes were intelligent and she gave her a knowing look. "Rosalia, ye know we couldnae stay," she said quietly. "Ye have been through much, my sweet lass, but ye have your whole life yet ahead of ye and I have a feeling it will be verra bright." Ealasaid paused, studying her for a moment. "Tell me, will ye take your leave for Glengarry or will ye stay?"

Now that was the question. Rosalia had no idea how to respond. She had begun to understand her own needs and recognized the fact she needed Ciaran. Needed? Who was she fooling? She wanted Ciaran. They had reached the point where their relationship needed to be resolved or defined, but she hesitated, not wanting to admit the inevitable.

"Ye love him," said Ealasaid with smug delight. "I can see it in your eyes, lass."

She did not know which frightened her more, the realization that the words Ealasaid spoke were true or the fact that she could not yet admit her true feelings to Ciaran. She had known there was something special about him from the first moment she saw him at court.

She clung to that memory and would never forget a single detail of his compassionate smile. He was the kindest and most handsome man she had ever met.

Ealasaid pulled her from her quiet reflections. "Lass?"

"I donna know what to speak to that," she simply stated.

Ealasaid raised her brow. "Lass, will ye take counsel from an old woman?" She paused, reaching out and grabbing her hand. "Ye clearly love him, Rosalia, and I think he is a fine and honorable man. I suggest ye speak openly to him and tell him what ye truly want and how ye truly feel. Donna make him guess. Sometimes when ye speak with men, ye must speak bluntly lest they *think* they know how ye feel. And believe me," she chuckled, "ye donna want them thinking on their own. Trust me on this matter. I have had many *years* to discover this."

Speak her feelings to Ciaran? She would never have enough strength within her to speak to such a matter. Although he showed her affection, he spoke no words of love. It was obvious he cared for her, but that was all it was or would ever be. His vow was his bond. He would not break it. Besides, Rosalia did not think her pride would ever recover if he denied her.

"Ealasaid, I know ye mean well, but I cannae speak to that," Rosalia said in a tone that was final but, unfortunately, not final enough to fool Ealasaid.

"Donna make this more complicated than it needs to be. Do ye wish to stay at Glenorchy or nae?" Ealasaid raised her brow searchingly, waiting for a response.

Rosalia rubbed her temples and lowered her voice. "I care for Ciaran and, aye, love him. I donna wish to stay if he doesnae return the same feelings for me."

A grin passed over Ealasaid's features before she quickly masked it. "How do ye know how he feels if ye donna speak to it?"

Rosalia sighed. "I know he cares for me, but he speaks nay words of love. I donna want my poor heart to suffer if he doesnae feel the same. I donna think I could bear it," she said solemnly.

"And how will ye ever know if ye donna speak to it? I have seen the way he looks at ye, lass. I think ye may be surprised by his response. I think ye make an error in judgment by nae telling him how ye feel and 'tis worth the risk ye take. If ye think upon it wisely, ye will agree," she said as she patted Rosalia's hand. Ealasaid rose, placing biscuits in a basket.

Rosalia pulled herself to her feet, taken aback by Ealasaid's advice and feeling more uncertain than ever. What if Ciaran did not share the same feelings? She had a quick and disturbing thought. What if he did? She stood motionless in the middle of the kitchen, and her stomach was still clenched tight when Ealasaid cleared her throat. She was clearly aware of her dilemma.

"Take the chance, Rosalia," she said in an encouraging tone.

She inclined her head in a small gesture of thanks and walked briskly away with a purpose.

❧

Ciaran reviewed the accounts in his solar and his mind fought for clarity. The harder he tried to ignore the truth, the more it persisted.

Declan would not change.

As far as he knew, his brother had not wenched within his walls, but as of late, he was deeper in his cups. And to think, there was a time when he'd believed his youngest brother had finally straightened his path. That only lasted for as long as the blink of an eye. When had his life become a bitter battle of the wills? Sitting back in his chair, Ciaran ran his hand through his hair and sighed. This is not how he wanted things to be. His vow weighed on him, choking him. He had no choice but to take Rosalia to Glengarry. It was a bitter decision.

"How goes it, Brother?" asked Aiden, walking into the solar.

Ciaran straightened, his mouth pulled into a sour grin. "Nae well." Aiden sat down casually and studied his brother, waiting for him to continue. "I will be taking my leave to Glengarry by the end of the sennight and ye will act in my stead. The accounts are in order, and I trust ye to keep watchful eyes on the border. I donna know if the Campbell vermin plot, but I want us to plan in case they do." He knew he sounded curt, abstracted. Frankly, he did not care.

Aiden stared at him with complete surprise upon his face. Leaning forward, he rested his arm on the desk. "Do ye think that wise, Brother? I mean to say, I thought ye cared for Rosalia and would make her your—"

"Declan doesnae change his ways." Ciaran ground out the words between his teeth. "And ye cannae say ye havenae seen him back in his cups as of late."

"Aye. 'Tis only because of Mother's death," said Aiden.

"'Tis always because of Mother's death. He doesnae cease. 'Tis nay easy decision for me to make, but 'tis my decision."

His brother smirked. "And what of Rosalia? What does she say of your *decision*?"

"I havenae yet spoken to Rosalia. She knows naught," Ciaran simply stated.

Aiden raised his brow questioningly. "And when were ye going to speak to her, Brother? The morn ye take your leave?"

Ciaran rose, not appreciating the tone in Aiden's voice. "*That* isnae your concern, but 'tis best to speak upon it at the last moment—for everyone."

"For ye or for Rosalia?"

"My decision is made," he repeated firmly.

He shook his head. "So ye say."

"So I say." Ciaran's annoyance increased when his brother rose, blocking his escape to the door. He knew the family had grown fond of her, but this was difficult for him. He did not need Aiden rubbing salt in an open wound.

Aiden's expression stilled and grew serious. "For being a great laird, ye can also be so daft. The two of ye have been inseparable for months. She doesnae walk past ye without ye giving her a raking gaze. Ye care for her and ye cannae tell me ye donna."

Taking a step away from his brother before he throttled him, Ciaran ran his hand through his hair. "It doesnae matter what I feel for Rosalia."

"'Tis where ye are verra wrong, Brother. It does matter how ye feel for the lass. If ye love her, ye wouldnae take her to Glengarry. Ye wouldnae let her take her leave. Ye would fight for her. Ye would make her yours," he said with determination.

Aiden had not made a promise to his father. Had he done so, he would have done the same as Ciaran was doing. "I made a vow to Father and I *will* honor my word," he said curtly.

"Aye, the *bloody* vow. How many times must we speak to this? Father didnae want ye to cease your life only to look after Declan. Declan chooses his own path, and he is a grown man whether ye admit it or nae. Donna let the love of your life go, Ciaran," Aidan said in a raised and angered voice.

Love of his life? He had to admit that he cared deeply for Rosalia, but love of his life? At one time he believed he could have made her his wife, but his vow was not fulfilled. And he would honor his vow. He grew tired of Aiden's prodding. "Aiden," he warned.

"Ye donna listen to reason. I see the way ye look at Rosalia. 'Tis the same way I look at Aisling. Can ye imagine Rosalia with another? Can ye imagine yourself without her in your life? Ye take her to Glengarry and there is nay taking her back. Think this through. She will be gone from your life, Ciaran," he said tersely. "Any blind fool can see ye love her. Just ask yourself if ye can live without her."

Ciaran strode to the door. "I willnae discuss this with ye again. My decision is made and 'tis final." He almost made it through the door when, almost as a second thought, Aiden spoke. Ciaran stilled at the tone of his brother's voice. It was ice cold and coolly disapproving.

"Ye are going to lose the only woman ye have ever truly loved."

Ciaran hesitated and a muscle quivered at his jaw. How many times must he have this conversation? Aiden was aware of his commitment to his father. He'd given his word. His word was his bond. His word was—everything. It did not matter what he did or did not feel for Rosalia. All he knew for certain was that he did not want to spend the rest of his days listening to his brother's lectures on finding a wife—or letting one go. He knew his duty. His father had taught him well.

With increasing intensity, Ciaran raised his voice. This time, he would ensure that his brother understood his purpose. "For the last time… I donna *love* Rosalia, and I will take her to Glengarry at the end of the sennight." As he turned on his heel and thundered through the door, azure eyes stared back at him, glittering with raw hurt.

Rosalia…

෴

Ciaran stopped dead in front of her. He attempted to pull her into his embrace, but she withdrew from his arms and moved to the right.

"Rosalia…"

She froze, mind and body benumbed. How could she be so foolish? She swallowed hard and squared her shoulders. "Pray excuse me."

Aiden stepped from the doorway and reached out, grabbing Ciaran's arm. "Donna…"

Rosalia ran at lightning speed, so distraught she did not recognize anyone in her path. A few servants scrambled out of her way on the stairs as she flew past them and down the hall. The first thing she did when she entered her bedchamber was latch the adjoining door.

Her pride had been seriously bruised by Ciaran's open declaration and she was intensely humiliated. After spending so much time together and sitting every eve in front of the fire, she'd actually believed they were closer than ever. Closer? She was a fool. They were never further apart. It seemed they even disagreed on the very nature and meaning of love.

Love? Who was she fooling? Ciaran did not love her at all. She shuddered, thinking of his warm kisses and the way he touched her. All of those moments meant naught. *She* meant nothing to him. In fact, she meant nothing more to him than—Beathag.

Her sorrow was a huge, painful knot inside. All of those months of pure heartfelt pleasure now left her with nothing but bitter memories. Her sense of loss was now beyond tears. There was only one detail that continued to surface—the undeniable and heartbreaking fact that Ciaran simply did not love her.

Fourteen

Someone knocked at her door. Maybe if she ignored it, they would walk away. All Rosalia needed was to be left alone with her misery to accompany her, but apparently she was not going to get that. A few seconds later, there was another rap. Surely Ciaran was not foolish enough to attempt such a feat.

"My lady? I come from the village. Our laird's brother needs ye," a young boy whispered through the door. Reluctantly rising from the bed, she swung open the door to find a young lad standing sheepishly before her. His tousled head glanced down the hall and back, and his clothes were dirty and torn. His hazel eyes darted nervously back and forth before her. "My lady? I come from the village. Our laird's brother told me to seek ye out."

She raised her brow questioningly and folded her arms over her chest. "Declan?"

He nodded. "Aye, my lady. He told me to seek ye out when ye were alone. He made me say these words over and over until I got 'em right. I am to speak them to ye the same as he told me." She waved her hand for him to continue and he held a determined look upon his features. "I am deep in my cups. I had a mishap with my horse and my clothes are bloody, but I am well. I need ye to grab clothing from my chamber and bring it to me in the treeline south of the *cabhsair*. Donna speak of this to anyone lest Ciaran has my head. Please make haste."

Rosalia closed her eyes and rubbed her temples. Did she not just tell him to have a care? Now the rogue involved her in his debauchery. She would be sure to give him a piece of her mind when she saw him. How would she be able to bring him clothes undetected? She would have to sneak like a thief in the night. If Ciaran ever discovered Declan deep in his cups again, there would be bloodshed. No matter her feelings toward his lairdship, at the moment, she still cared about Declan. She would not want anyone to face Ciaran's wrath.

The lad continued to study her, shifting from foot to foot. Declan's reckless behavior certainly was not his fault. She approached her trunk and pulled out her sack. Opening the pouch, she reached in and grabbed a coin. When she spun around to give it to the boy, he was gone. Declan probably had already paid him for his trouble. She tossed the bag back into her trunk and slammed the lid. Although Ciaran's words hurt her beyond belief, she did not like deceiving him. The sooner she got this over with, the better. One thing was for certain. Declan would receive an earful. How could he place her in the middle of his carelessness?

She donned her cloak and opened the door. Observing no one in the hall, she stepped out and gently shut the door. As discreetly as she could, she walked to Declan's chamber. Giving one last look down both sides of the hall to ensure no one was about, she entered. Latching the door with a soft click, Rosalia leaned back against it, breathing a sigh of relief no one had seen her.

Rummaging through his trunk, she searched until she found trews and a tunic. Pulling them out, she stuffed them underneath her cloak. Her mission was complete. It was time to take her leave. She did not want to remain in his chamber any longer than what was required. Cracking open the door, she peeked through the slit. If anyone saw her, she would have a lot of explaining to do. Not hearing or seeing anyone in the hall, she stepped out and silently shut the door. Rosalia glanced around sharply and breathed in a deep sigh of relief. She had made it.

Almost.

Turning on her heel, she bumped straight into Aisling, who held Teàrlach with an unreadable expression upon her features. Rosalia tried desperately to mask her guilt. God's teeth! What other reason would she have for being in Declan's chamber other than the obvious? She needed to think, but any plausible explanation escaped her. They both froze in a stunned tableau.

Trying not to panic, Rosalia smiled at her sheepishly. "Aisling. 'Tisnae as ye think."

Aisling shook her head, her eyes widening in astonishment. "And what do ye think I am thinking when ye sneak out of Declan's chamber?"

This was not going well. Surely Aisling knew she

would never let Declan woo her let alone... Before she had a chance to respond, Aisling stormed past her. She was reaching for the latch of Declan's door when Rosalia spoke in a rush of words. "He isnae in there."

Aisling glanced at her in nonbelief. "Then ye willnae mind if I look for myself." She pushed open the door and walked in. Studying his chamber, she cast a puzzled look. "Declan isnae here."

Rosalia met her accusing eyes without flinching. "As I stated," she said sternly.

Aisling studied her. "Then what were ye doing in his chamber?" Entering the room, Rosalia closed the door. She unfastened her cloak and pulled out Declan's clothes. "Are those Declan's?" asked Aisling, lowering her gaze in confusion.

Rosalia sighed. "Aye. Ye willnae believe what he did now." When she hastily explained the entire tale, they both flinched. At least Aisling no longer wanted to kill her. Now she had her sights on someone else entirely.

"I say we bring him his clothes and take him to task. He expects ye, but he willnae expect the both of us. If he is deep in his cups then I am sure his head aches." Aisling paused as she plotted against him. "We may as well get some enjoyment out of this. Let us nae speak of this to the men. There would be a battle for sure since Declan was daft enough to call upon ye. Come." She opened the door and pushed Rosalia through. "We will take Teàrlach, and if anyone asks, we go for a walk. Mayhap we should take his clothes and leave him bare as the day he was born." She giggled. "I think he would be daft enough to fall for something as that."

"He would deserve it." Rosalia chuckled. She tried to push back the ache of how much she would truly miss Aisling. She had become as a sister to her.

As they walked through the bailey, Aiden yelled after them. "Wife? Where are ye going?" He ran up beside them and Rosalia caught herself glancing uneasily over her shoulder. She had not seen him since Ciaran's open declaration. She cast her eyes downward.

"We go for a walk," Aisling said, kissing Teàrlach on the head.

He rubbed Teàrlach's curls. "Can I come along?"

"Nay," Aisling simply stated. When he looked as if he would question her further, she quickly added, "Ye see, I got my monthly courses, and Rosalia and I—"

He quickly waved her off. "I donna have to come. I will see ye later." They started to walk away when Aiden cleared his throat. "Aisling?"

"Aye, Husband?" she asked, turning around with a look of innocence.

"Stay to the front of the loch. If ye journey further, ye will need an escort. Ciaran doesnae want any of ye too far away." He gave Rosalia a compassionate smile and turned away.

Aisling giggled. "Ye are right, Rosalia. They run away as quickly as they can when ye mention monthly courses or birthing. I will remember to use that again."

They walked across the *cabhsair* and continued to walk south. Approaching the treeline, they looked for Declan. "I donna see him. Declan, are ye here?" Rosalia shouted.

"Over here!"

Aisling nodded toward the trees and they walked

into a heavily wooden area. Everything was silent and they did not even hear a cracking tree branch. Standing quietly with the exception of Teàrlach's cooing, they searched the area and still did not see him.

Rosalia shouted again. "Declan? Where are ye?"

"Over here!"

Aisling's skirts became tangled in some branches. "Och, he is going to get a good thrashing when I see him," she bit out, tugging at her skirts and balancing Teàrlach in her arms.

Rosalia helped Aisling to clear her skirts and turned her head around. "I still donna see him. Declan!" she shouted louder.

"Shh! Over here!"

They dredged further into the trees, pulling their skirts out from under the branches and thistles along the way. She finally spotted his mount. As they approached, he was sprawled out upon the ground. Blood smeared his face and head, and he was motionless.

Rosalia dashed to his side. She placed her hand under his head, which she found was wet with blood. "Och, Declan."

"I thought the lad told ye he wasnae hurt," said Aisling. Her tone held a degree of warmth and concern.

"He did," Rosalia said worriedly.

Declan moaned and started to move. "Declan." She gently shook him. "Can ye hear me? Declan, 'tis Rosalia."

"Rosalia? What are ye doing here?" he asked with a glazed expression, disoriented.

She hesitated, blinking with bafflement. "What am I doing here? Ye sent the lad from the village, ye big oaf. Aisling and Teàrlach are here as well. Ye called out to me only a moment ago to tell me where ye were. Ye donna remember?"

He lifted his hand to reach for his head and then noticed his blood. "Nay."

"Donna try to move," said Aisling. "Mayhap he is injured in the head."

"Aisling? What are ye doing here?" he slurred, staring at her, perplexed.

"Ye called for Rosalia and I came with her." She cast Rosalia a look of concern.

Sitting up abruptly, he reached for his head and screamed in pain. "Take your leave. Now!" he bellowed, grabbing his head in agony.

They regarded him with searching gravity and were halted by the tone of his voice. "What? We willnae leave ye here," said Rosalia. Perhaps he'd hit his head harder than they thought.

"I didnae call upon Rosalia! Run!"

Without warning, a hand closed over Rosalia's right shoulder and something was thrown over her. That was the last she remembered before everything went black.

⁓

Declan was swimming in a haze of confusion. He fought through the cobwebs, shaking his head in an attempt for clarity. Called for Rosalia? He did not call for Rosalia. Why would he call for Rosalia? And why was Aisling here with Teàrlach?

God's teeth! It was a trap!

He sat up abruptly, trying to ignore the shooting pain through his skull. "Take your leave. Now!" he screamed, grabbing his head in pain. Why were they not listening to him?

A man sprang out of the brush and threw a sack over Rosalia. He knocked her on the back of the head, and she fell to the ground instantly with a heavy thud. Declan felt like his heart was being torn out and shown to him. He was pulling himself clumsily to his feet, ignoring the shooting pain, when someone dropped him to his knees from behind. He raised his head as one of the men ripped Teàrlach from Aisling's arms. Another man covered her with a sack, knocking her motionless to the ground.

Declan continued to watch the scene unfold before him. The women lay upon the ground seeming completely lifeless while his nephew screamed in terror. He would be damned if they would take his own without a fight. He again pulled himself to his feet and was pummeled to his back with a massive thud. The pressure of a booted foot against the base of his throat caused him to gasp.

"Donna even attempt, MacGregor *arse*," said the man through clenched teeth. He spit in Declan's face and applied more pressure on his neck.

Declan was forced to watch, powerless and weak, as the men took Aisling, Rosalia, and Teàrlach before his very eyes. He was completely helpless, but a driving force kept him alert. There would be bloodshed. He would give his last breath to see every one of them pay, and there was only one payment he would accept.

Death.

"Strip him of his clothing," spoke a familiar voice.

Three men forcefully stripped him of all his clothing

and kicked him to the ground. He did not even notice the chill of the air brushing against his skin. The heat of his vengeance was smoldering from within and was enough to fire his blood.

"Bring him to his knees," someone ordered. The men shoved him onto his knees and he hobbled over, forcing himself to raise his head. He would look his attacker in the eye.

"Hmm… mayhap I did choose the wrong brother," murmured Beathag in admiration.

He glared at her and spat to the ground. "I told ye before… my brother and I donna share whores."

Some of the men chuckled around him, but Beathag silenced them all with a single glare. She stood directly in front of him and poured something cold and wet all over him. Leaning in close, she smiled. "Ye tell Ciaran he can come collect his ugly virgin, the MacGregor whore, and the brat from the Campbell."

❧

The memory of the hurt upon Rosalia's face swept over Ciaran like a punch in the gut. He never meant to hurt her. She did not deserve this. It killed him not to be able to offer her comfort, but maybe Aiden was right. He needed to let her cool her ire. He would speak with her later.

He found Aiden in the kitchen soliciting Ealasaid for biscuits—again. "And what are ye going to do when Ealasaid takes her leave?" he asked, raising his brow.

Aiden and Ealasaid jumped. "Och, my laird. Ye startled us." Ealasaid chuckled, holding her hand over her chest. "Donna ye worry. I showed Cook how to make them so your brother will always have his fill."

"Ye donna need to take your leave, Ealasaid. I am sure I can change your mind to remain," said Aiden, giving her a roguish grin.

She swatted at him. "Cease. Cook will make ye all of the biscuits ye require or all of the biscuits Lady Aisling will allow ye to have."

Aiden nodded at her. "There is that," he said, rolling his eyes.

Ciaran smiled at her warmly. "Duncan said ye will be taking your leave. As I told him, ye may stay at Glenorchy for as long as ye wish."

She patted him on the arm. "Ye have my thanks, but Duncan and I have overstayed our welcome and will take our leave in a few days. We thank ye for having us."

"Ye and Duncan always have a home at Glenorchy," Ciaran said sincerely, knowing they would be sorely missed.

"Just have a care with my lassie. Ye know she has been through much. I see how light of heart she is with ye and it truly warms my heart." She smiled at him.

"Ye donna have to worry about Rosalia," he reassured them. "We take our leave for Glengarry in a few days."

Ealasaid gave him a look of disappointment and cast her eyes downward. Was she actually clenching her teeth? She finished wrapping some of the biscuits in a cloth. "There," she said, placing them on the corner of the table. "They are for your lady wife and our lassie when they return. Please make sure they get them and ye donna eat them," she chided Aiden.

She approached Duncan as Ciaran nudged Aiden. "When they return?"

He nodded. "Aye. They went for a walk."

"Do ye think Rosalia speaks with Aisling?"

His brother gave him a look of utter nonbelief. "Why would ye care if she did? Ye donna love her. Remember, Brother?"

Ciaran scowled.

"I donna know of what they speak. All I do know is they went for a walk and had Teàrlach with them."

Shouts rang out in the great hall, halting any further discussion. They rushed into the hall where Seumas was bellowing orders to Calum. "Find our laird!" he said, trying to disperse the men.

"I am here."

"My laird, ye need to come to the bailey," said Seumas, lowering his voice.

As they strode into the bailey, the men were gathered. "'Tis Declan's mount," said Ciaran to Aiden. They pushed their way through the crowd. His brother swaggered before him, bare as the day he was born. He tried to disguise his annoyance in front of his men, but his patience was wearing thin. They flanked Declan as he continued to sway on his feet, the smell of ale overwhelming Ciaran's senses. He turned his head in disgust. He was a fool to think his brother would cease his debauchery, but he would not be made the fool again. "Seumas, clear the men. Calum, take Declan's mount to Niall," he ordered.

"Aye, my laird."

"'Tis the last time, Brother," he said through gritted teeth. "Ye brought this upon yourself."

Declan stiffened at his words. "Ciaran, 'tisnae as ye think." He raised his hand to steady his head.

Ciaran's face was a mask of rage. "Save your excuses, Declan. I grow tired of hearing them, and I nay longer have the patience for ye or them," he replied sharply. Aiden and Ciaran forcefully grabbed him, leading him to the solar. When they reached the door, they shoved him inside. Declan had gone too far. He actually rode his bare, naked arse into the middle of the bailey. What the hell was he thinking? Apparently, he was not.

Ciaran slammed the door in disgust. "I warned ye for the last time! Ye are knee deep in your cups, have nay clothing, and what... fell from your mount?" he bellowed, pointing to his bloodied head.

"Will ye cease the lecture and listen, *ye bloody fool*?" said Declan sarcastically.

Ciaran had just reached for the door to escape his brother's latest disaster when Declan slammed into him from behind. Aiden grabbed Declan and tried to pull him off.

"Ye will listen to me, ye bloody fools! The *bloody* Campbell has your women and my nephew!"

Ciaran shoved him off. "What? What is this ye speak?"

"Listen to me, ye bloody arse! I was knocked over the head. I am nae sure exactly how, but someone spoke to Rosalia and told her to come to me. I donna know why, but Aisling and Teàrlach were there as well," Declan blurted out.

Aiden punched him square in the jaw. "The *bloody*

Campbell has my wife and my son because ye were in your cups and couldnae offer them protection! I should kill ye right now!" he bellowed. "If they are harmed in any way, I will kill ye with my bare hands!" He attempted another swing at Declan, and Ciaran shoved them apart.

"Cease, both of ye! This doesnae help matters!"

Declan ignored Ciaran and grabbed Aiden by the tunic. "Look at me! I am nae in my cups, Brother! I ne'er made it to the village! They knocked me out and set a trap!" he bellowed, releasing Aiden.

Ciaran studied him intently. "If what ye speak is true, then why do ye reek of ale and where is your clothing?"

"Ye have your *bloody whore* to thank for that," Declan said through gritted teeth.

"Beathag?" Ciaran asked as a shiver ran down his spine.

Taking a deep breath, Declan sighed. "Aye. She stripped me of my clothing, poured ale over my head, and said ye can collect the women and Teàrlach from the *bloody* Campbell," he said solemnly.

A heavy silence fell.

Aiden stepped around them and opened the door.

"Where do ye think ye are going?" asked Ciaran, placing a restraining hand upon the door.

"I am going to get my wife and my son."

"And ye will get yourself and them killed as well. Think, Brother. Think how Father taught us. If ye let your anger guide ye, ye are nay help to anyone. We must think and we must plan. 'Tis the only way." He called for a maid to bring Declan some clothing. He also called for the captain of his guard.

Seumas arrived and they plotted their course for

hours. No one would take their leave until they devised a plan that held the lowest possible risk. Ciaran refused to take even a moment to think about how Rosalia fared for it would surely be his undoing. He knew he must maintain his collectedness or he would get them all killed. He was laird. He was trained for this. He was a battle-hardened warrior. The Campbell had gone too far. No matter what plan they chose to execute, the Campbell would die. Let that be a warning to all future Campbell lairds. No one harmed his own, and no one took what was so clearly his.

The sun settled against the horizon as Ciaran stood on the parapet. It was his favorite place with Rosalia and the closest place he could feel her right now. He briefly closed his eyes and prayed she was well. She had to persevere and know he would come for her. In the meantime, she needed to do whatever she could to survive and come back to him. There was no other recourse.

They would execute their plan in two days. That would give the bloody Campbell enough time to hopefully lower his defenses. He knew as long as he did not take action against the Campbell, he would let them live. What he could not do however, was ensure that the Campbell treated them well. This was one time where he wished he could seek his father's counsel.

It was completely dark by the time Ciaran descended from the parapet. He would seek a few hours rest and then review the plan again on the morrow. He needed to have his wits about him. He hoped his brothers did the same.

Fifteen

"We are reaching MacGregor lands. Keep a watchful eye," ordered Alexander MacDonell of Glengarry to his guard. Shifting in the saddle, he ran his hand through his hair. It was a lengthy journey to reach Glenorchy, but it would not be long now. He searched through the trees. Odd, it was silent. The tiny hairs on the back of his neck rose, sending a shiver of warning down his spine. Something was off and he could not quite place it.

"Do ye feel it, Alex?" asked John, the captain of his guard. John reined in his mount beside him, his eyes darting cautiously back and forth.

Leave it to John to sense his unease. He nodded his head, continuing to survey the surrounding landscape. "Aye. Something is amiss. We havenae been greeted by a single man, and I donna see any guards at the border. We are clearly on MacGregor lands. 'Tis too quiet. I donna like it. Make sure our men stay alert," said Alexander.

With a curt nod of his head, John rode ahead to speak with his men. Pensively, Alexander glanced around him. There was no trace of anyone. He could not stop himself from thinking the obvious. What daft fool would keep his borders unprotected? His father would surely not be pleased.

When the missive arrived at Glengarry from the MacGregor, it took some time for his father to cool his ire. The MacGregor had bollocks, he would give him that. Alexander did not exactly jump at the chance to travel to Glenorchy, but he would do anything his father asked of him, knowing this was important to his father as well as his aunt.

They traveled for some time before the smell of peat smoke billowed in the air from the village ahead. A few of the villagers looked upon them warily as they passed through. Alexander was pleased that his father bestowed this responsibility upon him. After all, his sire was reaching up there in years. If the man did not start entrusting him to do things, how would Alexander be able to prove he could act in his stead? It was so easy to lose track of how many times he had pleaded to assist with courtly matters, but ever so slowly, his father had been giving him more and more responsibility. Alexander could certainly not disappoint him now—he would not.

Raising his hand, he stopped his men. The massive stone castle stood before him—the home of the MacGregor. Alexander stiffened his spine, sitting up straighter in the saddle. He would make his father proud.

❦

The men reviewed the plan again—thoroughly. Ciaran needed to ensure everyone knew their strategy well. His brothers looked like hell, but they stayed true to their course. He was confident everyone knew their role and everything would be ready as planned. As they were ready to take their leave, there was pounding on the solar door. He rose to find a pacing Calum on the other side.

"My laird, there are riders at the gates," he said quickly. "I donna think they are the Campbell's men. Howbeit they insist to see Lady Rosalia and willnae leave until they do. They hold fast."

He paused, rubbing his brow. "How many men?"

Calum sighed. "At least a score."

"A score?" he asked surprised. Who could possibly be at his gates with a score of men if it was not the Campbell? Surely it was not Dunnehl. Montgomery had seen to that. Turning to Seumas, he gestured him forward. "Prepare the men and let them into the bailey under careful watch. Have the archers readied."

"Aye, my laird."

His brothers exchanged carefully guarded looks as they followed him into the bailey. Flanking him, they watched the men ride through the gates. "Do ye know these men?" asked Aiden, studying them intently.

"They arenae with the Campbell and I donna think they are Dunnehl's men, but I am nae sure. 'Tis the last thing we need right now. Keep calm and let us see what they are about," Ciaran said, placing his hand on the hilt of his sword.

Aiden and Declan followed suit.

A rider approached them and nodded. "Laird Ciaran MacGregor of Glenorchy?" the man asked as he dismounted.

Ciaran did not respond.

The man walked with an arrogant swagger and stood face to face with him. "Are ye Laird Ciaran MacGregor of Glenorchy?"

Ciaran noticed the arrogant arse was not as old as he initially thought. He might even be younger than Declan. "Who is asking?" asked Declan sarcastically.

Turning to Declan, the man smirked. Looking back to Ciaran, he smiled and raised his brow. "I will have your name," he ordered.

"Watch your tongue or I will have your head," Ciaran countered.

Declan and Aiden laughed when the man paled.

"Verra well," he relented, taking a step back. "I am Alexander MacDonell. I come on behalf of my father, Laird Dòmhnall MacDonell of Glengarry. Father's sister is Lady Rosalia's *seanmhair*. I request an audience with my cousin."

Ciaran studied MacDonell's well-armed men. "How many men do ye have with ye?"

Alexander stood to his full height. "A score," he said confidently.

"Can they fight?" Ciaran asked with a raised brow.

"Of course. I have some of my father's most skilled men. If ye attempt anything on my life, they are instructed to raise arms against ye," he said cautiously, glancing nervously at a man Ciaran thought to be the captain of his guard.

Ciaran gazed at his brothers with a silent understanding. They had recruitments. Adding an additional score of men would increase their chances and lessen the risk of injury to Rosalia, Aisling, and Teàrlach. He visibly relaxed and gave the man a playful slap to the shoulder. "Ye have naught to fear from me, Alexander MacDonell. Come. We have much to discuss. Tell your men they are welcome at Glenorchy."

It was time to revise the plan.

❧

Slowly opening her eyes, Rosalia blinked away the haziness. She was being pulled and dragged while the muffled voices of men echoed in the background. The sack was finally removed from her head, and she was shoved onto a stool. The light was blinding and she could not see. She attempted to move her hands and realized they were not bound. Praise the saints for small favors. She pressed both hands over her eyes and tried to focus on her surroundings. Where was she?

The last thing she remembered was Declan. What was it? Declan screaming about something, and then she... Why did her head ache so badly? She'd blacked out—well, she was knocked out. Several men were gathered around her in what seemed to be a great hall. Finely woven tapestries were displayed on the walls, and fine wood furnishings graced the hall in abundance. This was obviously the home of a man with great wealth.

A path was cleared as another group of men entered the hall, escorting Aisling. She staggered forward, her face streaked with tears. Her muffled cries echoed through the hall as she was pushed onto a stool next to Rosalia. They clasped their hands together in a futile attempt to offer each other comfort.

"How verra touching," said Beathag, ambling over with a sly grin.

Rosalia's eyes flashed with outrage. "I suppose we have ye to thank for this," she bit out.

"Of course. Donna say I didnae give ye fair warning," Beathag replied, her voice heavy with sarcasm.

"Where are we?" Rosalia demanded.

An older man in full Highland regalia approached them. He wore a kilt of green, black, and blue, and the light sparkled off the bejeweled rings he wore on each of his fingers. He carried himself in an arrogant manner, and something in his dark eyes chilled her to the bone. He gave an impatient shrug to Beathag. "Ye didnae tell them?"

Beathag shook her head at him without speaking.

"Then pray allow me to introduce myself," he said, placing his hand over his chest and giving them a slight bow. "I am Archibald Campbell, seventh Earl of Argyll."

Rosalia gasped. "Och, the *bloody* Campbell." She bit her lip, but it was too late.

The Campbell smirked and Rosalia stared back at the floor.

"Verra well done, Cousin. I didnae think your plan would work," he simply stated.

Cousin?

"I spoke to ye as such. Ye merely had to listen." Beathag held out her hand in front of him. "I expect the coin that was promised to me, Archie."

He laughed and patted her hand. "Ye donna get it that easily, my dear. I believe the deal was for the MacGregor."

Beathag huffed. Her coolness was evidence she was not amused. "And it will only be a matter of time before he storms your gates."

Ignoring Beathag, the Campbell took another step toward Rosalia, and his dark eyes examined her from head to toe. She held her breath under his silent scrutiny and did not dare look in his direction. "I think ye are losing your touch, Cousin. I wonder why the MacGregor chose her instead of ye? She is nay great beauty." He smirked, placing his hand over Rosalia's breast. "Mayhap she services him better than ye did," he said with a wolfish-grin.

Aisling jerked to her feet. "Leave her be!"

"And what have we here?" he said, taking predatory steps toward Aisling. He tapped his finger over his lip as he studied her.

"'Tis the second MacGregor's wife. The whelp belongs to her," said Beathag.

"Mmm… I only intended on capturing his woman," he said, gesturing toward Rosalia. He turned back to Aisling and took another predatory step closer. "How fortunate for me I find ye within my walls as well."

Aisling looked away hastily.

"Ye will look at me when I speak to ye," the Campbell ordered, his mouth twisted into a threat. Aisling glared at him, and he laughed with subtle amusement. "Och, I do love a challenge, and I love my women with some spirit. I think ye will be both."

Rosalia turned her head away. She could not let this happen. She had to do something. She silently prayed Ciaran would storm the gates and kill them all.

When Teàrlach's wails echoed through the great

hall, the Campbell made a dismissive gesture with his hands. "Take the bairn out and kill him." The man left with Teàrlach, and a woman with tresses as black as the night followed him out of the hall. Rosalia watched helplessly as Aisling dropped to the floor and sobbed with such a sound of loss that her cries tore through Rosalia's heart like a dagger—one that she would gladly put through the Campbell's black heart.

"Take her to my chamber," ordered the Campbell.

Aisling no longer fought, and the men had to lift her up and drag her away. Rosalia knew Aisling had just given up hope. She would do everything in her power not to let that happen to herself.

Everything in the hall went quiet.

The Campbell strode away from Rosalia, shouting, "Throw her in the dungeon." She was roughly pulled to her feet and escorted down a stone staircase. Upon their descent, the remaining light faded and the change in temperature made her shiver. One of the guards lit a torch and escorted her to the last door.

The guard pushed the door open with his foot and smiled with a toothless grin. "Your chamber, MacGregor whore," he spat, shoving her into the room.

She glanced around her small prison, seeing only a dirty, worn blanket thrown into the corner.

The guard slid the latch, barring the door, and Rosalia was embraced by darkness. She sat with her back against the wall, folding her arms over her knees. She prayed the gods would watch over Teàrlach.

Her eyes were playing tricks on her as light appeared to be coming closer to her prison. She wiped her tears and stood. She did not imagine it. The same guard escorted Aisling to the door. Unlatching the door, he opened it and shoved her inside.

Aisling fell to her knees and Rosalia embraced her. "Och, Aisling," she said, pushing her hair back from her face. "Please tell me ye are unharmed." The door slammed shut and the light again faded until they were in complete darkness. She pulled her close and rubbed her hands over her back. "Och, Aisling. Ye are freezing. There is a blanket in the corner. I will get it for ye."

She rose and carefully slid her foot toward the other wall. The only sound coming from their prison was the sound of her sliding foot. Aisling did not make a single sound or utter a single word. When Rosalia reached the wall, she felt for the blanket with her foot. Picking it up, she shook it out, praying there was nothing in it. It was probably fortunate they were in the dark. At least they could not see the muck.

Carefully making her way back to Aisling, she placed the blanket over her shoulders. "Och, Aisling. Please speak to me. Are ye hurt?" The only answer Rosalia received was a sniffle, and she repeated the question.

"It doesnae matter. My bairn is dead. He killed my Teàrlach!" cried Aisling, sounding unnatural.

Rosalia placed her arms around Aisling and held her tight while Aisling's body rocked as she sobbed. "My bairn... my Teàrlach, my Teàrlach," she cried over and over.

Blinking back her tears, Rosalia choked with emotion. She needed to be strong for them both or they would never survive. "Shh... Aisling. I am here with ye. We will get through this."

"Teàrlach is dead. Why didnae the gods take me? Why, Rosalia? I would have given my life for his! I donna understand why they wouldnae take me! Teàrlach was an innocent bairn!"

Rosalia rubbed her hand over Aisling's tresses in an attempt to soothe her. "We donna know why the gods do what they do, but I do know it wasnae your time, Aisling. They still have a plan for ye. I am sure the gods watch over Teàrlach."

"I hope Aiden kills every last one of those *bloody* Campbells," said Aisling through gritted teeth.

"I know, Aisling. Come…" Assisting Aisling to the far wall, Rosalia held her well into the night. Aisling would sleep and then wake up screaming for Teàrlach, but Rosalia tried to console her friend as best as she could. She must have fallen asleep for a short time because something pulled her from her sleep. It sounded as if something had fallen outside the door. Shuffling noises came from the other side.

"My lady."

Thinking she heard someone whisper from outside the door, she quickly banished the thought. It was probably her mind playing tricks on her. Listening for another moment, she did not hear anything and shook her head for clarity. The last thing she needed was to lose her wits.

"My lady," a woman's voice said louder.

This time she did hear something. "Aye?" Rosalia whispered in return.

"Please come to the door. I brought some blankets."

Aisling stirred and started crying out for Teàrlach. "Shh… Aisling," Rosalia murmured.

"Rosalia, where are ye going?" she cried with panic in her voice.

"A woman is here with some blankets." She attempted to rise, but Aisling hastily grabbed her skirts.

"Donna trust her! She will kill ye when ye reach the door! Donna!" She clung to Rosalia's legs.

"My lady, please be quiet. Donna wake the guards," the woman pleaded.

"Aisling, I only travel to the door." When Rosalia felt Aisling release her hold, she shuffled her feet and held her hands out in front of her, feeling her way to the door. "Who are ye?"

There was a heavy silence.

"Someone who doesnae agree with the ways of men," the woman simply stated.

Aisling bumped into her from behind and pushed her to the side. "Ye *killed* my son. I pray my husband slays every last one of ye *bloody* Campbells," she said through gritted teeth. "Take your blankets and shove them up your arse."

There was a brief silence before the woman spoke again.

"Your son isnae dead," the woman whispered.

Aisling cried out. "Ye tell untruths! Why would ye do this to me? Rosalia, donna believe her. We heard the Campbell order Teàrlach's death. She speaks untruths to make us only further suffer!"

"My lady, please lower your voice. I donna have much time, and the guards will be making their rounds soon. Ye have my solemn vow your son is safe."

"Aye, the solemn vow of a *Campbell*," Aisling bit out.

"I am handing ye the blankets through the slits in the door," said the woman.

Rosalia fumbled her way, pulling them through the bars. "Why are ye helping us?"

The woman gave a strong sigh. "If I can avoid the laird, I will bring your son late on the morrow. I must take my leave now," said the woman quickly, avoiding the question.

"Wait!" Aisling called out. "Are ye the one that helped me?"

"Helped ye?" Rosalia countered.

"Aye," the woman answered. "I will speak with ye on the morrow. Speak of this to nay one."

Rosalia heard muffling sounds in the opposite direction of the guards. Interesting... there must be another passage out of the dungeon.

Aisling sat back down next to Rosalia against the wall. "What did ye mean when ye spoke the woman helped ye?" asked Rosalia.

"The men took me to the Campbell's chamber. He was going to rape me," she choked out. "As he climbed upon the bed to perform the deed, a woman walked in and said he couldnae touch me for if he did, he would be cursed for all of eternity. He quickly rose and dismissed me to the guard."

"So ye werenae..."

"Nay."

"Thank the gods! I worried about ye so. I didnae know if ye were hurt," Rosalia choked out, barely able to get the words past her throat.

Aisling rested her hand on her shoulder. "His stench still lingers upon my body, but he didnae have me."

"Praise the saints for sending the woman." She remembered something from the great hall. "What color were her tresses?"

"'Tis odd ye ask me of that because even though I only remember parts, I do remember her tresses being as black as a raven."

"I thought as much. When we were in the great hall, I saw such a woman watching us with such a look of regret or sadness upon her face. I am joyful I didnae imagine it."

They were silent for a few moments.

"I am afraid to ask, but do ye think my Teàrlach lives?" Aisling could barely get the words to come out of her mouth before she choked on them.

She placed her arm over Aisling's shoulders and pulled her close. "I am verra hopeful. It doesnae make sense that she brings ye blankets and then would speak untruths about Teàrlach. I am thinking mayhap we have an ally."

"Rosalia, I cannae live without my son. I am his mother. I was to protect him."

"Aisling, ye are a wonderful mother and there was naught ye could have done. The Campbell is a black-hearted, cruel man. He finds joy in the misery of others. Let us hope he doesnae make us suffer further. Even if we stay in the dungeon, I think 'tis better than what he would place upon us. We have to do whatever we must to survive and pray Ciaran and Aiden come quickly."

It was difficult to tell what time of day it was since there was nothing but total blackness. It seemed they had been held in their prison for several long hours. Rosalia guessed it might be around mid-morning.

The sound of approaching voices reached their door, and the guards appeared with torches in hand. A guard unlatched the door and shoved the light through it. "Get up," the man ordered. "The laird wants to see ye."

Stepping out into the corridor, Rosalia glanced to the left and stared at a blank wall. She wondered where the entrance to the passage was located. A man pushed her firmly down the corridor and up the stone staircase. When they reached the top, they placed their hands over their brows to block out the sun. After being surrounded by darkness for so long, the blinding light took a toll on their sight.

Approaching the great hall, Rosalia heard voices raised in a heated discussion. "Why, Cousin? Ye claimed to know him well. Why doesnae he storm the gates? My men await for naught!" the Campbell bellowed.

"I donna know why he doesnae storm the gates, Archie. Mayhap he hasnae yet seen his brother," replied Beathag in exasperation.

"Then ye didnae complete your task now, did ye? Ye willnae receive coin from me," he said curtly.

"Donna ye go back on your word, Archie! We have an agreement."

"We *had* an agreement if the MacGregor doesnae storm my gates," he said tersely.

Upon their entrance to the great hall, the Campbell silenced Beathag with a glare. "Bring them forward," he said, gesturing with his hand. He started to pace. "I want to know why the MacGregor doesnae come for ye." He took a step closer toward Rosalia. "Are ye the MacGregor's wife?"

From the conversation Rosalia had overheard, Beathag was not currently in the Campbell's favor. Perhaps she could draw a wedge further between them. It was worth a try. Rosalia pointed to Aisling. "She is the MacGregor's wife."

The Campbell huffed. "She is the second MacGregor's wife," he said impatiently. "Are ye wed to the MacGregor or nae?"

"Declan?" She tried to squeak convincingly. "Declan is nae wed."

He grunted. "Are all women daft?" He slapped his hand to his head. "Nae the third MacGregor, ye daft woman. Are ye wed to the laird?"

Rosalia rolled her eyes as if she now understood his question. "Why didnae ye just ask me if I was wed to Ciaran? Nay, I am nae wed to him. Ye think he would take me to wife?" she said, gesturing to her body.

The Campbell looked at her in disgust. "Ye are his leman. Are ye nae?" he asked, folding his arms over his chest.

She purposefully looked offended. "Leman? I assure ye I am nay leman."

He approached Beathag with a trace of annoyance upon his face. "Mayhap ye have it wrong, Cousin."

Beathag's eyes flew wide open as if he had insulted her. She stormed over to Rosalia. "I donna have it wrong. Tell him ye care for Ciaran."

"I care for all of the MacGregors," she stated simply.

Beathag gritted her teeth. "Tell him ye are his leman," she spat.

"I am nay whore. That was your task, I do believe," Rosalia said, folding her arms over her chest. When

Beathag's face reddened, Rosalia had the feeling she had better cease this game before it led to serious trouble.

"It doesnae make sense. Even if he doesnae care for her, he would at least come to rescue his sister-by-marriage. Yet, Cousin, he doesnae. I wonder why that is." His eyes narrowed at Beathag.

"I donna know, Archie. Why donna ye send him a missive?" she offered.

"And chance it being intercepted by King James's men, ye stupid chit?" he bellowed, continuing to pace. "The MacGregor is loyal to a fault. He will come for his sister-by-marriage. We will wait, but my patience is growing thin. And ye better nae be wrong, Cousin."

Beathag paled.

"Take them back to the dungeon," the Campbell ordered. "I cannae stand the sight of MacGregors in my presence."

Rosalia and Aisling were escorted back to their prison and left again in total darkness. At least they were not made to suffer in the Campbell's presence or to put up with his machinations.

"Why were ye trying to provoke the Campbell?" asked Aisling.

Rosalia sighed. "His ire is raised against Beathag and I thought to use it to our favor. If he was angry enough with her, he might err, and that could only help Ciaran and Aiden. I think I was able to raise some doubt in the faith he placed in Beathag. That can only help us."

"I hope she gets what she deserves. I cannae believe she plotted all this time with the *bloody* Campbell. It doesnae come as a surprise they are cousins. Both are black of heart," said Aisling.

They sat for hours. They would talk, fall asleep, and talk again, trying to do anything to keep their minds from going mad in the blackness. Another muffled sound came from outside the door and Rosalia rose. "Aisling, did ye hear that?"

"Aye! 'Tis the raven with my Teàrlach," she said, rising and shuffling her feet toward the door.

"I brought some food and a wine sack for ye. 'Tisnae much, but it was all I could gather," said the woman. "I am handing ye the food."

Rosalia fumbled her way to find the food and pulled it through the bars. "Ye have our thanks."

"Where is my son?" asked Aisling.

"He is above stairs, my lady. I will try to bring him to ye late this eve, but he is well," the woman assured.

"If what ye speak is true, ye have my sincere thanks… er, I am nae sure what to call ye."

The woman paused. "Ye can call me Liadain, but donna share this with the laird lest I willnae be able to move about freely."

"We willnae speak of it," said Aisling quickly.

"Liadain, how did ye come to be with the Campbell?" asked Rosalia, wanting to put all of the pieces together.

"I have spoken too freely already. I must take my leave."

"Nay. Please donna. I am sorry for my questions. Ye seem kind of heart, and I donna understand why ye are here, 'tis all," Rosalia explained further.

Liadain sighed. "Some days I wonder that as well. I will try to return this eve with your son."

"Ye have my thanks, Liadain," Aisling choked out.

They both stood at the door and waited until they heard her exit through the passage. "Och, Rosalia. I pray my Teàrlach is well. I need to hold him and feel that he is unhurt. Waiting is misery in itself."

"I know, Aisling. I think Liadain speaks the truth. Let us hope she brings Teàrlach this eve so we know he is well."

They continued to sit. Once they realized their backs suffered, they took turns as one of them would lay their head down on the other. The food and drink Liadain had brought was gone hours ago.

Finally a shuffling sound made Rosalia spring to her feet. "I think Liadain is here."

"Liadain?" asked Aisling, making her way to the door.

"Aye. Your son sleeps and I donna want to wake him for fear of the guards. I will place his head near the bars so ye can feel him. There. Reach through the bars and feel your son."

Aisling sniffled. "Och, my bairn. Teàrlach, I love ye. My sweet, sweet bairn. Rosalia, feel through the bars and feel he is well. He only sleeps."

Her cheeks were wet with tears. "Aye, Aisling. He only sleeps. Liadain, we donna know how to thank ye for caring for Teàrlach."

"Will ye tell me when ye think your men will come for ye?" asked Liadain. Both Rosalia and Aisling were quiet. So far Liadain kept true to her word, but Rosalia did not know how much she was willing to share with her. Apparently, Aisling felt the same.

"Ye still donna trust me? I have been trying to search for your men in the woods, but I havenae even seen a scout. I only ask because I can lead ye out to them when they arrive, but I cannae lead them in."

"I donna understand what difference that would make. If ye are willing to help us, why cannae ye lead them in? We risk capture or worse if we take our leave," said Aisling.

There was a heavy silence.

"'Tisnae safe for ye with the bairn. I donna agree with the ways of the Campbell, and I will be willing to lead ye out when your men arrive. I willnae lead MacGregor men in and send the Campbell to his death. He has chosen his path, and whatever his fate, I willnae be the one to send him to it." She paused and then spoke in hushed tones. "He is my brother."

Rosalia was speechless, but Aisling found her voice. "Your brother?"

"We share the same father but have a different mother. Nay matter, he is still my blood."

Rosalia's fumbling fingers found Aisling's arm. "We understand, Liadain. Ye cannae choose your family as much as ye cannae control their actions. Our men willnae come for us now. Mayhap on the morrow or the following day, but nae now. We place our trust in ye with that."

"I will watch for them on the morrow then. I will take Teàrlach first to ensure his safety and then I will come back for ye. Would ye like to kiss your son before I take my leave?"

"Verra much," said Aisling joyfully.

"I will hold him up. Feel for him."

Aisling kissed Teàrlach and he stirred. "I owe ye much, Liadain. Ye saved me and my son."

"*Mòran taing,*" Rosalia said sincerely.

Sixteen

THE PAST TWO DAYS HAD BEEN HELL FOR ALL OF THEM. They had reviewed the plan so many times that Ciaran dreamt of every last detail in his sleep. It took all of his strength to physically hold back and not storm the Campbells' gates. Fear and anger knotted inside him. He had never prayed so much in his life. Rosalia was safe—she had to be for he would accept nothing less. Declan, Aiden, and Calum had left early in the morn to move into position. This had to work. They would have no other chance.

"My men are ready, MacGregor," said Alexander with an air of calm and confidence.

"My laird, the men, and the horses are readied," called Seumas.

Ciaran nodded and ran his hand through his hair. "Let us rescue our women," he said firmly.

Ciaran mounted Noonie. He would ride with Alexander and his men, and Seumas and Ciaran's own men would follow behind. When everyone was in position, they would make their move.

Declan, Aiden, and Calum secured their mounts deep in the forest and proceeded on foot. By the time the sun cast its first rays of light, they were ready and waiting. They would lurk in the brush to see if someone entered another way into the stronghold. If that did not work, they would force their way in when Ciaran and Alexander arrived.

Declan wished to slit every last one of the Campbells' throats, but he would be logical. He would at least wait until they were shown a way in. Each one of them was spread out strategically around the castle watching for an opportunity to present itself. The rustling of tree branches caught Declan's attention. A woman walked through the forest unaware of the danger that awaited her underneath the brush.

Her tresses were the black of a starless night and hung down her back. She wore a cloak, but when it parted, generous curves were displayed underneath. There was both delicacy and strength in her face. The flush on her pale cheeks was like the flush of sunset on the snow. She looked ethereal, unreal in the sun's early rays. She was... enchanting. Who was this woman who cast such a spell? She carried herself confidently and was unaware of the appreciative glances he cast upon her. As if she sensed his presence, she stopped. When a shadow of alarm touched her face, he knew he had to make his move.

Declan sprang from the brush as if his arse was afire and she let out a startled yelp. "Donna move," he threatened, placing his dagger to her throat. "If ye scream, ye will die. Do ye understand?"

She started to tremble. "Aye," she whispered.

"I see ye are a woman of intelligence. Move out of the view of the guards," he ordered. He continued to hold the dagger to her throat and moved her flush against the castle wall. He spun her around to face him, replacing the blade to her throat. "Who are ye?"

"Ye donna need the dagger," she choked out.

He tilted his brow, looking at her with uncertainty. "Nay? Why donna ye let me decide what is needed. I willnae ask ye again. Who are ye?" he repeated.

"Are ye Aiden?" she asked him searchingly.

His annoyance increased when he felt her hands trembling between them. He glared at her, frowning. "Howbeit I ask the questions since I am the one holding the weapon. Ye will show me the way into the castle." Removing the dagger from her neck, he pulled her away from the wall and gently pushed her to walk in front of him.

She stopped but did not turn around. "Please listen to me. I will bring your son and your wife out to ye now, but I cannae lead ye in," she said, slowly turning around to face him. She swallowed hard, lifted her chin, and boldly met his gaze.

Their eyes met and a shock ran through him. This woman stood before him visibly shaking, but boldly challenging him. He gave her a roguish grin. "My apologies. Did ye feel ye had a voice in which to bargain?" He simply raised his brow and waited.

She was obviously irked by his cool, aloof manner because she mocked his stance and also raised her brow, folding her arms over her chest. They simply stared at each other across a sudden silence and she showed no signs of relenting. He must find a way to breach the castle walls and did not have time for the foolish games of a woman. Forcefully, he grabbed her arm and led her in the same direction from which she had hailed.

Her feet stumbled to keep up with him. "Ye are hurting me," she said breathlessly.

He eased his grip but did not release her. "If ye donna show me how to get into the castle, ye will be dead."

"So ye have said," she said dryly, stopping again. "Aiden, please. I have spoken to Aisling and Rosalia. They know I will bring your son to ye. Ye must release me so I am able to get him out unharmed."

Declan tilted his brow, looking at her doubtfully. "Now isnae that convenient? I am to believe those words so ye can… set another trap for us?" He gave her a mocking smile. "I have had enough of ye *bloody* Campbells and your lies to last my life," he bit out. "Show me the way into the castle. Now…"

The raven beauty stood in front of him still boldly defying his demands. "Please let me bring ye your son, Aiden. When ye see he is unharmed and nay warning is called, ye will see I speak the truth. I will help ye, but I cannae lead ye in. I can only bring them out."

His face clouded with uneasiness. "Why should I trust ye?" he asked. "Who are ye?"

She bit her lip and looked away from him. "I am Liadain," she relented, pushing her black tresses out of her eyes. "I am the healer."

"If ye want to help and are willing to bring them out, why willnae ye lead me in?" he asked her searchingly.

She set her chin in a stubborn line. "The Campbell

is many things, but I willnae be the one to lead him to his death. He willnae die by my hand." She extended her hand and touched him on the arm. "Please, Aiden. Ye waste much time. Let me bring ye your son." She reached out and clutched his hand. "Please."

Declan prayed he was not going to regret this decision. "Bring them out safely. I will be here."

A thankful smile curved her mouth. "Thank ye. I will return as quickly as I can. Watch above for the guard." As she walked away with long, purposeful strides, he thought she had better be true to her word or he would—well, he was not sure what he would do to her. On that notion, he had better find Aiden.

He jumped at the sound of Aiden's voice. "God's teeth! I didnae even see ye," he said, grabbing his chest. "I found a woman who will help us. She is going to bring Teàrlach out. We need to wait for her here."

Aiden's expression stilled and grew serious. "How do ye know 'tisnae a trap?"

He gave an impatient shrug. "I donna, but she didnae raise a warning and took her leave to bring out your son."

"Then let us get my son."

Declan and Aiden waited impatiently for Liadain, deciding to leave Calum on the other side of the castle in case it was a trap. A branch snapped and they both drew their swords. Aiden let out a long, audible breath. "My son." When Liadain's steps slowed, he approached her quickly, sheathing his sword. He reached for Teàrlach, but Liadain continued to hold him in a protective embrace.

Her eyes were sharp and assessing. "I assure ye he is

well. Mayhap ye should let his father hold him," she chided him.

Aiden gave her a look of utter nonbelief. "Give me *my* son," he demanded, pulling Teàrlach from her arms.

"*Your* son?" Disconcerted, she crossed her arms and glared at Declan.

He shrugged dismissively. "I didnae tell ye I was Aiden," he countered.

She whipped her head away from him, clearly dismissing him and giving Aiden her undivided attention. "Aisling is well. I will bring her out next. I am thinking to bring them out one at a time lest I draw suspicion if guards are making rounds."

He offered her a forgiving smile. "That is wise. Ye have my thanks… er?"

"Liadain," she simply stated. She turned on her heel, walking away in the direction from which she came.

"Declan, find Calum. We need to get Teàrlach and the women far from here."

"Aye." It did not take him long to return with Calum. Aisling was out and Liadain had already gone back for Rosalia.

His brother exhaled a long sigh of contentment and kissed Aisling and Teàrlach on the head. "There will be plenty of time for us later, Wife. Take your leave now with Calum back to Glenorchy, and I will have Declan follow with Rosalia." He placed his hand to her face and brushed a soft kiss to her lips. "I love ye, Aisling."

"And I love ye, Aiden." She opened her eyes, and suddenly her smile faded. "Aiden, I want ye to kill the Campbell," she spoke with bitterness.

Declan cleared his throat. "Aiden, they must take their leave. 'Tis too dangerous for them here."

Aiden gazed at her intently. "Ye have my word. His fate is sealed. Ye must take your leave." He placed Teàrlach into her arms and watched them walk into the trees with Calum.

Declan placed his hand on Aiden's shoulder in a brotherly gesture. "They are safe, Brother."

He closed his eyes. "Aye," he said in a choked voice.

Liadain approached them with a pensive look upon her face. "The Campbell has Rosalia."

❧

When Liadain came to their darkened door and said that Aiden was waiting, Rosalia and Aisling were overjoyed. Teàrlach had already been delivered safely into his father's arms, and relief flooded Aisling. Liadain said, "Aisling, ye first and I will come back for Rosalia. If the guards come, she may be able to distract them long enough for ye to escape. If both of ye arenae here, they may raise a warning."

Aisling grabbed Rosalia's arm. "I willnae take my leave without ye."

"Ye can and ye will. Ye have Teàrlach to think upon. Take your leave quickly, and then Liadain can come back for me and we can escape this madness," Rosalia said reassuringly, squeezing her hand.

Aisling embraced her. "I love ye, Sister. Ye make haste."

"Donna ye worry," Rosalia said, pushing her gently out the door. She took a deep breath and tried to remain calm, waiting impatiently by the door for Liadain's return. Half in anticipation and half in dread, she prayed their attempts would not be discovered. Then torchlight approached from the opposite direction.

The guards swung open the door. One of them pushed the torch through the doorway and looked around. "Where is the other MacGregor wench?" he bit out.

Rosalia shrugged dismissively, and the man walked forward with purposeful strides. "The Campbell wants to see ye, MacGregor *whore*." She had no choice but to follow the guards up the stone staircase. When she reached the top, her steps slowed and she raised her hand over her brow. The light was painful.

Upon her entrance to the great hall, the guard informed the Campbell that Aisling was missing. He stood there, tall and angry. He bellowed instructions to a handful of guards, and they hurried away to do his bidding.

The Campbell whirled to stare at her, anger rising further in his eyes. "I donna know how that red-haired siren escaped my walls, but how fortunate for me that ye are still within my grasp," he said, his voice belligerent. "The MacGregor wishes to speak with me for your release. Verra clever of ye to attempt to deceive me that he doesnae care for ye."

She regarded him impassively.

"I told ye he would come for her, Archie," Beathag said smugly, clapping her hands together in front of her.

The Campbell ignored her as did Rosalia. Shouting to his guards, he instructed them to permit Ciaran in the gates. Beathag slithered over to Rosalia like a snake ready to devour a meal. "I warned ye to stay away from Ciaran. Now ye will watch him die," she said with satisfaction in her eyes.

At this point, Rosalia was beyond intimidation. Aisling and Teàrlach had escaped, and she had nothing more to lose. If this was her fate, so be it. She quickly waved aside any hesitation. "What do ye know? Ye are naught more than a whore. 'Tis ye who has sealed your fate, and I shall find great pleasure in watching ye die when Ciaran comes for me."

Beathag paled.

A guardsman walked toward the Campbell, drops of moisture clinging to his forehead. "My laird, 'tisnae the MacGregor at your gates."

"What do ye mean 'tisnae the MacGregor at my gates? Who else would it be?" the Campbell bellowed, his dark eyes showing nonbelief. The guard's voice drifted into a hushed whisper. The Campbell whispered a response and watched him depart. Running his hand through his hair, he began to pace.

Everything in the hall was so quiet that Rosalia could hear the sound of her own breath. She was not sure what was occurring, but it was obvious the Campbell was unnerved. He hesitated in mid-stride as a man entered the hall flanked by several guards in full battle attire. Additional Campbell guardsmen followed them in with watchful eyes, standing strategically around them. From her count, there was roughly a score of men including the Campbell's own guard.

The man's thick brown hair was tapered neatly at his neck. He was much younger than the Campbell but had an air of authority and the appearance of one who demanded instant obedience. He approached the Campbell with regal elegance and gave him a courtly bow. "Pray allow me to introduce myself. I am Alexander MacDonell. I come on behalf of my father, Laird Dòmhnall MacDonell of Glengarry, who maintains King James's alliances in the north. I have come to understand ye hold my cousin, Lady Rosalia Armstrong. I am here to escort her safely to Glengarry to my father."

Cousin? She did not even know she had a cousin.

The Campbell's eyes grew openly amused. "Pray allow me to introduce myself," he said, giving him a mock bow. "I am Archibald Campbell, seventh Earl of Argyll, who maintains King James's alliances as well. Mayhap ye have heard more of me, eh? Aye, I have your *cousin.*" He regarded Alexander then turned, casting Rosalia a look of disdain.

When Alexander spoke again, his voice was cold and exact. "Ye will release my cousin to me. Now," he demanded, his guards reaching for the hilt of their swords.

The Campbell was casually amused and started to pace in front of Alexander. He tapped his fingers to his lips. "Verra clever, but nae clever enough to outwit a Campbell," he smirked, taking an abrupt step toward him. Alexander did not move and simply raised his brow, a swath of wavy hair falling casually on his forehead.

"Your error was claiming the MacDonell is the cousin of the MacGregor whore. The MacGregor sent *this* whelp to rescue his woman?" he said tauntingly, turning and jesting with his men. The men laughed at his remark as he turned back to Alexander and snarled, "Ye see... she comes from Liddesdale and is merely a whore."

Rosalia remained perfectly still and tried weighing the whole structure of events. Frankly, she was perplexed.

"Archie," Beathag warned.

He silenced her with a cold stare.

Alexander stood to his full height and placed his hands behind his back as the Campbell studied him. "Ye donna understand what I speak. The MacDonell isnae the cousin of Rosalia. He is her uncle. *I* am her cousin," he said, his voice resonant and impressive.

Hesitantly, Beathag moved to stand beside the Campbell. "Archie," she said, raising her voice and reaching out to touch his arm. When he still paid her no heed, she awkwardly cleared her throat.

"What do ye want, cousin? Ye see I am speaking," he said in an irritated tone.

❧

Ciaran tried not to watch Rosalia, but he could not help himself. He needed to ensure she was well. She was obviously puzzled by Alexander's sudden appearance, but she was an intelligent lass. She would know he would plan to come for her. He placed his hand on the hilt of his sword. Although the Campbell did not recognize him due to his strategically placed head gear, he must be ready for anything.

What the hell? Beathag was the Campbell's *cousin*? He should not be surprised they came from the same soiled blood. How fitting that the pieces would finally come together. Now certain events started to make sense. Not only did they plot together, but now they would die together as well.

Beathag became increasingly uneasy and shifted her weight from foot to foot. "Archie, he speaks the truth," she muttered uneasily.

The Campbell stared at her, confounded. He dug his fingers into her flesh, pulling her forcefully to the side. "What is this? What do ye mean he speaks the truth?"

She flinched at the tone of his voice. "Archie, the MacDonell is her uncle and that man is her cousin. She was to travel to Glengarry, but I didnae think her—"

"Nay, ye didnae." The Campbell glowered at her and then turned away. He spoke to all, but gazed at Beathag. "It appears the MacDonell—"

"Will be taking his cousin," bellowed Alexander, unsheathing his sword and raising it high in the air. Ciaran and Alexander's men followed suit as their men came thundering into the hall from the courtyard. The Campbell stared with complete surprise upon his face.

Ciaran took out two guards and easily deflected a few choice blows. He would slay every Campbell that got in his way and held him from his purpose. Alexander's men fought by his side and showed no mercy. No one touched his own. Ciaran glanced over as the Campbell tried to slither out of the great hall. He would not escape that easily. He knew for certain that Archibald Campbell, seventh Earl of Argyll would die this day by his hand—the hand of the MacGregor.

Rosalia had backed up against a far wall and Alexander was fighting his way over to her. She would be safe. "Ciaran, behind ye!" shouted Aiden, working his way toward him.

Ciaran turned in time to lunge his broadsword into the neck of a Campbell. Looking back over his shoulder, he saw that two men held Aiden at bay. He was about to move when Declan stormed into the great hall with his sword raised high and screamed, "*Ard-Choille!*" He took down one of the guards and held his own.

Ciaran continued to maneuver his way over to his brothers and, with a deep thrust, took out another Campbell along the way. "Aisling?" he shouted to Aiden.

Aiden turned, deflecting another blow. "She and Teàrlach are out!" he shouted through the clanking metal sounds of battle.

Taking another glance at Rosalia, Ciaran saw that Alexander was almost there and would see to her safety. It was time to find the *bloody* Campbell. Deflecting several more blows, he fought his way out of the great hall and into the courtyard. The Campbell was making his way toward the gate. Ciaran let out a piercing whistle to his men who encroached on the barmkin wall and waved his arms for them to close the gate. Other than a few skirmishes within the courtyard, his men had already started to gather and secure the Campbells. It would not be long before all of the men were held.

Thundering across the courtyard, Ciaran pulled off his headgear. "*Ard-Choille!*" he bellowed, charging at the Campbell.

The Campbell's loyal guardsmen placed him at

their back and lunged at Ciaran. "Kill him! I wish to have his head!" the Campbell shouted, cowering behind his guardsmen.

Ciaran easily brought one man down but still held two at bay.

He pushed one of the guards to his enemy, then turned to deflect a blow aimed at his head. He knocked his opponent to his back and buried his sword deep into the man's chest with a crushing sound. A burning sensation ripped through his arm. As he turned, the last man was coming in on him fast. He did not get out of the way quickly enough and received another slice to the shoulder. He grunted, holding his blood-soaked shoulder.

Spinning with an upper cut, Ciaran sliced his opponent's chest, and he fell to the ground with a thud. Ciaran's chest heaved as he turned and gave the Campbell a mocking smile.

The Campbell paled.

"Ciaran!" Beathag screamed.

He whirled to stare at her, quick anger rising in his eyes. Beathag held a dagger to Rosalia's throat. Alexander moved out of the corner of his eye, but Ciaran told him to stand down with only a shake of his head.

The Campbell let out a great peal of laughter. "Verra well done, Cousin."

"Ciaran, have your men open the gates," Beathag said.

He gave the order for his men to open the gates. Beathag moved slowly, guiding Rosalia toward her means of escape.

Ciaran shifted his eyes to Rosalia and she gave him

a knowing look. Before he could figure out what she was about, she pulled on Beathag's arm and pretended to stumble. Lifting her leg, she pulled her dirk from under her skirts. Pivoting with a backward thrust, she impaled Beathag on her dagger.

Beathag yelled out in surprise, placing her hand to her stomach. When she pulled it away, it was covered with blood.

"*An diobhail toirt leis thu!*" *The devil take you!* Rosalia snarled, shaking with rage.

Ciaran whipped around and grabbed the Campbell. "Nae so fast. Where do ye think ye are going, ye *bloody* coward?" he said through gritted teeth. Raising his sword, he held it at the Campbell's throat. "Ye killed an innocent man. Ye left a wife without a husband and a child without a father. Ye attacked my brother. Ye took my sister and my nephew." He pushed the blade deeper. "Ye took my *woman*," he said, seething with mounting rage.

The color drained from the Campbell's face. His eyes became sharp and assessing. "King James—"

"Ye have nay honor," Ciaran bellowed, his voice echoing throughout the courtyard. "King James will know of your deceit and disregard of his orders. All of this madness and for what? To gain my lands?"

The Campbell's eyes widened as Ciaran raised his sword and swung the fatal blow. "I protect what is mine," he grunted, pulling out his sword, "and so did my father." He bent over and wiped his bloodied sword upon his jupon.

The Campbell stilled.

Rosalia still stood like a stone statue until he

reached her with purposeful strides. "Och, Rosalia…"
Ciaran pulled her trembling body to him. Shock, stark
and vivid, flashed in her eyes. She began to shake
uncontrollably and Ciaran shouted for someone to
bring him a blanket. Pulling her into the circle of his
arms, he whispered soothingly into her ear.

⌒∕⌒

"Rosalia…" someone called to her. She could hear the
voice in some faraway place in her mind.

"Easy, lass. Donna move too quickly," the voice
spoke silkily.

Rosalia took a moment to catch her breath. The solid
ground was underneath her and she felt a soft tapping to
her cheek. She sat up abruptly, the vivid recollection of
the day's events flooding her with emotion.

A warm hand rubbed her shoulder. "Donna move
too quickly," Ciaran instructed, pushing her tresses
out of her face.

Lifting her hand, she stared at Beathag's lifeblood,
blood she spilled. Ciaran grabbed her hand and placed
it back down. "Donna look upon it, Rosalia. Ye did
what ye had to do."

"Cousin, are ye well?" asked Alexander, kneeling
beside her and placing a comforting hand upon her
shoulder.

How was she supposed to respond to that? She was
not fine. She had killed someone. She opened her
mouth to speak, but words escaped her.

Fingers gently lifted her chin and she gazed into
eyes of compassion. Ciaran gave her a tender smile. "I
know how ye feel, but trust me when I speak this will

pass. Ye defended yourself, lass. Beathag deserved her fate." At the mention of Beathag, she pulled her eyes away from him and turned to view Beathag's lifeless body upon the ground. She gulped hard.

"Come…" Ciaran hefted her into his arms and walked several feet in the courtyard. Bending over, he placed her gently on a bench. His heavy arm encircled her shoulders and she leaned into him. Holding her tenderly, he continued to whisper words of comfort.

A woman wept in the distance. Lifting her head, Rosalia glanced around the courtyard. Liadain was kneeling upon the ground next to the lifeless Campbell. There was so much death.

She stood and released the blanket, hastily making her way to Liadain. She thought she heard Ciaran call for her, but it didn't matter. She could not allow Liadain to be alone. "Liadain, I am truly sorry for your loss," she murmured, her brow creased with worry and her own voice sounded strange upon her lips.

Hesitantly, Ciaran approached and cast a questioning glance.

"Ciaran, this is Liadain. She helped us and brought Aisling and Teàrlach to safety," she spoke solemnly.

He nodded in gratitude. "Ye have my sincere thanks."

Liadain nodded in return, turning her attention back to the Campbell, her eyes clouded with tears.

"Will ye stay?" Rosalia asked her searchingly.

She closed her eyes. "I donna know. I need to bury my brother." Opening her eyes, she placed her hand on the shoulder of the Campbell before she stood.

Rosalia turned to Alexander and raised her brow. "Are ye truly my cousin?"

He smiled in earnest. "Aye. I am your cousin, Alexander."

She embraced him. "Ye have my thanks, Alexander. I owe ye much."

"Ye owe me naught. Ye are my kin, Rosalia. We protect our own. Ye take your leave with MacGregor and rest, Cousin. Your *seanmhair* anxiously awaits ye at Glengarry."

Feeling a warm hand at her back, she settled back into Ciaran. She needed his comfort and strength.

Seventeen

CIARAN LIFTED ROSALIA AND PLACED HER UPON Noonie, but instead of riding his own mount, he swung up behind her. He grunted upon securing his seat and winced when he touched his shoulder.

"Och, Ciaran. Ye are injured," she said, leaning forward in the saddle and trying carefully not to bump into him.

He waved her off. "'Tis naught but a scratch." Placing his arm around her waist, he pulled her back against him. For a long moment, he looked down at her. "Please tell me ye are well," he said, brushing the tips of his fingers over her cheek.

As Noonie took his time walking along the path, Rosalia started to relax against him. "Lass," he murmured soothingly into her ear. "I need to ask something of ye and then I promise we willnae speak of it again." Silently, he waited for her response.

Almost as if she did not have the strength to do so, she nodded her head. "Aye?"

He sighed. "I know this may be difficult to speak, but I need to know... Did the Campbell touch ye?" There was no simple way to ask and he needed the truth.

"I mean to ask if the Campbell forced himself upon ye as a man." When she did not immediately respond, he raised his hand, gently rubbing her tresses. Terrible regrets assailed him. "It will be all right, Rosalia. I want ye for my wife."

Rosalia was stunned. Ciaran offered to wed her because he believed the Campbell ruined her. That was so... Ciaran. A few days past, she would have jumped at the chance to be his wife. Now it seemed they disagreed on the very nature and meaning of love.

She spoke with quiet firmness. "'Tis verra generous of ye to offer yourself as my husband, my laird, but there is nay need for such offerings. The Campbell didnae touch me as a man."

He blew out an abated breath. "I am relieved to hear it. I worried so," he murmured, leaning forward and kissing her on the top of her head. Weariness enveloped her, and with a long, exhausted sigh, she fell asleep in Ciaran's arms.

❧

Upon their return to Glenorchy, Ealasaid ran to Rosalia. That was exactly what she needed. She was safe. She was *home*. When Alexander and his brothers returned a few hours later, Ciaran met with Alexander in his solar. Sitting behind his father's desk, he sealed the missive to King James with the MacGregor seal. "Do ye think 'tis enough?"

Alexander sat forward in his chair, leaning his arm on the desk. "When I give this to him in person and the Campbell's sister confirms what ye stated in the missive, I think he will accept it. Will ye be sending Aiden with me?"

Sitting back in the chair, Ciaran contemplated the decision he already made. "Nay. Aiden needs to see to Aisling and Teàrlach. Aisling has been through much and needs him right now."

"Who will ye send in your stead?" asked Alexander, raising his brow.

Damn his shoulder. Although the stitches kept it closed, it throbbed more than the devil and caused him more pain than he cared to admit. He could not chance making the trip to court and risk infection. He had no choice. "I will be sending Declan in my stead."

Alexander merely studied him. "And upon my return, I will be taking my cousin to Glengarry."

Ciaran's eyes narrowed. "She willnae take her leave with ye. I willnae allow it."

Alexander smirked. "*Ye* donna have a choice, MacGregor. She isnae your wife," he simply stated.

"I will have her as my wife."

"We shall see," Alexander said doubtfully, rising and picking up the missive. "I leave for court on the morrow."

"Declan and the Campbell's sister will be ready on the morrow."

When Ciaran told Declan he would be representing him at court, his brother's expression was unreadable. Ciaran would just have to pray his reckless brother would take the task seriously and not end up on the gallows. He ran his hand over his father's desk. He hoped his father was proud.

His mind drifted to Rosalia. She deserved to be happy. He remembered the look upon her face when she was—with him. Looking up to the gods, Ciaran prayed for forgiveness from his father. The vow to his father plagued him, but realizing he almost lost Rosalia brought him back to reality. When she was taken, he had felt an extraordinary void. The thought of losing her was almost his undoing. He had to convince her to stay—to be his wife. He was a fool to think otherwise.

᳇

Rosalia slept like the dead. She did not even think she shifted her position the entire night. Pulling herself from the bed, she approached the washbowl. She donned her day dress and made her way to the only place she felt tranquility.

Looking out at the loch from the parapet, she sighed.

"I thought I would find ye here," said Ciaran, approaching her and giving her a sly grin.

She turned back and tried to imprint the picture in her mind. She would sorely miss Glenorchy. "'Tis truly beautiful." He gently took her hand and she yanked it away from him. "Please donna."

He nodded his head in consent and glanced out at the loch. "How do ye fare?"

"I am fine. When my cousin is ready, he will escort me to Glengarry to my *seanmhair,*" she said, casting her eyes downward.

"Alexander, Declan, and the Campbell's sister took their leave this morn to journey to court. When your cousin returns, I donna want ye to take your leave. I wish for ye to remain at Glenorchy."

"What?" She was bewildered by Ciaran's behavior. Frankly, he was driving her mad.

"Respond with the truth. I would expect naught less from ye."

She shifted her weight from foot to foot. "I donna know what to speak, my laird," she blurted out.

"I would want for ye to stay."

She gasped. "Why?"

He looked at her in utter nonbelief. "Why? I would want ye for my wife."

Rosalia rubbed her fingers over her eyes then flung them down at her sides. "Why, Ciaran? I told ye the Campbell didnae touch me. Ye donna have a reason to take me as a wife," she said, her breath came raggedly in impotent anger. Her expression bordered on mockery. "I wouldnae wed Dunnehl for coin and I sure willnae have ye wed me out of *pity*!"

"Pity?"

He was about to speak again and she abruptly cut him off. "Before I was taken by the Campbell, ye were bound and determined to take me to Glengarry. Ye openly stated ye donna love me. My answer is nay, Ciaran. I willnae wed ye."

She looked away from him and he raised her chin with his finger. "I would want ye to look at me when I speak to ye." Ciaran waited for her eyes to reach his and he held them intensely. "Ye are truly the most stubborn lass I have ever known." When she huffed and attempted to pull away from him, he held her in place. "Nay, ye donna. Ye will stand and listen to what I have to speak."

She closed her eyes and nodded her head in consent.

When he spoke again, his voice was softer and warm, and his mouth curved with tenderness. "I enjoy the speech we have every eve in front of the fire. I enjoy the jesting between us. Ye seem to have taken to Glenorchy and everyone around ye. Aisling has become as a sister to ye and Aiden and Declan as your brothers." He paused and took a deep breath.

"What ye heard me bellow to Aiden was my attempt to get him to cease his matchmaking. 'Tisnae how I truly feel for ye, Rosalia, and I believe ye know the truth to that. I hope one day to earn your love because I take ye as a wife *verra* willingly." He touched her cheek in a wistful gesture and she closed her eyes to hold back her tears. "I am nae done," he murmured.

"I have ne'er known a lass as ye and I donna want to know another. I want *ye*. I want all of ye—your kindness and compassion, your dislike of wearing skirts, your cut tresses, your nervousness when ye look down at your hands, your nightmares so I can will them away, your ire so I can kiss it away, and mayhap even one day I can earn your love." His eyes bore into hers. "*Tha gaol agam ort.*" *I love you.*

Rosalia choked back a sob. Grabbing his hand, she kissed the inside of his palm. She smiled, her cheeks wet with tears. "Ciaran, I donna know where to begin."

Patiently, he waited for her to continue.

"I wouldnae even be alive if it wasnae for ye." He started to shake his head, but she held him in place. "Nay. I listened to ye, but ye will also listen to me."

He nodded for her to continue.

"If it wasnae for ye, I wouldnae be here. Ye are the

kindest man. I see your compassion for your clan and it warms my heart. Ye are a great and honorable laird. I also enjoy our speech every eve in front of the fire, but I donna enjoy it when ye take your leave. I know I am nay great beauty…" He rolled his eyes, but she continued. "Come now. I know it, but ye make me feel as though I am beautiful."

"Ye *are* beautiful, Rosalia," he simply stated.

"I always felt as though I ne'er belonged. Being here at Glenorchy with ye and your clan has changed my view. I see how family should be and I see how all of ye have graciously welcomed me into your home. If ye want the truth, my laird, ye shall have it. I cannae think of my life without ye. It pains me too greatly. Ye speak mayhap one day ye can earn my love." Raising her hand, she touched his cheek. "Ciaran, ye have always had my love. I love ye with all my heart and soul."

He smiled and bent down on one knee. "Then Lady Rosalia Armstrong," he said, taking her hand, "will ye do me the verra great honor of becoming my wife? I cannae imagine my life without ye in it." She pulled him to stand and embraced him. When he lowered his head, he kissed her with passion and tenderness.

They stood there for some time, enjoying the warmth of their embrace. "I am so joyful," murmured Rosalia.

"As am I," he said, brushing her hair back behind her ear.

She raised her head. "Does your shoulder still pain ye?"

He chuckled. "My heart is overjoyed and I donna notice if it does."

"If ye donna mind, could we send a missive to James? I need him to know I will stay at Glenorchy."

"Of course. I will send Montgomery a missive later this morn," he said, rubbing her arms.

"I would also wish to send a missive to Glengarry to advise my *seanmhair* I am safe at Glenorchy and we are to be wed," she spoke joyfully.

"It will be done," he said in a gentle tone.

He kissed her with pure male satisfaction and then said, "Howbeit after we are wed, we travel to Glengarry to pay a visit to your *seanmhair*?"

"Truly?" she asked hopefully.

"Aye."

"That would be wonderful, my laird." She embraced him, reveling in the comfort and strength he provided her. "Ciaran, ye truly saved me."

"Nay, lass, it was ye who saved me."

More exciting Highland romance
Available now from Sourcebooks Casablanca

The Highlander's Prize

By Mary Wine

❧

Scottish Lowlands, 1487

"Keep yer face hidden."

Clarrisa jerked back as one of the men escorting her hit the fabric covering the top of the wagon she rode inside of. An imprint of his fist was clearly visible for a moment.

"Best keep back, my dove. These Scots are foul-tempered creatures, to be sure. We've left civilization behind us in England." There was a note of longing in Maud's voice Clarrisa tried to ignore. She couldn't afford to be melancholy. Her uncle's word had been given, so she would be staying in Scotland, no matter her feelings on the matter.

Better to avoid thinking about how she felt; better to try to believe her future would be bright.

"The world is in a dark humor," Clarrisa muttered. Her companion lifted the gold cross hanging from her girdle chain and kissed it. "I fear we need a better plan than waiting for divine help, Maud."

Maud's eyes widened. Faster than a flash, she reached

over and tugged one of Clarrisa's long braids. Pain shot across her scalp before the older woman sent to chaperone her released her hair. "You'll mind your tongue, girl. Just because you're royal-blooded doesn't give you cause to be doubting that the good Lord has a hand in where you're heading. You're still bastard-born, so you'll keep to your place."

Clarrisa moved to the other side of the wagon and peeked out again. She knew well who she was. No one ever let her forget, not for as long as she could recall. Still, even legitimate daughters were expected to be obedient, so she truly had no right to be discontented.

So she would hope the future the horses were pulling her toward was a good one.

The night was dark, thick clouds covering the moon's light. The trees looked sinister, and the wind sounded mournful as it rustled the branches. But Clarrisa didn't reach for the cross hanging from her own waist. No, she'd place her faith in her wits and refuse to be frightened. That much was within her power. It gave her a sense of balance and allowed her to smile. Yes, her future would hold good things, because she would be wise enough to keep her demeanor kind. A shrew never prospered.

"Far past time for you to accept your lot with more humbleness," Maud mumbled, sounding almost as uninterested as Clarrisa felt. "You should be grateful for this opportunity to better your lot. Not many bastards are given such opportunities."

Clarrisa didn't respond to Maud's reminder that she was illegitimate. There wasn't any point. Depending on who wore the crown of England, her lineage was a blessing or a curse.

"If you give the Scottish king a son—"

"It will be bastard-born, since I have heard no offer of marriage," Clarrisa insisted.

Maud made a low sound of disapproval and pointed an aged finger at her. "Royal-blooded babes do not have to suffer the same burdens the rest of us do. In spite of the lack of blessing from the church your mother suffered, you are on your way to a bright future. Besides, this is Scotland. He'll wed you quickly if you produce a male child. He simply doesn't have to marry you first, because you are illegitimate. Set your mind to giving him a son, and your future will be bright."

Clarrisa doubted Maud's words. She lifted the edge of the wagon cover again and stared at the man nearest her. His plaid was belted around his waist, with a length of it pulled up and over his right shoulder. The fabric made a good cushion for the sword strapped to his wide back.

Maybe he was a Scotsman, but the sword made him look like any other man she had ever known. They lived for fighting. Power was the only thing they craved. Her blood was nothing more than another way to secure what the king of Scotland hungered for.

Blessing? Not for her, it wouldn't be.

༄

Lytge Sutherland was an earl, but he ruled like a prince on his land at the top of Scotland. Plenty of men envied him, but the wiser ones gave him deference gladly, because they knew his life was far from simple. At the moment he was feeling the weight of ten lairds, only half of whom he called friends.

"If the rumor is true, we must act," Laird Matheson insisted. "With a York-blooded son, that bastard James will pass the crown on to an English puppet."

"Or a king who the English will nae war with because they share common blood," Laird Morris argued.

The room filled with angry shouts as men leaned over the tables in front of them to give their words more strength.

"Enough!" Lytge snapped. There were several cutting glares, but Matheson and Morris both sat back in their chairs. The tension in the room was so tight the earl knew he had to find a solution before the men assembled before him began fighting one another. "Let us not forget how important it is for us to stand together, or James will get his wish to disinherit his first son, a young man worthy of our loyalty. If we squabble among one another, we will have to be content with James remaining king."

Laird Matheson snarled, "That bastard has no' done what a king should. He gives riches to his favorites and refuses to punish thieving clans like the MacLeods! It's his fault we're fighting Highlander against Highlander."

"Which is why we're all here, united against him despite half our own kin calling it treason." It was a younger man who spoke this time, and the earl grinned in spite of his desire to appear detached.

"Young Laird MacNicols says it clearly. We're here because we're united—a bond that needs to remain strong. The York lass must be eliminated before she can perform the function James desires of her. We do nae need England's war on our soil."

"We'll have to find her first," Faolan Chisholms said. "Such will nae be a simple task."

The old earl looked around the room. There was plenty of spirit in the lairds' eyes, but thinking the deed done would not gain them success. It would take cunning and strength, along with a healthy amount of arrogance for the man willing to try and steal from the king. Such a man would have to believe himself above failure. The earl was sitting in the right place to find him, for they were all Highlanders.

"I'll find her and steal her." Broen MacNicols spoke quietly—too quietly for the earl's comfort.

"Ye've got vengeance in yer eyes, young MacNicols. Understandable, since James has slighted yer patience by refusing ye justice concerning the death of yer father."

The earl's son, Norris, slammed a fist into the table, sending several of the goblets wobbling. "James neglects us and leaves good men no choice but to feud when their neighbors commit crimes, since he will not dispense judgment upon the guilty."

"I tried to respect the king instead of falling back on old ways," Broen snarled. "I took the matter of me father's murder at the hands of the Grants to the king. The man would nae even see me, much less send an envoy to Donnach Grant to demand me betrothed be returned." He flattened his hands on the tabletop, leaning over it. "I made a choice, sure enough, for I'm here, and I tell ye I will make sure the king does nae get the lass he wants while he refuses me justice for the murder of the woman I was contracted to. She died on Grant land, and I deserved more than a letter telling me she's dead."

Lytge Sutherland nodded and heard several of the other lairds slap the tabletop in agreement. "We place our faith in ye, Laird MacNicols. Find the York bastard, and ye'll have me at yer back when ye demand that explanation from Donnach Grant."

There was a solid ring of endorsement in the earl's tone. Broen didn't enjoy it. His father had been dead for four months, but he still felt the sting of the loss like a fresh wound. He reached up and tugged on the corner of his bonnet before quitting the chamber.

"Ye're in a hurry." Broen didn't lessen his pace as Faolan Chisholms caught up with him. They'd been young boys together, and now fate had made them lairds in nearly the same season.

"There is no reason to sit at a table drinking and talking like old men. I've an Englishwoman to find, since that is the only way I'll possibly see an explanation to me father's death that will nae require spilling blood when the snow melts."

"Aye, Sutherland will nae be giving ye his assistance otherwise, but ye need to know where to look for her before ye ride out," Faolan insisted.

Broen stopped and faced Faolan. "If ye want to come along, ye should have stood up when the earl was looking for men to take on the burden."

Faolan grunted. "Ye did nae give me a chance."

True Highland Spirit

By Amanda Forester

Scotland, 1355

MORRIGAN MCNAB SILENTLY DREW HER SHORT SWORD, careful to remain hidden from the road. She checked to ensure her black head-scarf was in place, concealing her nose and mouth. The target of today's villainy clopped toward them through the thick mud. Twelve men were in the mounted party, their rich robes identifying them as wealthy, above the common concerns of daily sustenance… in other words, a perfect mark.

Concealed by the tree and thick foliage, Morrigan scanned the party for weapons. It appeared to be a hunting party, since all had bows slung across their backs and long knifes at their sides. The dead boar they carried strung between two riders was also a clear sign of a hunt. Despite their alarming arsenal, most looked complacent, paying more attention to the flask they were passing around as they laughed and joked amongst themselves. One man, the one carrying a metal-tipped pike, scanned the woods around him as if he sensed danger.

Morrigan glanced at her brother Archie, only his eyes visible over the mask he wore. He pointed to her then to the man with the pike. Morrigan narrowed her eyes at her brother. He always gave her the hard ones. Morrigan gave a curt nod and turned her focus back to the pikeman. He looked fit and vigilant. She preferred fat and careless. The war horse was a fine specimen too, tall and strong, trained to stand his ground in battle. It would not be easy to take him down.

The hunting party clomped closer, and a man walking behind the riders came into view. Morrigan wondered why he was left to slog through the mud behind the hunting party. Many of the horses would carry two men with ease. The walking man was dressed in a worn traveling cloak and a brightly colored tunic with a lyre strapped to his back. He must be a minstrel. Those wealthy hunters must not consider him worthy of a ride. Damn rich bastards.

Archie gave a bird call, the signal. Morrigan tensed in anticipation, coiled, ready to strike, and counted. The men jumped at twenty; she always leaped at nineteen.

Morrigan sprung onto the road and charged the man with the pike, screeching like a fey creature from hell. Archie and the men surged into the fray, the men's shouts blending with the surprised cries of the beset hunting party. The pikeman lowered his weapon toward her with a snarl, but Morrigan dropped to the ground and rolled under the nicely trained war horse, which was obliging enough not to move.

Regaining her feet on the other side of the horse, she pounded the hilt of her sword into his elbow holding the pike, now fortunately pointed the wrong direction.

The man howled in pain, his black teeth showing, and swung to hit her. She anticipated the move, ducked out of the way, grabbed the pike and flipped it out of his hand. She had her sword tip stuck under the edge of his hauberk before the pike sunk into the mud. She applied just enough pressure to give him pause.

Her fellow bandits had likewise subdued the rest of the party. It was quiet for a moment, an odd silence after the explosion of sounds a moment before that had terrified both man and beast into mute submission.

"Good afternoon, my fellow travelers." Archie McNab stood before the hunting party, a scarf covering his nose and mouth. He gave a practiced bow with an added flourish. Morrigan rolled her eyes. Her brother liked to think of himself as a gentleman thief. True, he was laird of his clan, but Morrigan had little tolerance for petty niceties. They were there to rob them. What was the point of being genteel about it?

"I see ye are burdened wi' the evils o' worldly possessions. But ne'er fear, my brethren, we have come to relieve ye o' yer burdens."

Morrigan held out her free hand, hoping the man would readily hand over his pouch of coins like the other wide-eyed members of his party. He did not comply and instead nudged his horse, causing it to step sideways.

"Grab the reins," Morrigan commanded a young accomplice. The lad took up the reins of the war horse and holding the animal's head while Morrigan kept her eyes and her sword on the black-toothed man. He snarled at the lad, who balked and stepped back.

"Hold its head!" Morrigan snapped. The last thing she needed was this man making trouble.

"Now if ye fine gentlemen will make a small dona-
tion to the fund for wayward highwaymen, we shall
set ye on yer way in a trifle," said Archie.

On foot, Morrigan mentally added. The warhorse
Black-tooth sat upon was a fine specimen. She reckoned she would look better than he on such a fine
animal. The rest of the hunting party readily handed
over their money pouches and weapons easily, but not
Black-tooth. He glared a silent challenge. Morrigan
sighed. For once, just for the novelty of it all, she'd
like things to be easy. It was not to be on this day. Not
any day, truth be told.

Morrigan stabbed her mark harder but other than
a scowl, he made no move to comply. She could kill
the man, but Archie was firm in his orders not to kill
unless necessary, and Morrigan had to acknowledge
the wisdom of it. Robbing folks was one thing,
murder was another. The last thing they needed
was a band of Highlanders come to rid the forest of
murderous thieves.

The man still refused to hand over his money bag so
Morrigan grabbed the pommel of his saddle with her
free hand and put her foot on his in the stirrup and
hoisted herself up. It should have been a quick move.
She grabbed his purse and pulled it free. Suddenly
he shouted and kicked the horse. The lad dropped
the reins and the horse lunged forward, throwing
Morrigan off balance. One punch from Black-tooth
and Morrigan fell back into the mud.

The black toothed terror charged the horse in front
of him, causing the mount to spook and rear. The
result was chaos, as the remaining horses broke free,

urged on by the hunting party who sensed a chance to break free.

"Grab the horses, ye fools!" Morrigan jumped up shouting. "They be unarmed, get them ye bastards!"

But more than one thief, having secured the desired reward, melted back into the shrubbery rather than face the angry hunters. The hunting party broke free and galloped away down the path they had come.

"Damnation!" Morrigan yelled at her thieving brethren. "What is wrong w' ye cowardly knaves?"

"We got the coin," grumbled one man in response.

"But not the horses, ye fool! Now they can ride for their friends and come back for us. And ye," Morrigan turned on the spindly-legged lad who had dropped the leads of the warhorse she had coveted. "Ye ought to be more afeared o' me than any bastard on a horse." Morrigan strode toward the boy with the intent of teaching a lesson that would be long remembered, but her brother caught her arm.

"Let him be, he's only a lad."

"I was younger than that when I joined this game," Morrigan shot back.

"Aye," Archie leaned to whisper in her ear. "But we all canna be heartless bitches like ye." With teasing eyes he straightened and said in a louder voice. "Besides we have a guest."

Standing in the middle of the muddy road was the colorfully dressed man with a lyre slung on his back. Damn hunters had left him with a bunch of thieves. Morrigan cursed them once again along with their offspring and their poor mothers for general completeness. She was nothing if not thorough.

Despite being surrounded by thieves, the man appeared surprisingly calm, though perhaps after their pathetic display of incompetence he rightly felt he had nothing to fear.

"Allow me to introduce myself," the stranger said with a seductive French accent and an equally appealing smile. "I am Jacques, poor traveling minstrel, at your service." He gave a polished bow that put Archie's attempts at gallantry to shame. Morrigan caught her brother's eye to make sure he knew she had noted it.

"And what brings ye to be traveling with such cowardly companions that they would leave ye at the first sight of trouble?" Morrigan asked.

"The hunters I met on the road, and they invited me that I may walk behind them to their hunting lodge." Jacques gave an impish grin. "I can only assume my services are no longer required."

"Ah, then they are doubly fools, for a minstrel is a rare prize indeed," said Archie.

"You mean for me to be ransomed?"

"Nay, nay, ye are our guest. We are but humble thieves, but we shall take ye to…" Archie swallowed what he was going to say and coughed. "We shall take ye to the doorstep o' the great Laird McNab. We dare no' cross the border o' his domain for he has no tolerance for our kind, but I am assured he will welcome ye. And he can pay for yer services," said Archie McNab jingling his ill-gotten gains.

Acknowledgments

A very special "thank you" goes out to the following people:

To Sabrina Jeffries, for making me realize it's never too late to try something new.

To Hannah Howell, for her support while I was bogged down in synopsis hell.

To Eliza Knight, for giving me the courage to put myself out there.

To my agent, Jill Marsal, for her endless support and encouragement.

To my editor, Deb Werksman, for giving me a chance.

To my production editor, Rachel Edwards, for trying to make me "perfect."

And finally to my critique partner, Mary Grace, there are really no words to express the tremendous amount of gratitude I hold for you. All those times I ruffled your feathers about having your nose planted in a book, even when you walk…

For your brutal honesty and endless reads, your unwavering support and encouragement, these *Bad Boys* came to life. Thank you for believing in me.

About the Author

Victoria Roberts writes sexy, Scottish historical romances about kilted heroes and warriors from the past. An avid lover of all things Scotland—simply, she writes what she loves to read. Prior to ever picking up a single romance novel, she penned her first young adult novella (never published) at sixteen years old. Who knew her leather-studded motorcycle hero would trade in his ride and emerge as a kilt-donning Highlander wielding a broadsword?

Victoria lives in western Pennsylvania with her husband of nineteen years and their two beautiful children—not to mention one spoiled dog. When she is not plotting her next Scottish romp, she enjoys reading, nature, and antiques. For more information about Victoria, visit her website at www.victoriarobertsauthor.com.

A *Booklist* Top 10 Romance Fiction of 2011

The Return of Black Douglas

by Elaine Coffman

─────── ❧ ───────

He'll help a woman in need, no matter where she came from...

Alysandir Mackinnon rules his clan with a fair but iron fist.
He has no time for softness or, as he sees it, weakness. But
when he encounters a bewitching young beauty who may or
may not be a dangerous spy, but is surely in mortal danger,
he's compelled to help...

She's always wondered if she was born in the wrong time...

Thrown back in time to the tumultuous, dangerous Scottish
Highlands of the sixteenth century, Isobella Douglas has a
lot to learn about her ancestors, herself, and her place in the
world. Especially when she encounters a Highland laird who
puts modern men to shame...

Each one has secrets to keep, until they begin to strike a chord
in each other's hearts that's never been touched before...

For more Elaine Coffman, visit:

www.sourcebooks.com

Sins of the Highlander

by Connie Mason with Mia Marlowe

ABDUCTION

Never had Elspeth Stewart imagined her wedding would be interrupted by a dark-haired stranger charging in on a black stallion, scooping her into his arms, and carrying her off across the wild Scottish highlands. Pressed against his hard chest and nestled between his strong thighs, she ought to have feared for her life. But her captor silenced all protests with a soul-searing kiss, giving Elspeth a glimpse of the pain behind his passion—a pain only she could ease.

OBSESSION

"Mad Rob" MacLaren thought stealing his rival's bride-to-be was the perfect revenge. But Rob never reckoned that this beautiful, innocent lass would awaken the part of him he thought dead and buried with his wife. Against all reason, he longed to introduce the luscious Elspeth to the pleasures of the flesh, to make her his, and only his, forever.

"Ms. Mason always provides a hot romance."—RT Book Reviews

www.sourcebooks.com

The Highlander's Sword

by Amanda Forester

— ❧ —

A quiet, flame-haired beauty with secrets of her own...

Lady Aila Graham is destined for the convent, until her brother's death leaves her an heiress. Soon she is caught between a hastily arranged marriage with a Highland warrior, the Abbot's insistence that she take her vows, the Scottish Laird who kidnaps her, and the traitor from within who betrays them all.

She's nothing he expected and everything he really needs...

Padyn MacLaren, a battled-hardened knight, returns home to the Highlands after years of fighting the English in France. MacLaren bears the physical scars of battle, but it is the deeper wounds of betrayal that have rocked his faith. Arriving with only a band of war-weary knights, MacLaren finds his land pillaged and his clan scattered. Determined to restore his clan, he sees Aila's fortune as the answer to his problems...but maybe it's the woman herself.

— ❧ —

"Plenty of intrigue keeps the reader cheering all the way."—Publishers Weekly

For more Amanda Forester books, visit:

www.sourcebooks.com

The Highlander's Heart

by Amanda Forester

―――――――――― ⧆ ――――――――――

She's nobody's prisoner

Lady Isabelle Tynsdale's flight over the Scottish border would have been the perfect escape, if only she hadn't run straight into the arms of a gorgeous Highland laird. Whether his plan is ransom or seduction, her only hope is to outwit him, or she'll lose herself entirely…

And he's nobody's fool

Laird David Campbell thought Lady Isabelle was going to be easy to handle and profitable too. He never imagined he'd have such a hard time keeping one enticing English countess out of trouble. And out of his heart…

―――――――――― ⧆ ――――――――――

"An engrossing, enthralling, and totally riveting read. Outstanding!"—Jackie Ivie, national bestselling author of *A Knight and White Satin*

For more Amanda Forester books, visit:

www.sourcebooks.com

True Highland Spirit

by Amanda Forester

— ❧ —

Seduction is a powerful weapon...

Morrigan McNab is a Highland lady, robbed of her birthright and with no choice but to fight alongside her brothers to protect their impoverished clan. When she encounters Sir Jacques Dragonet, she discovers her fiercest opponent...

Sir Jacques Dragonet is a Noble Knight of the Hospitaller Order, willing to give his life to defend Scotland from the English. He can't stop himself from admiring the beautiful Highland lass who wields her weapons as well as he can and endangers his heart even more than his life...

Now they're racing each other to find a priceless relic. No matter who wins this heated rivalry, both will lose unless they can find a way to share the spoils.

— ❧ —

"A masterful storyteller, Amanda Forester brings new excitement to Scottish medieval romance!"—Gerri Russell, award-winning author of *To Tempt a Knight*

For more Amanda Forester books, visit:

www.sourcebooks.com

Highland Hellcat

by Mary Wine

❧

He wants a wife he can control...

Connor Lindsey is a Highland laird, but his clan's loyalty is hard won and he takes nothing for granted. He'll do whatever it takes to find a virtuous wife, even if he has to kidnap her...

She has a spirit that can't be tamed...

Brina Chattan has always defied convention. She sees no reason to be docile now that she's been captured by a powerful laird and taken to his storm-tossed castle in the Highlands, far from her home.

When a rival laird's interference nearly tears them apart, Connor discovers that a woman with a wild streak suits him much better than he'd ever imagined...

❧

"Deeply romantic, scintillating, and absolutely delicious."—Sylvia Day, national bestselling author of *The Stranger I Married*

For more Mary Wine books, visit:

www.sourcebooks.com

The Highlander's Prize

by Mary Wine

Clarrisa of York has never needed a miracle more. Sent to Scotland's king to be his mistress, her deliverance arrives in the form of being kidnapped by a brusque Highland laird who's a bit too rough to be considered divine intervention. Except his rugged handsomeness and undeniable magnetism surely are magnificent...

Laird Broen MacNichols has accepted the challenge of capturing Clarrisa to make sure the king doesn't get the heir he needs in order to hold on to the throne. Broen knows more about royalty than he ever cared to, but Clarrisa, beautiful and intelligent, turns out to be much more of a challenge than he bargained for...

With rival lairds determined to steal her from him and royal henchmen searching for Clarrisa all over the Highlands, Broen is going to have to prove to this independent-minded lady that a Highlander always claims his prize...

"[The characters] fight just as passionately as they love while intrigue abounds and readers turn the pages faster and faster!"—RT Book Reviews, 4 stars

For more Mary Wine books, visit:

www.sourcebooks.com

Highland Heat

by Mary Wine

———— ❧ ————

As brave as she is impulsive, Deirdre Chattan's tendency to follow her heart and not her head has finally tarnished her reputation beyond repair. But when powerful Highland Laird Quinton Cameron finds her, he doesn't care about her past—it's her future he's about to change...

From the moment Quinton sets eyes on Deirdre, rational thought vanishes. For in her eyes he sees a fiery spirit that matches his own, and he'll be damned if he'll let such a wild Scottish rose wither under the weight of a nun's habit...

With nothing to lose, Deirdre and Quinton band together to protect king and country. But what they can accomplish alone is nothing compared to what they can build with their passion for each other...

———— ❧ ————

"Dramatic and vivid...Scorching love scenes threaten to set the sheets aflame."—*Publishers Weekly* starred review

"A lively and exciting adventure."—*Booklist*

For more Mary Wine books, visit:

www.sourcebooks.com